White as Bone, Red as Blood

The Storm God

D1118225

In twelfth century Japan, Seiko Fujiwara, a young woman believed to be a sorceress, is caught in a deadly conflict between the Heike and the Genji, two clans battling for control of the throne. The peaceful Heian period is giving way to the rise of the Samurai; Japan trembles on the edge of a time of darkness.

Seiko's mother, priestess of Inari, the deity of abundance and sorcery, predicts that if Lord Kiyomori's daughter Tokushi, Seiko's closest friend, becomes Empress and gives birth to the next Emperor, their world will be saved.

If he lives...

It is Seiko's responsibility to make sure the prophecy comes true.

Journey with Seiko as she navigates through a world of assassins, palace intrigue, warfare and enchantments, struggling to honor her giri, her sacred destiny, while longing for the fulfillment of love.

Praise for Cerridwen Fallingstar's first book,

The Heart of the Fire

"Ms. Fallingstar's writing style is so captivating that you find yourself totally engrossed by the first chapter. I simply could not put this book down. I felt not so much as if I were reading a book, but that I was experiencing Fiona's life with her, as she did. A MUST READ! Highly recommended."

--The Index

"The author brings us an exciting novel filled with edge of the seat adventure which is hard to put down."

--Omega New Age Directory

"The Heart of the Fire is an unforgettable book, compelling the reader, arousing passionate emotions on every level. Read it and you will laugh, love, cry and remember."

--Green Egg Magazine

"Fallingstar is a consummate story-teller who brings her characters to life in all their fullness and complexity. She lets the characters define themselves through their relationships, especially those involving Fiona and her lovers—Annie, her young gypsy friend; Sean, the son of the village laird; and Alain, the magical wandering minstrel. I cannot remember the last time that a book moved me so deeply."

--Fireheart Magazine

"The Heart of the Fire is a gripping and disturbing look at a vanished world and way of life. The story of Fiona and Annie, their families, Alain the minstrel, the dour priest, the half-pagan nobility and the other people of the village is a story that deserves to be heard."

--Rave Reviews

"In the business of writing, few authors can successfully write about their own experiences and have them accepted by the reading public. Very little has been published by authors who were actually writing about experiences they had in another life-time. Taylor Caldwell claimed to have lived her own novels, but nobody really believed her. Fallingstar, on the other hand, augments her past life experience with meticulous research into the period and a stunning use of detail. There are no anachronisms in The Heart of the Fire. A vividly written and compelling book that is next to impossible to put down."

--New Directions for Women

"The characters in this book are rich and full. They cover a wide spectrum and are all completely believable. And the writing is brilliant. The love scenes are the most erotic I have ever read, and the pace and timing of the story are flawless. Highly recommended."

--Sage Woman Magazine

White as Bone, Red as Blood
The Storm God

A Novel

by

CERRIDWEN FALLINGSTAR

CAULDRON PUBLICATIONS
SAN GERONIMO, CALIFORNIA

Published by Cauldron Publications
P.O. Box 282, San Geronimo,
California, 94963

Book Design, Production and Cover Design:
Paige Cheong, Pacifica, CA 94044

Cover Art:
Heather Brinesh

Author Photo:
Susanna Frohman

Library of Congress Catalog Card Number: 2010919429

First Printing: January 2011
ISBN 978-0-578-07355-2

This book is dedicated to my beloved
Elie Demers, my Sessho.

Husband, lover, and partner
in sacred marriage, in this life.
And so many others.

And to our son, Zachary Demers,
our finest collaboration

Acknowledgements

The generosity of two beautiful women made the publication of this book possible. They are:

Deborah Phillips, quintessential Taurus, kind-hearted supporter of the arts.

And

Marjorie Jennings, my unofficial fairy Goddess-Mother, whose quirky brilliance shone as a beacon of creativity throughout my childhood, gently beckoning me onto my unconventional path.

Thanks also to:

Cindy Wadsworth, heart friend then, as now.

Judith Johnson, who helped me locate my past life memories within the context of Japanese History.

My wonderful editors, Lisa Alpine and Marjorie Rhea.

Heather Brinesh, who created the beautiful cover art.

And my husband, Elie Demers, whose last words to me were; "Go home and work on your book."

Foreword

I bowed happily to the girl in the mirror with the black hair, slanted eyes and embroidered silk jacket. Granted, this look had been achieved through my long-suffering mother's application of temporary hair dye, eyebrow pencil, and a trip to Chinatown to buy a 'happi' coat. But I looked into the mirror and drifted through silver space to another life.

By age ten, I knew that I had been other people; a Scottish girl raised as a Witch, a Japanese girl writing poems about cherry blossoms and maple leaves, a Greek Priestess in a temple by the water. I also knew better than to talk about it. I was glad there was one holiday a year—Halloween—where I could dance in my old skins.

The White as Bone, Red as Blood series is the story of one of those lives. These books have been thoroughly researched in all the conventional ways, but they are based on past life memory. In my early thirties, memories of a particular Japanese lifetime became so intense and pressing that I began taking notes on them and researching Japanese history to see if they were valid. I discovered, with shock, that the people I remembered as friends, lovers, and enemies were historical figures from a critical time in Japanese history known as the Gempei Wars, which spanned the end of the artistic Heian period and the beginning of the warlike Kamakura era. During the Heian period, the 'ideal man' was measured by how perfectly he matched the colors in his layers of garments, the elegance of his poetry and the eloquence of his 'morning-after' letter to the lady with whom he had spent the previous night. The Kamakura Period, which violently ended and supplanted the Heian, saw the rise of the Samurai; in this era the ideal man was one who could knock an enemy off his horse at a distance of five hundred yards with his bow and arrow or split him in half with a single blow from his sword.

White as Bone, Red as Blood; The Storm God, is the second and final book in this series. While it can be read on its own, a fuller, more satisfying experience will be obtained by reading *White as Bone, Red as Blood: The Fox Sorceress* first. To understand the true cost of war, one must understand what a culture was like in times of peace. *The Fox Sorceress* offers a window into the courtly life of the Heian period before that highly sophisticated and beautifully artistic way of life vanished into the maw of the Gempei Wars. *The Storm God* depicts the unraveling of that peace, as the Genji clan regains its strength and challenges the Heike to a series of shattering battles whose outcome will forever alter the course of Japanese History.

Through weaving together memory and research, I have endeavored to bring to life individual people and their way of looking at the world. Neither memory, nor what is recorded as history, is infallible. If I have made any errors, I ask the forgiveness of the ancestors who breathe again in these pages, and their living descendents.

Cerridwen Fallingstar
Dec. 5, 2010

"*The sound of the Gion Shoja bells
echoes the impermanence of all things;
the color of the sala flowers
reveals the truth that the prosperous must decline.*

*The proud do not endure, they are like a
dream on a spring night; the mighty fall at last,
they are as dust before the wind.*"

--*The Heike Monogatari*

Chapter One

"Susanoo!"

"Hachiman!"

Two huge Gods gallop through the night sky towards each other.
Hachiman's horse is white as bone, and the banner streaming from
his spear is pale as a sliver of moon. Susanoo's steed is jet; black
storm clouds roil about him. Puffs of flame red as blood spurt from his
horse's nostrils.

"Follow me!" Susanoo, the storm God shouts. Winds of the
hurricane lash before him. He disappears into the form of a tornado.
As it whirls down the mountain, trees fly up before him as if they were
no more than twigs. Hachiman lowers his sharp spear for the charge
and yells, "Yoritomo!"

A thousand white cranes, or seabirds, swirl in his wake. No, not
birds, but banners, brandished aloft by a thousand demon-haunted
skeletons, riding skeletal horses. They spread out like a huge tsunami
of white foam, hurtling down the sacred mountains toward Kyoto.

I gasp and bolt upright. The chodai I am sharing with Sessho is shaking. Overhead, the tinkling clatter of tiles being ripped from the roof, rumble of thunder, surging of rain against the walls. I leap from the bed. My maidservant, Machiko, instantly slides across the floor to me. "Mistress, what is it?"

"Seiko—Seiko, what's wrong?" Sessho calls, but I am already through the door, running down the hall to my daughter's room.

"Peony!" I cry, as I run into her room. The twins' nurses sit up, rubbing their eyes sleepily. I scoop four year-old Peony up out of the bed she shares with her nurse. She grabs my hair. "What's wrong, Auntie?"

Her brother sits up crying. The next instant, Sessho's hand is on my shoulder.

"Seiko, what is it?"

"The storm. We have to save them from the storm!"

"Seiko—it's not that bad…"

"There's going to be a tornado!"

Alarm flicks through his eyes. I am not the powerful sorceress most think me to be, but my visions are generally accurate.

"Take the children under the house," he orders. "I'll get Seishan and the others." He moves quickly.

Matsu's nurse grabs him up. We all make our way to the ladder leading to storerooms beneath Sessho's mansion.

Seishan clatters down the stairs next, her nine year old, Tomomori, and eleven year old Nori following. Seishan was my best friend and lover at the Empress' court in Kyoto, until she left to marry Sessho and moved here to Tanba province. I was terribly jealous until I met Sessho and fell in love with him myself.

"Where's Sessho?" I ask fearfully.

"He has to warn his brothers to get into their store rooms as well, and all the servants. How long until…?"

"I have no idea. I dreamed it." Both the four year-olds in my lap start to wail, and I realize I must calm myself to soothe the children.

"I could be helping Father to warn the servants!" Nori says. "Mother, let me go! Father shouldn't be alone!"

"I'll go too!" Tomomori leaps to his feet.

"No, neither of you will go, you will sit down right now!" Seishan says. "Oh, my poor birds!" She starts to weep.

"They'll be all right, Mother," Tomomori puts a hand on her shoulder, the way Sessho would. "Birds know what to do."

"They're in a cage. They can't flee."

My heart pounds fiercely until finally Sessho descends with the sleepy cooks and their families, maidservants and stable boys. The storeroom is tightly packed. Some of the servants run back up the ladder and return with folding screens, boxes of jewelry and Sessho's most precious manuscripts. Jars are set up behind screens in the corner and soon the fetid stench of emptied bowels permeates the cellar. We curl up on the sleeping mats the servants have brought. The twins fall asleep in my arms. We call Matsu and Kiku Botan, my Peony, the twins although it was I who bore the girl, and Sessho's wife, Seishan, who bore Matsu three weeks before her. To avoid scandal we claimed she gave birth to both. Although the children do not look alike, they are as close as if they had truly come from the same womb.

Sessho is the husband of my heart, but my service to the Empress prevents me from marrying him and living here. Outside of these walls, no one even knows we are lovers. Seishan is usually happy to share him with me, enjoying the rare solitude in which to re-anchor herself when I am here to distract him. But now, in a crisis, with the storm God battering our eaves, it is she that he wraps in his long arms. It's all right, I tell myself; we're all safe, the twins are safe.

The house shakes. "Ooh, that was a good one," Tomomori exults.

"Shut up you idiot, do you want to encourage Him?" Nori snaps, 'Him' being Susanoo, the storm God.

"Just because *you're* afraid of thunder and lightning," Tomomori gibes.

"I'm not afraid of it!" But she jumps when the next peal shakes the house.

"Like a mouse isn't afraid of a fox," he smirks.

She shoots him a baleful look. Nori and Tomomori have always been competitive with each other. She likes to fancy herself every bit as tough as the men and boys.

"Susanoo, you are beautiful in your fury," Tomomori intones. "We ask you to spare our house, and the houses of our people—and mother's birds. We thank you for your rain and the bright beauty of your lightning."

I smile. Tomomori is going to be very much like his father. His beauty is more like his mother's, but his personality is calm and unflappable, and, like Sessho, he is able to see the blessing in every circumstance. Nori has a more turbulent nature, unlike either of her parents. Matsu is wild, like Nori. Where they get that strain of wildness I cannot say. My daughter, Kiku Botan, is calm and graceful like my mother, and resembles her more with each passing year. I marvel at the two young ones being able to sleep in my arms as the storm rages. Machiko, my beloved servant, as close to me as my own shadow, sits cross-legged beside us. She is calm, as poised as a warrior, as if she could leap up and fight Susanoo himself. Machiko's lover, an older woman who is a kitchen servant in Sessho's household, creeps over, kneels beside her and clasps Machiko's hand.

I am unable to sleep, clutching the children more tightly to my chest with each roll of thunder. As the house ceases to shake I become even more agitated, knowing that things become very calm just before chaos and destruction ensue. Time passes: nothing but eerie silence.

"My Lord," one of the guards kneels before Sessho, "Shall I go out and see what is happening?"

"Yes, Koei."

"I shall go too." Koei's young son stands up. Several of the guards climb up the ladder.

"Susanoo, do not harm my loyal, brave servants," Sessho breathes.

After a time, they return.

"The worst of the storm seems to have passed, my lord. The rain is gentle now," Koei reports. "There is little damage."

"It seems your prayers have been answered, son," Sessho beams at Tomomori.

"Susanoo doesn't have any quarrel with us," Tomomori replies. "He just likes to gallop around and fling thunderbolts."

"Like you know Him personally," Nori gripes.

"I'm not afraid of Him like *some* people," Tomomori sniffs.

"What say you, sorceress?" Sessho asks.

"Let's stay down here for the rest of the night. It could come back."

"All right. Anyone who wants to return back upstairs may." Most of the guards and a few of the other servants rise to go. Most of the others look at me and then curl up on the floor.

4

Dawn comes. The rain is dropping lightly, the sky a pale gray. Sessho takes me out in the garden to look around. Shattered tiles from the roof are everywhere.

"It's the new tiles that have taken the brunt of it," he says, picking up pieces of the decorative sea turtle tiles he had placed around the edge of the roof to celebrate the birth of Emperor Antoku a year ago.

I look at the shattered tile in his hand, horrified. I can't imagine a more vile omen. When Antoku was born, I thought all of our worries were over. After so many years of prayers and spells for my childhood friend Tokushi, now the Empress, to bear a son, finally she gave birth to an heir, surviving a hellish labor. Now the claim of her family's clan, the Taira-also known as the Heike-is complete; it would seem that their right to protect the throne could not be questioned. But since then, terrible storms and foreboding prophecies have swept the Capital. And the news that Yoritomo and his brothers, heirs to the Genji clan, the Taira's greatest enemy, have been gathering allies and raising armies in the north has made our lives more insecure than ever.

"I'm afraid the tornado may be happening in Kyoto."

"You do not think the tornado will strike here?"

The rain is falling straight down now. There is barely a wind to ruffle the treetops.

"My dream..." I look around at the servants and guards who are close by.

"Let's discuss your dream inside." Sessho takes my arm and escorts me to his study. As governor of Tanba, Sessho keeps as far from court politics as possible, but having lived in the court for all my adult life, I have learned to be cautious of the talk of servants.

"Tell me your dream. Leave out no details."

I sip my green tea and describe the dream, trembling again as I recall Susanoo and Hachiman and the white flags behind them pouring like a tsunami down the sacred hills towards Kyoto.

"I am sorry I had us all go to the basement. It was Kyoto in my dream, but I was just so afraid."

"I understand. It is best to be cautious. Imagine if we had ignored your fear and the worst had occurred. Shall I send a messenger to the court now?"

"If anything has happened, we will hear from them."

Sure enough, that night, as we are eating dinner, one of Sessho's servants runs in, panting. "Two messengers have arrived from Kyoto. They say they must see Lady Fujiwara without delay."

"Bring them in." Sessho orders.

"They're—wet and muddy, sir."

"Shigata na gai—it can't be helped." Sessho says, glancing apologetically at Seishan. "Make sure their horses are well cared for."

"I shall." The servant bows and runs off.

Faster than you would think people could move, two messengers are kneeling before me. The one bearing the Empress' insignia naturally takes precedence, proffering his message first. "My message also concerns matters of state," the other grumbles. He wears Shigemori's colors, and the butterfly of the Taira clan is featured prominently on his clothing. Tokushi's older brother, he is technically head of the Taira clan now that Lord Kiyomori has taken Buddhist vows. Shigemori is loved and respected, yet everyone knows it is still Kiyomori who makes the decisions.

I question a third messenger who has just arrived, kneeling behind the first two.

"Who has sent you?"

"Lady Taira Tsunemasa."

On'na Mari. One of my oldest and dearest friends. A merchant's daughter who managed, through her great beauty, to marry Tsunemasa, one of Kiyomori's nephews. Her status is now high, but nowhere close to that of the Empress and her brother.

I unroll Tokushi's missive first, dreading what will be inside.

"You must hurry back immediately. I am sorry to cut your visit short, but a terrible tornado has destroyed a great portion of Kyoto. Thousands are dead. As usual, it is the poor who have suffered the most. The palace has not been touched, but most of the great mansions, including those of my father and brothers, have been severely damaged. We have word that the traitor Yoritomo has hired evil sorcerers and rebel monks to conjure the terrible wind. I can't be without my personal sorceress another day. It is your duty to be here, protecting the heir, rather than amusing yourself in the countryside. Regretfully, I must order you back home."

My heart sinks. I had remained by Tokushi's side throughout her entire difficult pregnancy, and pulled her through a birth which would have killed most women. She had been promising me this trip to Tanba for months. Now, after only a few days, it is to be taken away from me. I press my lips together to keep from crying. I know how selfish it is to think of myself instead of all the people killed in Kyoto. But it is like death not to be seeing my daughter grow up, not to feel Sessho's strong arms around me.

"A tornado struck Kyoto last night. The palace was untouched. But many mansions are damaged and some areas are destroyed."

"Just like you thought!" Tomomori exclaims. "We're so lucky to have a sorceress as our Auntie! Nothing bad will ever happen to us, 'cause you'll always know, right?"

Touched by his faith in me, I give him what I hope is a confident smile. "Well, I hope so."

"What's a tornado?" Matsu asks.

"It's a very bad storm," his mother says, shooting a warning glance at Tomomori so that he will not say anything that will terrorize his younger siblings. I can see how badly he wants to describe what a tornado is really like, his hand twitching in a swirling motion, but under his mother's glare he restrains himself.

I take the scroll from Shigemori's messenger.

"Alas, my dear Lady Fujiwara," Shigemori writes, "Things are even worse than we thought. The Gods have left an unmistakeable warning on my doorstep. I--and the nation—are in urgent need of your divinatory advice. I have been ill for the last fortnight, but would appreciate a visit from you at your earliest convenience. My gardeners were killed, their cottage rendered into fragments smaller than chopsticks. Other than that, those in my household are well, and my mansion, though damaged, is reparable. My garden, in which we have spent so many happy times together, is, sadly, utterly destroyed. But it is not my own losses that concern me.
Praying this letter finds you well in Tanba--"

"I'm being called back to Kyoto. The Empress and Lord Shigemori are demanding my return immediately."

"Oh no!" Seishan gasps, then smacks herself on the hand. "What a selfish creature I am."

"You just got here," Tomomori complains.

Nori droops, looking disconsolate.

"I know. The timing is so bitter. But, as your mother says, we can't be selfish."

On'na Mari's messenger shuffles up on his knees. I take the paper and unscroll it.

"My dear Seiko,

Did the tornado pass through Tanba, or did you miss all the excitement? We lost virtually our entire roof, though it is true as they say, that one man's disaster is another man's fortune. Now at last I can order some of those beautiful cerulean tiles my father has in his storeroom. Oh, our roof is going to look so magnificent when I get through with it! And, best of all, that horribly ugly warrior statue that I finally persuaded Tsunemasa to move out to the garden fell over and broke into a million pieces. Tsunemasa is distraught—it has been in his family for three generations. From the look of it, you would have thought it was thirty. It seems even Susanoo cannot resist my charms, as the only destruction to our house was absolutely to my benefit. Sadly, some of our servants were killed; the only difficulty will be interviewing for new ones. Akoyo slept through the whole thing, but then, he does seem determined to sleep his life away. I received a letter from the Empress this morning, so sweet of her to be concerned for us. Fortunately the palace was not touched. It seems Amaterasu still holds sway over her tempestuous brother."

I smile. The quarrels between the Sun Goddess Amaterasu, divine ancestress of the royal family, and her Storm God brother, Susanoo, are legendary. It is so like On'na Mari to have a childish enthusiasm for such stories.

"There is quite a bit of damage to Munemori's mansion," the letter continues, "and trees like battering rams smashed down much of the wall surrounding Lord Kiyomori's Roduhara residence. He's not happy with those omens, you may be sure. Tsunemasa is quite anxious about the omen of the warrior being smashed. Goodness, can't a wind just be a wind? Maybe it means we won't have to fight because Yoritomo will just slink off with his tail between his legs, don't they ever think of that? Many of the peasant homes and shops were blown down, but you know how it is, the slightest gust will blow them down. In any case, no one we know was killed, so I think the only logical conclusion is that the Storm God, like everyone else, considers peasants to be expendable. Still, I imagine you will be called back to court, since

8

Tokushi seems ready to have a nervous breakdown about it all. I am on my way over there now to try to console her. I plan to bring her some of my little opium candies. That should settle her down. I do hope it doesn't take too long, because I want to get back in time to supervise the work on my beautiful new blue roof! Travel back safely; I hear many of the roads are impassable. Your loving friend—"

"No one we know has been killed, but there is quite a bit of damage," I say, and read On'na Mari's letter to the group. Sessho's sisters-in-law gasp with sympathy. "How lucky we are to be away from the Capital!" one exclaims.

"Surely you're not suggesting the Capital is an unlucky place to be," her husband chides.

"Oh no, I never meant to suggest that."

" I wish we'd been there, I would have liked to see the tornado," Tomomori says. "I've read about them, but I've never actually seen one."

Nori shakes her head and rolls her eyes as if to say, 'What an idiot.'

"At least I'm not scared of them," Tomomori punches his sister in the arm. She grabs his wrist.

"Stop that now," Seishan warns.

"Fine, I'll come sit by you." Tomomori stomps over, sits beside Seishan. "Why you ever put us together anyway..."

"I like being able to look at my handsome children across the table." Already my heart aches so much with missing the family even the children's bickering seems endearing.

Sessho puts a hand on my back. "When does the Empress want you to return?"

"As soon as possible. She'll be sending her palanquin in a day or two."

"Well," he says consolingly, "Many of the roads will probably be impassable, at least for a palanquin. It will take a while before enough trees can be cleared for them to get here. What with all the other repairs—it might be awhile before I can spare the workers to go remove those trees."

It is all I can do to refrain from hurling myself into his arms. Since we are at dinner with the whole family, I just give him a grateful smile and squeeze his thigh under the table.

"There's a lot of destruction in the garden," Seishan chimes, wide-eyed. "The gardeners are going to be very busy."

9

"Oh, *yeah*," Tomomori says, as the purpose of their deception dawns on him. "Yeah, the garden's a *mess*. Wait till you see how much better I am with a bow and arrow," he says to me, "Now that the winds have stopped…"

"I can't wait to see."

I know Sessho won't be able to put off removing the trees from the roads forever. But it is a relief to think I have at least three or four more days to spend with my family. Whether the tornado is a sign foretelling crises, or an attack sent by Genji sorcerers, it will just have to wait.

Chapter Two

Destruction is everywhere. Looking out the window of the carriage, I see people sifting through splintered wood, torn fabric, shattered tiles. At one house a small boy dressed only in a breechclout dances triumphantly, waving a metal pot that has been barely dented. A woman, perhaps his mother, sits on a pile of rubble nearby absently caressing a small doll in her lap, looking towards us but not seeing us. I wonder what happened to the girl who owned that doll.

By the storm it reached Kyoto, the storm had become the terrible tornado of my nightmare, destroying these houses and ripping me away from my true home. I unscroll the chiding letter from Lady Daigon-no-suke. "Demons conjured by the Genji sorcerers roiled the whirlwind. The palace is safe, but Kyoto is devastated. It is absurdly selfish for you to go off visiting, leaving us unprotected at a time like this. The Empress and the young heir need all the protection you can afford them."

I shake my head, looking outside my window again. People shoveling broken crockery and splintered ridge poles into carts. At several points our carriage comes to a standstill, the road so covered with debris we must turn and find another route. How can they think any human can stand against the whirlwind? I was so glad when the storm passed through Tanba and left us safe, when it seemed the dream was only a dream. But not for these people. For these people, the nightmare is quite real.

We pass through an entire block where there is nothing but rubble. I try to remember what was here before but can't visualize it. A three-legged stool sits at the edge of the road as if waiting for its owner to return.

It is a relief to see the palace intact. Lady Daigon-no-suke is waiting for me under a parasol held by a servant to ward off the strong summer sun. She rises, looking resentful. "What in the world took you so long? We were told you were on the outskirts of the city hours ago."

"Have you seen what the city looks like?"

"Actually, I have been rather busy here, trying to calm the Empress," she snorts.

"Well, many of the roads are impassable. We had to keep changing our route. After awhile it was impossible to avoid the day's unlucky directions."

"Well, none of us are feeling particularly lucky at this time."

"I notice the palace seems to have escaped all harm."

"The courtyard was thick with Shinto priests and Buddhist monks alike, all chanting and reciting charms to turn back the storm from the palace. The Empress was hysterical, not having you there."

She escorts me to the Empress' quarters. Tokushi gets up and grabs me fiercely. "I *needed* you! I needed you and you weren't here!" she cries. "You're never here when I need you!"

"I was very relieved to hear you were all right."

"Takakura was here. *He* came. But you didn't come."

"No one could have traveled during that storm."

"Antoku kept screaming and no one could stop him!"

She has led me into her chodai and now weeps on my shoulder. "You can never, ever leave us again. Terrible things always happen when you leave."

It is no use telling her that I was here when fire destroyed much of the city two years ago, and for her son's birth, and that usually things are utterly quiet and boring the whole time I am gone. "I'm here now, I'm here now," I keep saying. "Look, all the talismans I made you, all the spells woven around your bed are still here. The spells I gave you and Antoku kept you safe, didn't they?"

"I needed someone to hold me," she sobs.

Yes, and I need that sometimes too, I think to myself, longing for Sessho's strong arms. There and only there can I be vulnerable and afraid, not the strong one--Seiko, not the powerful sorceress. Tokushi seems to have forgotten that it was her own invention about me, saying I could change myself into a bird, which caused my reputation as a sorceress to begin. Now she is as convinced as all the rest that I have powers beyond their mortal understanding.

"You must do battle with these evil sorcerers who sent the tornado," she whimpers. "The Genji have bewitched all these lords in the north to turn against us. And now Susanoo appears to be on their side."

I shudder when she says that, remembering it was not just Susanoo, but Hachiman, god of war, calling out the name of Yoritomo, raising the demon army of my nightmare.

I will never tell Tokushi my dream.

"Your father defeated Yoritomo's father, Yoshitomo. Do you really think the sons are any match for him, or for Shigemori? Now Lord Kiyomori is even more powerful, surrounded by his powerful sons. Shigehira and Tsunemasa will set things right. If those fools from the north ever try anything except talk, the only regret will be theirs, you know that."

"We need someone to fight for us on the plains of heaven."

"Thousands of monks and priests are doing just that. Have you sent word to the High Priestess of Ise?" I ask, referring to Amaterasu's mouthpiece, who occupies the highest spiritual office in the land.

"Of course. We haven't heard back yet. All the priests will be doing divinations soon. Shigemori wants you to do one at his mansion."

My heart sinks. "Well, of course. Whatever he desires."

"I had them draw a bath for you, but it is probably cold by now." She rings a bell to call the servants.

"It has to be from supernatural forces," Tokushi whispers. "Whoever heard of a tornado in the middle of June?"

"We'll have a bath and a massage, then we'll sleep. It will all seem better tomorrow."

Shigemori is busy helping to organize the rebuilding of the city and the restoration of his own residence. Kiyomori is very efficient. He sees to it that merchants who have been devastated receive expedited loans from the Ministry of Finance so their shops can be rebuilt immediately. He negotiates with the temples so that teams of woodcutters can bring logs back from the forest. The woodcutters and stonemasons are paid overtime to work from cock-crow to cock-crow.

It is well over a week before Shigemori can receive me, despite all his messages of urgency. Every day the women of the court go over again and again the terror of the storm, even though they were nowhere near the worst of it.

There is not a single girl here that I am interested in now. Cross-eyed, Sallow, Foolish, Pious, Self-important—the nicknames I privately assign the girls currently under Tokushi's care are not flattering, but all too accurate. It is all I can do to hide my resentment. 'Battle the Genji sorcerers', Tokushi implores me, then hands me a robe to embroider. I almost wish I had been here for the tornado. At least it would have been something interesting.

13

Chapter Three
1179

I am sitting with Shigemori in a room adjacent to the gardens of his elegant mansion. Close to forty, he is the oldest of the Kiyomori children; Tokushi in her mid-twenties, is the youngest. His robe is dark green embroidered with gold dragons. When the silk ripples it looks like the dragons are alive, breathing fire. He is toying with a small knife. We are kneeling on tatami mats; the doors to the outside are wide open. Most of his garden was devastated by the tornado, but this alcove was spared. Bushes trimmed to curve like waves are studded with ripe red pyracantha berries. Many birds are feasting on the berries, accompanied by loud cheepings and bursts of song. The finches and sparrows love the fermented berries; they get as loud and raucous as the courtiers on feast days. It is a charming sight, but Shigemori's smile is bitter.

"Heike birds," he comments.

"What makes them Heike birds?" I ask.

"Eating the fermented berries with abandon, oblivious to the cats lurking beneath the bushes which they cannot see."

I don't see any cats beneath this particular bush, but it is true that when the birds get too drunk to fly, the cats appear and polish them off.

Again, his rueful smile. "So we feast on all the bounty they offer, and become drunk on our own riches. Anything the birds don't notice, the cats do. There is a penalty for too much excess, a penalty with claws and teeth."

At first I think he is referring to his brother Munemori, who is fatter than any autumn sparrow and infamous for his decadence. But then I realize he means the whole Heike clan. It is true that all the plum positions at the court are even being given to the farthest-flung cousins, regardless of their age or ability. Clan supporters are rewarded for their loyalty, but the clan itself is taking the juiciest parts. Certainly many other hereditary nobles have been enraged that young Heike with no experience are given advancement over nobles whose lineage may be Fujiwara or some other equally ancient line, that competent, hard-working courtiers are replaced by fifteen-year-old boys who use their offices for drinking and sporting with maid-servants. Experienced men in their forties are often forced to give way to youths whose hair is barely out of boys' loops. Of course, Kiyomori prefers to have young people of his own family around him, because then he can simply tell them what to do.

But when Shigemori continues, I realize he refers to situations more pressing than the jealousies of the court.

"I have always been so proud of my father for sparing the children of his greatest enemy, even Yoritomo who was a young warrior of fourteen at the time. One would expect karma to reward such generosity." He shakes his head. "It would have been fitting for them to spend the rest of their days in the monasteries, praying for Lord Kiyomori's well-being. But instead each of them in turn—Yoritomo, Noriyori and Yoshitsune—has used his time in the monastery fasting, praying, drinking only from the purest mountain waterfalls, developing ascetic powers to obtain supernatural strength and prowess, to become a warrior worth a thousand. And now they have gathered in Kamakura, with clouds of warriors—even some from my own family— pledging their support every day. Already the monks of Todaiji and Kofukuji are said to be secretly siding with Yoritomo and the Genji. Meanwhile, my father continues to make enemies of the monks on Mt. Hiei and half the court."

I am drinking green tea brought by Shigemori's servants. When I realize he is drinking only water, I switch to water. He says he feels that someone in the clan must seek the path of purity to counterbalance the excesses of the rest.

"Do you think one man's sacrifice will be enough?" I ask.

He shakes his head. "I know very well that my sacrifices are meaningless. Still. I feel a sacred obligation to make the attempt." There has always been something of the ascetic in Shigemori. It is a spiritual quality Tokushi shares. Where they come by it, given the insatiable drive for power both their parents display, is a mystery. I often think Shigemori would take the tonsure of a monk, but he could never be permitted to depart the court for a monastery: he is far too valuable to Lord Kiyomori, as essential to him as roots or legs, for all their quarreling. And his bonds of affection for his wife and children are great.

15

"Birds will fly," I say, trying to allude delicately to the fact that Kiyomori will die one day, upon which Shigemori will be leading the clan and can impose his own vision of how things should be.

"Often eggs do not hatch," he says, shaking his head. "Come and walk with me?"

We go out and walk in the garden where servants are busily planting new trees and flowering plants. He orders the guards accompanying us to walk quite a long ways behind so that our conversation can be private.

It seems silly to have guards trailing us through the garden anyway. I suppose an assassin could be lurking, but despite my own success at having invaded the palace garden, I think danger here is unlikely.

"Your sister sends her regards."

"Yes, and mine to her." We walk in silence a bit. "I'm wondering, would you do a brazier reading for me, for my family?" asks Shigemori.

My heart sinks. I don't like to do readings. One can never control what one sees. Most of the people consulted for such things simply determine in advance what they are going to say while under apparent possession, hoping it will offend no one and seem too obscure to be held against them later. But if I take the proper teas and light the brazier fire, it is almost certain that I will fall into trance and things will speak themselves through me that perhaps should not be spoken. I understand why he wants to look--to know what must be done to secure the rights of Tokushi's son, Antoku, and preserve the influence and the bloodlines of the Heike. *If the line goes through Tokushi's womb, Japan will thrive...*so my mother predicted before her death. Did she foresee the return of the Genji, and their threat, when she said that Japan stood at the edge of a time of darkness?

"Well, of course. You or Tokushi may command me at your will."

"And do I need to command you?" he asks. "Would you not do it out of friendship for us?"

"I would rather not, for I cannot control the outcome."

"That is precisely why I value your scrying, and why I would like you, and only you, to do it," he says. "You are the only one I can trust to do it honestly and not to simply say what you believe I want to hear."

"What small skills I have are always at your disposal."

"I sense harsh times coming for the Heike," he says. "We have alienated too many people. My father seems to think he can chop off a few of his fingers

16

and it won't affect the working of his hand. The problem is, he is a warrior. Making war is what he knows. He knows how to intimidate, how to crush opposition..."

"Your father has built some good coalitions."

"Perhaps in the past," he says impatiently, "but now...now he is too certain of himself, now he offends right and left and thinks nothing of it. A coalition built on fear will dissolve like soot into ink. There is talk everywhere, like the scuttlings of mice. Right now, yes, he keeps a tight rein, and if the horse's mouth is sore, the horse will obey. When it is my turn..." he shakes his head. "So I implore you, will you look in the brazier for me?"

I cannot refuse Shigemori a direct request. He is a good man, his strength tempered in gentleness, the man I value most after Sessho and Tsunemasa. I have often wished that he would fancy me, but he seems devoted to his wife and his primary concubine, and it seems he has no use for any further distractions, unlike Munemori who has bevy upon bevy of beauties to wait on him hand and foot. Munemori spends a fortune giving large sums of money to those he gets with child, so they can marry a man interested in a large dowry and be resettled out in the country in a respectable manner. Shigemori does not do anything that the most upright man could not be expected to do. He reminds me of Tokushi; though they are separated by many years, they are like twins. Shigemori is always inward, thoughtful, restrained, unlike his father, Kiyomori, who, while shrewd and perceptive, conducts the game of statesmanship like a war. Kiyomori offers rewards for unflinching loyalty, true, but his demands are always backed with the threat of force. Shigemori seems to have almost none of that will-force: he is strong, like a sword, yet almost without his own volition, as if he were just a tool in his father's hand. But Shigemori is loved. Men follow him because they trust him to truly have what is best for all the country in his heart.

We pass the pond, hearing the frogs croaking. As we draw close we see them abandoning their lily pads for the shelter of the cool green water.

"They too are the Heike," observes Shigemori. "They brag and croak about their own position, each seeking to be louder than the next. But at the first sign of danger..." he indicates the empty lily pads. "That braggadocio will be our undoing."

He has chosen an appropriate night to ask for a channeling, the third night before the moon is entirely gone. When the moon hides her outer face, that energy may be pulled into the head of the diviner, to shine forth from there. Servants are sent to the marketplace to fetch the mugwort, poppy pods and other herbs I will need for the divination. I spend the remainder of the day playing poetry games with Shigemori's family, admiring the calligraphy of the boys, and their archery as well. I also nap briefly, to gather and store energies for the work of the night. Shigmori's home is sumptuous, yet almost spartan compared to the dwellings of most families of comparable wealth. Everything he has, each vase, statue and extraordinary wall hanging is of the finest quality but his place is not cluttered. The effect is very restful; I am asleep within moments of curling up on a futon.

Regretfully, I must stay in my room and skip dinner so as to be purified and allow the teas I must take to achieve their maximal effect. Servants come to escort me outside when it grows dark. My loyal Machiko accompanies me.

The garden is so different at night. The birds are silent. Frogs and crickets rule the night, weaving melodies as complex as any exchange between drums and lutes. But their sounds are almost drowned out by the droning of the monks Shigemori has hired, the deep throbbing sounds they make similar to that of the frogs. At first I am annoyed to see them there--my mother always did her divining work surrounded by silence--but as the thrum of their sounds enters my body it weaves together with the teas to close the mind of Seiko and open the path of the channel.

Shigemori's friend Kaneyasu sits with his scrolls near a small scented-fat lantern to write down everything I say. I light the brazier, which has been prepared with a combination of herbs, salts and alcohol. The blue flame takes hold, spreads across the liquid, more sensuous and fluid than any ordinary fire can be. I see the blue snakes of flame roll, twist, grapple, then turn into blue dragons, wrestling. The dragons assume different colors and their struggle grows more fierce; their claws and teeth draw blood. A dragon of white flame grabs a younger, smaller dragon of red and gold and devours it. In the next moment the white flame becomes a white wave, seizing the dragons and carrying them under. Herbs burning on the surface of the brazier become boats burning; figures detach themselves from them and leap, screaming, into a burning sea.

I hear Shigemori's voice without understanding the words; pull myself back from the scene so as to make out what he is asking. He is asking about the fate of the Heike. I see waves coming in, smoothing the sand; a peaceful image,

18

yet I take it to mean that all of the deeds and the knowledge of the Heike will be erased. I see a man hoeing with a baby in his arms. I see rice fields, burnt, blackened and smoking. The smoke is thick, choking. I cough, acrid smell of flame, blood, fear...the smoke parts, revealing men battling, flags white as bone, red as blood, swords slashing, men and horses screaming, and the smoke...the palace burning, boats burning, Kyoto burning...

"Mistress, mistress, oh please, mistress..." I wake to find Machiko holding a bottle of aromatic oil under my nose, dabbing my face with cool cloths soaked in a lemongrass decoction. Her face is bathed in tears.

Shigemori is kneeling on the other side of me. "Thank heavens you have returned. Your breath and pulse had both stopped. My sister would have never forgiven me if I had sent you on to the ancestors with my greed for future knowledge."

I feel dizzy, pounding in my ears. It would be unthinkable to vomit in front of Shigemori, but it takes all my will not to do so.

"What did I say?"

"Many things. Many battles. But at the last...the Kami of the sea, flanked with the Sea Nagas, took the Heike, who were on the brink of defeat, to their undersea palace. You said that there the bones of the innocent dead would be an irritant, until those in a future time should make their deaths into pearl."

I lay back in Machiko's lap. "Forgive my tongue for uttering such an ill-omened speech. Perhaps demons prevailed on my mind and disordered my trance."

Shigemori shakes his head with a wry smile. "No. The Kami of Prophesy was within you. Your flesh was only the lantern, her wisdom the light. I myself had a dream--marked with a Torii so I would know it was from the Gods-- heralding the end of the Heike. And Kaneyasu came to me that very night to tell me of a dream he had experienced which proved to be identical to mine. Yet I thought perhaps demons had swayed us both. But when you spoke, you spoke with the authority of Inari, the voice of the land. And if the sea itself turns against us, when our clan is descended from the first sailors and it is we, the Taira, who keep the shrine at Itkushima--then we are lost indeed."

Kaneyasu steps closer to Shigemori, looking down on me. "An amazing journey back from the dead," he mutters. "Truly we thought the spirit world had claimed you."

"Your hands are like ice," worries Shigemori, and only then do I realize he has been holding one. "We need to get you inside."

I sit up. The wave of dizziness and nausea has passed. They help me into Shigemori's chamber and ply me with restorative tea and sake until my normal breathing and circulation has been restored.

Shigemori looks over at the scrolls Kaneyasu is holding. "The Heike think only of the rice cakes, not of the fields. So Inari said, and then she spoke of the rice fields burning...what else? Did you write it all down?"

Kaneyasu looks at his notes. "The time of planting has passed and the green growth. The rice hangs heavy and the time of winnowing is upon us. The whirlwind is coming. Nothing can stand before it."

"Yet perhaps this ill fortune can still be averted," Kaneyasu says. "Perhaps it is not the will of the Gods but a result of miscalculation on the part of Lord Kiyomori. You have been trying to heal the rift between him and Go-Shirakawa. And the other courtiers--he has forgotten the sweet rice and uses only the whip. Even a horse will rebel against such treatment."

"My father was wily when he was younger. Now he lacks patience," Shigemori despairs. "He showed great cunning in the acquisition of power, but little in the maintaining of it. He of all people should know that 'after the battle is won, never turn your back on the vanquished.' 'A sword must be kept sharp.' 'A dull sword is not a plow.' I learned those proverbs on his knee! He is drunk on power, like a lesser man becomes drunk on sake."

"But you are his best beloved, his eldest son, his heir and his wisest advisor," I say.

"So he says when others are present. When we are alone he treats me like a small child having trouble with nightmares. He says I lack the will to command."

"The man who knows how to ride does not injure his horse's mouth," Kaneyasu murmurs. He lays a hand on Shigemori's arm. There is such affection in his touch I think they must be lovers.

"We must tell Lord Kiyomori of this remarkable series of events," Kaneyasu says.

Shigemori shakes his head. He is as pale as parchment. "The judgment of the Gods has been rendered. There is no escaping karma. Still, I will build and dedicate a temple in the hopes of cleansing the ill deeds of Lord Kiyomori against the temples. Even if our prosperity cannot be preserved, perhaps the Amida Buddha will look kindly upon our prospects of rebirth."

"It is the Kami, the Old Ones, who have sent us the visions of warning," I say.

"Yes, but it is the Buddhists against whom we have sinned. So it is the Buddha whom we must petition to restore the balance."

I sigh, but hold my counsel. Like his sister Tokushi, Shigemori is infatuated with the foreign Buddha. He had explained his philosophy to me on one of our walks. "The Kami are our mother-line. They gave us life. They come from the womb of Inazami, from the age of Queens. But the Buddha is our father, only now revealed to us, whose realm is not the body and the beauties of creation, but the ineffable serenity of spirit. To him we owe the fealty of a son to a father."

How have Lord and Lady Kiyomori, whose only concerns are power and wealth in this world, spawned two such spiritual dreamers like Shigemori and Tokushi, who are so enchanted with the next?

Chapter four
1179

Shigemori sets to work immediately building the temple of his vision. Construction ceases everywhere in the capital as he commandeers every carpenter, journeyman and laborer for the task. The hall is finished in an astonishingly short time, a beautiful structure at the foot of the eastern mountains. It has forty-eight bays for each of the Amida Buddha's forty-eight vows, and in each bay hangs a lantern. Even I, who have minimal patience for Buddhism or its trappings, feel transported to the edge of the spirit world when I accompany Shigemori, the Empress, and the most important court dignitaries to attend the dedication ceremony.

It takes place at night; the lanterns gleam and twinkle like the weaver's stars in a constellation of wonder. Six beautiful girls stand at each of the bays, representing the six paths. Many are from the Empresses' court, all are from the best families. Each girl is dressed in colors symbolic of the path of Buddhism which she represents. They all chant the Amida's name in unison, until we are lost in a sea of sound and light.

Sessho and Seishan have come all the way from Tanba. Seishan chants with tears running down her face, lit up from within like one of the lanterns until she weeps so hard she can no longer move her lips. Even Sessho has tears in his eyes, the girls' voices and the beauty of the lanterns are so moving.

After this, everyone refers to Shigemori as the Minster of the Lanterns. But though he seemed filled with purpose throughout the construction of his dream, afterwards his melancholy returns, though his being is still suffused with a gentle radiance. He worked himself unstintingly during the construction of the temple, insisting he oversee every aspect of the project, demanding that the simple laborers maintain an attitude of reverence while they worked. Meanwhile, he did not shirk his duties as Minister of State, but carried on his meetings and paperwork late into the night, sleeping little and eating less. Despite his work on a holy enterprise, he continued to have vivid nightmares, but considered them messages from the gods and so would not take my sleeping draughts to stop them. Now that the project is over, I note that he is painfully thin, with dark circles under his eyes. I express my concerns to Tokushi, who sends me to him.

"Now I regret having denied his request for you to share his bed," she frets. "By all means, if he has the energy and you think it will comfort him, embrace him."

"Shigemori asked for me? When?"

"Oh, many times," Tokushi says, giving a nervous, airy wave of her hand.

"You never told me."

"It was mine to decide. As if you did not have enough...distractions! I told him to find his own Inari Priestess. I offered him his choice of the other ladies. Anyway, what he needs now are your healing skills, so gather your herbs as quickly as possible. You may stay there as long as you deem necessary."

Shigemori is surprised to see me, his sister having written only that she was sending a healer. Four servants and Machiko accompany me, carrying every sort of herb and charm in my possession, and our healing entourage quite fills up his study. He has received me at his home, which is in Kyoto but some distance from the palace.

"It looks as if my sister has sent many gifts, but you are the best gift of all," Shigemori says, embracing me. "What is the occasion?"

"Actually, my lady is concerned for your health. These bags are not gifts, but merely a selection of herbs and charms with which she hopes . . ."

"To turn back the tides of karma?" Shigemori asks gently.

Seeing my expression, he lays a hand gently on the side of my face.

"Well, let us retire to my chambers and you can take my pulses," he says, taking me by the hand.

We enter his bedroom. His wife seems startled to see me as well.

"Tokushi has sent her physician to care for me," he tells her.

"Thank the heavens!" she cries, pressing my hand in welcome. "We are honored by your visit, Lady. Anything you wish, my servants are entirely at your disposal, and our fortunes as well."

"I only hope I will be able to help."

Shigemori reclines on a futon, moving as if his bones hurt. His pulses are faint, erratic and slippery. Running my fingers along the inside of his arms I find several mysterious swellings. He says he had sustained no injury at any of the sites. The glands at his throat and groin are swollen also. Clearly this is not a simple matter of overwork and concern for the state. The swelling of the glands bespeaks inflammation, but his overall system is cool, overly yin. I ask the servants I have brought with me to brew him a restoring tea, not knowing if I can trust the servants in his household.

"Have you been receiving acupuncture? Your whole system requires both tonics and a redirection of your chi."

"The Amida Buddha and his tender mercies is all the physician I require now."

"If you wish to continue ministering to the state, you must let others minister to you," I say gently.

Tears fill his eyes. "My poor family. My poor country. Only the Amida Buddha can save us now."

I sit him up to give him the tea when the servants return with it, shocked at how easily I can feel his vertebrae through the cloth of his garments.

"But you are the instrument of the Amida Buddha," I advise him. "Only you can chart a peaceful course between Lord Kiyomori and Retired Emperor Go-Shirakawa. Only you can unite the capital and the surrounding provinces against the unstable forces in the East. Your health is the health of the nation."

His eyes gaze beyond me. "I supported Father in ending the tradition of sacrifice. I thought it was the best thing he had ever done. But perhaps we were wrong. Perhaps a sacrifice is needed in this time of trouble."

"Not you, Shigemori. Not you," I chide, rubbing his glands with aromatic unguents and chafing his limbs with Machiko's help to restore circulation. "Your body is ill and your mind is full of sick fancies. Forgive me for saying so, my lord, but your judgment is weakened."

He nods vaguely. "I grow weaker." I administer a draught to put him into a deep, restorative sleep, and while he drowses, I seek out his wife.

"Lady Shigemori, I fear demons have taken advantage of his tired mind and have gained possession of him. Have you called in the shamans to drive out the evil influences?"

Tears spill out of her eyes. "Aiee, pardon this foolish woman's emotions. No, he will not hear of it. And the only prayers he will allow to be said for him are prayers for his soul's rebirth in the Pure Land."

"And the physicians his father sent earlier? What do they say?"

"He will not see them. Not even the esteemed Chinese physician Wu Shan Tzu sent by Lord Kiyomori at great expense. He has agreed to see no one but yourself." Tears fall from her eyes, spots of darkness blooming on her kimono. "Thank the heavens you are here, now there is some hope."

"He needs acupuncture and he needs, badly, to be exorcised. Surely he will see some of the monks from the Hall of Lanterns?"

"Perhaps if you advise it," she says tremulously. "He has always said you had the finest mind of any woman at court."

The next day, as Shigemori and I sit sequestered in the shade of a wisteria trellis, I say, "Your wife tells me that you refused to see the great physician sent by Lord Kiyomori." He sips his tea moodily, staring off into his garden. There are still holes in the ground left when the tornado of June twelfth uprooted trees. At a distance, we can see servants dredging the waterways and ponds, plopping surviving carp and turtles into buckets. Other workers are rebuilding a miniature replica of Mt. Fuji. A shaft of sunlight illuminates our bower. Shigemori sighs, as if the sun hurt him.

"No one can stop the whirlwind," he says at last.

"True."

"But why not?" he probes.

"It is a force too great for any but the gods to control."

"Would you say that karma is also such a force?"

I grit my teeth, seeing too late where the conversation is leading. "It is true that the laws of karma are beyond mortal comprehension," I admit, refilling his cup. "Let me pour you some more of this tea." I shake my head at the maidservant crouching unobtrusively behind a curtain of wisteria pods.

"Yes, not even the great Wu Shan Tzu, traveling all the way from China can stop the whirlwind, nor cease the inevitable progress of karma. You have heard no doubt that several of the smaller shrines were smashed as the tornado passed through?"

"Yes."

"A torii was ripped up, whole," he says, "spun through the air, ripped in half, and deposited here in my garden." He exhales as if exasperated by my

25

obtuseness. "How could there be a more blatant sign from the gods? My mountain…" he points towards the wreckage at the other end of the garden, "laid low. Chopped down as if it had never existed. The oldest plums and cherries, whose fragrant canopies had given me pleasure for years…" He exhales another shaky breath. "All gone. All gone before the wind."

"As I said, it is not we who determine the ways of karma. Nor, perhaps, is it even within the realm of our intelligence to discern whether the cause of such a storm is natural or supernatural. As to interpreting its meanings…"

"Do not treat me like a child. I may not have your powers of divination, and I cannot lay any claims to sorcery…but I am not a fool. Like any man, I may ignore it when the gods whisper to me. But when they shout…" He finishes his tea, and I pour him another cup.

His despair is so profound as to be contagious. A broken torii laid on one's doorstep would be a sign to quail the strongest of spirits.

"The roof was torn off along the long hall," he continues, gesturing to a pillared hallway connecting parts of his mansion.

"The new tiles look lovely," I say, wincing at my trite response.

"Yes," he sighs, "the new tiles look lovely."

"Perhaps the message is only that when our dreams are destroyed, we must have the courage to build anew," I suggest.

"You weren't here for the storm. You didn't see the tornado."

"The palace was not touched."

"No. But every mansion of the Heike was affected."

"But none destroyed."

He smiles. "You are relentless." His dry fingers pat my hand. His skin feels like thin parchment. "It was like the howling of a hundred thousand demons. Munemori's pleasure pavilion was utterly destroyed. A pillar from the pavilion was hurled through the central gate, into the front doors, quivering there like an arrow from a giant's bow. What do you think of that? The whole sky was black, with flashes of supernatural red and green. Thousands of tiles, whole cedar roofs, shrieking humans, bellowing oxen--all caught up, tossed helter-skelter across the city. The rivers overflowed, wresting houses from their foundations, because the bridges were so clogged with bodies. But you think this was simply a storm…a natural occurrence. No one who was here could possibly question that this was a dreadful communication from the gods. And after Kaneyasu and I had the same dream, marked by a torii…"

26

"Did you receive signs during your pilgrimage to Kumano Shrine?" I ask, knowing that he and his three sons have just returned from making prayers and offerings in the wake of the storm.

"I have told no one except Kaneyasu this. I prayed, all night, at the Hongu Shojoden Hall, asking if the sins of my family might yet be forgiven. And I offered my own life as atonement. Though Kaneyasu did not know the content of my prayer, he said a light as brilliant as that of the full moon poured from me as I was praying, then was suddenly extinguished, making it seem as if the whole hall had been plunged into darkness. My illness began later that night."

"But you've been exhausted from your work on the Hall of Lanterns, all the politics, the insubordination of the North--any man would fall under such strain."

"The next day," Shigemori continues as if I had not interrupted, "as we were returning from Kumano, Koremori and the other boys plunged into the river, knocking each other off their horses, mock-battling, letting off steam from the enforced silence and solemnity of our visits to the shrines and temples. We were all still wearing our white pilgrimage robes. As they became wet, the lavender under robes they were all wearing began to shine through, making it appear as if they wore mourning garb." He takes another deep breath. "The gods have granted me clarity," he says. "Do not try to deprive me of it. It is one of the only comforts remaining to me."

He crumbles some of the almond cookies, scattering them under a newly planted privet hedge beside him. A sparrow which has been cheeping unseen inside the hedge hops down and begins pecking up the crumbs.

"If we are speaking of signs, what of the sign that this physician happens to be in Kyoto right when you are ill? What of the sign that I am beside you now? We cannot pick and choose only the signs which suit our mood."

"If a Chinese physician were to cure me, it would imply that Japanese medicine is inferior. And if he can't cure me, what's the use? No, karma cannot be cured. It is my father who will heed no signs unless they suit him. It would take something...like the loss of his eldest son...to get him to pay attention. But I am drinking your tea." He smiles wanly. "I appreciate how you have used jasmine flowers and peach juice to mask the bitter parts. I only hope to live long enough to enjoy this season's peaches."

"What of your sons? They are far too young to be without their father."

"Sometimes an old tree must fall before a young one can flourish," he quotes. "It is too sad being in the garden now. I will go lie down. I hope you will forgive my rudeness."

"No, you should rest as much as possible."

"I will have my servant Jozen give me a massage."

"Excellent plan."

"Please don't trouble yourself, Lady Fujiwara," he says, indicating I should stay seated as he struggles to rise. Two of his servants leap nimbly through the sliding door and take him by the elbows. "There's not much to enjoy out here," he croaks. "But at least there is still the sunshine."

"I'll come back in with you."

"I need to sleep."

"Forgive me, my lord, I did not mean to be intrusive."

"I'll call for you when I wake," he promises.

I walk out into the garden, Machiko gliding beside me. "He does not look well, mistress," she ventures. That is an understatement; he is more gray today than when I arrived.

"Perhaps the ginger and ginseng and dried peach will take effect in another few days. Their power takes time to build in the blood," I reply.

"Of course." She takes my left hand and starts massaging it, knowing that when I am tense I clench my hands unconsciously. It is true that Shigemori's garden is barely recognizable. I walk through a cluster of maples that survived, the green leaves providing some welcome shade on this humid day. I cross over a bridge traversing a dry stream into the bamboo grove where Shigemori, after a full moon gathering, once proposed that we should be lovers. The day is so heavy and still, the bamboo is silent. The bamboo symbolizes long life. I cup my hand around one of the cool green stalks, trying to find a hopeful sign in the fact that this grove was spared. But my hope feels as hollow as this reed.

Throughout the summer, I spend more time at Shigemori's mansion than at the palace. Towards the end of August, when he is too weak to resist, Japanese physicians begin treating him with needles and moxa. But by this time, I despair of anything working. He no longer seems in any way depressed or sad. In fact, he is entirely peaceful, making gentle jokes, playing the occasional game of Go with his sons, reading to them from the sutras.

On the twenty-eighth, a Buddhist Abbot shaves Shigemori's head as Shigemori takes his vows, changing his name to Joren. Kaneyasu excuses himself from the ceremony, black rivers of makeup streaming down his face. Lady Shigemori remains calm. She has lost almost as much weight as Shigemori in the last month.

September first, I send a message to Tokushi, letting her know it will not be long. Rows of droning monks fill the halls and gardens. As I am clasping Shigemori's feet in my hands, he slips into unconsciousness. Koremori continues reading to him from the sutras. I tell servants to fetch the rest of the family. Less than an hour later, with Tokushi stroking his head, his wife and sons clustered around him, and Kaneyasu standing in the corner sobbing, Shigemori breathes his last.

Chapter Five
1179-80

Women are sewing, reading, or otherwise quietly occupied in Tokushi's quarters. The technical time of mourning for Shigemori has passed, but Tokushi is so grieved by the loss of her favorite brother, and her sister Moriko, who died soon after, that her court continues to be very quiet and somber. Tokushi and her sister Sotsu-no-suke, who is helping to raise Antoku, are playing with him in Tokushi's chodai. Tokushi is reading Buddhist texts to Antoku though, being only two years old, he doesn't seem particularly interested. But Shigemori's death has propelled Tokushi far more deeply into other-worldly matters and since life is so uncertain, she feels she cannot delay in introducing Antoku to the more important Buddhist beliefs, particularly those which pertain to obtaining transcendence in the afterlife. This obsession of hers is very like Shigemori's own preoccupation, towards the end of his life, with death and enlightenment. He was so concerned with his afterlife needs that he sent an envoy to the Emperor of China, donating a vast sum of money to be given to a Buddhist temple in China where his soul could be prayed for eternally, apparently not trusting the Japanese monks, many of whom were biased against the Heike, to pray sincerely enough. Or perhaps he thought that Buddhism in China would be more pure, more refined, since it has been practiced there longer. Certainly many in the court believe that Chinese monks are more efficacious, and many monks are supported here by nobles wishing only the highest quality of prayers, but I suspect that it is simply the feeling that anything exotic, particularly from China, is better than what is common, familiar and close to home.

A disturbance arises outside the curtains separating us from the hallway. "I must see her! I must see her! I have a message from the Retired Emperor!" a woman's voice cries. Several of us look up from what we are doing, exchange glances. A woman messenger? One of Tokushi's servants strides across the room to see what the commotion is, but is almost knocked over as two guards slide into the room, trying to restrain a disheveled woman in servant's dress from entering. "Lady! The Retired Emperor! I must speak with you!"

Tokushi motions with her hand for the guards to bring the woman closer and makes a gesture with her chin for her sister to take Antoku from the room. When he objects to being scooped up Sotsu-no-suke hushes him, saying, "We'd better go see about your rabbits. They are probably feeling lonely."

The guards bring the woman over. She falls on her face, prostrating herself before the Empress so abruptly she drags the guards down to a kneeling position beside her.

"This is an honor, your ladyship," the woman pants. "Forgive this unseemly intrusion but I have a message of greatest urgency."

"Then give it to me," Tokushi responds with uncharacteristic impatience.

"Oh, alas," the woman wails, "Your august father has ordered the Retired Emperor seized and carried off from his mansion! None of his servants were allowed to go with him. The soldiers said he was being taken into exile! Perhaps he will be executed! Oh, oh!" she cries, banging her forehead against the floor in anguish.

I set my writing down in mid-line. All around the room the women have hushed, some with their hands over their mouths, staring at Tokushi, waiting for her cue to see how they should react. Tokushi is clearly shocked, her eyes wide, lips pressed tightly together.

"Are you certain it was my father's soldiers you saw?" she asks.

"Oh forgive me, I'm a miserable, miserable wretch, ignorant of the world..."

"Continue," Tokushi orders icily.

"The soldiers who came...wore emblems of the Taira. There was a battle... the Retired Emperor's soldiers fought to protect him...one of the wounded... was my brother...he said it was Lord Kiyomori's men before he died." She bursts into fresh tears. "The carriage they put the Retired Emperor in bore the Taira insignia. They said they would set fire to the mansion...we all poured out like ants from an anthill. We thought we would be burned alive. But they left without setting fire to the mansion. They took only the Retired Emperor and his sister, who is a nun. None of us were allowed to accompany them. We scattered like partridges before the hunters. When they left, I found my brother bleeding. He said I should come to you--fair, generous, an emanation of Kannon. He died with Kannon's name on his lips."

Tokushi is too stunned to reply, sitting there with her mouth slightly open. I make my way over to her side on my knees. When I put my hands on her, she recovers herself enough to ask, "Where did you say they had taken him?"

"I don't know. They said he would be banished for his role in the Shishi-no-tani rebellion."

"Who said that?"

"The men who took him."

"Did you recognize any of them?"

"Oh, my lady, it is not for me to recognize men of that station. Above the clouds."

"You might have recognized them," Tokushi persists.

"A thousand apologies, but I did not."

"Did his guards not defend his august personage?"

"There was a clash. Many were dead. I dared not look too closely. Most were killed. One or two may have fled. Oh, lady, if you would only provide your blessed intercession, surely your honorable father will not execute the Son of Heaven."

"Hush!" Tokushi says vehemently, coming out of shock. "I will not have any rumors to that effect!" she says loudly so that everyone in the room hears her. "I am certain Lord Kiyomori is in no way involved with this travesty. I shall go and speak with him immediately so the perpetrators impersonating his soldiers may be apprehended at once!"

She nods to the guards. "This woman is under my protection. Take her to the servants' quarters, see that she is fed and bathed. When she has recovered, find some work to occupy her hands."

The woman squirms a little closer to Tokushi, trying to touch the hem of her robes. "Oh, thank you, thank you."

"As for you, I expect you to hold your tongue," Tokushi warns her. She makes a shooing motion with her hands; the guards yank the woman up and drag her off.

Tokushi makes a subtle gesture with her head; immediately the scribes and messengers run over, sliding into kneeling position at her feet, prostrating themselves, then pulling paper from their sleeves while servants run to fetch their inkstones. "Ichiban," she nods to one, "take this message." A servant frantically mixes the ink.

She dictates a letter to her father, requesting an immediate audience
for an issue of grave importance to the nation. She understands that he is
tremendously busy with affairs of state, but, regrettably, this is a matter that
cannot be postponed. She regrets that she cannot wait for a reply, and informs
him that she will be arriving at his mansion shortly.

Immediately after the messenger leaves, servants flock around and start
dressing her formally, draping her in her most elegant robes, so many layers
she can hardly move. The top layer is so heavily embroidered with gold thread
it is almost blinding. She orders her servants to put up her hair, inserting
two dozen shining gold hairpins dangling with golden tear-drops. Around
her neck she wears a heavy necklace of jade and mother of pearl. Her women
blacken her teeth and apply her makeup. When she is done she looks like one
of the dolls she had back when she named one for herself and said she would
be Empress. She is not Tokushi anymore, but Kenreimon'in, Mother of the
Heir, Wife of the Emperor, vessel through which the flame of Amaterasu
passes and lights the next generation. She is not going as the dutiful daughter
of a powerful father, but as a power in her own right. She seems so remote at
these times, as if she disappears into the stiffness of the robes, the formality of
the role. I cannot see the Tokushi that I love in there.

"I will take Lady Daigon-no-suke," she says in response to my offer to
accompany her. She also takes Ben-no-taishi, one of the younger women, a
very recent addition to the court, a serious girl who strives hard to emulate
the Empress in every way. I am both relieved and insulted that she does not
want my presence at such an important meeting, but I understand. I am one
of her most controversial associates, and she wants to appear before her father
only with those of her ladies who are beyond reproach. Ben-no-taishi has
a spotless reputation, and Lady Daigon-no-suke is an extremely formidable
woman married to a formidable man; it is almost impossible to imagine who
would have the courage to confront her on anything. Lord Kiyomori has great
respect for her. She is his favorite daughter-in-law; she carries herself with a
fierce arrogance equal to his own.

Kiyomori executed some of the men implicated in the Shishi-no-tani plot
against him in particularly gruesome ways; only Shigemori's intervention kept
him from exiling the Retired Emperor at the time. He has been raging about
since Shigemori died; reports of his behavior and what I have seen lead me to
worry that he may have become unhinged by grief. He has shown little mercy

to anyone crossing him of late, and has doubled the number of young men who move around the Capital spying on people's conversations. The slightest hint of disloyalty or impropriety is greatly punished. If any more nobles and merchants are exiled to the misty islands they will become more populous than the capital.

In some ways I am not surprised that he has not moved against Go-Shirakawa sooner. The Retired Emperor was implicated in the Shishi-no-tani plot by the unlucky conspirators, yet strongly denied his involvement. Shigemori persuaded Kiyomori to look the other way, but in spite of owing him so much, Go Shirakawa has shown little grief for Shigemori. Though he attended Shigemori's cremation looking solemn and sad, and made offerings on his behalf to the temples, he then proceeded to make pilgrimages and throw parties with dancers and musicians before the time of mourning had run its course. To do such a thing while Shigemori's soul was in the intermediate stage, when a caring friend would dress only in mourning and say constant prayers, was a grave insult to Shigemori's memory.

"I have seen him mourn longer for a cat!" Kiyomori had cried with humiliation after learning of the first of these parties. Even worse, Go-Shirakawa then issued an edict saying that the lands that had been given to Shigemori for his services to the crown, which had been originally reserved in perpetuity for Shigemori and his descendents, had now reverted back to the throne and been given to someone else, "as it seems likely that Shigemori's descendents should have no trouble acquiring fortunes of their own." This was a direct slap at Kiyomori for placing Shigemori's young sons in positions of power. The tension that had always existed between Go-Shirakawa and Kiyomori, a natural tension between two stags in a herd of deer, has now boiled over into something more lethal. Shigemori was a loyal retainer to the Retired Emperor, always trying to walk the fine line between filial duties and his responsibilities to the throne. It was he who always sought to steer a middle course between them. He was the iron cauldron separating the fire and water, helping them to work together rather than seeking to extinguish each other. Munemori has tried to steer that course since Shigemori died, but he is too easily cowed by his father's anger and always ends up giving in and groveling to him rather than standing firm as Shigemori did. It does seem shameful for Go-Shirakawa to cruelly disregard the sacrifices and skills of such a loyal subject as Shigemori; I don't blame Kiyomori for being enraged and hurt.

Still, even in his madness, I cannot believe Kiyomori would be so foolish as to order the Retired Emperor's execution. I truly think the nation would rise up against him should he attempt such a thing.

Once Tokushi and her ladies are dressed, they depart in a carriage for her father's mansion. The Rokuhara mansion is very much a fortress, with sharp stakes planted all along the walls, though vines have been trained over them to diminish the visual impact of the stakes. Many political meetings are held there, but few parties. I hope Kiyomori is home rather than elsewhere in the Capital; anyone would faint in a matter of hours wearing as many robes as Tokushi.

They do not return until very late that night, which I know is not a good sign, given how early Tokushi prefers to go to bed. I have a servant posted looking out at the courtyard who notifies me as soon her carriage returns. I rise from bed, waiting, my hair flowing down around me. One of her maids comes to request my presence—actually, she says the Empress 'requires' my presence at the baths. Her women are pouring the bath when I get there. We both are scrubbed, then enter the bath, along with a servant who immediately starts massaging her. I massage her hands while Naniwa works on her neck. Tokushi is sniffling, and soon I see tears creep down her face. "They kept me *waiting*," she says. "At first he tried to tell me he would see me *tomorrow*. As if I were a *merchant*. I declined to leave. He has turned into an old man," she says wonderingly.

"He has not been himself since Shigemori died," I say.

"Oh, yes he has," she says, "he's just more of himself, and you know it. If he cared about my brother, he would not be so quick to undo all of his good work, to forget all of his good advice. He should follow Shigemori's filial precepts. He should remember that all of us are children of the Emperor, who is the Son of Heaven. 'As a father loves his son, a sovereign loves his people,'" she says, quoting the Chinese scholars.

"Lord Kiyomori will not do anything to harm the Retired Emperor," I assure her.

"But he has taken him to a much inferior mansion and placed him under house arrest! He is discussing banishing him! An Emperor--Retired or not--cannot be banished! What's next? Shall he banish the sun? Shall it shine only on the Northern Provinces and not on the capital? Everyone will be talking about the wickedness of the Heike now."

I try desperately to think of something comforting to say.

"I am glad Antoku is too young to understand what one grandfather has done to the other," Tokushi cries. "I have never been so ashamed."

"You have nothing to be ashamed of," I say, stroking her back. "It is not your fault."

An older maidservant enters the bathing chamber. "Forgive me, my lady," she says, kneeling and tapping her forehead on the wet tiles. "But there is a messenger from your august husband, the Emperor Takakura. He will not give the letter he carries into the possession of another and he says he will not leave until he receives a reply. He has been here all day."

"If he will not surrender the letter, he will have to wait." Tokushi snaps.

"Yes, of course, mistress," the woman replies, backing out of the chamber like a crab.

It used to be a rare thing for Tokushi to snap at the servants, but she has been more brittle since Antoku's birth, and especially short-tempered since Shigemori's death. All of our nerves are frayed since we lost Shigemori. All carry a deep fear that without Shigemori's steadying hand, Kiyomori will act on impulse. While Lady Kiyomori has little or no gentleness in her makeup, she has a pragmatic side that sometimes leavens her husband's impulsive rages, but she is heavily in grief for Shigemori also.

Still, Sessho believed that the Retired Emperor was part of this Shishi-no-tani plot, or that he at least knew of it. Too many of the people involved told the same story for it not to be true. Kiyomori might have found some more discreet method of containing Go-Shirakawa, but Shigemori's death has torn open the silken sleeve concealing the iron fist. Shigemori made Kiyomori's policies more palatable, often succeeding in softening their harsher aspects. But Munemori is no statesman; he fears his father and rarely dares to disagree with him. He gave himself over to the privileges and pleasures of a second son, never thinking he would have to fill the shoes of the first. Now he is next in line, without Shigemori's talents for personal or political restraint. He is far more easy-going than his father, and in that sense is like Shigemori, but while one always sensed a steel beneath Shigemori's calm, Munemori's relaxed attitude seems to stem from laziness.

Ben-no-taishi, a little less than sixteen years old, stands quietly, showing no signs of tiredness from her long day. She is calm as an ivory statue, but her eyes are alert to anything the Empress might need. She is clearly Tokushi's favorite among the girls. Perhaps if Tokushi had a daughter, she would be like her.

"The Retired Emperor had nothing to do with the plot of Shishi-no-tani," Tokushi says firmly.

"How can you be certain of that? It seems there is much evidence that he at least knew of it and neglected to warn Lord Kiyomori," I say.

"It's just gossip!" she insists. "I talked to him soon after it happened, and he assured me he had no knowledge of it at all. He promised me he would never do anything to hurt me or my son. If he wanted to destroy the Taira, why did he pray for Antoku? Why did he pray for me? He could have easily prayed for me to die, and then the Taira line would not be mixed with the bloodlines of Amaterasu."

I nod. She will never believe that Go-Shirakawa could ever betray her or act against her interests after his brave invocations on her behalf during her labor. She will always be certain that she and Antoku owe him their lives, and that they would never have been spared without his intercession with the divine.

But I have seen another side to him--a crafty old fox, a consummate player of the game of politics, perfectly able to switch sides at a moment's notice if he thinks it will benefit him. He and Kiyomori have been in power struggle from the beginning. Narichika, Naritsune, Saiko, and the other plotters all claimed they had acted upon the Retired Emperor's behest. Shigemori told me before he died that only his intercession had kept Kiyomori from exiling the Retired Emperor and persuaded him to exile rather than execute some of the higher officials in the case.

"The only argument I could make that swayed him was that Go-Shirakawa was too dangerous to let out of our sight and that it would be safer to keep him here at the capital where we could have our spies watching him constantly," he had said. "The proper filial argument, that we owe him our loyalty no matter what, only made him laugh." He also revealed that it was only because his brother Norimori threatened to become a monk if Kiyomori executed his friend Naritusune that Kiyomori agreed to banish him instead.

But I must not betray Shigemori's confidences by sharing them with Tokushi. He always thought to protect her from the harsher realities of

37

court life, and now that he is dead, it is up to me to do the same. Without Shigemori's cool waters to douse Kiyomori's hot head, I fear for Go-Shirakawa's life, never mind his tenure here in the capital. Angry as Kiyomori is, however, surely he would never risk publicly flaunting the gods by destroying the Son of Heaven. It would set a precedent that would endanger his own seed and almost certainly spark a rebellion. Go-Shirakawa counts on his immunity from Kiyomori's revenge, but he made a grave error in giving his tacit or explicit consent to Narichika's plans to overthrow Kiyomori. He underestimated Kiyomori if he thought the men in that group were strong enough to bring him down. One of the plotters, Yukisuna, betrayed the others before a blow had been struck; that gives a fair idea of the quality of courage and intelligence of the conspirators.

After our bath we dress in simple robes. We go to the audience room where Tokushi sits hidden behind a kicho--a screen of state--to receive her husband's messenger. I kneel unobtrusively over on the side of the room so I can see everything and describe it to her later.

The messenger is not a servant, but one of the pack of noble young men Takakura surrounds himself with. This particular young man, Kentetsu, is very skilled at kemari, a game in which the men stand in a circle and see how many rounds they can kick the ball to each other without it touching the ground. They also play at archery, but mostly they hold drunken poetry evenings, attended by the most beautiful women at court. Not young women of their own class, whose reputations would suffer irreparable harm through their association with these young men, but girls from merchant or warrior families, the sort that make concubines rather than wives. Emperor Takakura is known for his love of pretty women, always having several simultaneous affairs; some serious romances, some temporary playthings. Though he composes passionate letters protesting his love for one lady or another, and his love poetry is renowned and quoted often in the court, it is also noted that the same phrases turn up again and again, only slightly altered for different ladies. And alas, none of his love poetry is directed at his wife.

Whatever this messenger has come to say, I am glad he cannot see Tokushi's face, for anything having to do with Emperor Takakura makes her stiffen visibly. She has never gotten over her disappointment that her sacrifices in bringing forth a son did not result in Takakura being more loving and attentive to her. Indeed, now that he is relieved of his duties to supply an heir, his visits are more infrequent than ever.

Kentetsu is elegantly dressed, a moth-wing brush of mustache, his eyebrows drawn very high up on his forehead giving him that same effete look that Takakura and his associates all affect. His skin is painted very white. He prostrates himself before her curtains.

"Emperor Takakura inquires after the health and happiness of his Empress and asks her to receive this missive."

"Proceed."

"Emperor Takakura sends his deepest affection and respect to his cherished wife, mother of his son, heir to the throne. He asks for an audience with her, and asks if she has heard this most grievous news, that Lord Kiyomori has captured Retired Emperor Go-Shirakawa and placed him under house arrest, in conditions far from suitable to one of his station, depriving him of his household and the comforts of his own mansion. Emperor Takakura requests an interview with honorable Kenreimon'in to discuss possible remedies to this unfortunate situation."

From my vantage point I can see both the messenger and Tokushi behind her curtain and watch as she bows her head, taking a few moments to master her feelings.

"Naturally, I am always available to his Lordship. I will be most delighted at this rare opportunity," I notice she cannot resist slipping in this subtle jibe--"to see the august father of the nation. Please advise your lord, your sovereign, that my household is at his disposal and if he will give me notice as to his arrival and how many retainers he is bringing I will attempt to provide a suitable feast."

The man prostrates himself again. "I shall take this message back immediately. As to the time--I know his Lordship would like to see you as early as tomorrow."

"We shall be ready for him."

After he leaves, Tokushi and I retire to her chodai. I hold her head on my chest.

"If I could only persuade my father to restore the Retired Emperor to his mansion and all his former privileges, perhaps it would be a new beginning for Lord Takakura and myself. If there were not such tension between our families, I really believe he would be a more devoted husband," she says.

I hold her tightly, my heart aching for her. Although her parents engineered this marriage only with political gain in mind, Tokushi convinced herself from the beginning, that she was deeply in love with Takakura, though he was only a child when they first wed. Unfortunately, he has not returned the compliment. While always respectful and courtly in his manner towards her, he has not seen fit to feign a passion he does not feel.

Emperor Takakura passes almost three days, an unheard-of extravagance of time, in our quarters. He and Tokushi bed together twice, and we all hold our breath, hoping that another child will result, and are bitterly disappointed when her courses arrive a week after his departure.

Due to Tokushi's ardor and gratitude to Go-Shirakawa, she and Emperor Takakura are entirely of like mind regarding the injustice of the Retired Emperor's confinement, and she promises Takakura that if it is within her power to sway her father, she will see the Retired Emperor freed.

I accompany her to an interview with Lord Kiyomori where she plans to argue that Go-Shirakawa should be restored to his former estate. Under our most sumptuous robes, we are webbed with strings of talismans and charms. She has persuaded the High Priestess of Ise to side with her in the matter, although the Priestess, being an intelligent woman, sent only a letter from the Sun Goddesses' shrine, declining to appear herself, and couching her arguments in extremely vague and respectful terms. I have been brought along as testament that Inari favors the Retired Emperor also. Lady Daigon-no-suke has stayed behind, pleading headache. Privately she told me her husband, Shigehira, supports his father, Kiyomori, in this matter.

We are shown into a room containing several altars, some improbably pairing various Buddhas with Hachiman, the god of war. The largest shrine is to the Itkushima deity, their family kami. Kiyomori is seated in front of it on a dais. Pillows for us have been placed at the foot of the dais.

Tokushi stands before her father, gazing haughtily down at the pillows.

"You would place the head of your Empress below your own?" She turns to one of the servants who ushered us in. "Bring a chair and set it on the dais," she commands.

The whites of the servant's eyes show as he looks towards Kiyomori. A long moment ensues where father and daughter regard each other coldly. Finally Kiyomori nods curtly towards the servant, who swiftly fetches a bench

40

for Tokushi which elevates her head above her father's. I sit beside her on the floor, wishing I were shorter and less visible.

"It is my strong back you stepped on to reach that throne, daughter," Kiyomori observes.

"It is destiny, written in the stars before either of us was born," Tokushi returns icily. She hands the letter from the High Priestess to a servant, who proffers it to Kiyomori. He reads it, then yawns ostentatiously.

"Daughter," he says, "you have a good heart. But you are a woman, and matters of politics are not for you to decide. It is your nature and destiny to provide heirs for the throne. My destiny is to protect the kingdom. It would be better if you did not insert yourself into matters that do not concern you."

"The Retired Sovereign..." she starts.

"Is sadly lacking in judgment. He is a man swayed by the bitter and envious. It is as much for his protection as *ours*," he emphasizes the word, "that I have placed him under guard where he cannot be unduly influenced by his inferiors. Really, my dear, such squabbles are beneath you. Do you not trust your old father to see to your best interests?"

"My best interests--and the best interests of the country--are for Emperor Takakura and I to dwell in harmony and peace, for our families to dwell in harmony and peace."

"How will your 'harmony' be served by assassins stalking and destroying the Taira!" he flares.

"He had nothing to do with--"

"He had everything to do with it, daughter! I regret you are so misinformed! There is no need to sully your purity with this quagmire of deception and betrayal!"

"My husband Lord Takakura is gravely depressed. If his father continues to languish in captivity I fear there is no hope for any future heirs."

Kiyomori shrugs. "Too many heirs just confuse the succession anyway."

Tokushi's mouth drops. I see her fighting not to cry.

"Do you really think you could survive another pregnancy?" her father says cruelly. "No, and if you die, Takakura remarries and more sons are born which threaten our claim."

"It is only because of Go-Shirakawa that I survived the last one! You are deliberately sabotaging my marriage! Takakura will never forgive me if you do

41

not free his father! I'm nothing to you but a white stone on your board!" she bitterly accuses, referring to the strategic game of Go favored by courtiers.

Kiyomori rises, moves toward her, reaching his hand out gently. "Ah, my little one, my pretty one..."

"Don't touch me!" she cries, rising and backing away. "Shigemori would never have countenanced such an attack on the throne! You dishonor his memory!"

Tears stream down the old man's face at her rebuke. I can't help but feel sorry for him. He wipes his face with his sleeve. "Are you done with your harangue? I have business to attend to. I hope you will stay and partake of our hospitality before returning to the palace." He steps heavily off the dais and strides out, not bothering to turn and bow to her at the doorway.

Instead of freeing Go-Shirakawa, Kiyomori decides to help Tokushi's marriage by banishing Takakura's favorite concubine from the court, thinking this will encourage the Emperor to spend more time with his wife. His concubine, a lovely young woman named Aoi, is a quiet, modest girl who is a surprisingly accomplished musician. It is a terrible blow to both her and her family, and Emperor Takakura appears to be utterly devastated. He throws no further parties; instead, he and his entourage travel from shrine to shrine and temple to temple, making prayers and offerings for his father's release.

Tokushi, observing how dejected, thin, and pale Takakura appears at the state dinners they attend together, generously picks out one of her young attendants, a beautiful but sober girl she deems loyal to her, and sends her as a gift to Takakura to cheer him out of his despondency. Given how much she envies Takakura's devotion to his concubines, this is truly a noble gesture. This girl soon becomes pregnant, and Kiyomori has her banished as well, enraged that the Imperial bloodline is flowing through wombs other than his daughter's.

Kiyomori continues to rage like a wounded animal, unpredictable and dangerous. His grief for Shigemori is unabated. All of us are still deeply sad, but Kiyomori is despondent to the point of madness. Perhaps he blames himself for creating the burdens that led to Shigemori's despair and decline. There is, unfortunately, much truth to that, for Shigemori had exhausted himself trying to mediate constantly between his headstrong father and the rest of the nation.

Emperor Takakura grows more and more depressed. Frequently he stonewalls Kiyomori's requests, refusing to agree with such and such an appointment, leaving various positions at court unfilled. Kiyomori's increasingly impatient messages are frequently returned unread, with no reply except that the Emperor was indisposed, or that worry over his father's condition makes it impossible for him to concentrate on matters of state at this time. Takakura does not have his father's craftiness, nor can he withstand the gale-force winds of Kiyomori's anger, but I admire the courage it must be taking for him to pull in like a turtle and refuse to accede to Kiyomori's wishes.

Chapter Six
1180

After several months of frustration, Kiyomori seizes upon Takakura's despondency as cause to have him forcibly retired from the throne, pointing out that the Emperor appears to be too ill to attend to his duties. Takakura realizes too late his stalling tactics have succeeded in portraying him as too weak and infirm to govern. Takakura is far from the consummate politician his father is. He does not have the heart to oppose Lord Kiyomori. While remaining totally loyal to his father, his own despair takes precedence. He agrees to stand aside so that Antoku can ascend to the throne. Antoku is not quite three years old, and there is great talk all through the capital, and I imagine, even the countryside, of how shocking it is that a child so young should ascend the throne while an Emperor so youthful, deeply loved and respected by the people as Takakura, should step aside. Popular opinion whispers that he is being forced from his position, and rumors abound that the monks from various temples will take arms and descend to the city to prevent it.

But in the end nothing comes from such talk--perhaps because Munemori, Shigehira, and other sons of Kiyomori shower the monasteries with gifts of money. Some scholars of history point out that young Emperors had been elevated in the past, but others argue such examples had always preceded times of unrest and instability, and therefore are worse than no precedences at all. Of course, there is nothing the rich and idle like better than being scandalized, for otherwise they would suffocate in boredom. So much of the horrified whispering is simply a matter of what is fashionable. When I ask Machiko what the other servants are saying, she says nearly all are delighted at the thought of such a marvelous child as Antoku being on the throne.

The whole court thrums with excitement as the day of Antoku's ascension draws near. With Emperor Takakura out of the way, and Go-Shirakawa safely cloistered under heavy guard, Lord Kiyomori rules as brightly as any king descended from the sun. The Regent in charge of speaking for Antoku is clearly Kiyomori's mouthpiece that he is called 'the Royal Seal' behind his back, acknowledging that he is no more than the stamp that makes documents official.

In spite of the presence of Kiyomori's young spies, the city crackles with gossip. But at the court itself, the Taira clan, even down to the most distant cousins, are treated as gods on earth. Families offer their most marriageable daughters as consorts for Kiyomori's sons and grandsons. Older men fawn on the adolescents who now hold the richest posts, offering themselves as their underlings.

Tokushi is so torn between her concern for Takakura's humiliation and her pride in her son's ascension, she bursts frequently into tears and even throws things at the servants, though only soft objects such as slippers. She sets all our maidservants and twenty others hired just for the occasion to sewing night and day on the most splendid, costly garments anyone has ever seen, laden with jewels and far more ornate than her usual style. She herself walks up and down tirelessly observing the servants work, though the best tailors in the capital are there guiding them. She storms and rages if she believes one of the women is making the stitches too big, or frets that one dragon's claw in a pattern is bigger than another, insisting all the offending stitchery be taken out and the whole thing started anew. For the first time, I see her father in her, and I pray the difficult, domineering traits will pass once the ceremony is over.

At last the auspicious day chosen by the court astrologers arrives. The ceremony itself is very solemn, as befits such a momentous occasion. Antoku is far too young to understand its significance or comprehend what is happening, although he enjoys the attention. He sits on the throne wiggling his feet happily, having peeled off his splendid but uncomfortable golden shoes, and he cranes his neck with great interest when each of the sacred treasures of the ceremonial regalia is ritually presented to him. He chortles on catching a glimpse of himself in the sacred mirror, fondles the bead strand, and gazes solemnly at the sword without reaching for it, causing a visible sigh of relief to run through the ladies who have all been watching anxiously. We are all very grateful for his cheerful mood. He had been affected by the tension running through the palace over the last several months and we had seen him go through many interminable jags of crying and temper tantrums when he did not get his way. Later, his nurse, Tokushi's sister Sotsu-no-suke confides that some of the sweets she had slipped into his hand throughout the ceremony had been concocted with the slightest whisper of opium. Tempestuous behavior is not uncommon in a child of that age, but children of the Sun Goddess are held to a higher standard. On the day when it mattered he was a cheerful sprite, and everyone took that to be a good omen, which was much needed due to the questionable circumstances of the event.

After the ceremony, the court and the capital, fickle as always, immediately agree that for such a mature, precocious, brilliant prodigy such as Antoku to ascend the throne at age three could not be considered premature at all. No, it is clearly the will of heaven, and an age of prosperity and peace would no doubt follow.

As grandparents of the new Emperor, Lord and Lady Kiyomori now hold positions comparable to that of their daughter, the Empress. Tokushi undergoes a ceremony investing her with a certain amount of power as the mother of the current sovereign. I have little doubt it will be Lord and Lady Kiyomori making all the decisions, with Tokushi only the mouthpiece through which they make their will known. Much as her father's behavior disappoints her at times, she does not have the strength Shigemori possessed to stand against him.

Alas, her worst fears for her already tenuous relationship with Takakura are realized. After the ascension, Takakura--now Retired Emperor Takakura--ceases visiting her altogether. The moment the ceremonies have ended, Takakura leaves on a pilgrimage to the Shrine at Itkushima, dedicated to the Taira family's patron Goddess, in the hope that praying to the Goddess closest to Lord Kiyomori's heart may soften him in regards to Go-Shirakawa. While he is gone, Tokushi prays daily to the Itkushima deity to turn Takakura's heart towards her, to let their son's ascension be a source of joy and a new beginning for them, that they might come together and create a brother for Antoku, a crown prince. But Takakura's return brings no such scenes of connubial bliss, and one of Takakura's sons by a concubine is declared crown prince instead.

While I have been frequently disappointed in Takakura's treatment of Tokushi, no one can fault his filial loyalty. He clearly feels each slight directed against his father as if it were a blade being stabbed into his own body.

Whether through the agency of Takakura's prayers, or whether Lord Kiyomori simply repented of a move that had proved increasingly unpopular, shortly after Takakura returns from his pilgrimage to Itsukshima, Kiyomori permits Go-Shirakawa to return to his own mansion, though still heavily under guard. All of his correspondence is read by Kiyomori's trusted scribes, and he is allowed only limited visitors, only those who Lord Kiyomori feels confident are either loyal to him and or too timid to cause the Heike any further trouble. Every audience Go-Shirakawa holds is attended by one of Kiyomori's loyal generals who relays the content of every conversation to Kiyomori.

I agree with Sessho that Kiyomori is justified in these precautions, despite the unpopularity it causes him, but due to Tokushi's strong feelings on the subject, I remain silent on the matter. I agree with her that Go-Shirakawa is being treated cruelly, but in my heart of hearts I do not feel his treatment is unfair.

Chapter Seven
1180

Tokushi and I and several other ladies have traveled to Tsunemasa's mansion for a banquet to be held later tonight. While the other ladies are napping, I walk in Tsunemasa's garden with him, watching the ornamental pheasants pecking the grain the servants have set out for them. The persimmons are burning golden orbs on a bare tree. "They look like lanterns in the sunlight," I comment to him, indicating the tree.

"Yes, they light up the garden during the bleak times, don't they?" Tsunemasa smiles. "The cooks will be preparing some of the persimmon delicacies that you like so much. Hopefully that will tempt your appetite."

"Indeed. You know me so well," I say. I look forward to this time of year when we can enjoy specialties made with persimmons and yellow squash.

"We have some very fresh fish as well, prepared six different ways," he assures me.

"The table is always perfect at your house."

"I have spent enough time sleeping rough and eating rough during campaigns. When I am at home, I like to enjoy the best the countryside has to offer," Tsunemasa says. "Those egg and crayfish squares you enjoyed so last time will be on the menu also."

"Stop!" I laugh, tapping him with my fan. "You're making me hungry!"

He chuckles and leads me over to a bench where we can watch the carp swimming lazily against the current of a waterfall cascading over artfully placed rocks.

"I have a favor to ask you," he says.

"Name it."

Tsunemasa is dressed in a hunting costume of grays, browns and greens patterned with gold. It complements his rugged looks.

"My brothers will be here tonight, Tsunetoshi and Atsumori."

48

I nod. I am familiar with the much younger half-brothers his father, Tsunemori has had with his third wife. Tsunemasa's mother has been dead for many years. Though they are very young, Tsunemasa's brothers have already received enviable positions and titles, due to their status as Kiyomori's nephews.

"Atsumori...well..." Tsunemasa shifts uncomfortably, tapping his fan against his thigh. "Atsumori is much infatuated with you."

"Atsumori?" I say. He is so young, fourteen or fifteen at the most. I am twice his age.

"Not that I blame him, of course," Tsunemasa says gallantly. "You are a woman to capture the imagination. And Atsumori is a very sensitive young man. He is already quite talented with the flute. He is a great admirer of your poetry. I don't know if you noticed how at the last banquet, every time you presented a poem, he would attempt to make one to follow it. Of course, his poetry is by no means the match of yours. But he has confided in me that he is wasting away for love of you."

"Wasting away! That is absurd! I am far too old for him!" I protest.

"It is too much of a difference for a marriage," Tsunemasa agrees, and I bristle a bit, for he is twice as old as On'na Mari, and between an older man and younger woman that much age difference is thought to be perfect for a marriage. But he is quite right; it is not seemly for a young man to marry a woman so much older that her fertility might seem in doubt. "But you are so youthful looking," Tsunemasa continues, "and as I said, Atsumori is a young man of refined taste. He is to be seated next to you tonight. All I am asking is that if the poor love-sick pup starts sending you notes during dinner--well, if you could treat him kindly, I would appreciate it."

"Well, of course I will treat him kindly." I had never considered Atsumori for myself, but I am flattered that such a young man would find me attractive. "Has he always fancied older women?"

"He fancies *you*," Tsunemasa says pointedly. "You, and I think no one but you, since he was twelve. He always says how he envies me for our friendship, and naturally, he is right."

I can see that Tsunemasa is not comfortable with the role of matchmaker.

"He is a good boy, and if you would consider him--I can't imagine any young man being fortunate enough to have a better teacher," Tsunemasa says gruffly. Now he is unquestionably starting to redden about the cheeks and I find it most amusing that Tsunemasa should be so embarrassed. I wonder if he is remembering our one occasion of pillowing at Itkushima. My own face heats at the memory and I snap open my fan and position it between us. I wish Tsunemasa were courting me for himself. But while Seishan has always so generously shared Sessho with me, I know better than to think that On'na Mari would be similarly inclined. Despite how many lovers she had since coming to court, she is extremely jealous where Tsunemasa is concerned.

"Well, that's settled then," Tsunemasa rises, adjusting his robes. He looks uncomfortable, and I wonder if his jade stalk has risen in response to our conversation.

"If you would be kind to him, I would appreciate it," he concludes. "And frankly, I envy him his opportunities," He strides off, leaving me to hustle to keep up with him, in spite of my tendency to take long steps.

Back at my room, I inform Machiko of the conversation.

"Oh, yes, mistress. He has been staring at you like a love-sick puppy for years," she says matter-of-factly.

"I have never noticed this. Are you certain?"

"Oh quite, mistress, quite." She looks at me mischievously. "They say a young man can be very entertaining. They never get tired, neh?"

I laugh. Machiko is utterly inexperienced in the ways of men. For her to make such a comment is most humorous. "Ah yes, I have heard that too, Machiko. Though I can't imagine what we would talk about."

"Perhaps conversation is not one of the chief charms a young man has to offer," she says with a sly smile.

I whack her on the shoulder with my fan. "Impertinence!" I giggle. "I had best get a nap before the banquet, lest my young admirer be shocked at how haggard I look."

That night I have Machiko arrange my hair in a girlish style with just a few pearl- encrusted pins rather than a more formal look that might seem intimidating.

On'na Mari glitters, resplendent in gold and red at one end of the table, wearing a headdress of miniature lanterns and mirrors which looks so heavy I am surprised her delicate neck doesn't snap under the strain. She tosses her head flirtatiously, speaking animatedly to the Empress on one side of her and Tomomori, one of Tokushi's brothers, on the other. The table is ebony, so polished I can see my face in it as clearly as in any mirror before the plates are brought out and set before us. The plates have a crushed shell glaze in the center, bordered by raised sea goddesses and dragons around the rim. Tsunemasa had them made for On'na Mari, honoring her legendary status as an ocean kami. I find them a bit gaudy.

I am seated with Atsumori on my left and a friend of his of the same age, Kiyosune, on my right. Kiyosune is about my height, I notice, before he kneels down on the cushions beside me. Atsumori is still half a head shorter. But both men are so young, it is likely they will still grow. They are scarcely older than Sessho's oldest boy.

They are both very solicitous of me throughout the meal, piling delicacies on my plate.

"You must think I am far too thin, the way you are trying to fatten me up," I surmise.

"No, no!" Atsumori protests. "Who would choose a fat sparrow over a graceful egret?"

"Shoulders in the clouds, like Fujiyama--and equally worthy of pilgrimages!" Kiyosune chimes in.

I laugh at their extravagant flattery and start picking up the morsels they have piled on my plate and placing them in their mouths, like a mother bird feeding the baby birds--an analogy that, alas, is not so far from the truth.

Atsumori is wearing black robes rimmed with a brilliant azure. As I have chosen to dress as a somewhat younger woman, he has chosen a costume evocative of an older man; the pole through the shoulders of his puffed gown support sleeves that ripple like waves past his wrists, making him look more filled out than he is. Kiyosune is dressed more modestly in a gray-green outfit with salmon inner-sleeves. He seems far more shy than Atsumori, mostly just nodding at the conversation or adding a word or two in between Atsumori's bouts of grandiloquence. They have only recently graduated from wearing their hair in boy's loops to the top-knot style favored by courtiers and warriors alike.

Atsumori is doing his best to impress me with his knowledge of ancient literature, offering poems heavily laden with literary allusions at every opportunity.

"My father has just bought me a war-horse," he mentions, letting me know his status is now that of a young warrior. "He is jet black. I wish to be able to sneak up on the enemy at night without being seen."

51

"I hope it will not come to that. We can ill spare courtiers with your education and wit." I nod, indicating both young men. "Surely we should leave war to those with a more simple nature. The best rice should be held back for planting."

"Well-spoken," Kiyosune says, bobbing his head shyly.

"We would cut a poor figure and set a poor example for those simple folk," Atsumori says heatedly, "if we were not willing to take those risks ourselves." He quotes a couple of noble, stirring poems of warcraft from centuries past to illustrate his point. "As I was saying--I have decided to call my horse, 'Midnight Battle.'"

"A noble name," Kiyosune remarks, nodding solemnly. "You are fortunate your father supports you being a warrior. My father won't let me ride anything except my old dappled mare, Mist-on-the-Lake. She's a fine horse, but I can't see her going off to war. And I would hate to risk her."

"Yes, you need a stallion that can be trained for battle," Atsumori frowns. "I shall speak to your father the next time I see him. He must be persuaded. Of course, my family--Tsunemori and Tsunemasa, all of the Taira--we have a reputation to uphold."

"Oh now, I'm half Taira too," Kiyosune admonishes.

"On your mother's side," Atsmori says, trying not to sound too disparaging, but letting me know that he is the true Taira of the two of them.

"You and my brother have been friends for a long time now," Atsumori remarks to me, changing the subject.

"Much to my honor, I am fortunate to count Tsunemasa among my friends," I reply.

"Yes, it takes a real man not to be threatened by a sorceress, but I find a woman who stands between the worlds to be most intoxicating," Atsumori asserts. His eyes look hotly into mine for a brief moment before looking away. I find his admiration stimulating and find I am actually toying with the idea of taking him into my bed. I hide my thoughts behind my fan however. Tokushi and the girls shall certainly tease me if I embark on such an autumn-spring romance. Still, it is not uncommon for an older woman to be a younger man's mentor. I see no real reason why I should not step into that role. Usually I find men's bragging to be repugnant, but Atsumori's swagger, so transparently eager to impress me, seems amusing and touching rather than annoying.

"Would you flatter us with some poems?" Atsumori requests.

I shake my head, hiding behind my fan, feeling flustered.

I gaze down the table. The men are laughing, pounding on the table, relating military exploits. At the other end of the table, Tokushi is laughing animatedly in response to something On'na Mari has said, while Ben-no-Taishi, sitting on Tokushi's right, smiles benignly. She is only a couple of years older than these boys, but her remote manner makes it clear she is saving herself for marriage and will not consider dalliances. Inari being the Goddess of Love, among her other attributes, one would expect a daughter of Inari like myself to be amenable to erotic suggestion.

Atsumori is fiddling with a piece of paper in his lap. I rest my arms on the table in such a way that my sleeves hang open, making it look like a careless gesture. He makes use of my position to pop his letter into the sleeve nearest him. I give no indication of having noticed the mulberry paper brushing against my forearm, though inwardly I shiver with anticipation of what the contents of the letter will reveal.

Tsunemasa leans toward us and makes a suggestive jest.

I laugh, hiding my smile behind my fan.

"Laughter, like a beautiful clear stream. I could only wish to drink from it," Atsumori says immediately.

It is not an original thought, but certainly appropriate for this situation. I follow it with another proverb.

"A slender waterfall, hidden in the woods--who knows how deep it plunges in the pool?"

The sexual subtext of the poem strikes both young men into silence. Fortunately we are all saved from embarrassment when the servants bring trays of fruit and sweetmeats to the table and we occupy ourselves by setting an assortment of sweets on each other's plates.

"Shall I peel you an orange?" Atsumori offers.

"I would be most grateful."

I take some mochi with persimmon paste from Kiyosune, grateful to have the orange fruits my body craves in autumn. I hope all this feasting has not worn away the black stain on my teeth.

Atsumori excuses himself, and when he returns I notice he has repainted his mouth a bright crimson. He has a large mouth, which most would consider a defect, but I find it sensual.

At the other end of the table, guests are trading poems about the autumn.

"Autumn: the birds fly south, searching for a nest," Atsumori whispers to me. Then, in a normal voice, he ventures, "Everyone knows you are the best poet in the capital. Won't you favor us with something original?"

"Your older brother is better than I," I demur.

"I heard that!" Tsunemasa declares loudly. "That is the most outrageously untrue compliment I have ever received."

"Oh, not so!" On'na Mari chimes in at the end of the table. "When you were writing love-letters to me, it was indeed your very sense of style that endeared you to me. I had never seen such perfect handwriting and such perfect sentiments all put together."

I twist my hands under my sleeves. It seems a bit awkward for her to mention their correspondence now that he knows it was really I writing him under her name.

"I thank you," Tsunemasa says, bowing in her direction. "I was most impressed by your correspondence as well. Truly, your compositions almost rivaled our Murasaki's."

Pink blooms in my cheeks as he compares me to the most famous writer of the previous century. Fortunately, Tsunemasa keeps his attention on On'na Mari, who continues to flirt with him. Who would choose an author of poems when he could have a woman whose beauty is poetry itself?

"I would be most gratified," Atsumori says in a lowered voice, "if you would look over my own unworthy attempts and lend your expert eye to improving my puerile scribblings."

"I would be happy to help, though talent such as yours needs no improvement."

"With your help, perhaps I shall grow to rival Tsunemasa's renown," Atsumori says eagerly.

"That is an excellent idea," Tokushi says, having overheard at least part of our conversation. "Perhaps you could tutor all the young people who wish it. It would raise the quality of our poetry exchanges hugely, I am sure. Perhaps a class."

Atsumori droops visibly.

"It is likely that a short amount of time tutoring each person individually would see more improvement. I should have no idea how to teach a class. Writing is such an individual thing," I explain.

"Oh, as you wish," Tokushi replies airily, returning to the conversations nearer to her, apparently unaware of the flirtations occurring at my end of the table.

"Is it agreed then?" Atsumori whispers to me.

"Agreed. Do not be shocked at my handwriting. It is not as neat as many."

"No one concerns himself over where a pearl comes from."

An interesting response. I certainly hope he refers only to my thoughts and my writing, and is not equating my mind with the pearl and my body with the oyster. I have a moment of worry that perhaps his true ambition is simply to become a better writer, and that he does not fancy me as Tsunemasa thinks he does. As the flirtation progresses we shall see what his motives are. I turn to Kiyosune.

"Are you also wishing for writing lessons. Or do you find me too intimidating?"

"Oh, yes, that would--no you're not at all--I could never hope--never aspire, so far beyond--" he stutters, blushing wildly.

"You do me far too much honor," I admonish, tapping him on the hand with my fan. "I should be more than happy to assist you with your writing. It is a skill that can never be too finely honed, like a sword blade that must always be kept sharp. And," I hide my face behind my fan, "I imagine both of you will be needing all your skills for the morning-after letters you will be writing soon."

Both of them flush deeply at this comment. It is wicked to enjoy flustering them like this, but I cannot help it. I have tutored many sexually inexperienced young women but never a young man, and each of them in his own way appeals to me. I do not wish to come between the friends, however, so I suppose I shall have to choose. Since Atsumori is so much bolder, and Tsunemasa has interceded for him, if I must choose it will be him. But it seems unfair for the shy one to be rejected.

Finally the evening's festivities draw to a close. Machiko lifts the hems of my robes and helps me back to the room set aside for us. She brings over a lamp so I can read Atsumori's missive. It is a shy poem about a mouse looking for shelter in the face of an oncoming storm. I am touched. After all his presenting himself as a soon-to-be-seasoned warrior over dinner, in his private letter he compares himself to a vulnerable mouse. Machiko mixes my ink. I lovingly touch the dragon and cloud design swirling around the well of my inkstone, a gift from my father so long ago. On the parchment she brings me, I write:

'A mouse may be happy in his burrow
No matter how bitter the chill winds blow
Or icicles drip from the eaves.'

The sexual innuendo is almost obscene in its obviousness, but he is young, and I don't want him to miss my meaning. I sit for a few minutes, considering whether to send something more subtle, scratching out other possible replies. But every moment I delay is probably causing him agony, so I decide to send my original effort. I send Machiko to find a page to take the letter to his room. I lie awake for a time, wondering if he will come to me that night, but he does not. Immediately after we all return to court, however, a messenger arrives with a branch of pine dusted with the first snow, and a letter from Atsumori hoping I have not forgotten my promise to tutor him. I send him a reply suggesting he come late at night, since 'my duties to the Empress occupy my every hour during the day'.

The messenger returns with Atsumori's agreement to arrive at the appointed hour. He also bears a gift: a thin silk inner robe of shocking red folded inside a white quilted outer robe trimmed with fox fur.

That night I have servants prepare two writing desks side by side. I have the privacy of my own room, so I shall dispense with the 'curtains of state' a lady should sit behind when discoursing with a man neither her relative nor her intimate.

He arrives early. He bows low as he enters, and I bow in return. I am dressed in light green outer sleeves with pink and green inner sleeves--the red silk he sent me as the innermost layer, barely visible, with a light gold brocade on top, warm but still pretty, a light, girlish look. Machiko tends the braziers, but it seems to me the room has grown warmer with Atsumori's arrival. He seems uncomfortable. I indicate that my maids should depart, with the exception of Machiko, who retires discreetly to her resting place behind a screen. Atsumori's manservant places his inkstone on the table not occupied by mine and departs. I settle beside Atsumori at our tables.

"Show me what you have brought," I say encouragingly. He is wearing a purple robe so dark it is almost black, bordered with gold. The pole extending his shoulders sticks so far out past the end of his body I must adjust my table in relation to his. I smile at how he is trying to impress me.

"It is not the plumage of the nightingale which impresses, but the quality of his song," I say.

He calls his servant, who brings in a bamboo carrying case full of scrolls. The sheer output is impressive. I scan through several of them. Some are quite a bit better than others. I think he must have brought everything he has written since he was a child. It never fails to amuse me how convinced men are that is the size of their endeavors or personal attributes that is what matters.

"This one is quite good," I say, pointing at one comparing the oak and the maple, showing him a couple of small ways in which it might be improved.

"Which do you prefer? The sturdy oak or the bright colors of the maple?" he asks.

"Each in its season," I reply.

Atsumori takes a scroll out of his sleeve and passes it to me shyly.

'The young stag

antlers still sheathed in velvet

brushing up against a branch of purple wisteria.'

"That's magnificent," I respond, touched at his allusion to my nickname, Murasaki--purple. He does indeed seem like a young stag, apricot fuzz still on his antlers. I am inclined to rub that soft velvet off and feel the ivory it leaves behind. I write him a quick reply:

'The wisteria sighs

under the soft touch of velvet antlers

longing for the ivory hidden beneath.'

Atsumori unrolls a blank scroll on his writing desk and sits frozen, hand on his brush, his cheeks flushed, his breathing shallow, too aroused or nervous to think of a reply.

"Let us look at some of these older ones," I suggest, indicating the pile of mulberry scrolls he has brought with him. He nods mutely. I pick one out of the pile. It is a love poem;

'Some say the wisteria

blooms only in spring;

But that lavender memory dances

throughout each season in my heart.'

Since wisteria, or Fujiwara, is my family name, it is clear who he is referring to, but I feign innocence.

"What a fortunate lady to have inspired such devotion!"

"That lady is none other than yourself," he says in a barely audible voice.

"I am honored if that is so," I say. "But the wisteria cannot long hold its purple," I continue, delicately alluding both to the evening remaining and the fact that I am no longer in my youth.

"In my heart, that purple can never fade." This time he is bold enough to look at me. I let my hand peep out of my sleeve, letting the white flesh contrast with the ebony lacquer of my writing desk. He lays his hand, big and puppyish, on top of it.

"If the door to your garden were left open," he says huskily, "I would be honored to see where the wisteria blossoms."

"It is only a simple brushwood gate.
But few know the secret of entering
into the autumn garden on the other side," I respond.

"If only I knew the secret!" he exclaims.

"Poetry crosses all the barriers of time and space. May not a poet do the same?" I encourage him.

He clasps my hand tightly. "They say only a great lover can become a great poet--and you agreed to tutor me--I would gladly study--all night with such a tutor. For truly they say that to master poetry is to transcend death."

The word shi means master, poetry, and death. To his three 'shi's' I add a fourth.

"Shi...shi." I say, hushing him, placing my finger against his lips. "It is true that to be a poet, one must enter death, one must die into love. Words are only the first layer, and," I say, suggestively loosening my outermost robe, "there are so many--yet to be revealed."

Atsumori nearly capsizes both his desk and inkstone in his haste to embrace me. His throat is moist with perspiration and his heartbeat, thudding like a Taiko drum, pulses through all of our silks.

"He is named the Impetuous Male," I murmur between kisses, invoking the Creator God Izanagi. I lead him behind the screens where Machiko has already prepared a futon draped with some of my most erotically colored silks. He plunges into the silks with me with an intensity that reminds me of a cat pouncing on a bird, with the subsequent explosion of feathers.

"Shall I call Machiko to undress me?" I ask as he struggles to free me from my garments.

"No! I want to experience every layer," he insists.

I restrain him from removing the last bright silk, the crimson kimono of his gift, knowing the contrast of the red against the white of my skin will inflame him further. He slides his warm arms under my back and lies on top of me, kissing my mouth. His jade pillar is as hard as its namesake. His hands fumble at my gateway, not knowing what to do to arouse me. I guide them to my breasts instead, which are less complicated. His ardor is all the stimulation I need anyway.

"Show me what to do!" he begs.

I guide him slowly into my cleft. His cock is slender, not like the comfortable thickness of Sessho's wand, but I welcome it nonetheless. I wrap my legs around him to bring him as deeply into me as I can. His body shakes with the effort to control his passion, but he comes almost immediately, after three quick thrusts.

"I'm sorry!" he gasps, collapsing on top of me.

"It's all right. The night is young," I murmur, caressing his face. I undulate beneath him, massaging his jade stalk with my vaginal muscles, hoping it will revive. After only a few minutes he begins moving inside me again and I am happy to feel that he is as hard as ever. He rears up above me, arching his back in pleasure; I hold his hands as he rides me.

"Faster….deeper…yes, like that…" I coax. He closes his eyes in an ecstasy of concentration. I move my hips, guiding his with gentle touches until his strokes hit the rhythm I require and our moans and movements begin to sing together. An agonized groan bursts from his throat and I take a deep breath, willing the white fire of his coming up my spine and into my brain. My crest is small but exquisite, leaving me laughing with delight. My body vibrates with relief. It has been months since I have been with Sessho, and I have been craving a male body.

"Ah, my young tiger," I pant, grasping his shoulders, "I am overcome."

"I am drunk on the sweetness of your fruit," he whispers back to me. "No sake shall ever touch me now that I have drunk the true nectar of Inari." He withdraws from me, collapsing by my side, and my temple gate quickly flows into a temple pool. We will need a whole new set of bedding.

"Truly," I ask, "have you not had other experience in another garden?"

"Tumbles with serving maids. But you are the lady of silk I have lived for, since I was a child."

He is only fifteen now, not so far from being a child. Still, he is a handsome youth, and I am surprised if I am the first court lady he has bedded. Perhaps he says it to be polite. But he seems sincere, and his inexperience is real enough.

As if he read my mind, he says, "You will excuse this young buck his inexperience? Perhaps soon I shall grow horns branched enough to be interesting. Under your tutelage my skill can grow from this slender stream to an ocean of knowledge fit to match yours."

"You are remarkable for one so untutored," I say, believing that praise encourages skill more than criticism. "If this bee comes often enough to the flower, he will soon know all the flavor of the nectar."

"I would not just take from you, I would give," he declares with ardor.

"Well, perhaps now you can give me some restoring tea," I suggest.

I am pleased to find that the tea on the table beside us is once again hot; the incomparable Machiko has slipped in invisibly as we made love, to refill it. She can glide as noiselessly and unseen as any spirit while I am reveling with my lovers. I am always hungry after making love, and I think it is safe to assume that my young man is hungry also.

"Your strength must be restored after such exertions," I say. Placing the hot towel Machiko has brought on his lower back, I ring the small bell by my bed and she appears instantly. I ask her to bring us an assortment of pastries and fruit. I eat just as much as Atsumori, to his unspoken astonishment. But I suspect he is restraining himself somewhat, not wishing to appear crude and animalistic, which is what people say about others whose appetites appear too hearty. After we have eaten, Atsumori is eager to make love again, but sleepy and mindful of the fresh silks Machiko has arranged for us, I coax him to slumber instead. He changes intent quickly, dropping into sleep swiftly as a stone plummets through a well.

When I wake the next morning he is already getting dressed. Custom demands that he be gone before the household is awake, which leads to the amusing spectacle of disheveled men stumbling past each other throughout the palace halls in the dim light before dawn, all pretending they have no idea where anyone else may have been.

Atsumori kneels down, his garments charmingly disarrayed, and caresses my hair.

"I do not think I can bear leaving if I do not know that I can again return," he says.

"So many have tried this gate, it must remain locked," I reply. But as he looks downcast, I add, "But I shall have the gardener open it, just for you."

He gives me a look of such relief and happiness, I feel pleased. I like how readily he shows his feelings in his face, as so few men would do.

"Do not forget to blacken your teeth as part of your ablutions. I seem to have kissed you white!" I admonish.

"I shall," he says like an obedient child, wrapping his sash and tying back his hair. "But I do not know if I can bear to wash my fingers. What help I shall be to my father today, I do not know. My heart and mind are so full of you, I fear there shall be room for nothing else. I am a monk to this temple now, and matters of the world are nothing to me anymore."

"Part of keeping our secret is to do well in all that you attempt throughout the day. To be too moody or dreamy leads to talk."

He bows to me, head touching the floor. "I will endeavor to follow your advice." A few more sweet comments, and he departs.

I allow myself to drift back into a contented sleep.

Chapter Eight
1180

Though late in spring, the weather has turned as cold as a winter day. My writing desk is near a brazier whose decorative dragons are glowing red with the heat. I pull my quilted purple robe around me closer. It used to be Tokushi's and is worn but its soft familiarity makes it a favorite garment. Whenever she sees me in it she says, "Oh, that old thing; get rid of it." But it is one of the first gifts she gave me after I came to court, so for me it holds the essence of love and comfort and I never intend to give it up. In the summer I have a green kimono of Sessho's that I wear to write in. It is ludicrously long for me, but I pin back the sleeves and the way it envelops me makes me feel treasured, as if I were in his arms and not merely in his garment. Whenever I go to visit, I coax him to put it on so I can take it back to court with his smell lingering in it. The scent doesn't last very long, but my nose imagines it. Sometimes he sends me home with a jar of his own blended incense, so I can burn it and dream of him. But the smell of his body is far more intoxicating than his incense, and that, alas, cannot be duplicated.

I am writing to Uryo-on-dai, who tantalizes me in her absence as she did when she was my passionate and infuriatingly ambivalent lover. I'm conveying the latest gossip to her as if she had been gone only a week or two, when in reality it has been years and many of the faces at court now are ones she would not recognize. I report on which girls have gotten married, which ones have left the court, what the new girls are like, speculating on whether she would like them or not (mostly not). Each month I send her a long scroll, and I still believe she will eventually write back something more personal than her bland recitals cataloging the health of her household. I finish the letter and sigh, wishing she were here right now, her strong fingers massaging my neck, saying, "You shouldn't hunch over like that when you write." Scolding, from her, was a sign of affection.

Machiko goes out in the hall to find a page to take my letter. We are visiting at the Rokuhara mansion, which is far roomier than our quarters at the palace. I have been writing in this large room by myself, which would be an unheard-of luxury in our palace quarters. There is a sliding door opening out onto a platform overlooking the garden but the cold prohibits me from stepping out. I take a peek at the garden, seeing how the cherry, plum, and willow trees are drooping under their unseasonal load of snow. The thin coat of wet heavy snow is most decorative, limning all the trees, miniature pagodas and stone outer walls with white. I etch the scene in my mind, then huddle by the brazier trying to think of a poem to describe what I have just seen, knowing Tokushi will be pleased with my efforts.

Even by the brazier, I still shiver. I will ask Machiko to fetch a servant to build up the coals when she returns. Machiko comes back still bearing the letter, saying she can't find any pages.

"That's ridiculous. That's like saying there are no ants in an anthill, no bees in a hive."

"I asked a servant, mistress. She said the young men and boys, including the pages, all went running out of the mansion hours ago. Taira soldiers galloped in earlier, and soon all the men who had armor had thrown it on and those who didn't went as they were, on horse or on foot according to their station. All left with the soldiers except for a small group of guards left to watch over us."

"Why did no one tell me of this sooner?"

"I am so sorry, mistress, but I have been with you all day and I do not know."

"I know you did not know, Machiko, but someone knew and they should have alerted us immediately."

Dread bores a hole at the pit of my stomach. First the troubling omen of the strange snowstorm, now this. Men galloping off in armor never leads to good news. What terrible thing can be next? Who can be challenging Kiyomori's authority now? Kiyomori lets the gray and silver shine in his hair, not dying it like most men and women of the court do as they age, but anyone who thinks his vitality is waning has not spent any time with him. He can still draw a bow as heavy as that used by the most muscular young soldiers, and age has sharpened rather than dulled his ruthlessness.

I ask Machiko to go back out and find a servant who knows more about what is going on, giving her a couple of coins to offer as a bribe if necessary. I cannot leave the room myself, as I am having my monthly bleeding and therefore must remain isolated. Normally many women would be bleeding at the same time, so it is unusual for me to be alone. I suspect some of the younger women may have simply lied about having their courses because they did not wish to miss the trip to the shrine ceremony Tokushi and most of the rest of them are attending today.

Machiko comes back saying she has not been able to find anyone who will admit to knowing anything. Being a woman and being shut out of everything is frustrating enough; being a woman in monthly seclusion even more so.

A few hours later, Tokushi and her ladies return. I am laying quietly on cushions near the brazier while serving women massage me and lay hot stones on my belly to draw out the pain. Machiko is stroking my head and placing fresh cucumber slices over my eyes when we hear the commotion of the returning women. I brush off the maidservants, pull on some clothes and have Machiko slide open the screen separating us from one of the main rooms. Tokushi and most of the other women have disappeared into their own quarters. I motion to one of the young women remaining. She comes over, an apprehensive look on her oval, small-featured face.

"What has happened?" I demand, not taking time for preliminary niceties. "All of you are blowing in like autumn leaves, storm-tossed."

Aikyo Sashie casts an anxious look in the direction Tokushi has disappeared. "Terrible news, my lady, terrible news."

"Go ahead, you can tell me."

"Prince Mochihito has rebelled against the Taira. He has sided with the Genji--Yorimasa is with him."

The Genji. Kiyomori's old clan enemies. The ones who killed my mother. The relaxation brought about by the massage vanishes.

"Surely they are not successful! What has happened? Have there been battles?"

"No, not yet."

"Then how do they know a rebellion has occurred?"

"I don't know. Somehow Kiyomori found out. He knows everything... he sent soldiers to arrest Prince Mochihito and found that he had already disappeared. His retainers fought hard to keep Kiyomori's men out. By the time they were defeated and the mansion searched, Prince Mochihito was gone; no one knows where."

"Yorimasa! He was the only one of his clan to side with Kiyomori during Yoshitomo's rebellion of twenty years ago. He was completely trusted!"

"It is shocking," she agrees, "completely shocking." A couple of the other women come back into the room looking for Aikyo Sashie who alas, is not as delightful a picture as her name, 'charming illustration', would indicate. She clumsily hustles over to them. "Like a water buffalo" Tokushi had whispered in my ear when the girl first appeared at our court a month ago, demonstrating a lack of refinement both piteous and laughable.

Yorimasa is an old man, over seventy, an excellent poet with whom I have enjoyed many stimulating exchanges. I cannot imagine how enraged Kiyomori must be at this betrayal from the one Minamoto he had come to trust. And if Uryon-dai's husband, Yorimada, is with him, it is unlikely they will receive the mercy of mere banishment.

For once I am not enjoying the luxury of solitude, wishing as Machiko again closes the screen to our room that I had the company of the other women-- even the softer and sillier among them--to share all the gossip they have heard today. A month ago I had thought myself pregnant, which proved not to be so, but my courses were late so I am off rhythm with everyone else.

A couple of days later I rejoin the others and find they know nothing more than what has already been disclosed to me. After an anxious week, it becomes known that Prince Mochihito has taken refuge with the monks at the temple of Miidera and that they have vowed to fight for him. Worse, they are sending letters to the monks of other temples trying to rouse them to fight beside them against Kiyomori and the Taira Clan. This in spite of the fact that Kiyomori has become a Buddhist monk and his wife, Lady Kiyomori, a Buddhist nun, and that every member of the Taira family has given generously to various Buddhist temples, enriching many beyond all measure. The monks are a formidable adversary. "All those men without women," On'na Mari used to laugh. "No wonder they're so angry!"

Whether that is the case, or whether, as they like to claim, their spiritual purity makes them strong, even the simplest peasant monks armed with cudgels lay about them with such ferocity that they can unseat a accomplished warrior from his horse. Shigemori's devotion to the Buddha no one doubted, but many believe that Kiyomori's money and ostentatious conversion are cynical political ploys. He has a history of uneasy relations with the monks dating back to when he was a young man and dared to shoot arrows at a sacred palanquin during a skirmish. He has often declared the Way of the Kami to be the only true Japanese religion and publicly questioned why the Sons of Heaven would adopt a foreign God when we have our own deities in every rock and tree and waterfall. I respect him enormously for this stand, since it echoes my own feelings, but I also know that one does not prod a hornet's nest unless one wishes to be stung. His recent politicking is only prudent; the monks are too powerful to be flouted or ignored. Fortunately, each temple considers their way of worship to be superior, holding the others in contempt, and as long as they snap at each other's throats they do not have the strength to rip out Kiyomori's. But if anything can unite them, it would be an appeal to defend the throne, which Mochihito is now claiming to be his, though Antoku is the rightful heir and it seems shameful that Mochihito should challenge the clear rights of his own nephew.

Soon the monks issue edicts, which of course make their way around the capital, stating that Kiyomori has gone against the will of heaven, first by imprisoning Retired Emperor Go-Shirakawa, then by forcing Takakura to retire prematurely, and now by seeking to arrest Prince Mochihito, Takakura's half-brother. I don't really know Prince Mochihito; he has been isolated in his own mansion most of the time I have been at court. On the rare occasions when he has appeared at a gathering he seems much like Takakura, with a refined, somewhat melancholy air, the sort that women like to think betrays a sensitive heart. He is older than Takakura, but as the son of a concubine rather than an empress, was passed over in the succession. Takakura's mother, the Empress Kenshunmon'in, had been jealous of Mochihito's mother and had seen to it while she was alive that they were socially isolated in a mansion at the outskirts of the city. Mochihito has been crown prince all this time, however, so it does not look good for Kiyomori to be seeking to arrest him, given the devotion everyone feels for the royal family.

Still, we have an Emperor, and though only three years old, Antoku is the Emperor nonetheless, and popular with the people. It seems naive of Mochihito to think he can replace him at this late date. Still, in spite of how inappropriate his bid for power seems to those of us in Antoku's court, it is impossible to say where others' sympathies may lie.

Though our house is initially bereft of men, soon we are put under tremendous guard. There must be close to a thousand of them, literally rows encircling our mansion. After a week we are taken back to our quarters at the palace, which is more easily defensible, which frees up some of the soldiers to await the next move by Mochihito and his allies. It is ironic: the Retired Emperor had been confined to the Toba Mansion for nearly two years, and Kiyomori had just decided to release him back to his own mansion. It had appeared, publicly at least, that the Royal Family and the Taira were back on better terms at last, but now...

I wonder if Go-Shirakawa encouraged Prince Mochihito to embark on this foolish endeavor. I am sure Kiyomori wonders also. As the days pass, I am somewhat surprised that neither he nor Lady Kiyomori has summoned me to perform a divination for them. Perhaps they think that my emotional proximity to Tokushi would taint my reading. In any case, I am grateful not to be placed in such a position.

A pall falls over the palace; there is such a lack of the customary gaiety and frivolity, one would scarcely recognize it. The men who are fit enough are garbed in armor, off training their forces for upcoming battles. Even many of the high-ranking courtiers who are far more deft with their ink-brush than their swords are mobilized; there is strong pressure from Kiyomori for everyone to show their loyalty.

The Hollyhock Festival, normally one of the most important celebrations of the year, is very subdued. We wear our garlands of the flower, and perform the dances, but a visit to the Kamo Shrine is deemed too dangerous, as the monks are constantly threatening to invade Kyoto. Tokushi looks very pale and solemn in her lavender robe embroidered with silver.

After our abbreviated ceremony, Tokushi sits with a few of her most trusted ladies. Three of her ladies are Minamoto, or Genji, so we are all quite uncomfortable around them, as their loyalties cannot be counted upon.

"Have you had news from Shigehira?" Tokushi asks Lady Daigon-no-suke in barely audible tones.

Lady Daigon-no-suke nods. "The monasteries are still quarreling amongst themselves, which is good--but I have evil news as well."

Tokushi nods anxiously for her to continue.

"Kio, a very high-ranking palace guard, has defected to the other side, and there is great concern that he will betray his knowledge of secret entrances and all the weaknesses of the palace to the enemy."

Ben-no-taishi clutches her arms about herself so tightly the blossoms on her costume are crushed.

"How many troops have Yoritomo and the other Genji managed to organize? How close are they to the monks?"

"Our spies are not certain of their numbers. Rumor has it they are delaying, trying to persuade more of the northern clans to join them."

"How can Yorimasa and the Prince betray us like this?" Tokushi wails.

"Lord Kiyomori should have killed Yoritomo and Yoshitomo's other demon-spawn sons when he had the chance," Lady Daigon-no-Suke growls.

On'na Mari writes, beside herself with anxiety, that Tsunemasa is going off to lead one of the battalions against the rebellion. I receive letters from her daily, she is so worried and upset about her husband. I take this as a sign that she has become genuinely attached to him, though she phrases her concerns in her typically self-centered manner: "What will become of me if anything happens to him," and, somewhat ridiculously, "How could he leave us at a time like this?"--ignoring the fact that 'a time like this' is precisely when a soldier must leave his family.

I try to reassure her that he is only doing his duty and that he had no choice but to leave. She responds with a rather silly, petulant letter about how Tsunemasa should have stood up to Kiyomori, should have refused to go--as if anyone in their right mind would stand up to Kiyomori and defy his will at a time like this. Knowing Tsunemasa's reputation for unquestioning loyalty, I am sure it never occurred to him.

Martial law has been declared all through Kyoto; no one is allowed out after curfew, nor indeed are social visits permitted, so there is no question of our seeing each other. It is amazing that she manages to send a messenger to me each day with her letters, but bearing Tsunemasa's seal, he is above suspicion and is allowed to pass. One hears of unfortunate peasants being killed as spies for violating curfew, though perhaps they are only innocently trying to fetch a doctor for an ailing child, but no one seems to be in a mood to take any chances. In one letter On'na Mari writes that she is taking consolation from the 'stalwart presence' of one of Tsunemasa's most trusted guards, and I can only pray that the comfort she is finding is not of an intimate nature. I do not dare address the topic in written form, and she does not mention it again.

Everyone goes about as if sleepwalking until news of an impending battle arrives, and then the whole palace is charged up as if by the wild currents advancing before a thunderstorm. The rains pour down, turning the garden into a sea of mud. The rains are depressing, but when the sun dries the land, then the battle will begin, so it becomes more depressing and ominous to see sun than clouds.

At last word comes that Kiyomori's forces are ready to attack the Temples at Miidera. Even the formidable Lady Daigon-no-suke is moping; her husband Shigehira is leading a large section of the army. Munemori is in charge of the troops, having been drilled in the art of commanding night and day by his father, Kiyomori, since this conflict began. We all pray he is capable of the task. But of course, Kiyomori's commanders, like Tsunemasa, are the ones who really make the decisions; Munemori just nods when they 'suggest' what to do.

One morning, Lady Daigon-no-suke rushes panting into Tokushi's room.

"I just received a letter from my Lord. Prince Mochihito fled the Miidera Monastery, realizing that invasion was imminent."

"How many of the traitor Genji are with him?" Tokushi shrills.

Lady Daigon-no-suke smiles. "None, my lady. The Storm God sent hail and snow to harry the north, leaving the mountain passes difficult to traverse. Mochihito, Yorimasa, Kio, and the Miidera monks are heading for Mt. Hiei Temple, hoping the monks there will come to their aid. My Lord assures me they will never make it. This letter was sent last night. The battle may be decided by now."

Tokushi pulls her prayer beads out of her sleeve and we all begin praying for the safety of our troops. I pray fervently that Tsunemasa will see to it that my young lover Atsumori and his friend Kiyosune will be kept far from harm's way.

Shortly before dusk, a messenger arrives for Tokushi. All of her most trusted ladies wait with her in the audience hall. The messenger slides on his knees to the kicho concealing Tokushi, touches his head to the floor, and announces, "I am honored to report the rebel forces have been crushed. Your brother Tomomori requests an audience to convey news of the battle personally."

Tokushi claps her hands together happily, "Send him right in!"

"He is bathing and changing into something more presentable. He will be with you shortly," the messenger promises. Lady Daigon-no-suke clears her throat. "Oh!" Tokushi says, taking her cue. "Is Lord Shigehira well?"

"Yes. He will be arriving with prisoners and the heads of the traitors later."

Lady Daigon-no-Suke releases an audible sigh, thankfully dropping her head to her folded hands.

The messenger leaves before I can signal Tokushi to ask about Atsumori, leaving me shifting from side to side with nervous anticipation until Tomomori finally enters.

Servants remove the kicho and Tokushi rushes to embrace her brother, kissing him on both cheeks. Tomomori is her favorite, after Shigemori. He had been quite ill with a lung ailment shortly before the battle and I had urged him to stay home to recuperate further, but his prideful sense of duty would not permit it. He looks well now, however, his boyish good looks fresh and gleaming from his bath, clothed in a sumptuous array of blue silks patterned with the gold butterflies of the Taira crest.

"Thank heavens you are well, and victorious!" Tokushi exclaims. "Quickly, assure me that the rest of our family has survived!"

"Of course! Amaterasu was on our side!" he says, smiling impishly as they kneel together on cushions, clasping each other's hands. He nods to Lady Daigon-no-suke, who joins them. "Shigehira is such a masterful commander! I can only hope to prove a pale imitation of him one day! He inspires the men with his courage!" He turns back to Tokushi. "Munemori did well, too. Our father has trained him well," he assures her. I slide across the brightly polished wooden floor to join their cluster.

"What of Atsumori and his friend Kiyosune? And Tsunemasa?" I ask.

"I said everyone in our family was fine," he says. "I don't know this Kiyosune, but I saw Atsumori after the battle and he was laughing with some of his young friends."

"Thank you. I am much relieved," I sigh.

"What of Prince Mochihito and Yorimasa? Were they captured?" Tokushi asks. Tomomori fidgets and glances away before answering.

"The battle was brutal. All the rebel leaders were killed."

"Not the Prince!" Tokushi gasps, "Who would dare to spill royal blood?"

"It's not entirely certain the Prince was slain," Tomomori hedges. "Heads were taken--forgive me for mentioning it--leaving bodies hard to identify. One of the captured men swore the Prince died in a hail of arrows--but the body he pointed out had no identifying characteristics."

Tokushi sways, looking a bit green. "Yorimasa?" she asks hesitantly.

"The traitors Yorimasa and Kio both committed suicide after being injured. Yorimasa fought well for a man his age, though he fought for the wrong cause."

"What of Yorimasa's son, Yorimada?" I ask.

"You hadn't heard? He's been sick with the bloody flux for a month or more. He sent a letter declaring his loyalty to Emperor Antoku and gave all his soldiers to us."

Uryon-dai knew at least three different herbal formulas that would cause such symptoms. I suppress a smile. My fox girl found a way out of the trap. Now her family is safe.

Lady Daigon-no-suke lays her hand on Tokushi's arm. "May I put on my traveling cloak and wait in the courtyard for Shigehira's triumphant return?"

"Of course. I'll go with you," Tokushi responds, still looking troubled.

"So sorry, but that is impossible," Tomomori interjects. "The others will be returning stained with battle, carrying hundreds of heads on their pikes--it will be no sight for ladies."

Tokushi shudders. "Oh, how dreadful! Thank you for warning us, brother."

The next day, one of Mochihito's concubines identifies his head, confirming his death. Shockingly, the Prince's head, along with the heads of his supporters, are left rotting on stakes all along the main streets of Kyoto. Where before we ladies had not been permitted out for fear of violence, now that the rebellion has been put down we cannot venture forth because "the sight and stench could never be endured by a lady," as Shigehira informs us when he returns to the palace.

Tokushi is prostrate with horror at the realization that her husband's brother--who resembled him--has his head rotting on a stake just outside the palace walls. "This is the most dreadful thing that could possibly have happened. Yorimasa must have tricked him into it; he would never have thought of such a thing on his own," she weeps. "Doesn't my father see what a ghastly precedent this sets? A prince cannot be disrespected in such a manner! My own brother-in-law!" she says brokenly. "Such a beautiful musician--so incomparable on the flute! And so like my dear husband…"

Her grief causes her to come down with a terrible chest cold, and many of our ladies fall ill with the same thing. Our court undergoes constant exorcisms to placate the angry ghosts assumed responsible. Whispers come to us that in the capital that many are questioning Kiyomori's judgment, wondering why

Prince Mochihito could not have been exiled, or placed under guard like his
father. One anonymous poem circulating widely includes the lines:
"A shining Prince
in the belly of a crow.
The sun in eclipse."
At least Kiyomori spares Mochihito's young sons, sending them off to
temples to take vows, even though Yoritomo, Nori Yori and Yoshitsune,
whom he had spared with similar kindness, have turned on him like a pack of
ungrateful dogs. Kiyomori's kindness is forgotten, however, when he orders
his soldiers to march on the Miidera monastery. All of the soldier-monks
who resist the invasion are slaughtered, and every one of the hundreds of
monastery buildings is put to the torch. Heike soldiers supposedly went
through the smoking wreckage scooping up bits of the melted gold and silver
Buddhas, a great sacrilege. Most of the monks who surrendered were exiled;
the majority of their order had been killed in the two battles. So everyone
gossips about the destruction of the Buddhas, ignoring Kiyomori's kindness in
sparing the children.

Kiyomori has always exhibited a soft spot for children; his general
ruthlessness dissolves and he seems the kindly old sage when they are near.
He frequently sends for Antoku to visit him. He plays Go with him, patiently
teaching him strategy, and reads him military texts. But not all the games are
lessons; he has been a willing horsie more times than I can count, and a wise
dragon, and he never comes to Antoku's quarters without gifts and sweetmeats
hidden in his sleeves. "Dig, little badger, dig!" he coaxes his grandson, who
happily burrows into his grandfather's sleeves, disappearing entirely in his
quest for hidden treats.

The badger is a Taira Clan symbol, so Kiyomori encourages Antoku to
identify with them. When Kiyomori heard that his imperial grandson was
afraid of the dark, he had a large cylinder of black silk made which he brought
to the child's room. "Badgers aren't afraid of the dark," he said stoutly. "Badgers
dig tunnels and make their homes in the dark. Courage lights up the darkest
tunnel and makes it bright as day! The descendent of Amaterasu carries his
own light!" Then Kiyomori announced that he was the Grandfather Badger
and Antoku was the Imperial Grandson Badger, and together they tunneled
into the cylinder of black silk and sat in there with Kiyomori regaling Antoku

with badger stories both heroic and humorous until Antoku felt quite contented in the dark and was not afraid of it again.

The courtiers who trembled in Kiyomori's presence would not have believed their eyes to see his silliness in his grandson's presence. Once, when Antoku was two, shortly before his accession, Kiyomori put his finger in his mouth and poked a hole in the paper folding screen they sat beside, encouraging Antoku to wet his own finger and do the same. Then the two of them together poked many holes, big and small, big fat finger holes for Kiyomori and little tiny finger holes for Antoku. Kiyomori was so charmed by the result that he kept the screen in its damaged state and always let loose with a booming laugh when it was unfolded.

Of course, anyone would adore Antoku. He really does possess an unearthly, radiant quality; no one could question his descent from the Sun Goddess. He radiates a purity that is obviously from the spirit world, though his light does not have the fiery, robust brilliance of the sun, but more the delicate, refined quality of the moon. His ever-expanding collection of pet rabbits, symbols of the moon, are his favorite companions. He likes his birds, and the turtles and fish in the palace ponds are a constant delight to him, but the rabbits are like his personal family; he will not go anywhere unless members of his entourage tuck his favorite rabbits into their voluminous sleeves and bring them along. The rabbits frequently escape into the garden, and then the whole court must go out searching for them, sometimes by torchlight if night has fallen, for Antoku cannot sleep until he knows they are all safe. He is a gentle boy, and strong men weep to see the tenderness with which he strokes his rabbits and whispers into their ears.

Antoku frequently asks for 'Grandpapa Badger' and sees far more of him than he does his own father. Takakura always seems stiff and uncomfortable around the child, whereas Kiyomori never fails to greet Antoku's rabbits and knows all their names, rarely failing to tell them apart even though there are thirty or forty of them. They have many serious conversations on the merits of rabbits, though Kiyomori likes to expound upon the superior nature of badgers, who are too fierce to be kept in captivity, "Like our clan, which can never be subdued," he boasts. They also spend hours feeding the carp. Kiyomori has taught Antoku not to be afraid of them, with their big blubbery lips, but to see how wise they are. He always speaks to Antoku as if the boy can comprehend everything, and I do believe he understands a surprising amount.

Chapter Nine
1180

I am invited to Tsunemasa's house for a small gathering to celebrate Atsumori and Kiyosune's first battle. Tokushi is still ill, but she urges me to go. Atsumori and Kiyosune had been a part of the force sent to subdue Prince Mochihito's rebels. Even knowing the young men survived the battle unwounded, I am stiff with anxiety. It is absurd to think that boys of fifteen should put on armor and be exposed to the hardships of war.

A group of brightly clad maids greet our carriage when we arrive at Tsunemasa's mansion. They are all wearing red cherry-blossom patterned kimonos and bow enthusiastically as we exit our carriage. Machiko holds her head high as they escort us to our suite. In the hierarchy of maidservants, as a lady's personal maid she is far above the status of these household servants.

Shortly after we come back from the bathhouse, a young page arrives with notes from Kiyosune and Atsumori. The page kneels down outside my doorway while I peruse the notes. Machiko is drying my hair and combing warm orange-scented oil through it to make it glossy. I am wearing a soft peach quilted robe. Atsumori has sent a poem:

"A sword pounded in the heat of the forge
Longs for the cooling embrace of the waters."

He refers to the technique of smith-crafting whereby the sword is shaped in the forge, cooled in the water, then shaped anew in the fire. I hope the forge of battle has not hardened my young man.

Kiyosune's name is close to kitsune—fox--and I am sometimes referred to as kitsune-majo--fox sorceress. He makes a play on words with his name in his letter, implying that we are two of a kind and that he is grateful to return to me. His tone is more intimate than our relationship would suggest. I find his presumption endearing. Luxuriating in the comfort of Machiko's touch, I contemplate my replies. No doubt they are expecting my admiration, but I am anxious and heartsick with the thought that this is only the first of many battles if the Genji win more converts to their rebellion. If the seven hundred monks from Nara who had been coming to join forces with Prince Mochihito had arrived in time, this battle might not have had such a happy outcome for the Taira. Shigehira told Lady Daigon-no-suke that the Genji persuaded ten thousand warriors to join them, under the pretense that the crown was threatened. Yoshitomo's three sons are behind it all, and their true aim is revenge against Kiyomori, who slew their father. The death of Mochihito won't change anything; they'll find some other excuse for their rebellion.

I'm never fearful for Tsunemasa. He is so strong and has been through so many conflicts it is impossible to imagine ill befalling him on the battlefield or anywhere else. I don't worry about him dying on the battlefield any more than I would worry about a carp drowning in a pool. But the thought of these slim young men whose bodies can scarcely sustain the weight of their armor confronting seasoned Eastern warriors makes me shudder.

"What can I say that would be encouraging when I want to shake them until their brains rattle?" I say to Machiko.

"Oh mistress," she chuckles. "Male pride, neh?"

"If it wasn't for male pride we wouldn't have all this stupid warfare," I grumble.

"Yes, but they have come back safe," she says logically. "Really mistress," she chides as her hands massage my shoulders, "you are as stiff as a suit of armor yourself. Men will be men. It cannot be helped. You know Lord Tsunemasa will never let anything happen to them."

"So what shall I say?" I am not generally in the habit of asking Machiko's advice on my writing, but my unreasoning anger has erased my capacity for useful thought.

"Say that you are honored to be in the presence of heroes," she advises.

"I don't want to encourage them!" I protest.

"Mistress, they will go to war whether you encourage them or not. It is a matter of honor, neh?"

"Yes, you are quite right," I admit. I start and crumple several different scrolls. I want to say "Don't ever do this again," though I know it is useless.

Finally I simply write the truth.

"I have been so frightened I did not know which way to turn. I am grateful that you have come back safely," I write to Atsumori. Perhaps he will be shocked to receive such a non-poetic and blunt communication, but I do not care. To Kiyosune I write:

"The clever fox slips away
From the farm unharmed,
His prize between his teeth."

After the ink has dried, Machiko takes my messages to the page waiting for them. Then she comes back, slips off my robes and massages musk and orange scented lotions all over my body.

"You will entertain Atsumori tonight?" she asks.

"Yes, of course."

Late afternoon, before the victory supper, I meet with Tsunemasa and On'na Mari in a room adjacent to the banquet hall so I can visit with their son Akoyo. On'na Mari is wearing sheer red outer layers bordered with gold; as I embrace her I can feel that the material of her robes is of the highest quality. Her outer robes are embroidered with the characters for luck, wealth and happiness. Her inner robes are pale green and yellow.

"Look at our little man!" She gestures to Akoyo, who is nearly a year old and sitting up, waving his chubby fists. More like a dumpling than a miniature man, he is so plump there are rolls of fat where his neck should be, so pudgy I fear he will never learn to crawl but instead will have to be rolled from place to place. Tsunemasa greets me. He is wearing rich robes of dark green edged with gold. His inner robes are in shades of brown and yellow. Akoyo begins to fuss. On'na Mari motions for a servant to bring a tray piled with soft bean-filled dumplings. She takes one from the tray and pops it into Akoyo's mouth, then utters a shriek as he bites down on her finger with his sharp baby teeth.

"Ow! Unfilial little brat!" she mumbles, putting her finger in her own mouth.

"Pity poor Yukie!" Tsunemasa says, referring to Akoyo's nurse who still gives him suck, in spite of his seed-pearl teeth.

"He's so...." I stop mid sentence, thinking I should not say the word, 'big', as it could be interpreted as a criticism of his bulk. "So...handsome," I finish.

"Next time you see him, he will be walking." Tsunemasa says with pride.

"And running the time after that," I agree. "Congratulations on the successful outcome to a sad chapter," I add, referring to the recent rebellion.

He returns my bow. "Yes, no one can take pleasure in such a tragedy, but I have brought your young man home safely," he says, a slight twinkle of amusement in his eyes.

I want to snap, "You should never have taken him in the first place!", but I swallow that impulse, nod and smile, saying, "I am forever grateful for your care."

"Atsumori and Kiyosune acquitted themselves nobly, but I shall let you hear the tales of their exploits from their own lips. Shall we?" He nods towards the banquet room.

Machiko helps me to rise. I am wearing the full complement of layers considered proper for a banquet and am already sweating underneath them all. She untangles some of the pearls from the headdress adorning my hair and quickly pats them into place. My outer robe is a pale lavender-blue embroidered with branches of wisteria edged with silver.

It is only a small gathering, as too much celebrating the conclusion of a battle that resulted in the death of a member of the royal family would be in very bad taste. As Atsumori and Kiyosune enter the room, my throat goes dry. They seem taller, their gestures more manly and assured. Kiyosune is wearing a dark blue robe figured with lighter blue clouds. Atsumori is wearing garments of bright red and yellow. We all bow and sit down at the table. Atsumori and Kiyosune are seated across from me. Tsunemasa heads the table, On'na Mari is on my left. Tsunemasa's brother Tsunetoshi and his wife come next, and a couple of his other friends and their wives complete the party, the men on one side of the table, the women on the other.

Cloudy cold unfiltered sake is brought for all. Tsunemasa toasts the brave warriors who fought against the rebels to preserve the Imperial line, "especially our two young cubs whose swords tasted their first blood on this sad yet triumphant occasion." We all assent to the toast and drink the sake thirstily. Tsunemasa's reference to 'swords tasting blood' has left me dizzy and light-headed, remembering my own blood crimes, and how I was forever changed and hardened by them. I grieve to think of these young men being hardened in such a way.

Kiyosune bows his head towards Tsunemasa. "We did nothing more than our duty."

"As any warrior would do," Atsumori adds.

"We must all fulfill our duty," Tsunetoshi nods.

"I can't even imagine what horrors you have all been through," a young wife of one of the other noble warriors shudders.

"Like it could be any worse than child-birth!" On'na Mari whispers to me behind her fan.

"Tell the ladies of your exploits," Tsunemasa encourages the young men as the food is laid out and set before us. For a few moments, the only conversation revolves around the delightful qualities of the food.

"There is nothing worth reporting," Atsumori says modestly.

"Other than the fact that you saved my life," Kiyosune notes wryly.

"And you mine," Atsumori admits.

"We rode hard for three days pursuing the traitors," Tsunetoshi starts. "We caught up with them at the Uji Bridge, and men were racing to see who could take the honor of being first across. But the rebels had removed some of the planking, and two hundred men were lost as they fell into the churning currents. It seemed impossible to cross such a raging torrent with our horses, and the Prince's archers were showering us with arrows."

"But our own archers lost no time in returning their volleys," Ieyasu puts in.

"We dismounted from our horses while deciding what to do," Tsunetoshi continues.

"Our archers were knocking traitors off the bridge left and right--" Ieyasu interrupts.

"But their warrior Tajima held the bridge, wielding his spear so furiously he knocked the arrows aside before they could reach him. Everyone calls him 'arrow-scattering Tajima' now." Kiyosune chimes in.

"Yes, it was quite a performance. Admirable," Tsunemasa nods between bites of meat.

"He is a warrior worth a thousand," Atsumori acknowledges. "I wish he were ours."

"There is no understanding the web of karma that caused him to be on the other side," Tsunetoshi comments. "Men on foot tried to take the bridge, but the flights of arrows made it impossible, and many brave warriors went to their deaths."

"We discussed taking our soldiers down to the next bridge, but we feared that in the time it took, the traitors would escape," Tsunemasa says.

"Being spring, the river was in full flood," Tsunetoshi explains. "Finally we decided if we tied our horses together into horse-rafts, with the foot soldiers clinging to the pommels of the saddles and the tails of the horses, we might make it across."

"And if not, we were prepared to drown nobly," Atsumori boasts.

"My heart is in my throat at such a thought!" one of the young wives gasps.

"It is a technique that has been done many times in history," Tsunemasa reassures her.

"As we were crossing, my roan mare was shot in the throat," Kiyosune says "She rolled over into the water kicking, and I was nearly drowned. But as I struggled to free myself from the stirrups, I felt a strong hand grab me by my top-knot and drag me to the surface. It was Atsumori." He gazes at his friend fondly.

"Lucky you're such a bean-pole. I could see your top-knot even through the churning water," Atsumori teases.

"Yes, he ripped half the hair out of my head. My helmet had been lost when my horse went under. I grabbed onto Atsumori's pommel, and holding onto his pommel and leg I made it across," Kiyosune says.

"As soon as I got to shore, an arrow bounced off my armor," Atsumori says. He bows towards me. "But your wonder-working charms preserved me from injury." He brings his hand to his throat and I see he is still wearing the charms I had made for him. "The arrow glanced off harmlessly, unable to penetrate the web of magic you had woven about me."

"Atsumori said, 'Hold on and I'll get you a horse,'" Kiyosune continues. "So my manservant and I huddled behind our shields with the arrows singing around us."

"Tsunetoshi had engaged with the enemy right away," Atsumori says, "So I galloped up to help him."

"After we finished cutting off the enemy's head--" Tsunetoshi begins.

"I grabbed his horse by the bridle and took it back to Kiyosune," Atsumori finishes.

"It was a red and white horse with a gold-edged saddle," Kiyosune says, "so it must have belonged to someone important.'

"Yes, but we didn't bother to stop and ask his name before taking his head," Tsunetoshi chuckles.

"My servant helped me into the blood-soaked saddle," Kiyosune continues. "I looked around for Atsumori, and saw he had taken on three of the enemy at once."

"And I was hard-pressed," Atsumori says grimly.

I have given up all pretense of eating as I listen, gripped by the dreadful tale. Only at a warrior's household would this be considered dinner-table conversation. Beside me On'na Mari eats as unconcernedly as if we were discussing gossip in the Empress' quarters.

"And where were you during all this?" Tsunetoshi's wife gasps.

"I had taken off pursuing the enemy, trying to battle my way through to wherever Prince Mochihito might be," he confesses. "I had lost sight of Atsumori."

"I was leading my soldiers, pursuing Yorimasa. We had been friends. I wanted to be the one who took his head," explains Tsunemasa.

"So suddenly," Atsumori bursts forth, "as I am fighting for my life, trying to keep these warriors at bay, Kiyosune without a helmet, hair every which way, looking like Hachiman himself appears, slashing madly with his sword, his horse rearing, fighting with its hooves!"

"Yes, fortunately for us," Kiyosune laughs, "the horse was a traitor, just like that traitor Kio who betrayed his own people. She fought like a thousand demons! Indeed, I felt myself turn into a demon on her back when I saw you surrounded; a wild spirit took possession of my brain."

"You fought like a man possessed!" Atsumori laughs. "Kiyosune, who was so modest, claiming to fear battle, was utterly fearless when the occasion came!"

"So between the two of us--"

"We slew them all!" Atsumori boasts proudly.

"You could have handled them by yourself," Kiyosune says modestly.

"One of their swords hit my helmet so hard I was seeing stars," Atsumori shakes his head. "If you had not come up when you did, I fear they might have had my head. I always liked to think of myself as one who could best a dozen warriors like one of those heroes in the war chronicles. But," he adds ruefully, "its quite a lot harder than it sounds."

"Yes, my sword was so battered, my father says I will need a new one," Kiyosune says.

"It can be repaired. And you got a fine new horse out of it. What a warhorse she is! What are you going to call her?" Atsumori asks.

"Mistress of Demons," Kiyosune says with a broad smile.

"That she is! I must train my horse to fight like that. Midnight Battle didn't flinch, though," Atsumori notes proudly. "He held his own."

"Hai, I was glad for his strength crossing that river."

"We are truly brothers now," Atsumori says, clasping Kiyosune's hand. "We have each saved the other's life."

"There is no stronger bond," Tsunemasa says. "Not even the bond between husband and wife can compare to the bond between comrades in battle." He raises a cup of sake in silent toast to his friend Ieyasu, then to each of the other men in turn.

On'na Mari gives a derisive snort behind her fan. "Let Ieyasu give him a son then!" she whispers disgustedly.

"It's a male thing," I whisper back to her. "We'll never comprehend what they go through."

"Now you see what I have to live with every day!" she complains. "All this boring talk of war, war, war, battles, battles, battles, swords, arrows, armor, strategy! You have no idea what a strain it is to try to act interested in all of this. All I care about is whether I can redecorate these dreary halls or not! I want bright colors for my new wall hangings, and jade sculptures, not moldy armor on pedestals and swords hanging from the walls. Parts of this house are like living in a barracks!"

"Well, Tsunemasa probably finds talk of decorating boring," I whisper back to her.

"He hasn't the faintest idea of what looks presentable! He has no sense of style!"

"What deep thoughts pass behind those fans, ladies?" asks Atsumori.

"Oh," I say, fluttering my fan, "we were just saying how we cannot even imagine the courage needed for such deeds. I feel I am about to faint on the spot."

"Yes," On'na Mari agrees, batting her eyes and fanning herself, "we are overcome with your bravery."

"They can be proud of their first battle," Tsunetoshi nods. "We are all very proud of them."

"Well, and you are one of the ones who caught up with that traitor," Kiyosune says.

"Yes, I am proud to call you my brother," Atsumori says.

"Well," Tsunetoshi shrugs, "there were so many of us. It is true that my arrow was one of the ones that found the traitor, but there is no telling which of us was responsible for his death. There were so many crowding around, at least five are claiming they took his head, though he only had one head to take."

"Goodness, we ladies can scarcely eat a bite," one of the other ladies complains. "Remember, our sensibilities are so much finer than yours. All this talk..." she stops, thinking that she has been rude. "Please forgive me, my lord, our sex is fragile," she begs Tsunemasa.

"No, you are quite right," Tsunemasa nods gallantly. "I am forgetting my manners, letting this coarse talk of war occupy all of our dinner. I have called this event to honor our new warriors, so I wanted them to have a chance to tell their story. Meanwhile, let us have a moment of silence to honor all those who died--on both sides--for bravery is always honorable, even if a man's choice of allegiances is not." There is a quiet pause.

"I only wish that traitor Kio had been captured alive!" Atsumori snarls.

"He had the good sense to cut open his belly," Tsunemasa says. "Ah, forgive me ladies, that was far too graphic. Yes, had he been taken alive, his fate would have been grievous. Munemori did a fine job with his first command," he assures us. "He is quick to learn."

I can tell by the way Tsunemasa casts his eyes down as he says this that it is not strictly the truth, but naturally he must honor his commander-in-chief. I imagine that as long as Munemori will take Tsunemasa's advice, all will be well. "As for Tomomori--he is pure genius in the field. The men are calling him 'Kiyomori's talons.' And Shigehira is a warrior among thousands," he adds.

"Yes, he has always seemed like a doughty soul," On'na Mari agrees. "But if Lady Daigon-no-suke would ride beside him, I do believe they would be an unconquerable force."

Everyone laughs at this. Lady Daigon-no-suke is known as a woman whose will is not to be broached.

"Hai, thank heavens she is on our side!" Atsumori chimes in, and we all laugh again.

The dinner continues. Some of the ladies mention how darling Akoyo is. On'na Mari preens herself.

"Yes, he is clever, and his skin is like silk and his dimples are charming, but underneath it all he is a savage beast." She holds up her bandaged finger. "He bit me just now, most ungratefully, as I was feeding him a dumpling! He has teeth as sharp as a stoat's! Obviously he is going to be a warrior like his father."

"Yes, he's a fierce little badger, a proper Taira boy!" Tsunemasa puffs proudly.

The rest of the evening passes convivially. No sooner have I returned to my room for the evening than a messenger arrives from Atsumori. I open the scroll he has sent. He has enclosed a poem which ends, 'My sword seeks your sheath, to bring me to peace.'

I am somewhat displeased that the image is war-like and blunt, rather than more romantic.

"What's the matter, mistress?" Machiko asks, ever-alert to my shifting moods.

I read her the poem. "Dismayingly blunt, don't you think?"

"Oh, mistress," she laughs indulgently, "he's a young man."

"Yes, that's true."

"He's probably too excited to think of anything more elegant," she says.

That casts the situation in an entirely more cheerful light.

I unroll some paper, on my desk. I should incorporate some of the images of his poem, but I find war references quite distasteful. Machiko trims the wicks of the oil lamps to make sure they are all even and will not flare up, distracting from the romantic glow intended. The dappled light sways back and forth like a tide.

She pulls back the shoji doors. It is now late enough that most of the mosquitoes will have retired. The doors face a tiny inner garden featuring a small waterfall. The sound of the water gurgling over the rocks is very pleasing. I leave my desk for a moment to step outside. The weather has changed completely since the battle, moving now into the balmy weather more typical of late spring. The stars are twinkling. I take a deep breath and feel content. I return to my desk and write:

"There is no peace
Without the preceding passion.
The battle for my heart
Has already been won."

I blow on the ink to help it dry faster, causing it to smudge on one character. I don't care. I hardly think Atsumori will be all that concerned about my handwriting.

After the messenger leaves, Machiko brushes my hair out with camellia nut oil to make it glossy and dresses me in a few gauzy layers--a dappled midnight blue over a pale lavender will look lovely in the flickering light. She moves my bedding near the door so we can feel the soft kiss of the air and hear the coaxing voice of the fountain all night long.

At the first knock, Machiko patters over to slide the door to the hallway open. Atsumori slips in quick as an eel, enjoying the secretive nature of the intrigue.

"All evening I have been longing for this moment," he says.

"And I."

He crushes me to him, ignoring Machiko's nearness. She quickly scuttles into a sheltering alcove and pulls a screen in front of it.

"Do you want anything?" I ask.

"Everything! All you have to give me!"

"I meant something to drink!" I laugh.

He pulls me over and down onto the bed. "Only your love can quench my thirsts!" he declares ardently.

I love this wild passion of his. I feel tossed about like a small boat on the swells of the deep ocean. The way he pulls open my robes makes me think he doesn't notice how lovely they look in the light. But when he says, "My sweet lady Wisteria, you're so beautiful!" I don't mind at all. An arbor of wisteria hangs over the entryway to the garden; its scents blend seamlessly with the oils of wisteria and musk that Machiko added to the lamps. Soon those scents are made heady with the addition of our own salts and musks. He barely pauses after each climax, coupling with me five, six, seven times, stopping only when I beg for mercy.

"You're relentless!" I pant. "Makes me feel sorry for your enemies!"

"I never want to leave you unsatisfied."

"I don't think that would be possible."

Machiko brings an iron teapot and pours barley tea, which is good for restoring strength. We sit sipping it, gazing at the night sky, exquisitely framed by the rippling shadows of wisteria.

"I would go through a thousand battles for this reward," he laughs.

"May the gods grant you never have to. I can't stand the idea of you being in danger," I admit.

"How can I be in danger?" He puts his hand to his throat, to the talismans I have made. "I'm protected by the greatest sorceress in the kingdom."

"Don't be so confident of that," I plead. "Magic is like the wind. It can fill your sails--but it doesn't mean the boat is safe from storms."

"Between your powers and mine...I'm not a child you know."

"I'm well aware of that!" I laugh giddily.

He chuckles again, delighted at his ability to leave me limp. I imagine a young tiger would look like this. I run my hands through his hair, which has been thoroughly disheveled.

"You missed me?" he says.

"Oh yes."

"And you worried about me?"

"I did."

He lies down, happily crossing his arms under his head.

"That must mean you love me."

"It must mean just that," I admit.

"Because I'm so good in bed."

"Mmm hmm," I agree.

"And a fearless warrior."

"Mmm, mmm. I don't know about that." I put my hand on his finally limp cock. "This is the only spear I have any interest in."

"As it should be," he says. "I was determined to cover myself in glory in this battle. So you would think I was worthy of you."

"Well, you're quite wonderful enough now! Please don't prove yourself to me any further--except between the quilts, as you did tonight. No woman requires any more proof than that. Courage is highly over-rated as an aphrodisiac."

"Before, I was a boy. Now, I am a man. And I can tell, by the way you respond to me, that you respect me more."

"I do hope you don't expect me to ride into battle so that you can respect *me*." I pick a cluster of purple wisteria and trace it over his body.

"Don't be silly. No one wants a woman warrior. I heard the Genji are training women to fight. Isn't that insane?"

I personally think war is insane, but not wanting to damage his pride, I simply nod.

"Do you think Machiko could find us something to eat?" he asks.

Before I can reach the bell to beckon her, she pads out from behind her screens.

"Anything particular you would like?" she bows towards us.

"Oh, it doesn't matter, as long as there's a lot of it--and some sake," he says.

She bows and goes out into the hall to find someone to fetch the food.

We get up and walk into the garden. He lifts his face, drinking in the stars.

"I'm so happy to be alive. You can't imagine--until you've faced death like I have--the smells, the tastes--" he buries his face in a clump of wisteria. "Oh, that smell! Almost as good as yours. You can't imagine until you face death-- how sweet life is. In battle you're always dancing on the edge of a sword. You don't know how it will turn out. You don't know if you'll live to see another day. And when you do live, when you leave the battlefield and someone else's blood is soaking your sleeves and not your own--I can't explain it."

I nod.

He wanders over to the pond. "The water lilies aren't blooming yet," he comments. He takes my hand, drawing me down beside him. "Ah, but to be so deep in your lily--how sublime!" he says. "Pleasure means so much more now. Everything does. After the battle, I rode past the weir at the third bridge over the river Uji. So many warriors had been washed up against the weir-- bobbing there--all different colors of armor and armor lacing--like a rainbow quilt--so beautiful--and so horrible. I thought how easily that could have been Kiyosune if I hadn't managed to get him to shore. How easily it could have been me if I had been one of the first to cross the bridge, one of those men who fell through the torn-up planking. If Tsunemasa hadn't held me back, that could have been me."

"Thank the gods it wasn't," I say.

He brushes his hand through the water, shivering the star pattern. I touch some of the water to his neck, his forehead, his hands, his chest. "May the gods always protect you," I pray.

"I never want to die. Life is too sweet." He takes my face in his hands and kisses me. Then we hear the faint sshhing sound of the door to the hallway sliding open.

"Let's go eat!" he says.

We sit cross-legged on our pile of quilts enjoying baked buns with meat filling and a vast array of pickled vegetables with some cold grilled fish.

"You know," he says, as we lay together after eating, "if it wasn't for Kiyosune, I wouldn't be holding you right now."

I shudder. "Don't say such a thing."

"It's only the truth. You like him, don't you?"

"Of course I do."

"He so envies me for the privilege of your bed. Remember when you said…
you would give him poetry lessons also?"

"Mmm…" I murmur non-committally.

"He wants it badly, but he's afraid to ask."

"Are you saying you wouldn't mind?"

"No, I wouldn't mind. I told you he saved my life. He's my brother.
We share everything." He looks at me cautiously to see how I regard that
statement. "When my right hand caresses you," he says, pulling down the
shoulder of my thin silks, "the left hand doesn't get jealous."

"That's a very…provocative idea," I stall, trying to judge whether he is
sincere or whether he is testing my loyalty.

"I might be a little jealous. I can't swear that I wouldn't. Well, it would be
up to you, of course. But what a shame if such a brave warrior should have no
reward, no lady's love to help keep him alive."

"I'm not giving out any further rewards tonight, I can assure you of that."

"No, no, of course not. Just--just a thought. If you wanted me to," he adds
carelessly, "I could tell him you might still be willing to…" he drapes his soft
cock across my thigh, "teach him how to use his brush properly?"

"You're incorrigible!" I tap him lightly across the cheek.

"But you'll think about it?" he coaxes, curling up to me spoon wise as I turn
away from him.

"If you insist," I say, tingling at the thought.

Chapter Ten
1180

When I return to the palace, a pile of scrolls awaits me in my room. I know I can ignore the one with the peacock feather in it; it is from a very tiresome courtier who refers to himself as 'Lord Peacock'. He is convinced that because I smiled at him once when he delivered a well-composed poem that I am interested in him in other ways. The Empress' unmistakable perfume leads me to a letter from her containing a sweet poem, which I set aside to answer first. Two scrolls contain longing love letters from two young girls of the Empress' court who are currently smitten with me. Next, an invitation to a banquet to be held at the Rokuhara mansion rewarding various warriors who fought for the Taira. Finally, I eagerly open the very last scroll, which must have just been delivered since it is attached to a fresh sprig of wisteria twisted together with soft hawk feathers. Kiyosune's familiar scent wafts up from it.

"In the black of ink
All the colors of life are hidden.
The hawk's eye is poetry
And nothing is hidden from it.
No one is a poet unless the moon smiles on him."

A second poem follows the first.

"In a secret moonlit arbor,
Covered over with wisteria
Poetry entered my mouth.
I would have ink running in my veins,
If it could be wisteria ink."

An enclosed note reads; "My brother Atsumori informs me it is possible you would consider taking another, even so young and unworthy, as your pupil. If so, I should study as if my life depended on it. If not, to breathe the fragrance of the wisteria, only for a moment, is to remember it forever." He includes an address in Kyoto where I can write to him, as if I did not know the location of his uncle's mansion.

Excited as I am, I must attend to my duty and answer Tokushi's message first. If she is feeling completely recovered from her illness, she will probably want me to share her bed tonight. 'It would be a shame for the late-blooming wisteria to go to waste,' I scribble on a piece of paper, thinking I may use it as part of a poem to send Kiyosune later. I quickly compose a poem for Tokushi;

'The wisteria can never stray far
From the trellis to which it clings.
The hawk returns from the beckoning sky,
To the hand it loves.'

Shortly after the message is delivered, the messenger returns asking me to meet Tokushi in the garden. We walk about, admiring the wisteria that has bloomed so late.

"Everything is so topsy-turvy this year," she says. "But now spring is finally here. I think everything is going to be well, don't you?"

"I hope so." Rumor has it that all the monks are up in arms over the burning of the Miidera temples. It seems all too likely that more battles are just around the corner. But I would never introduce such a topic unless she brought it up first.

"I spoke with my father while you were gone," she says. "He says Tomomori did an extraordinary job as commander in chief of the last engagement. Munemori's good with strategy, you know, but he's not a fighter."

I nod. Even in his magnificent armor, Munemori's corpulent form upon a horse he has to be hoisted onto does little to inspire confidence. Tomomori, on the other hand, is becoming known as a masterful warrior.

"Your parents had at least one child with a talent for absolutely everything," I praise.

"That's the advantage of a big family," she agrees, looking downcast. I could kick myself. Why did I not anticipate that mention of a big family would remind her she has only one child? Still, when someone is as sensitive as Tokushi, it is hard to anticipate every comment that might make her unhappy.

"How was the party at Tsunemasa's?" she asks.

"Lovely."

"And Atsumori?" she questions, archly raising an eyebrow.

"He's really a young man now. Battle has changed him, but I think not for the worse."

"That's good. Enjoy it while you can. Those young men are very distractable," she says, obviously thinking of her straying husband.

"Speaking of young men--when I returned this morning I had a message from Kiyosune waiting for me."

"Isn't he a cousin of yours?" Tokushi asks.

"Very distantly--probably a closer cousin to you on his mother's side."

"Yes, I think he's a second cousin of mine--or is it third? So many cousins, I can't keep track of any except the first ones, really. He came back safely, didn't he?"

"Oh yes. Quite. I was wondering if it would be all right with you if I were to…entertain him."

"One young man isn't enough for you?" she says incredulously.

I blush and fidget, uncharacteristically at a loss for words.

"Oh, well, whatever takes your fancy," she laughs.

Kozaisho comes towards us across the garden, stepping very daintily. She is stunning, with prominent cheekbones and velvety white skin. She is married to Michimori, one of Kiyomori's nephews, and though not part of our court, comes to visit from time to time.

"May I join you?" she asks, twirling her purple parasol as she steps gingerly towards us over a stone pathway set across the water.

"Of course!" Tokushi says.

Kozaisho is known for being one of the most happily married women at court, so I don't know that she'll be very tolerant of my peccadilloes. "We'll finish our discussion later," Tokushi whispers in my ear. We wander about the garden gossiping how several of the girls at Tokushi's courts have succumbed to the blandishments of youths newly returned from battle.

"I can't imagine what it is that makes war such an aphrodisiac," Tokushi complains.

"Well," Kozaisho says, "speaking for myself, the thought that my beloved is in danger…" she flutters her fan. "The morning dew…" she says, referring to a poem that equates the brevity of our lives with the transience of the morning dew.

"Yes, I suppose that's it," Tokushi considers pensively. "And if such dangers are to persist…"

"It's one way of supporting the men who are fighting so bravely for us," I interject, thinking that it will encourage her to turn an indulgent eye on my affairs.

"That's quite true," Tokushi rejoins humbly. "I cannot believe I was so selfish as not to think of that."

"Oh, you, selfish? Never!" Kozaisho says before I can frame my own protest.

"No indeed. You are the most generous woman alive," I add.

"Hardly," she says. "But then again, in my position, I can't go about comforting warriors, can I?"

"No, of course not," Kozaisho says, "nor would I ever consider being with any man other than my husband. No one's suggesting...ah, but you are very lucky that your husband will never be called upon to fight."

"Seiko, on the other hand, who's not married..." Tokushi says, giving me an amused look.

"Seiko's free to do as she pleases," Kozaisho agrees.

"And she does," Tokushi murmurs.

"Do you think you are with child yet?" she asks Kozaisho.

"No, I'm just gaining weight because I'm so happy! It's terrible!"

"Oh, you're not gaining weight at all!" Tokushi and I chime together.

"I want to give you one of Antoku's old baby robes," Tokushi offers. "You can sleep with it under your pillow for good luck.

"Oh, Lady..." tears sparkle in Kozaisho's eyes. "I do hope we shall be so fortunate--though no ordinary son can compare with Antoku--he's such an amazing child. But then again, he is Amaterasu's grandson, so I suppose it is only to be expected."

"Yes," Tokushi says. "I'm very blessed."

"The whole nation is blessed, Lady," Kozaisho says. "Thanks to your courage." She nods towards me. "And your awesome powers."

We go inside and spend a couple of hours with Kozaisho before she returns to her mansion.

"What a lovely woman," Tokushi says. "What a pity she served at the Retired Empress' court instead of mine. But now that she's married to my cousin Michimori, we are getting to be good friends. I do hope the gods will bless her with a child soon."

"And another for you as well," I add.

"So be it," she says, fingering her prayer beads piously. Then she remembers our previous conversation. "What in the world are you doing with *two* young men barely out of their boy's loops?" she demands.

"Fulfilling my duty as an emissary of Inari," I say, referring to Inari's reputation as a love Goddess.

"Well, leave a little time for me, will you? Honestly, I've never known anyone who liked pillowing as much as you."

"Oh now, you know I have scarcely slept with any men the whole time I have been with you," I protest.

"Well, you are certainly making up for lost time recently," she says, raising an eyebrow. Her servant Naniwa brings her various pieces of jewelry to examine as she plots out what she will wear at her next formal occasion.

"Perhaps you should go and rest, since your young man will be coming shortly," she suggests.

"Thank you for being so understanding." I kiss her hands and bow. I almost skip back to my quarters.

Machiko laughs, "Ah, mistress, these young men are like a tonic for you. I swear you do not look a moment past the age of twenty today."

"You flatter me too much, Machiko," I say. "But my heart is fluttering so, I feel as if I *am* a maiden. I wonder how he will compare to Atsumori?"

"When eating persimmons, spit out the bitter parts." Machiko quotes an old proverb. I quickly write a message to send to Kiyosune:

"Wisteria can only blossom,
Filling the air with its lavender scents,
When it has a strong oak lattice to cling to."

I add a note saying that I would be pleased to be his 'poetry instructor' for the evening, and specify an hour that would be good for him to arrive. The messenger returns so quickly with an acceptance, I wonder if Kiyosune has been waiting by the front gate all day with his pre-written reply.

I lie down, but I am too excited to sleep, or even to rest. I keep twisting around on my futon. Finally I get up and ask Machiko to find me scrolls containing poetry referring to foxes. I sit with the scrolls piled around my desk, studying them to see what allusions to foxes and their relationship with Inari I might quote in my poems to Kiyosune. I write:

'Inari's mountain grows white with snow.
In their den, the foxes nip and chuckle

All winter long."

I inscribe another;

'Foxes change their coats in the winter
But towards my young fox
I could never change my heart.'

He's slightly late, which I find annoying. Finally he arrives, bearing a pot with iris growing from it. His servant sets it down. Kiyosune nods towards it. He seems quite nervous. I see that he has taken care to make his teeth very black and his hair is freshly oiled. He is wearing a subtle combination of grays. While I might wish that he had dressed more decoratively, he is in truth like the fox who hides and sees everything without being seen himself. I nod towards the two writing desks I have had placed side by side.

"Might I trouble you for a sip of water?" he asks.

"Do you prefer water, sake, or tea?"

"Water and sake?" he asks shakily.

"Certainly," I nod to Machiko who goes to the door and tells one of the other maidservants what to fetch.

One of Kiyosune's manservants brings his inkstone and inks and sets them on the desk, along with brushes and paper.

"Oh, what elegant paper," I say, indicating a textured scroll.

"You think so? I made it myself," he says, spreading it out across our desks for my inspection. "It is made from birch."

"It is wonderful," I say, running a finger along its nubbly surface. "I would want to write a very special poem on that."

"If you would be so kind," he says, bowing and handing me the empty scroll. "I would put it on my wall and regard it as a sutra."

"You do me far too much honor," I reply. "Let me see if I can think of anything suitable."

The maidservant arrives bearing a tray she hands to Machiko. She pours us sake and sets the cups of well water by our desks.

"To the Goddess of the rice, who gives us intoxication as well as nourishment," he toasts, acknowledging Inari and complimenting me for my association with her.

"Well said," I nod.

We sip our sake. I carefully inscribe the poem I had already composed about the foxes and the snow, decorating it with a quick brush sketch of Inari's mountain on the bottom. He smiles as he reads it.

"It's wonderful…you're so amazing," he stutters. "I can't believe I am fortunate enough to be kneeling beside you."

"I would be a strange Priestess of Inari if I did not welcome a fox."

He bows his head, looking both pleased and abashed.

"Now then, you must write one for me," I prod, indicating another of his handmade scrolls,

"I am so unworthy," he mutters.

"Now then, show me how you mix your ink," I coax.

He mixes it with assurance. "Alas, that is the easy part," he says, dawdling with his brush in the ink. Finally he writes:

'No matter how deep the snow
On Inari's mountain
Two foxes will always stay warm,
Together.'

He draws a charming image of two foxes curled together at the bottom.

'It's lovely," I purr. I stroke my neck and hair in a manner that invites him to touch me, but he merely gazes around nervously. If I could take him walking through the garden that might settle him, but it would be improper to have a man in the Empress' garden, even at night, and we might be challenged by the guards, which would hardly be relaxing.

"There is a dinner coming up shortly where many of the heroes of the recent battles will be honored," I say.

"I hardly think I qualify," he blushes.

"You are a hero to me," I murmur, stroking his hand. "You saved Atsumori's life. I will always be grateful."

"It was nothing."

"Well, in any case, I need to pick out some jewelry that I will wear for this occasion, and I simply can't make up my mind. If you would be so kind as to help me…"

"Oh, certainly, certainly…I don't have much of an eye for jewelry, but if I can be of assistance…"

Machiko opens a drawer on a lacquered chest by its metal handles. We slide across the floor to kneel by the jewel chest. I remove a hairpin with pearls.

"What do you think of this one?"

"Beautiful...lovely..."

"Could you put it in my hair and tell me what you think?"

I am wearing a thin and gauzy outer robe of scarlet with inner layers ranging from madder to reddish purple. He can hardly mistake the message of my clothing if he would just stop trembling and look at me. His hand is shaking as he holds the hairpin up next to my hair. I am beginning to think seducing this young man will be harder than I anticipated. He is so much shyer than Atsumori.

"What about this one with the golden leaves? Machiko, show him how it goes over my hair." I turn my back, and while lifting a hand up to my hair, push my robes back so the nape of my neck is exposed, making it look as if I had done it accidentally.

"It's quite beautiful."

Since his touch on my neck does not follow, I turn back to face him. "What do you think of this jade clasp? Have you seen my rose-colored robes? I was thinking perhaps this light green broach," I say, indicating how I would place it between my breasts. "Of course it doesn't go as well with what I am wearing now. Perhaps if I take off this outer garment, you would get more of the idea...." Machiko slips my outer layer off. I put the broach in his hand and press his hand between my breasts. "What do you think?"

"That would be...irresistible."

Well, I have certainly given him every opening. I wonder if this young man really only wants a writing lesson after all. But I imagine Atsumori knows his friend's mind. Finally I see that I am going to have to be the one to take matters further. I indicate for Machiko to bring us some more sake.

"Do you like the sake?"

"Oh, yes. Silver mountain sake, is it not?"

"Yes, yes it is. Tell me, do you think it is better warm or cold?"

"I really haven't had this type warmed, I don't think...."

"Try it cold, and then I shall give you some warm."

He swallows some obediently. Meanwhile, I hold some in my mouth to warm it. I lean close to him and let the sake I have warmed in my mouth flow into his mouth. He puts both arms around me, draws me to him. Our tongues explore the taste of each other beneath the sake.

"The warm is definitely better," he says huskily as we come up for air. "Perhaps we could lie down."

"That would be a wonderful idea."

He takes my clothes off very slowly. Unlike Atsumori, he seems to be in no rush at all. He proceeds to explore my body with his mouth. I am astonished at the expertise with which he circles my nipples with his tongue. I am even more astonished when he spends enough time with his face between my legs to bring me to a shuddering climax.

"And that is the best sake of all," he says, then swirls his tongue back up my belly to my breasts, and finally to my mouth.

"Where did you learn that?"

"I have been spending my entire salary exploring the pleasures of the floating world," he admits.

"Show me," I say, grasping his stiff jade stalk. "Show me what they have taught you."

He enters me so slowly I grow impatient and wrap my legs around him, drawing him in.

"I don't want it to be too fast," he says.

"If its fast the first time, the second time will be longer," I reply.

"This fox has longed for this den," he breathes.

"You are always welcome here."

He does come quickly, but I rock with him a bit longer until a subtle orgasm washes through me as I am looking into his eyes. When he grows hard again he pulls me on top of him.

"Ride me."

After another hour or so of enough positions to illustrate a pillow book, I protest that I have had enough.

"But we have only done four of the sixteen major positions," he says.

"The other twelve will have to wait for another day, Kitsune..." I laugh, knowing that I will call him Kitsune—fox--during our tender moments from now on.

"Kitsune-Majo," he murmurs back. "You are pure magic," he whispers in my ear as we drift off to sleep.

Chapter Eleven
1180

At last Tokushi arranges for an armed escort to bring Tsubame to court. She is thirteen. When she steps out of the carriage this time I gasp. The shape of her eyes, the slant of her cheekbones, her black, glossy hair, the insolent expression with which she glances about the courtyard--she is like a small, feminine version of Sannayo. A cuckoo flies over the courtyard, calling plaintively. Other birds are shrilling from the nearby magnolias, which are in blossom. She is wearing a padded outer kimono of a pink that is so light it could be mistaken for off-white at first glance, embroidered with branches laden with both snow and cherry blossoms that echoes a famous poem. I had sent the material to her because the poem refers to how sorrow and joy occur together, represented by the snow and the blossoms. It symbolizes the sweetness of having a daughter who is coming into blossom, contrasted with the bitterness of our long enforced separations. I am pleased to see that she is wearing it.

I go to embrace her. She bows to me instead. Her posture as she bows is elegant, but she does not bow as deeply as a child should bow to a mother. Her hands are tucked into her sleeves, perhaps for warmth. It must have been very chilly traveling in the carriage. It has been unseasonably cold the last few days, though today is more mild. I make a slight bow to her in return.

"My heart is full," I say.

"My belly is empty," she replies, lifting an eyebrow the way Sannayo used to do.

"Lunch is being prepared even as we speak, and the Empress is very much looking forward to seeing you again. On'na Mari is also here, looking very much forward to this visit."

"We value the blossoms for their transience." Her tone is light, ironic, but there is a coldness at the core of it that reminds me of my husband, who always had an amusing observation, whose mind and wit were so quick, whose heart never thawed. I have my own hands inside my sleeves, twisting them together. Since her last visit, it seems her letters have become progressively more distant and formal, where initially they had seemed warm and effusive. Once again it occurs to me how much I would love to have her grandmother poisoned. My hands convulse against each other, as if I were grasping the old woman's neck.

I lead the way down the winding corridors of the palace. My daughter walks with her chin very high. No one would guess that she is from one of the poorer noble households in the countryside; a princess could not regard the costly wall hangings and sculptures we pass along the way with more disdain. Her nurse strides behind her, glancing about importantly when it would be far more appropriate for her, as a servant, to keep her eyes cast down.

"I don't wish to see On'na Mari," Tsubame says as we pause in my quarters. Machiko takes the towels she has had soaking in lily-scented water and gently daubs my daughter's neck and hands, then replaces the white powder she has removed.

"She's very fond of you. She has known you since before you were born."

"She married Tsunemasa," my daughter hisses. "And you let it happen!" She darts an angry glance at me. So she has nurtured her crush on Tsunemasa all this time. He is so dear to my heart, I understand how she feels.

"It is better for you to wait, daughter. You are still very young."

"I'm not a child any more, Mother! Grandmother says I should be married within another year."

"I believe sixteen or seventeen is a more appropriate age," I say, more sharply than I intend. "A girl younger than that is not ready for childbirth, and if you are not ready for childbirth, you are not ready for marriage. I will find you an excellent husband, daughter. Have no concern for that. There are many fine young men with excellent pedigrees here at court."

"You could have made an arrangement! You could have asked him to wait! He could have taken a concubine!"

"He has concubines, like every man of his stature. Or had, up until his marriage. On'na Mari won't tolerate it."

"The Genji married Murasaki when she was only twelve," Tsubame sulks, referring to the famous romance *Tale of the Genji*, which is so popular among young women.

"There is often quite a gap between romance and reality," I respond. "Now I want you to take that sulky look off your face before we see the Empress, and I want you to be..." I hesitate, "...absolutely appropriate with On'na Mari, who is virtually your aunt. Your infatuation with Tsunemasa is a childish notion, and if you are no longer a child, then perhaps you should outgrow it." I don't think I have ever spoken so harshly to Tsubame, but it is shortly before my moon and my temper is not at its best. I am so disappointed that she has not fallen on my neck and embraced me with the passion with which I am longing to embrace her. She has so many layers on, I can't see if her body has really begun to develop yet. She has gotten quite a bit taller, but nowhere close to as tall as me, perhaps up to my shoulder. Tall or not, I want to drag her into my lap and ruin her make-up kissing her face.

"As you wish, Mother," she says listlessly, as if the fight had gone out of her.

"Come," I say, squeezing her hand. "You will feel better when you have eaten. It is such a hard journey. After lunch we will bathe, and Machiko will give you a massage. By dinner time you will feel restored."

"I'm sure you're right," she says dully.

We enter the room where we are having lunch. On'na Mari gets up with a happy squeak and shuffles over to Tsubame.

"Look at you towering over me! Like your mother!" She grabs her by the shoulders. "Look at you, you're a young princess now. Oh! Won't the boys be fighting over this one!" she says, rolling her eyes. "Time for me to start your education," she says. I shoot her a warning glance. This is my baby girl we are talking about and she is certainly not ready for erotic instruction yet.

"She's only thirteen," I say sharply.

"Older than I when I joined your household," On'na Mari reminds me.

I grit my teeth.

"I am very happy to see you returned," Tokushi says, indicating a seat beside herself where Tsubame may sit.

"You are too kind." Tsubame bows and slides into her place beside Tokushi. Tokushi indicates that I should sit on her other side, which rankles me since I want to sit beside my daughter. I kneel there while On'na Mari takes a place across from Tsubame. Other ladies from the court fill in the rest of the table. Tsunemasa comes in.

"I hear our beautiful swallow has flown back to the nest," he booms.

I glance past Tokushi and see Tsubame stiffen, her face becoming a mask at Tsunemasa's unexpected entry.

"Won't you join us for lunch?" Tokushi offers.

"Oh, thank you," he says, holding up his hand. "I have much to do. I must see to it that all the soldiers and servants who have accompanied our little swallow are provisioned and settled. I just wanted to see for myself how she has grown." He bows towards Tsubame. "You are just as breath-taking as your mother. I will look forward to an exchange of poetry this evening."

Tsubame's lips are quivering, but she manages a shy bow. Tsunemasa bows towards all of us and takes his leave, and the servants enter with a first course of a light broth. I hold my breath, hoping that Tsubame does not slurp her soup. Fortunately her manners seem to have improved since her last visit, and I sigh with relief. People will sometimes make exceptions for a child whose manners are not the best, but a young lady cannot expect to receive any such favors.

"Your grandmother, is she well?" Tokushi asks.

"Well enough. She has swelling in her knees that makes it difficult to kneel and rise. She is hoping you will use your influence to find me an appropriate marriage."

Tokushi laughs. "Marriage! I think we have plenty of time to think of that, dear child. But it doesn't hurt to start thinking about it." Tokushi is a most enthusiastic matchmaker who happily spends many hours considering all the possible permutations of courtiers who might wed her ladies. I can see her mind already working, pleased with the thought of another young woman safely esconced in an appropriate matrimony.

"Are you still practicing your biwa? I remember you showed much promise."

"Yes, my Lady," Tsubame replies. "I was most humbly grateful to receive your letters of encouragement to spur me onwards."

"It is only the truth. Your musical skill was quite precocious. I am hoping you will honor us with a performance tonight."

"As you wish." I see the spoon shake in my daughter's hand at the prospect of entertaining the Empress in a public setting.

"If you are not too weary," Tokushi says.

"I am always eager to serve you."

I am happy to see my daughter being so pliant with the Empress. Though it seems premature, I am pleased the Empress is already mulling over Tsubame's matrimonial prospects. Perhaps she will be willing to keep her this time and not send her back to her grandmother. She is nearly at an age where a girl might be expected to go to court. Usually the girls are fourteen or fifteen when they first arrive, but her fourteenth birthday is only half a year away.

"Or, you might consider keeping your freedom," On'na Mari chirps. "I kept mine for quite a while, though I am happy enough to be wed to Tsunemasa. But I do miss my more carefree days," she sighs, giving her hair a delicate pat, gazing with a far-off look in her eyes. Painted glass ornaments in her hair tinkle together like wind chimes. She is wearing an abundance of red and white jade and lavish robes of deep red and blue. Tsubame keeps eating without replying.

"Oh, you must try some of these," On'na Mari says with her tinkling laugh, placing some of the newly arrived delicacies on Tsubame's plate.

"Is it dangerous where you are?" one of the other young women asks. "We have been hearing such dreadful tales of uprisings and terrible things going on up north. I can't imagine how frightening it must be to live--well, anywhere outside of Kyoto."

"Nothing ever happens in my neighborhood," Tsubame says. "I'm sure a few battles would liven things up, but no such luck so far."

Many of the young girls make dramatic exclamations with their hands pressed over their hearts.

"Oh, how brave you are!"

"Oh, I could never imagine..."

"Surely you don't mean that!"

"They say they have women warriors," a young woman named Miyumi exclaims. "Can you imagine a woman astride a horse? It's unnatural!"
The other girls titter.

"Absurd!"

"Well, they can't possibly win that way."

"Oh, I don't know," Tsubame says. "If you knew my grandmother, you might think twice about that."

Tokushi gives her throaty little laugh. "Or my mother, for that matter. My mother has ridden into battle with my father on more than one occasion. Well, she didn't actually fight. But she certainly is good at giving commands."

A nervous silence descends, since no one else would be entitled to comment upon Lady Kiyomori in a manner which might be construed as unflattering. Finally one takes the courage to speak again.

"Everyone says Lord Yoshinaka--the cursed traitor--" she hurriedly amends, "has taken two of his concubines--and made them into generals."

Once again there is an excited tittering of disbelief.

"Yes, Tomoe and Yusinuga--is that their names?" another asks.

"Yamabuki," corrects another girl. "And they are captains, not generals. But they go with him everywhere."

"He's not the only one. They say many of their commanders have wives who are just as fierce as they are."

"Imagine what a campaign out in the broiling sun would do to one's complexion!" one of the girls exclaims.

"I hear they don't wear make-up--or blacken their teeth!" another one says.

"Well, if you are spending your days in the saddle, who can be bothered with such fripperies," another one sniffs.

"Women who live in the country often go hunting and hawking with their men. Lord Sessho allows his daughter to practice with a small bow. I understand that for a child, she is quite good, at least as good as her younger brother," I say.

"Women shouldn't handle anything sharper than a needle," one of the other girls asserts.

"Yes, I've pricked myself often enough with that!" another laughs.

Tsubame smiles at that and shoots an appreciative glance at the girl. "I can't wait to meet the young Emperor," she says.

"Oh, yes." Tokushi beams as if Amaterasu herself was shining out of her face.

Immediately all the girls start talking about what an amazing child he is, so handsome and wise, clearly the reincarnation of a powerful Emperor or Boddhisatva.

"Yes, the future of the country is secure now that Antoku is here," one of the girls says. "It is silly to even think about the northern rebels."

Lunch passes pleasantly enough. I am pleased to see several of the girls chattering with Tsubame. I hope Tokushi can see how perfectly Tsubame would fit in here, how improved her manners are.

We go to the baths. I am eager to see what my daughter looks like with her clothes off. She keeps her eyes downcast as her maidservants remove her robes. She is rather bony, as one would expect for a girl who is growing up faster than she is growing out. Her hips have started to flare and she has slight swellings on her chest where her breasts will be. Still, it is laughable for a girl of her proportions to think herself marriageable.

"Has the moon visited you yet, daughter?"

"Not yet," she admits, looking peeved that the answer is no.

"We shall have a wonderful celebration when it does."

"I'll be a million miles away by then."

"You are nearly old enough to be at court. I plan to ask the Empress to keep you this time, or to bring you back right after your fourteenth birthday. There are many girls who come that young. There is no reason you should not be one of them."

Her maidservant starts soaping Tsubame's hair. Will she be as tall as I? She is already average height for a woman and may still grow a great deal in the next couple of years. After all the scrubbing and rinsing outside the tub we enter the tub together, our maidservants with us, massaging our shoulders.

"I am so glad to see you, daughter." I say softly.

"It's good to be back," she says grudgingly, avoiding my eyes.

Later that night the Empress holds a feast celebrating Tsubame's return. A select number of men have been invited. Tokushi confides to me that she had not really thought of Tsubame as being eligible for marriage yet, but she will hold several other feasts during Tsubame's visit and invite young men she considers potential choices.

Kiyomune and Tomoakira, Munemori and Tomomori's sons, are present, though their fathers are not. Atsumori and Kiyosune, Tsunetoshi and Tsunemasa are here, as is Shigehira, Lady Daigon-no-suke's husband. I notice Kiyosune passing a note over to my daughter, who artlessly tucks it into her sleeve, having not yet learned the tricks of discreet flirtation. My heart nearly stops at the thought that he might be courting my daughter while sleeping with me. While I know that Kiyosune and Atsumori are fine young men, I could not bear for my daughter to marry a man I had slept with. I do hope Tokushi will keep this in mind when considering who to introduce my daughter to. I wonder if he and Atsumori are miffed that I have no plans to

sleep with either of them during the precious nights of my daughter's visit.
They are too young to understand a mother's natural feelings.

After dinner, Tokushi says that she would like to hear some music, and
looks encouragingly over at Tsubame. Kiyosune plays a tune on the biwa.
Atsumori and Tsunemasa play a stunning flute duet. Atsumori is truly a
virtuoso. His father recently gave him the flute, 'Little Branch', which is a great
family treasure. He is certainly worthy to play it. It is remarkable to see him
hold his own with Tsunemasa, who is known as one of the best flute players
at court. Tsunemasa then sings a love song with Kiyosune backing him up
with the biwa. He casts many mischievous glances towards On'na Mari as he
sings it but he occasionally glances at my daughter as well. Unfortunately he
cannot imagine how each of those glances, which for him are merely playful
acknowledgements of the guest of honor, is rending her heart. Naturally I
have kept her confidence and never mentioned her childish fondness for him.
I am certain he is not aware of it.

"Now we must have something from you," he nods towards Tsubame when
they have finished. "Let us see how your biwa playing has progressed since we
heard you last."

Most women practice the koto, which is thought of as a more feminine
instrument. While my daughter can play both, she has written to me that she
has a strong preference for the biwa.

"I am not worthy to play in such august company," she demurs. I cannot
tell if she is merely being polite or truly is afraid to perform.

"Oh, it is just a simple little gathering," Tokushi says, waving a hand airily.
"We are all friends here, nothing to fear."

"Yes, please," Tomoakira coaxes. His younger cousin Kiyomune, who can't
be much more than ten, nods his head.

One of Tsubame's maidservants unwraps her biwa and passes it over as
another helps her rise and settle herself upon a cushion on the dais set up
for the musicians. Her biwa is a beautiful light-colored wood inlaid with
mother-of-pearl. She takes a moment to tune it. Then she holds it with
her fingers on the strings, closes her eyes and takes a deep breath, and as she
exhales, she starts to play. My throat swells with pride. She has chosen a
very challenging composition, each plucked string reverberating into those
touched before, making a complex weaving of sound. She starts to sing; her
voice is a lovely alto. I had not noticed how strong her hands and fingers are

until now, watching them move over the strings. I start to shiver. Her hands are like his. The way she holds the instrument, the confidence with which she touches it. Her voice, a slightly higher version of his. Her expressions, the way the lantern-light gleams off her cheek and makes rainbows in her hair. It is as if my husband had stepped tauntingly from his grave and into the body of my child. I can't control the tears slipping down my face, though I know my make-up will be ruined.

When she finishes the song, there is a moment of silence, then an outburst of hands clapping, and fans tapping against hands. Some of the men bang their cups against the table and call out loudly in admiration. She does not tuck her chin to her throat as a shy maiden would do; instead she raises her chin and boldly looks at her audience. The glance of veiled triumph that shoots from her eyes is identical to Sannayo's. Somehow, through the biwa which was probably his, he has possessed her soul. I will call for an exorcism tomorrow.

Tsubame acknowledges the praise, then moves into another song without being coaxed. This is a classic song of Amaterasu, how the Sun Goddess hid in a cave and came out when tricked into seeing her own face in a sacred mirror. The song praises the Imperial line descended from Amaterasu and is aimed at Tokushi, a roundabout way of praising her for the birth of her son.

Tokushi beams afterwards, tapping her fan against the palm of her hand. "Well done, well done!" she says. "Truly, you have exceeded my expectations!"

"You are too kind, my lady," Tsubame says. Her words are humble, but her tone is not.

Later, as some of the men are congratulating Tsubame on her debut, On'na Mari beckons to me. I slide down the table over to her.

"I got the chills when she was playing," she whispers to me from behind her fan. "What did I tell you? She's the spitting image of him."

It is all I can do to keep my nails out of On'na Mari's face when she says this, though I had been thinking the same thing myself.

"It doesn't matter. She's nothing like him," I whisper back. "Not where it matters. Not in her heart."

"Well of course not," On'na Mari replies, glancing at me with a slight shade of alarm. "I did not mean that--didn't you feel it too?"

"Yes, it was most disturbing," I admit, "but if she had to inherit something from him, it is well that it is his musical talent, is it not? That part of him was delightful, after all."

"I don't know," On'na Mari says. "After being with the Beast, I couldn't have married a man who was good at the biwa. Tsunemasa's flute is as far as I go with music these days. Speaking of Tsunemasa, he and Atsumori are quite the pair, aren't they?"

"Yes," I say, relieved to have the subject change from my daughter's uncanny resemblance to her father. "I truly think those two are the best at court."

"Well, yes," On'na Mari preens, "Tsunemasa has won almost every competition at court for years now. Hopefully Akoyo will inherit his talents. The way he sucks at his poor nurse, he certainly has the mouth for it."

"Yes, but the flute is blowing, not sucking."

"Just a matter of whether you're breathing in or out."

"Atsumori will give Tsunemasa a run for his money from now on."

"Since it's his younger brother, he doesn't mind. He taught him after all, so it is all to his credit. And of course, Tsubame is a credit to you. I did not meant to offend..." she drifts off, still obviously as shaken as I am by Tsubame's metamorphosis.

As we go back to our quarters, I turn to Tsubame. "I am so proud of you. Truly your talent is beyond the stars. Your singing and playing is very much like your father's," I say, trying to make that sound as if it were a good thing.

"That's what grandmother says. She says I am just like him. Except for being a worthless girl."

"She's just teasing when she says that."

My daughter gives a sharp laugh. She turns, black eyes boring into me. I quail at the intensity, so like her father's. "Most wives can't stand their husband's concubines. How did you and On'na Mari get to be such good friends?"

I am struck dumb for a moment. The accusing look in her eyes...once again I feel Sannayo is in possession of her, and that it is he himself, knowing well the answer to the question, who stands accusing me.

"Not all wives are jealous," I finally manage to stutter. "On'na Mari was just a child, your age. I thought of her as the younger sister I never had. She reminded me of Tokushi, who was like my younger sister when I was growing up."

"*She* reminded you of *Tokushi?*" she says incredulously.

"Not exactly. She was young and...sweet."

"*Sweet,*" my daughter sneers, "I wonder how many people would describe On'na Mari as being *sweet.* Maybe if you think sake is sweet. You're lovers with her, aren't you?"

"It was your father's wish!" I say defensively. "You are too young to have seen pillow books, but many men like--I can't talk to you about this!"

"Aren't you and On'na Mari the ones who teach the girls about such matters here at court? I'd think you would be used to teaching girls like me."

"It's different when it is your daughter. I can't explain it." I turn and look imploringly at Machiko, though I don't know what I expect her to do about the situation. "Anyway, there is nothing wrong with ladies, either here at court or in a man's household, having pleasures together. It preserves our honor and makes us more relaxed and soft and able to attend to the man's needs. It is quite accepted." I feel her eyes on me, but don't meet her gaze, fearing that she will see what I have kept hidden for so long.

"Sit on my lap, let me brush your hair."

"Sit on your lap! I'm not a child anymore, Mother. I wouldn't fit in your lap."

"We could try."

"I have servants to brush my hair. They do a better job than you." She nods to a maidservant who begins brushing her hair.

"On'na Mari wrote to me."

My heart somersaults. "What did she say?"

"She said you helped her give birth to Akoyo. She said she would have died without you."

My heart starts beating again.

"You could have let her die!"

"Tsubame! I won't hear anything like this. This is unspeakable. On'na Mari has been my dear friend since she first appeared at your father's house. We shared him happily," I say, stumbling over the word 'happily', "until his tragic death, then we grieved together." I can barely get the lies out. She can never know. "I am sorry you are so jealous of her. I promise you there will be other men. There are as many men as stars in the sky, we will find you--by the way, what is that note from Kiyosune in your sleeve?"

"Mother! It's my business, not yours. Anyway, I haven't read it yet."

"I believe it is my business as well, if he is courting my daughter. Give me the note."

"No! I won't."

I plop down on my knees before her, outraged. "I am your mother!" Due to the change in subject, I can easily look her in the eye, while it is she who looks away. "And if I say I shall see the note, I shall see the note!" I reach into her sleeve and pull it out, rise and walk across the room.

"You could at least read it out loud!" she protests. "I haven't ever had a love note! If it's a love note I want to hear about it!"

I open the small scroll, a pang in my heart as I see Kiyosune's familiar hand.

"The snow fox kit, white as jade
soon will grow to be as beautiful as its mother."

"Read it!" my daughter whines. I read it out loud to her. At least he made a kind reference to me, but he may have thought I was likely to read it. I don't like the idea of any man flirting with my not yet nubile daughter. I will tell him in no uncertain terms that if he is looking for a wife, he had best look somewhere else. I hand the note back to her.

"I don't expect you to be carrying on flirtations at your age. That was most inappropriate, and I shall have chiding words with him."

"Oh, mother, he probably thinks I'm older than I am. Don't ruin everything!"

I can't help smiling, because the way she is whining is not at all like the adult she fancies herself to be.

"Are all girls so eager to grow up?" I sigh. I spent my twelfth year being unconscious. I really have no idea what a girl this age is like. I know by the time a girl is thirteen or fourteen her thoughts have turned to marriage, but since I last saw Tsubame when she was eleven, I can't adapt to this terribly sudden sprint towards womanhood.

"I would like to sleep over by the garden doors," she says.

"Most inappropriate for a maiden. Besides, you are sleeping here with me and I don't want to hear any arguments about it. I have been longing for you all this time, and I'm not taking no for an answer."

"Oh, fine then," she flounces down beside me. I enfold her in my embrace. In spite of all her trying to assert her independence, after awhile she snuggles up to me spoonwise and her hand holds my arm tightly until she relaxes into sleep.

Chapter Twelve
1180

The next day, On'na Mari arrives with Akoyo for a visit, and Setsu-no-suke, Tokushi's sister, brings Antoku. Whereas Akoyo merely sits there like a lump--a particularly plump lump--Antoku, who is three, dashes about, giggling madly. He likes to pretend that he is running away, causing us all to chase him.

"I hide in the cave!" he chortles from under a table, already having associated the tale he has heard over and over of the Sun Goddess retreating to a cave with his own games of hide and seek. He rushes off to hide behind a screen, or drapes a kimono over himself, causing us all to exclaim, "Oh! Alas! Where is the young prince? Where could he be? Amaterasu, shine your light, let him be revealed!" At last he will pop out from under the kimono or from behind the screen, and we all give relieved praises that he has once again reappeared as miraculously as he had disappeared.

Akoyo loves this game too, and claps his hands together giggling wildly at Antoku's antics. Antoku likes making Akoyo laugh and does various endearing things to create that effect. Seeing them together, I reflect that it is entirely possible that Akoyo weighs more than Antoku, despite their difference in age. Perhaps owing to the fact that his mother could eat so sparingly when she was pregnant, Antoku has always been slim, with barely a swell of belly where most children his age have quite a noticeable pot. He is quite agile, nimble on his legs, and it seems, constantly in motion. Tsubame seems a bit frozen, watching the younger children. She seems stiff beside the other young girls who so enjoy spoiling Antoku and Akoyo. The other girls take turns lugging Akoyo about, or swirling a colorful ball in his direction for him to bat or kick. Tsubame never makes a move towards him. Perhaps she has never been around small children. When I was a child, I had no younger brothers or sisters, but other families showed up at my mother's house so frequently, I was quite accustomed to smaller children. I wonder if some of her reticence has to do with her upset at On'na Mari having married Tsunemasa and so quickly giving him a son. Then again, perhaps she is unhappy with how familiarly Antoku climbs all over me. She can see by the way I play with him how close we are, and of course, he is just about the age she was when I had to leave her.

On'na Mari plays patty-cake with Akoyo.

"Any signs of..." one of the girls makes rounding motions over her belly.

"Certainly not," On'na Mari shudders. "No, this is the one and only heir for Tsunemasa."

"Well, only the gods can decide that," asserts another young girl.

On'na Mari rolls her eyes at me. "Time for another class."

"It's so wonderful that our sons can grow up together," Tokushi gushes. "Perhaps Akoyo will be the minister of Antoku's household," she speculates, referring to the role Tsunemasa plays in managing the Empress' household.

"That would be wonderful," On'na Mari purrs. "Yes, I'm sure they will be the best of friends, though right now he's a bit of a boring lump, isn't he?"

"Well, he's too young to walk," says Tokushi. "It will happen soon enough! How old was Tsubame when she walked?" she asks me.

"About fourteen months."

"She was the cutest thing you ever saw," smiles On'na Mari.

I catch a glimpse of Tsubame clenching her small fists before they disappear into her sleeves. She looks down with what I hope is being interpreted as modesty, though I am not so sure that modesty figures much in her make-up.

"Akoyo isn't nearly as cute as Tsubame was," On'na Mari continues.

"Everyone prefers sons." Tsubame looks up, eyes glittering like anthracite.

"Well, sons are necessary to inherit," Tokushi reminds her. "It's not that we wouldn't be thrilled to have daughters as well. And no matter what On'na Mari says, of course she wants a daughter."

"Oh yes, then our daughters can play together, too," says On'na Mari, nodding enthusiastically.

"My grandmother says daughters are essentially worthless," Tsubame says in a neutral tone.

"Now, then, we are all daughters," Tokushi says. "A daughter may marry an Emperor, after all. We shall certainly see that you are married well."

"So that I can finally be useful by producing some sons."

"Tsubame!" I glare at her.

"I just mean to say how lucky On'na Mari and the Empress are, to have such wonderful sons."

Everyone smiles as if that was indeed all that Tsubame meant, except for Akoyo who begins howling for his third lunch, and then our party is disbanded.

Back in our room, Tsubame turns to me. "If I had been a boy, you wouldn't have left me, would you?"

"Tsubame...we've been through this. I had no choice but to leave you."

"You like the baby Emperor better than you like me. Well of course! He's the Emperor, after all! He's a boy! He's everything!"

"Oh, sweetheart," I pull her down beside me. "I would give anything to spend every day with you. No other child can ever replace you in my heart." As I say this, I feel a twinge of guilt, thinking of my other daughter, Kikuko, whom I have allowed myself to love more fully, knowing she will never be stolen from me the way Tsubame has been.

"You *say* that, but you're here with them."

"I have no choice. Your grandmother must have taught you about obligation. The child has obligation to the parent, the parent has--"

"Of course! I know all about obligation. It's the only reason I'm even alive. Is that why you bring me here? Is it just obligation?"

"You know that's not true. My heart is bleeding the whole time you are gone."

Machiko sets an ebony folding table before us, and a pot of tea steaming with calming, harmonizing herbs. Tsubame takes a cup from Machiko and holds it to her mouth, waiting for it to cool. The steam from the cup casts a fan of moisture, like tears, across her cheeks.

It's unbearable, thinking how lonely Tsubame must be in that house with her horrible grandmother and her nurse, who seems as cold and unyielding as an icicle. It is ridiculous to judge her for being rude. It is a miracle she has even survived in such a bitter climate, like a persistent flower growing out of the rocks.

"Why doesn't the Empress make a nice marriage for you?" Tsubame asks.

"She wants me by her side."

"Why doesn't she want *me* by her side? I could be here and help her do... whatever you do."

"I plan to ask her for just that. Of course you want to be married eventually, but it would be perfect for you to spend the next four or five years here. That is exactly what I want."

To Kiyosune I write a letter with a quote from the I Ching; "If the young fox kit, crossing the river, should get its tail wet, misfortune follows." I certainly hope he takes my meaning that Tsubame is far too young to be sending courting letters. She is closer to his age than I am, but nonetheless...

He sends back a poem in response, saying that if the young fox crosses the river on the moon bridge, great good fortune is to be had. I study the poem. He probably means to convey that his thoughts towards my daughter are lofty, high ones. The moon bridge is also famous for its reflecting quality, which could mean that he has reflected on this. However, the moon bridge's reflection in the water makes a perfect circle, symbolizing completion and therefore is often used to symbolize marriage. Surely he cannot think to dally with the mother, then marry the daughter. I give a great deal of thought to my response, unsure as I am as to what he means by his. While I am still stewing about it, another note from him arrives, saying, "The male fox admires the kit, because of how it resembles her mother." Tsubame bears almost no physical resemblance to me at all, except for that pearly skin tone that we share. Perhaps he sees some resemblance of spirit.

The next morning, at my request, Tsunemasa has arranged for a carriage to convey Tsubame and myself to a local shrine, where he has placed a heavy purse in the hands of the priest-shamans to perform a very private exorcism.

I have told Tsubame that, in order for her to stay in proximity to the royal family, she must undergo a purification ceremony. As the shaman begins banging loudly on bells and shouting, Tsubame turns to me in panic.

"Mother! What kind of ritual is this? Do you think I am some sort of demon?"

"Hush, daughter! Of course not! It is typical for people to be purified before spending time with the young Emperor. It is a precaution, nothing more."

A young girl attached to the shrine sits quietly with a veil over her face, waiting for the priest to draw any unfriendly spirits out of Tsubame and into this girl, where they can be questioned and banished. As the chanting from the priests reaches a crescendo, she falls to the ground and starts writhing like a wounded caterpillar. Tsubame looks in horror at the girl, who is only a few years older than she.

"What has happened?" she cries out.

"Shh. You must stay silent unless the priests ask you a question."

The priest sternly addresses the uneasy spirit possessing the body of the shrine priestess, asking who now inhabits her.

To my horror, the girl twists brokenly, finally hissing the word, 'Sannayo.'

"What business have you with this girl?" the priest demands loudly.

"I am her father," the ghostly voice declares.

All the hair on my neck is standing straight up. Tsubame, shaking violently, looks as if she will be sick.

"It is understandable for a father to be concerned with the daughter he left behind, but it is time for you to journey to the windy land now," the priest insists.

The girl who has taken on Sannayo's spirit trembles convulsively; her heels drum on the ground.

"Banish it! Banish it!" I urge, "Don't talk to it, just banish it!" I am sick with fear that my secret will be revealed. Mindful of who is paying him, the priest shouts loud incantations over the girl until she goes limp, head lolling.

"The spirit is banished," the priest says, wiping the sweat from his brow. Tsubame is so white her eyes are like two black smudges on rice paper. The girl who did the channeling is carried off to recover. Machiko and I half-carry, half-drag Tsubame back to the carriage. Almost all the way back to the palace, she sits beside me like a child made of wax.

"It's all right now," I say, chafing her cold hands between mine. Machiko peers into her eyes, looking worried. "It's fine now, young mistress," she chirps.

"Why did you do that?" Tsubame finally gasps. She suddenly turns and starts punching me. "You banished my father? You banished his spirit out of me? At least he cared enough to be around. At least he cared! Not like you! Not like you!" she shrieks. I'm so shocked, I can't even defend myself. Machiko wraps her arms around Tsubame, restraining her. My mind whirls, wondering if we should return to the shrine. Certainly the exorcism does not seem to be complete.

"Perhaps we should go back, mistress," Machiko says, verbalizing my thoughts. I would be embarrassed for even the shrine attendants to see my daughter in such hysteria.

"Now I have no one, I have no one, I have no one," Tsubame keeps wailing. She has no idea what kind of man her father really was, and I have fed her illusions of him by speaking only of his talent and charm. To reveal to her who he truly was could only throw her into more terrible despair. How could she bear thinking that she was descended from a monster, when she has always imagined him as a shining prince? Perhaps all this time she has imagined his spirit being around her, praying for her, comforting her. Is it possible that when he passed into the windy realms, only the good in him remained, that he became in truth the beautiful spirit I thought he was when we first met? Is it possible he has been watching over his daughter in a loving way?

As we pass through the avenue lined with firs on the way to the palace, Tsubame calms.

"Machiko, fix my make-up," she implores.

Machiko pats a thick layer of skin lightener all over her, trying to conceal how red and puffy her face is. At least Tsubame wants to look presentable at court.

When we return to our room, she asks Machiko to pull out the bed, and lies there staring at the ceiling.

"Tell the Empress I am ill and cannot attend dinner tonight. Give her my apologies."

"I'll stay with you then." I lay down beside her. "It is probably best that we maintain our fast for the rest of the evening anyway."

"Sometimes I have dreams about it," she says.

My heart skips a beat. "About what?"

"About the robbers who killed him. They caught them and executed them later, didn't they? That's what Grandmother says."

It is true that a few months after Sannayo's death, five men were arrested for robbing poor folk and carriages alike. They had committed many crimes warranting a death sentence, so I had not felt guilty when they were blamed for Sannayo's death and executed.

"Sometimes I'm scared that maybe some of them got away, that they might ambush me when I am out of the house. That's what Grandmother's afraid of, too. That's why she won't let me out."

"We always send plenty of soldiers to accompany you. You have nothing to fear. Your father went out at night, without guards. He was very brave, but sometimes foolhardy."

"Grandmother says he did stupid things when he was drunk."

"All men do stupid things when they are drunk. And women too, which is why we must always be careful not to drink enough to make us behave in an unseemly manner."

"Did you miss him very much?"

"Terribly," I lie. I certainly missed the person I thought he was.

"Grandmother says he liked On'na Mari better. Is that true?"

"Oh, well, I was pregnant and then had a baby...and On'na Mari was very young and beautiful...he was much besotted with her, certainly, but I was so busy with you, I didn't mind."

"Really? You didn't mind? I would mind."

"You can never be certain how you will respond to something like that. Sometimes two women can love the same man and love each other as well."

"I'm sorry I hit you," she turns and cuddles up to me. "But they were acting like my father was a bad spirit, and he was not."

What do I say to this? I stroke her hair, buying some time.

"Even a good person," I explain finally, "can have a bad impact. It's just not right for one person's spirit to inhabit another. When a person dies, their spirit must travel on to its rightful spot. And particularly, a male spirit cannot inhabit a female body. It is a matter of everything being in its right place.

Shall I read to you?"

She gives a shaky sigh.

"All right."

Machiko brings out some of my scrolls. Tsubame lays her head in my lap. We are both exhausted from the exorcism. It is only a short while before my daughter's eyes close, and I ask Machiko to blow out the lamps.

116

Chapter Thirteen
1180

Tokushi finally permits me to visit Seishan and Sessho. Machiko and I pack happily. She is also looking forward to being away from the court and seeing her lover, Yanagi. The journey for her, as for me, is a reunion with her beloved. Being unable to write, they do not have the satisfaction of exchanging letters.

Tokushi sulks and occasionally fakes a reproachful cough, even though I know perfectly well from having kept my ear to her chest night after night that her lungs are clear. Antoku is also crestfallen to see me go. I tell him I will be back soon, though I know three or four weeks is an eternity in the mind of a three year old.

The weather is more like May than June. Birds weave an intricate tapestry of song and the wildflowers are a riot of color, as if a rainbow had melted over the fields. The rice is a brilliant green. It has been a very rough time, but it is impossible not to feel hopeful on such a glorious day. Perhaps everything is going to change for the better. We pass farmers in their rice paddies with their oxen, and hold our noses against the stink of the night soil. Some fields are tall and green, but others are just being plowed; the rice harvest in this part of Japan is almost continuous.

Finally our carriage rolls up to the gate. The twins, four years old now, run out and hug me, calling, "Auntie Murasaki, Auntie Murasaki!" I wear a new kimono dyed in unusual shades of pink with peonies embroidered on it, which my daughter notices instantly since her name is Peony.

"Yes, I had it made for visiting you!" I say. Her brother Matsu is more entranced by the pink jade rabbit pin Antoku gave me for my last birthday.

He is even more excited when he learns that the boy Emperor, who is close to his age, gave it to me. Tokushi has sent me presents for all the children, which are to be from her and Antoku. Matsu and Kiku cling to me, their mother remonstrating with them, "Now, now, your Auntie Seiko is very tired, don't pull on those nice sleeves..."

"No, no, I'm never too tired for my little ones." I hug my daughter again and again. She is an extremely affectionate child, and obviously glad to see me. I was so afraid they would have forgotten me in my long absence, and so relieved to find that they have not. Matsu eagerly tells me that they have been making kites, "...dragon ones and owl-eyed ones and hawks with long tails..."

"As soon as it gets more windy we shall take them out," Tomomori says, placing a hand on his younger brother's head.

There is a slight breeze today, fluttering the two cloth carp representing the sons of the house, but not enough yet so that they seem to swim through the air. Normally they would be taken down after Boy's Day. Sessho reads my thought. "Matsu insisted on leaving the carp up so you could see them."

"Mine is the blue one! With the silver scales!" Matsu cries, hopping up and down with excitement. "Tomomori's is red!" He leaps about singing, "Two boys, two boys, two boys..."

"Wait until you see Nori's writing," Seishan boasts.

Nori shrugs, "Oh, it's nothing, I'm no good at that. I would never consider boring the Murasaki with my prattling."

"Oh no, I want to see it. You are too modest I am sure. No true writer likes her own writing at first."

"No, it's just a journal, and a few dreadful poems--"

"That's wonderful. You will so enjoy looking back on what you have written now when you are older."

She fidgets and tries to look displeased but I can see she is secretly excited to show me her writing.

After tea and refreshments and the giving of gifts, Seishan is eager to show me her birds. Her father-in-law has passed on, but Seishan has kept up the tradition in their huge walk-in bird cage. She calls it a bird sanctuary, and it is so large I am sure the finches and nightingales feel they lack for nothing in the way of foliage and space to stretch their wings. Many of the finches have laid eggs, which she proudly shows me, in perfect miniature nests the servants have woven for them. I would think the birds might prefer to make their own nests, but she says they sing for happiness when the nests are presented to them. Outside, ceramic homes for the swallows have been built all around the roof's perimeter.

"It was so awful when the swallow's mud houses sometimes fell apart in the storms, and the babies would tumble to the ground. Now they are always safe," she says, eyes shining.

It is dusk, and swallows are dipping all around, catching mosquitoes and gnats with their strange, erratic flight. As the sky darkens the swallows enter their homes and the bats emerge, harvesting what the swallows have left. I feel sad, thinking of my older daughter, Tsubame, whose name means swallow, but I smile at Seishan's love for the birds. Who else would ever think of constructing ceramic bird nests?

"They seem to like their new homes very much," I say.

"Yes," she beams, "they still bring mud and decorate the inside of their homes with it, so it seems familiar to them."

Sessho complains good-naturedly that it is a full time job for a dozen servants, cleaning up the bird droppings that carpet the courtyard and the roofs of the compound.

Seishan links arms with him, looking up saucily. "I could have an opium habit, I could pester you for all the newest and finest clothes and jewels. Instead, all I ask is a few things for my birds."

Sessho hugs her. "With such a beautiful bird to help feather my nest, how can I complain?"

They take me on a walk around the garden, which is flourishing.

"You've put in so much just since the last time I was here!"

The bushes planted around our garden swing have become a huge, impenetrable hedge. Later, after the evening feast, when the children are in bed, we follow a path gaily delineated with a rainbow of paper lanterns to our bower, which is lit up like a faery land, heady with the scent of night-blooming jasmine. We explore a few of the swing positions favored in pillow books, but mostly we do our pillowing on a hillock of the finest, softest baby grasses, made softer with the addition of down stuffed quilts. It is cool in the night air, but our exertions and the stream of hot sake brought to us by servants keeps us warm enough. Seishan has become rounder and softer with age. I rock my pelvis beneath hers.

"Your haunches are so pillowy," I murmur appreciatively. "You're like a heavenly mochi--toothsome and tender."

"And sweet, too," Sessho agrees.

"Oh, stop, don't remind me. You're still elegant and polished as a piece of bamboo, and I'm as lumpy as an old pillow."

"Well, what is better than a pillow for pillowing?" Sessho says. "Or a nice round plump fruit for eating…yum!" He moves his head up and down her body making gobbling sounds while she squeals and giggles.

Silver streaks Sessho's hair, and his smile now crinkles his eyes. Otherwise, he is exactly the same as ever.

As we mop each other with the warm, damp, scented cloths the servants have brought, Sessho says, "I look forward to all of us growing old together,"

"Ha! I expect you to show up with a fourteen-year-old dancing girl any day now!" Seishan scoffs.

Sessho grimaces with disgust. "What would I do with a girl Nori's age? You two are more gorgeous than ever. The sparkle of youth has been replaced with something more ineffable, like a work of art that grows more precious with time." He pulls us close, one on either side of him, massaging our necks with his strong fingers.

"Like an amulet worn smooth by monks' fingers, which becomes more holy and powerful with use," he whispers.

About three nights after I arrive, we have an evening of Gosechi dances. The two older children entertain us with the dances they have practiced. Twelve, tall and gangly, Nori will never be a brilliant dancer. She will be like me, more of a book person than a dance person. Tomomori is more graceful, and executes a crane dance that would draw applause at court. The twins perform a firefly dance that is very charming, each bobbing up and down with a small paper lantern, singing, "We light up the night, we light up the night!" Then Matsu and two of his cousins perform a hopping frog dance, leaping from side to side with broad, frog-like smiles, chanting, "Gadunk! Gadunk!" Kiku and three girl cousins skip through a butterfly dance, twirling with colored scarves.

I had requested in my letter before arriving that we not talk about the rebellion. Sessho and Seishan have studiously avoided the subject. We talk of the children instead. Tomomori is making remarkably fluid brush paintings for someone so young, having inherited his father's skills. I tell them of Tsubame, what an incredible musician she is becoming, and how Tokushi has promised to bring her to court. I wonder what talents shall bloom in my Peony, if she will be a poet like her mother. If so, it will not betray her parentage, for Sessho is very eloquent, though Seishan has always hated writing of any sort. She writes me dutiful short notes, while Sessho sends me scrolls of descriptions of their life at Tanba, illustrated with brush drawings so feathery and evocative they could hang on the Empress' walls.

Kiku does resemble me somewhat, though she looks more like my mother. Her hair is not as wavy as ours; only a slight hint of wave around her face. Her skin tone is in between Sessho's and mine, gold as lantern light. She has a pointy chin, and her cheekbones will be prominent. Her hands are like mine, and she is long and slim for a child her age. Seishan sees me studying her as we all bathe together, and gives me a raised eyebrow, as if to say, yes, that's your girl. Matsu is sturdy, like Sessho, and a constant blur of running, jumping, yelling motion. His ears are delicate shells, like his mother's, really too perfect for a boy, and his hair is that same inky black, alive with rainbows, though caught up in boy's loops.

One windy day, we go out kite flying. There is a wonderful owl kite, staring down with huge yellow eyes, a hawk kite, and a brilliant long-tailed phoenix.

"Watch out, field mice!" Tomomori calls out as the hawk and owl kites climb the air. I imagine that if the mice are looking up, they are indeed cringing with terror. There is also a collection of box kites, flying fish, and a long dragon kite that swoops with serpentine sinuousness. The servants get them up and flying, then the older kids take over. Tomomori and Sessho maneuver the hawk and owl kites, darting them at each other in feints and swoops. Matsu sits on a servant's lap, tugging on the string of his box kite. Machiko tries to get Peony to sit on her lap as she spins out the twine attached to a butterfly kite, but Peony does not want to sit still, instead dashing from person to person, tugging on their sleeves, shrieking with excitement. I brought Nori an inkstone similar to mine, with a dragon swirling in clouds around the well, and some new brushes, so she sits narrowing her eyes at the brilliant display above her, trying to think of a poem. We have spent time together every day, poring over her father's Chinese texts. She is far better at reading Chinese than I am; together we discuss the poems and write poems in answer to them. We read them to the rest of the family later. This inspires the twins to dictate poems to a scribe sitting cross-legged near Nori.

"My kite will ride in the sky forever!

Better than a dragon!" Matsu boasts. He is so pleased with his effort that for days after one can hear him muttering to himself, 'Better than a dragon! Better than a dragon!'

Kiku, not to be outdone, rushes to the scribe and says:

"Up in the sky, I thought I saw flowers,
But they were kites."

Of course, neither of the twins can write yet, but it is never too early to encourage children to think poetically.

Some nights the three of us sleep together, sometimes Sessho and I alone, as Seishan enjoys having time to herself. Normally her moon time is the only time she takes to meditate and read apart from her family.

"If Sessho hadn't been so handsome, I'd have made an excellent nun," she observes. "When you are here, I can take time to remember who I am without feeling the slightest bit guilty."

I never feel as much like who I truly am as when I am with Sessho, but of course, I have no idea what it is like to be married and sleeping with someone night after night for years. I am deeply grateful for the nights when it is just the two of us, though I love our triadic times as well. And it is also sweet when Seishan and I have overlapping moons to sleep just the two of us together. This visit, Nori is bleeding too, so the three of us enjoy time in the moon cottage. She asks us about sex, birth, and babies, though most of our explanations elicit a sour face.

"*I'm* never having any babies," she says.

Her mother shakes her head. "I felt the exact same way when I was your age. But you'll see. One day you'll have them, and you'll be glad, and you'll be talking to your daughter like I am talking to you now."

Nori shrugs. "Well, maybe." She was not there when either of the twins was born, but she knows that Peony is my daughter, having observed both of us with big bellies, and aware that the children were born three weeks apart. She knows about my relationship with her parents, and knows that it is normal for men of her father's rank to have multiple wives and mistresses. It is less usual for the wife and mistress to be lovers and get along as Seishan and I do. Nori loves to hear the story of how we met and how we were best friends at court before Seishan met Sessho and married. This visit, she asks about the secrets of pleasing a woman. She has not experimented yet, but she is certainly curious about it. We look over some pillow books with her and talk of positions and pleasures. At night we make offerings of our blood to the moon kami, burying it in the garden in various places, and talk of the marriage to the moon women have. We soak our bleeding cloths in water, and pour the pink mixture over our secret moon garden. Those plants always do especially well.

I wish I could have been here for Nori's first blood ceremony. I vow not to miss Kikuko's no matter what. Kikuko is a completely different child than at my last visit; she has grown taller and acquired so much new vocabulary. If only I could be here always. I talk again with Sessho about the possibility of him taking me as a primary concubine, if not as a secondary wife.

He sighs. "For a woman of your status, it is unimaginable."

"Really, I have no care for my reputation at all. What difference does it make? If I am living here with you, I won't hear the tongues wagging anyway."

"I could never take you as a concubine. It would be shameful."

"But that's what I am now."

"No. No. You are the wife of my heart, you know that."

"I know, so what difference does it make what anyone thinks? They can call me your secondary wife, your primary concubine, or your whore. I don't care."

"Do you really think you could leave the Empress?"

I think of Antoku, who I love almost as much as my own children, with a pang. I have missed very little of his development. I was there when he said 'moon', his first word, and when he took his first step, he fell into my arms. I think of how Tokushi is always so sad when I leave.

"Would she even give her permission?" he asks.

"I think she would. Unwillingly, reluctantly, but still." But could I ask her for her permission, after all she has done for me? Soon Tsubame will be at court and I won't be able to leave until she is married.

He sees the answer in my eyes. "Oh well, we are better off than the Weaver and the Star Maiden," he says. "They can only meet once a year, over the Bridge of Birds. We see each other at least twice a year, sometimes more."

"Perhaps, after Tsubame is settled..."

"She would always be welcome here."

"Yes, but her grandmother would never stand for it. But in a few years, perhaps I could write a letter..."

"Would it be better if I wrote the letter, asking the Empress for your hand?" he asks.

"No. She could say no to you more easily than she could say no to me. Of course, she could also say no more easily in a letter than in person. But I can't do anything that would risk Tsubame's chances. I wish *I* were twins. Then one of me could always be here, and one could always be there."

"In my heart, you are always here." He kisses me on the forehead.

I don't mention it, but there is also the question of whether Seishan would want me here permanently. She is always happy to see me, but perhaps if I were here all the time, jealousy would arise between us, and that would be terrible. It has been so peaceful throughout.

Then I think of the fun we three had during our moon-time, with Machiko and some of Seishan's good-natured servants, including Machiko's lover, Yanagi. She is older than Machiko, and no beauty. She has a very high forehead, and a couple of teeth missing, but she has something Machiko responds to. She is tall and thin, like me. At first glance, one would dismiss her as homely, but when she smiles at Machiko, her whole face changes, and she is suffused with such love that in that moment she seems completely beautiful. The two of them must share an old karmic bond. They rarely leave each other's sides during our visits. To move here would be as heavenly for Machiko as it would be for me. If I could bear to part with her, I would let her stay, but I cannot imagine life without Machiko.

Of course, that is exactly how Tokushi thinks about me. Is there any way I can free myself of my obligation? I add up the things I have done for Tokushi, the birth of Antoku being the greatest. All the Chinese texts say that obligation to a sovereign is life-long. I cannot count the nights I have nursed Antoku through an ear infection, holding my hands over his hot little ears packed with garlic oil and camphor until his fever broke and his ears cooled. The last time it happened, he snuggled into my sleeves and said 'thank you for taking care of my ears' in his childish lisp. Who would take care of him if I were not there?

My eyes spill over. It is terrible to be split in two like this, to never be entirely happy one place or another. When I am in Sessho's arms, all worry, doubt and fear melt away, leaving me completely at peace in a way few people experience until they reach the Blessed Lands. I think of how Tokushi falls asleep with her head on my chest. I provide that safety for her. She can be with no man save Takakura. How I wish she would take another favorite from among the women. But she could never have the same level of trust as she does with me, who has cared for her since she was a child.over. It is terrible to be split in two like this, to never be entirely happy one place

"Maybe half your time here, half there," Sessho says. "As of now, we see you less than a quarter of the year. If we could see you for half, it would be a big improvement."

"Yes, it would be a big improvement." I know it is selfish to even think about following my own heart and my own pleasure when clearly my karma, my fate and my duty place me caring for the royal family. My mother thrust that giri upon me, to insure that the Imperial line passed through Tokushi's womb, to teach the young Emperor to rule in the way of love. But I am Inari's creature, not Amaterasu's. Inari is the goddess of the pleasures and comforts of the earth. So perhaps I cannot be expected to be a servant of the light without wearying of that incandescent purity which is really too refined for someone like myself.

When Sessho holds me, it is like being cradled by the earth itself. I think of Kiyomori and Antoku being badgers in their black silk tunnel. Just as the burrow is the home of the badger, Sessho's arms are my home. I rarely let him rise in the morning without making love to me first. He often says, "If it were up to you, we would never get up." Whatever pleasures and pursuits the day holds cannot compare to the joys of horizontality. But eventually Seishan sends the children in to roust us out, and we are called upon to come and paint with them, help with their lessons and such, and so another delightful day begins.

It makes me uneasy to see Tomomori practicing his swordplay and archery with his tutors. I pray the Genji will be completely defeated before he is grown enough to fight. Boys of fourteen commonly accompany their fathers into battle. Sessho assures me that he has no intention of letting his boy go off to war.

"Only a direct order from Kiyomori himself would stir me out of my peaceful home. I am a rice warrior; he needs me to stay here and oversee the rice production that feeds his troops. Everyone knows I am no fighter; I would just get in the way."

All the anxieties that seem so pressing in the Capital fade like bad dreams. Sessho practices with Tomomori, and even lets Nori try her hand at the warrior arts. Sessho's guards drill regularly, as they must, be it a time of peace or war, but there is always a bit of a catch in my stomach when I see it, and I find myself avoiding their practice sessions, retreating to the garden with Seishan and Kiku. I tried archery, under Sessho's tutelage, but I was never any good at it. My arms were never strong enough and my aim was wretched. Nori is quite good, however. She is very excited by the tales of women warriors of the north, who are reputed to fight by their men's sides. Women at the court, too, love to trade such rumors, but even if they are true, I imagine the women warriors must be very rare. It may be that the tales are just a way of expressing how barbaric the Genji chieftains are, to let their wives and daughters fight alongside them. I know perfectly well from incidents in my own youth that women are just as capable of violence as men. I still pray for the souls of the innocents whose deaths I caused, but I don't pray for Sannayo's soul. He can burn in the seven hells, or be reincarnated as a mosquito to be swatted. My deeds seem like sins of a past life already. But I paid dearly for them, losing Tsubame. Hopefully that is all the penalty the gods will require from me.

I confessed the truth to Sessho, even though On'na Mari and I had sworn not to tell anyone else. Soon after, he engaged a Shinto Priestess to bless and take the blood-guilt from me in the cleansing ceremony offered to returning warriors, at the appropriate shrine near the ocean. I was veiled, so the priestess did not know who I was. Sessho occasionally teases me about it. One night when he was assuring me that he would never go to war, he took my hand and kissed it mischievously. "But if I ever do, this is the sword arm that I want beside me. I'm going to take you along, just like that northern barbarian Yoshinaka who never goes off to battle without a warrior concubine on either side of him. A man after my own heart!"

"You'd be safer with Nori. But it is true that if danger came near you, I would fight to the death for you without any hesitation."

"I know you would Seiko, and truthfully, I would feel safer with you than anyone."

"I'm not that strong."

"You have a strong heart," he says, placing his hand over my heart.

"You don't think I'm a terrible person for what I did?"

"No. Sometimes a great warrior has to be ruthless. You did what you had to do. You fought for Tsubame. You fought for On'na Mari, for Machiko, for yourself. You fought a woman's war." He chuckles. "I will always be *very* careful to treat you well."

"I could never raise a hand to you. Even if you changed."

"I'll never change. You know that."

"Yes, I know." I put my head on his chest, hearing the strong, steady thud of his heart, his heart that loves so much, and the throb of that great river carries me into sleep.

Chapter Fourteen
1180

Tokushi had agreed to let me stay in Tanba six to eight weeks, depending on the travel auguries. But just two weeks after my arrival, I receive an urgent message from her revealing that Kiyomori has decided to move the capital to Fukuhara, by the Inland Sea. He was already dismantling everything that could be dismantled, loading it on rafts and shipping it down the rivers to the coast.

Fukuhara is an area of traditional Taira power; apparently Kiyomori felt that being surrounded by hostile monks and menacing northern forces was a poor position, and he wanted to seat the Capital in his stronghold surrounded by his shipping allies, an easily defended position with the mountains on one side and the ocean on the other. It makes sense, as a military move, but the decision had been announced suddenly and was immediately being implemented. He did not want the enemy forces in the north to have time to regroup and attack at Fukuhara before fortifications could be made and the new capital built.

In her letter, Tokushi says:

"The same day the order was given, people started dismantling their homes! Father says he cannot spare a single soldier to come and fetch you now--I was barely able to wheedle a messenger! The monks from Enryakuji are attacking the city again. The common people are fleeing to the Inari shrine at Fukushima in the south. It is in no way safe to travel. You will simply have to join us later, when things are more settled. I must see to the packing. Do send us your prayers."

After a fortnight, we receive a letter from Fukuhara.

"Antoku is loving the beach. Tsunemasa constructed a huge sandcastle for the boys, who stomped it flat in minutes. Construction of the new capital proceeds rapidly. No doubt we shall be quite happy here. I wish you to arrive as soon as possible, but do not take any untoward risks. The passage would be far too perilous now. Shockingly, it appears that Yoritomo is still planning a rebellion. After my father spared his life and that of his brothers after his father's revolt! Really, I suppose my father is too kind-hearted. He has commanded that the traditional sacrifice of a workman under each corner of the palace and other important buildings is to be discontinued. He says it is barbarism from the past, and the new capital is to be free of that. Even at his age, he is so modern, always thinking ahead. I am so proud of him!"

Tokushi sends a messenger about once a week, who then returns with a letter from me. After a gap of a fortnight, a messenger arrives, and the letter asks,

"Did you receive my message of a week ago? Is my messenger ill? I have received nothing in return. If he failed to reach you, then he must have been killed, for his loyalty was unquestionable. I do hope Hiroki-sama is all right. With things so unsettled, it is not just rebels we must contend with but more brigands, more robberies. With the soldiers busy here, the lawless element feels free to attack travelers with impunity. We have heard terrible stories of the monks ravaging Kyoto since our departure. How can they possibly claim to serve the Buddha?"

On'na Mari's letter, which accompanies Tokushi's, is more sardonic.

"They say Buddhism is about letting go of attachment, but it seems that in this case the Buddhists were eager to help others recover from their attachments. Ah, the noble, raping, pilfering monks, who suffer from attachment in order to free others from it."

Sessho sends out spies who report back that angry hordes of monks set fire to many of the remaining structures in Kyoto; the whole city has been laid to waste. I wonder about Uryo-on-dai and how she and her husband are faring. I send a messenger who returns saying that their home is still standing, but that he was not admitted past the front gates and was offered no letter in return.

I am sorry to have to inform Tokushi that her messenger must have been slain. She writes back:

"Under no circumstances must you leave Tanba! I miss you dreadfully, but it cannot be helped. You would be most amused at the rumors which declare that you have dematerialized entirely, or transformed yourself into a bird and flown away! If only you could truly turn into a bird, and fly to me here!

"Retired Emperor Go-Shirakawa accompanied us here, somewhat
reluctantly I fear. He is confined to a structure known as the 'prison palace'.
While it is as nice a mansion as anyone else has in Fukuhara, the walls are
high and it is constantly guarded. That rebel Yoritomo claims that the Retired
Emperor is on his side. How absurd! I visited him with Antoku the other day
and they enjoyed each other hugely. He is teaching Antoku to play Go, and
he is so patient! If only Takakura were as concerned for Antoku's welfare. I
have invited him to dinner many times, and he is always 'too busy'. He has his
own mansion, separate from the palace, and passerbys have noted that there
is music and laughter pouring out at all hours of the day and night. Rumor
has it that he now has over twenty concubines, dancers, and shrine attendants
entertaining him and his friends, and that he installed a fountain that flows
with wine instead of water. The facade consists of beautiful carved ivory,
which must have cost a fortune. As to the inside, I do not know, for I have
never been invited there."

Sadly, Sessho's own scouts have reported that the Genji leader Yoritomo
has been displaying an official edict from Go-Shirakawa, gaining converts to
his rebellion thereby. A monk named Mongatu gained access to the Retired
Emperor under spiritual pretenses and received a scroll that he smuggled
to Yoritomo. The scroll contained an Imperial Edict that commissioned
Yoritomo to 'crush the Taira forces, take power and restore the monarchy'.
Since the monarchy is in fine hands with Antoku, I suppose that means 'to
restore Go-Shirakawa'. Tokushi writes that Go-Shirakawa is a pious old man,
past politics, who would do nothing more radical with his freedom than go on
pilgrimages, traveling from temple to temple and shrine to shrine to pray for
the good of his people. The old fox has her much deceived. It is possible that
Yoritomo has invented this story of the edict, which so conveniently justifies
his rebellion. But my gut says otherwise.

Lady Daigon-no-suke writes, making no bones about her disgust with the
situation.

"After we moved here, we discovered there is not really room for a proper
capital, with nine sacred avenues; there is only room for five! Five avenues in
a city? Who has ever heard of such a thing? And yet, they are proceeding as
if nothing is wrong. The dismal roar of the waves goes on unceasingly; even
if you put your fingers in your ears you cannot stop the noise. I never see

Shigehira any more. But he assures me that soon they will fix things so that within a year, those rascally monks will be unable to do any further mischief."

On'na Mari describes the bleakness of their new habitation in even less uncertain terms:

"There are *swamps* and the insects are not to be believed! Mosquitoes, gnats--there are CLOUDS of them! They fly up your sleeves and they bite and they leave hideous welts. They are biting Akoyo, biting me--the other day there was a banquet at the new palace and there was an ugly welt on my neck no amount of rice powder could conceal. Our house is very near to the palace, much closer than it was in Kyoto. But then, everything is much closer together. Tsunemasa has been rewarded with many honors for his services. I rarely see him, but I am very proud. We have been given four lovely carved jade horses, and an exquisite statue of Kannon with her rabbit, and a Sea Goddess of green and white jade as well. Lady Kiyomori gave me a headdress with a pearl as big as a turtle's egg.

"While the new palace is looking very magnificent, with splendid tiles and alabaster steps, the nearby forest, which was so lovely to look at when we first arrived, has been virtually destroyed, all the wood cut down to build the new city. Now the peasants who depended on hunting and gathering in that forest to supplement their diet of rice and fish are left with nothing and have no wood for their cooking fires. So they are stealing anything that is not nailed down! I have told Tsunemasa I am going to double our number of servants. Someone has to feed these people, after all, and anyway, one can never have too many servants."

A warm feeling envelops my heart. Not too many people at court would even notice the common people. On'na Mari cares what becomes of them, and this endears her to me even more.

Ben-no-taishi writes that she is now engaged to a young man at court. She has always seemed so serious, I expected her to end up with someone much older, but this young man of twenty-three has a rather serious demeanor also, so it will probably be a good match. Selfishly, I am dismayed, since I had hoped she might be the one to take my place with Tokushi.

Tokushi writes that her husband has been given permission to visit the Itkushima Shrine. The Itkushima deity is the traditional Taira clan deity, the clan mother from ancient times. Now that they are at Fukuhara, they are much closer to the deity's sacred island and boat trips may be made there easily. Sadly, she writes, she was not able to go with him. But she does not write as to why she was unable to accompany him--whether it was through his own indifference to her company or if her father forbade it, or if she herself felt her duties would not permit her to leave. She encloses several pictures Antoku has drawn for me. I send him stories I have written about the adventures of the young Emperor and his rabbits, and how they traveled to the Inland Sea, for her and her sister, Sotsu-no-suke, to read to him.

The situation only worsens in terms of battles and lawlessness between here and Fukuhara, so there is no question of leaving my safe haven. I feel guilty about my happiness, especially when On'na Mari writes that people are falling ill because of vapors from the swamps.

"Four more deaths this week, and so many people are sick that a palace banquet was cancelled. Some people are afraid it is because Kiyomori omitted the sacrifices. But everyone knows there is pestilence in the marshes. Ugh! This place reminds me far too much of the Beast's mansion surrounded by those ghastly fetid swamps..."

I feel badly that people are ill, and I not there to help. Here in Tanba, we are all happy and healthy, without so much as a sniffle amongst us. The sun is warm, summer is at its height, and our table is filled with abundance from the vegetable gardens. There is plenty of fish from the eastern coast and our ponds, and we eat chicken and duck, which is rarely served at Tokushi's table. In spite of Seishan's fondness for singing birds, she does not seem to object to eating those whose voices are less sweet.

Chapter Fifteen
December, 1180

"Will there be enough for snowballs?" Matsu asks, jiggling up and down. We are all in one of the garden-viewing rooms, observing the first ragged pieces of snow swirling outside, sticking wetly on bushes, bare branches and bamboo gates. The rest of us are kneeling at our writing desks to compose poems for the year's first snowfall. Kikuko is snuggled under my quilted outer robe, pretending to be a rabbit in her den.

"It's very unlikely, Matsu," Sessho says. "The first snow rarely sticks. The earth isn't cold enough. Look at Shirata, the snow kami, dancing for us! Have you thought of a poem to honor her?"

"I want a snowball fight! I want a snowball fight! I want a snowball fight!" Matsu bounces out on the deck and scrapes a pitiful amount of melting snow into his palm.

A servant enters. "Pardon me, my lord," he bows to Sessho. "A messenger from the Empress has arrived for the Lady Fujiwara."

"Send him in then," Sessho says, still smiling at Matsu's antics.

"Matsu! You're getting your clothes wet! Come back in!" Seishan shakes her head in exasperation. Machiko takes the scroll from the kneeling messenger and brings it to me. I inhale the delicate scent of aloes and spring blossoms as I unroll it; Tokushi's signature scent.

"My darling, our long separation is coming to a close. Lord Kiyomori has decided to move the court back to the original capital in Kyoto--just when I thought our removal to Fukuhara was quite permanent. The new Imperial Palace is finally finished, and quite stunning, and the consecration ceremonies were the most elegant ever witnessed. But so many people have fallen ill, and so many are dying, the coastline is obscured by smoke from the funeral pyres. Everyone is saying the new capital must be jinxed or cursed in some way. You will be dismayed to hear that my beloved husband and lord, Retired Emperor

Takakura, is among the sick. Thank the powers Antoku is well! So many are ailing that a feeling of panic is sweeping the new capital, and though my father has banished any necromancers who dare state that the illness is the result of angry ghosts, fear of supernatural retribution has gripped both nobles and the common people who serve us. Sacrificed children and animals have been found at points throughout the city, whether killed by ghosts or by frightened people to appease the ghosts no one can say. I wish you were here with your healing powers. You must come quickly as soon as we have returned to Kyoto. The remarkable health of my women's court is no doubt due to the amulets and teas you provided us with before you left. If only you could have left some of your wonder-working cures with my husband! Please be packed and ready to return as soon as I can persuade my father to release enough soldiers to fetch you--within a fortnight."

I read the letter to everyone, and desks are pushed aside as thoughts of poetry are abandoned. The sullen gray sky has ceased its flurries anyway. Matsu's nurse carries him off to change him into dry clothes.

"Knowing how stubborn Kiyomori is, the situation must be drastic indeed for him to reverse himself in such a short period of time, after so much labor and expense," I sigh.

Sessho nods. "My spies say the move to Fukuhara seemed like a surrender on his part. The Genji are gloating over the fact that their mere threat, combined with the monks, were enough to drive the Heike forth from the capital to the edge of the sea. 'We the nets and they the fish!' and 'Into the sea!' have become rallying cries in the North and more disloyal vassals are joining the Genji by the day. A show of power is needed."

We knew our idyll could not last forever, but we are all drooping with the news.

"We'll miss you horridly," Tomomori finally ventures.

Suddenly realizing the meaning of the discussion, Kikuko pops her head out from the lair she had formed in my robes. "You can't go! You're the big rabbit and I'm the little rabbit! You have to stay and take care of me!"

Seishan comes over and puts a hand on my daughter.

"She's not going anywhere yet," she comforts.

It is all I can do to hold back my tears.

A week later, I receive a letter from Lady Daigon-no-suke, brought by Shigehira's soldiers.

"The new capital was dismantled with astonishing speed, and we weary exiles have poured back into the ashy ruins of Kyoto, determined to make a new, glittering phoenix of a city arise from those ashes. The country houses that remained are full of courtiers sleeping all crammed together like peasants. Reconstruction of the city is proceeding at an astonishing pace. Every peasant within walking distance who can wield a saw or dig a foundation has been put to work. A huge army stands guard all around the perimeters of the city, while an army of carpenters work night and day, barely pausing for food or rest. Oxen load after oxen load of lumber arrives from the mountains under heavy guard, as well as many entire buildings erected in Fukuhara, dismantled and brought back to the capital. The city is going up so quickly it is rumored that our sorcerers have enlisted friendly kami--Genji propaganda says goblins--to restore the city by magic. Our spies inform us that frightened monks and country-dwellers alike now refer to Kyoto as 'the City of Sorcery'. We even heard that the Empress' personal sorceress (that would be you, my dear Lady Fujiwara), though now invisible, is directing an unseen army of ghosts to complete the task."

"See, you don't have to go back," Sessho interrupts happily. "We'll just tell everyone that you *have* gone back but you are busy directing your unseen army. What else does she say?"

I scan the rest of the letter. "She says Kiyomori plans to attack and defeat the monks of the four hills surrounding Kyoto. The Heike army has increased dramatically in size, its numbers swollen by soldiers from Shikoku and the southern provinces who sailed to join with Kiyomori at Fukuhara. Shigehira asks you to send a company of soldiers back with this armed escort as a token of your loyalty and devotion to our cause."

Sessho sips his sake, nodding thoughtfully. "Probably that was the true intention behind Kiyomori's moving the court to Fukuhara, to raise support from the southern armies, from the people more traditionally aligned with the Heike and friendly to them," he speculates. "Kiyomori doesn't retreat, he regroups. Fukuhara has served its purpose. He'll crush the rebels now, like he crushed them before."

To my delight, a note from On'na Mari is enclosed within the gold-tasseled scroll covering which contained Daigon-no-suke's letter.

On'na Mari writes, "Though Akoyo and I have been forced to move back with my family for the duration, I am *ecstatic* to be back in Kyoto. Munemori's patronage has made my father an exceedingly wealthy man, as you know, and he is giving me my pick of statues, vases, and furniture *at cost* to refurnish our new home! This war is turning out to be the best thing that could have happened.

With my husband's family home burned to the ground, now I can have it rebuilt much larger, and with a more modern look. Before, Tsunemasa never wanted to change anything because it was all dreary family mementoes, suits of armor, old paintings crackling into dust, libraries of moldy scrolls no one ever read anyway. While Tsunemasa is away preparing to make war on the monks, I am marshalling my armies of furniture makers and curtain makers and rush weavers. He calls me 'the little general of the house' and now I shall have everything exactly the way I like it. Father lets me have the best pick of everything in his warehouses, though everything is still fearfully expensive because of how long it has been since we could get shipments of goods from China. He is grateful that I advised him to donate gold statues and ancient scrolls to the monasteries--the monks didn't touch his mansion, or any of his warehouses. Most of the trees on our property are still intact. I have a dozen gardeners making a miniature Fuji with a reflecting pond for moon viewing in the back--it will be the most magnificent garden in the capital when I am done, mark my words."

I reread On'na Mari's letter aloud to Sessho, shaking my head at the irony of it. The Buddhists preach detachment from the world, yet their temples are crammed full of costly statues, censers, lush materials and artwork. They burn the houses of commoners who have nothing, and spare the warehouses of the merchants who provide their luxuries. People go there to pray for their spiritual advancement, and as a token of their sincerity bring gold leaf to smear over the statues of the Buddhas, some of which take on so much gold leaf they no longer resemble Buddhas, but rather crude snowmen made by children, glinting gold rather than white. And many of those images are solid gold to begin with, or jade. How different from the Kami-no-machi, the Way of the Kami, whose shrines are simplicity itself, which focuses on the life-force present in all things, rather than the afterlife. How can any idol compete with the brilliant beauty of a maple tree in autumn, a cherry tree in spring, a rushing waterfall, or the mist rising from the rice fields?

Sessho sends a contingent of his own army under the command of his brother Hyodoshi to join Shigehira, Tsunemasa, and Tadanori in their campaign, in spite of Seishan's distress.

"Are we sending soldiers to kill the very monks who prayed for our son to be returned to us?" she asks.

Sessho sighs heavily. "What would you have me do, wife? Tell Kiyomori to count us among the rebels? Are you tired of seeing my head on its shoulders?"

Eight days later, Hyodoshi and the troops from Tanba return.

"Tell my honored brother to meet me in my study as soon as he has washed off the mud of the roads," Sessho orders his manservant. "Return to your rooms," he tells Nori and Tomomori, who have been studying Chinese scrolls with us.

"Father," Nori says, standing very straight, "I'm old enough to hear about the war."

"So am I!" cries Tomomori. "And I'm your heir, so--"

"I'm older!" Nori asserts jealously.

"You're a girl!" he sneers.

Nori stamps her foot.

Seishan raises her eyebrows. "Your maturity is so evident," she says quietly. The children hang their heads, abashed. Nori looks entreatingly at her father, mouthing "please".

"Very well," Sessho agrees. We all read silently, trying to conceal our anxiety, until Hyodoshi enters, bowing low before his elder brother.

"Greetings, Eldest Brother. The gods granted us victory. I followed your instructions, risking our men as little as possible. The men of Tanba suffered only three significant injuries, one of them fatal. The others are safely returned."

"Well done." Sessho bows in return as servants bring a table and a flask of sake for Hyodoshi's refreshment. "Tell us all about it."

"The Heike army defeated the monasteries closest to Kyoto, then marched on Nara, where the largest constellation of monasteries is clustered. All the monks too old to fight, and those defeated in smaller battles, fled there to come together and stand against the Heike. Perhaps they did not think the Heike would dare to attack them there, in that holiest of places, in the oldest capital of Japan. But Kiyomori had vowed to 'take out the rotting tree at its roots,' so the army marched on Nara. The outnumbered soldier monks were pressed before us, until only a thousand were left to oppose our forces. We outnumbered them twenty to one, so the outcome was never really in question."

"So everything went perfectly?" Sessho questions.

"Well…" Hyodoshi's eyes glance nervously to Nori and Tomomori.

"Speak freely, and spare no details," Sessho says. "The children have assured us they are ready to hear the truth about war."

Hyodoshi swallows. "Either by accident or design, Kiyomori's forces set fire to the monasteries at Nara. Our soldiers were not involved," he assures Seishan. "The soldiers claimed it was an accident, that they had simply put a couple of commoner's residences at the edge of the temple complex to the torch so that they would have enough light to fight by, since the battle was at night. But the fire spread out of control, fanned by a wind, and virtually every building in two adjacent temple complexes burned to the ground. The monks remaining are spreading talk that Kiyomori ordered the temples burned, but I don't believe that…however it happened, thousands of innocents died terrible deaths. Elderly monks and women and children from all over the city of Nara had taken refuge on the upper floors of the largest temples, drawing up the ladders so that they would be safe from the profanest soldiers. At least three thousand civilians, maybe more, died screaming as the flames engulfed them…"

A small sound escapes Seishan.

"Lady, I swear, our troops were not involved," Hyodoshi insists.

"Two entire temple complexes…" Sessho says. "Was there no attempt to put the fires out?"

"Many soldiers broke rank and stampeded the temples, trying to rescue the artifacts…"

"Looting," Sessho says dryly.

Because of my own experience with the fire that took my mother, our servants, and our home, I can imagine all too well the terror of that scene, and to imagine entire families consumed in one terrible night…

"What of the Kofukuji temple?" I ask. One of the Fujiwara's traditional temples, this temple, sacred to my family, is one of the oldest in Japan.

"It's gone, my lady," Hyodoshi says.

I am glad my father did not live to see this.

"What of the Todaiji Buddha?" Seishan asks. The hundred and sixty foot bronze statue coated in gold leaf was the pride of Nara.

"Gone. Melted, my lady. And all the ancient Hosso and Sanron scriptures, turned to ash. Of all the great works of art and the sacred scriptures, nothing remains. Tadanori's soldiers--not *ours*," he emphasizes, "were seen looting the temples, taking what remained of the melted gold statues and pocketing them, searching through the cooling embers of wood and human bone for any jewels that might have been spared.

The heads of the soldier monks were brought back on stakes, but feeling in the capital was running so high against the burning of the temples that Kiyomori cancelled the victory parade and the heads, rather than being displayed around the perimeters of the city and on the avenues, were ignominiously discarded into various trash heaps. The monks who remained at the monasteries surrounding Kyoto received great gifts from the Heike family for not having joined the rebellious forces. They acknowledged the gifts with thanks and did not publicly criticize Kiyomori's actions. But while they remained quiet, I can only imagine how resentful they must feel."

"If the temples prosper, the realm will prosper; if the temples decline, the realm will decline," Seishan quotes in a whisper.

"You did well," Sessho acknowledges Hyodoshi. "Thank you for upholding the honor of this family."

Soon after Hyodoshi's return, a contingent of soldiers arrives to give me safe passage back to the palace. Tears stream down Seishan's face as we unroll Tokushi's letter.

"My beloved husband, Retired Emperor Takakura, is now exceedingly ill. I fear the violation of the sanctity of the monasteries has been a blow that his spiritual nature cannot endure. I need you to return immediately--our court physicians are seemingly helpless. I fear that vengeful ghosts may be hunting down the Heike and all who are tied to them. The Imperial Palace was rebuilt exactly as it was before. Your room is ready for you. Truly, I cannot distinguish the old palace from the new one, except for the pervasive smell of fresh cedar. The garden will require your tender care to be fully restored, but everything else is exactly as it was engraved upon our hearts. Virtually every vase and wall hanging is back in place. I am amazed at how easily the old capital has reconstituted itself. But you can see even the common people are dazed and disheartened by the burning of the temples, though it was completely an accident. Come quickly, or we may face the loss of our sovereign as well."

Selfishly, I feel like a prisoner who has escaped from jail, recaptured by soldiers coming to take her back to prison.

That night I sleep between Sessho and Seishan, but many tears are shed by all of us before sleep claims us. "The sea kami sleep drier than this," Sessho remarks as we finally drift off. The next morning I say good-bye to the children. "Don't go, stay here with me," my daughter whimpers, clinging to me until Seishan gently pulls her away, saying, "Auntie Seiko must do her duty to the Empress. We must all do our duty, child, and it is our duty to let her go." The breakfast mochi tastes like cotton. Finally Machiko and I climb into the Empress' carriage. I am grateful the curtains are so thick so that no one can see or hear as we both sob all the way back to Kyoto, as we are carried away from heaven, into a life which is shortly to become hell.

Chapter Sixteen
January 1181

I realize how serious things are when we arrive at the court and are immediately rushed to the Retired Emperor's side. Normally, to ask someone who had just made a journey like that to do anything without having been fed, bathed and rested would be a dramatic breach of courtesy. Clearly the situation is quite desperate. I regret my selfish indulgence in my own emotions, which has left me quite worn out. We are escorted to a house within the Imperial Complex, separated from the palace by a small courtyard, which is Takakura's new residence. As we arrive, I am shocked to see ox carts loaded with bodies wrapped in shrouds waiting to be taken to the burning grounds. Maidservants greet us and wash our hands and faces with scented cloths before taking us to see Takakura. He is alarmingly jaundiced, with dark circles under his eyes, and extremely hot to the touch. His breathing is shallow and ragged. His eyes roll about in his head and he is unresponsive to questions. Tokushi is there, looking very pale. I kneel before her. She waves me away. "I don't need your attentions now. He does. You must save him."

I try pouring cool water down Takakura's throat. It comes right back up again. He is wrinkled like an old man around his neck and arms, obviously dehydrated.

The Chinese physicians attending Takakura seem uncharacteristically glad to see me; unfortunately I take that as a sign that they consider his case hopeless and are happy someone else has showed up to share the blame. I draw them into a tight circle and discuss with them in low tones all that has transpired so far. His urine was dark and his pulses very weak. They had tried everything; nothing had helped. Takakura had been ill for some time now, at least two months, and during that time had seemed to almost recover and then relapsed at least four times. Tokushi shuffles over on her knees, weighed down by exhaustion and her many layers of garments.

"Speak," she says, "What can be done for him?"

"I don't know," I admit. "The physicians have done everything I would have thought of. We will consult all the texts, however, in case we have overlooked something. You need to rest and to leave us with him now. We cannot have you becoming ill as well."

She leans close, eyes glittering. "It's not contagious. It's a demon illness. The spirits at Fukuhara did not want us there; they never wanted us there." I thought about how members of the court had described Fukuhara as a swamp. I have seen people with this illness, usually commoners who came to my mother, almost always at the time of year when the swamps smell fetid and the mists rise out of them, and those affected are generally those farming rice paddies or living near stagnant water. My mother gave the people herbs to burn that would keep the mosquitoes away; she believed they were the harbingers of illness in some way. It is also true that many of the ill reported having seen ghosts arise out of the swamps. And who is to say that ghosts cannot take the form of mosquitoes, or ride upon their backs? The world of spirit and the world of flesh can never be separated. I recommend as many wonder-working monks as Tokushi can find.

Retired Emperor Go-Shirakawa, Takakura's father, arrives later in the evening, freed from his house arrest to tend to his son. He settles beside his son's bed, spreading his gold and ivory robes around him, and begins uttering sutras and demon-banishing charms in his stentorian voice. Soon monks join him, and the chanting spins a powerful, pulsating web of sound. The next morning, the physicians have Takakura carried to a sauna, to be steamed with herbs to help him sweat out the illness. Later, two of his concubines come with musicians, to sing his favorite songs. Shamans create a net of talismans throughout his quarters to baffle his soul's attempts to seek out the world of spirit. New Year's celebrations are cancelled; the time courtiers would normally have spent in parties and first of the year rituals are spent quietly in prayer.

But in spite of all our best efforts, within ten days Retired Emperor Takakura breathes his last. During that time, three other minor members of the court die as well. Sixteen had died since they returned from Fukuhara, and twice that many before they had left that ill-starred place. At least sixty with similar symptoms recovered. It seems the more robust were able to fight it off, though often with relapses after five or six months, a year, or even later.

But the young and the old, and those who had been weakened by sorrow and excess, perished.

The whole city, already shaken by the deaths of the monks, is plunged into mourning. Much construction and dedication of buildings is put on hold during the mourning period, though Kiyomori orders the mourning period to be shortened, out of necessity. He tries to mollify Go-Shirakawa, who is naturally prostrate with grief over the loss of his one remaining son, by giving him one of his own daughters who had been born to a priestess at Itsukshima. She's an ivory-skinned woman of eighteen, mature beyond her years. Go-Shirakawa does seem to derive great comfort from her presence. She is no fragile flower--not broad of shoulders in an unfeminine way, but not thinly built like so many court women. She has a great solidity of character, and the calm authority of a born priestess, no doubt from having grown up in the sacred precincts of Itsukshima; she carries the blessings of the Goddess wherever she goes. Everyone comments that in her company, they feel as if they have passed beneath the Torii and are standing on sacred ground. Her presence is an elegant solution to Kiyomori's need to simultaneously appease and comfort Go-Shirakawa, while keeping an eye on him.

My own energies are used up in trying to comfort Tokushi, who is crushed by her husband's death. Now all her dreams of reconciliation with Takakura, and the birth of future children are shattered. She grieves as bitterly as any widow I have ever seen, tearing her hair, dressing exclusively in robes of white and pale lavender, shrieking and sobbing like a disconsolate ghost, forcing me to give her higher and higher doses of poppy syrup to help her rest. Her moaning and sobbing make it impossible for anyone to sleep, especially me. She accuses herself wildly, saying, "If only I had loved him better, this would never have happened." I try to assure her that if all the wonder-working monks had been unable to prevent Takakura's death, then surely it was fate and in no way her responsibility. Then she raves that it is her father's fault, that it is karmic retribution from the deaths of the monks at Nara. I try to point out that Takakura had taken ill well before that event, but trying to appease her grief with logic is like offering fruit to a cat.

Antoku is also devastated by his father's death, though he really didn't know him very well. Nonetheless, he grieves piteously, and cuts off his loops of hair, insisting that they be cremated with his father. "Now he will never know the names of all my rabbits," Antoku wails, and we all wail with him, thinking of all the things Takakura will never know about his son. Everyday I must send my clothes to be washed, for they are saturated with Tokushi's tears, Antoku's tears, and the tears of Takakura's many lovers who come to weep on my shoulder, knowing I will comfort them and keep their sobbed remembrances secret. For all his faults, he was a man who inspired much loyalty in his women. I fear that Tokushi will blame me for her husband's death, but instead she blames herself. In spite of my denials, she remains convinced that if she had managed to get me there earlier, it would have made all the difference between life and death for him. He was a very young man, only twenty-six years old. It is never easy to accept the death of one so young.

Kiyomori spends even more time than usual with Antoku, to comfort him and give him a male presence--though there could not be two more different men than Kiyomori, commanding as a bear, and Takakura, slender as a reed. But whatever frailties of body or spirit Takakura possessed, he was still the torch that passed the fire of the Sun Goddess on to his son, and that pure light of divinity is always apparent in Antoku, whether he is happy or sad. About six weeks after his father died, Antoku solemnly says to me, "My father has gone to help Amaterasu shine on us. It's an important job, and he was too important to stay here." He seems more reconciled to the situation after that.

Takakura's mistresses, especially those who had borne him children, are also disconsolate, and naturally quite worried about their position at court now that their protector is gone. Some promptly disappear and return to their families rather than face a precarious existence under the Kiyomoris. Takakura sired three sons besides Antoku, and seven daughters, by various paramours. Kiyomori soon lays the mothers' fears to rest by sending an envoy promising that Takakura's children will be treated as lesser members of the royal family, with stipends going to each mother to ensure the children will be raised in a manner befitting their station.

Tokushi, still believing that the destruction of the temples at Nara had something to do with Takakura's death, sells many of her own possessions to raise funds to rebuild the structures, and sends many fine gifts to all the other temples as well. Her parents and others of the Heike clan contribute magnificent gifts, but in the case of her parents, and Munemori, the gifts are clearly for political purposes, whereas Tokushi's are from the heart.

She seems convinced that her family's evils will produce karma which will return to harm herself and her child unless it is assuaged in some way. She begins to talk of becoming a nun. Lord and Lady Kiyomori had already taken vows in an effort to identify themselves as being devoted to the Buddha rather than opposed to him and his followers. Needless to say, they did not retire to the monasteries, and indeed, continued to live their lives exactly as they always had. But they refuse to hear of Tokushi taking vows, saying that she must think of serving her country as the Empress instead, and that nurturing the lineage of the Sun Goddess will do more honor to her husband than any other action. They insist that her highest duty lies in guiding the nation. Of course, it is they who are doing the guiding, they pulling the strings and she the puppet. They can only appear to have retired from politics if she remains as their mouthpiece, and it is my impression that they have actually forbidden her to consider becoming a nun at this time. I am relieved, for I agree that grief has unbalanced Tokushi's ability to think clearly. Lady Kiyomori enlists my help looking among the men at court for one who would provide a suitably discreet lover for her daughter, feeling that if she took a lover or two she would recover from what Lady Kiyomori terms; "this excessive grief of hers." I know she worries that Tokushi, like her husband, will sicken and die. But in spite of Tokushi's grief, she remains remarkably healthy. She eats sparsely, and grows thin, but after awhile she stops looking bedraggled and starts to glow with an inner light, perhaps generated by spending so much time in prayer.

Unfortunately, in spite of being showered with hopeful love poetry from the best minds at court, the only men she seems interested in are the monks who pray with her, and Go-Shirakawa, whose grief is commensurate with hers. She becomes a frequent visitor at his mansion and always returns far happier. I give her every herb I can think of, and after six or seven months of abstinence, she allows me to console her carnally as well, though far more sake is involved in getting her righteousness to melt than in the past. She seems more relaxed when we visit On'na Mari, partly because of the isolation and distance from prying eyes at court, and partly due to On'na Mari's stealthy application of the appropriate aphrodisiacs. The three of us enjoy some bawdy and raucous evenings while Tsunemasa is off harrying the Genji. Rebellion is breaking out in so many places, it is like a lightning storm in a dry forest. Even many traditional Taira allies in Shikoku abandon their obligations, rallying around a traitor named Michinobu. No sooner does Tsunemasa return from triumphantly executing the traitor Yoshimoto than we hear that Kiso Yoshinaka of Shinano has promised the support of that whole province to Yoritomo. All the auguries and portents discovered in the New Year's divinations portend a year of deaths, warfare, and unsettling transformations.

Chapter Seventeen
March 1181

Ten months have passed since I have seen Tsubame. But the Empress could not be approached during her grieving period, so I am forced to send letters to my daughter telling her to be patient. One rainy spring night, Tokushi and I are sitting by the open shoji screen, listening to the patter of rain, the delirium of frogs.

"It's all so gloomy," she complains.

"I imagine Tsubame has learned many new songs by now," I venture. "Perhaps if she were here, it would cheer you. She thinks of you as a second mother, you know."

Tokushi brightens. "Yes, it is high time that young lady came. I only hope I will not be too depressed to find her a suitable marriage." She starts to sniffle. Before I can reassure her that Tsubame is still too young to marry anyway, a messenger arrives from Lady Kiyomori, informing her that Lord Kiyomori has taken ill.

"Dear me! He is usually so healthy. A fever! You must prepare some herbs, in case they ask for you," Tokushi says.

Later that night, as I am preparing for bed, several members of Kiyomori's personal guard appear and inform me that Lady Kiyomori has commanded me to her Lord's presence.

When I enter his quarters, Kiyomori's eyes start out of his head. "What, is she alive?" he croaks.

"That is Fujuri's daughter," Lady Kiyomori reminds him.

"But she's just a child," he wheezes.

"She is grown now," Lady Kiyomori says gently. "Of course, she is older than Tokushi, and Tokushi is the mother of the Emperor."

"I smell smoke! The palace is burning! The Genji have set fire to it!" Kiyomori snarls. "Where are my guards, the traitors--"

I note the dusky redness of his skin and a touch confirms my fears: he is hot as a kettle, his skin dry as parchment.

"He needs to have a cool bath," I order, and servants run for water.

"We were just about to order that," one of the Chinese physicians says coldly. I instruct Machiko to prepare a mixture of herbs for fever. I nod for the Chinese physicians to step aside with me a moment. "Let us put aside our differences for the sake of the nation," I urge, "tell me, what have you tried so far?" I see them bristle at my use of the word 'tried,' with its implication that they have failed. They inform me that they have given him various pills and concoctions, but he has vomited them before they had a chance to take effect. He has been restless, aggressive, seeing visions of the unseen world, and has refused moxa and acupuncture. I had heard rumor that Kiyomori, who so fearlessly faced the swords of his foes, had an aversion to needles and would not allow himself to be treated with them, but I could scarcely credit such a thing. But certainly there is no reasoning with him in his current wild state. The bath is poured and he is helped into it. His skin shows his age, but beneath it he is still ropy, muscular and strong. He shivers in the cold bath, breathing hard, but does not complain. A messenger enters and announces, "The priests from the temple are here to perform an exorcism."

"Tell them to go exorcise themselves!" Kiyomori hisses. "Snakes...snakes..." he mutters, and I am not sure if he refers to the priests, or to a vision we cannot see.

Kiyomori is unable to keep down the herbs I give him. The Chinese physicians put a plaster of heat-drawing herbs on his chest, and keep taking his pulses and jotting down notes. I return to my quarters, seeing there is nothing I can do, but the next day Lady Kiyomori calls me back again. Seeing her state of agitation, I give her a tea to calm her spirit, hang talismans around the room and bless it in the old manner.

Kiyomori's fever drops while he is in a second cold bath and he is able to keep down some of my herbs, so I have hope. But as he is being bathed, I notice a small wound, like a doll's mouth, on the inside of his arm.

"What is that wound?" I ask.

"A mere nick," his chamberlain asserts. "He took it in swordplay a couple of days ago. It scarcely bled."

I run my finger over it. The wound is indeed small and insignificant seeming, but the tissue around it has an odd, soft feeling, like rotting fruit.

The probing must hurt, for he bellows and backhands me across the room. The Chinese physicians barely raise a hand to disguise their contemptuous giggles.

Dr. Chin, one of the Chinese physicians I respect, enters the room and I share my observations about the injury. He checks it himself as he takes Kiyomori's pulses.

"Yes, it is most disturbing, most irregular," he whispers to me later as we watch Kiyomori sink into a labored sleep. "There is an evil humor in his blood and I fear that is its entry point. He sleeps now; I must put the needles in before he wakes."

I tell Lady Kiyomori that her husband is in the best possible hands and again retire to my chambers. It was the last good sleep I was to have in days, for she did not allow me to leave again while her husband was ill, in spite of my protestations that I could do nothing for him.

Word spreads throughout the palace that the demons have come for Kiyomori. I do not believe in the Buddhist hells or their demons, but it is true that as he grows sicker, Kiyomori comes to resemble a demon himself--his eyes bulging, face red and fiery, ranting and raving with incomprehensible rage-- and the mysterious fever which envelops him burns as hot as the flames which devoured the monks at Nara. Later it was said he was so hot that when he was placed in a tub of cold water it began to boil and steam. That was not true, but it is true that he bellowed like an ox and thrashed so that it looked like the water was boiling, and that between his exertions and his fever, the water did not remain cold for long.

One day when I enter his chamber, all the physicians are huddled in a corner, eyes bulging. At Kiyomori's command, a servant had brought him his sword, and he lurches around the room slashing at things no one else can see, stabbing through screens, slashing down paintings and draped fabric, adopting sword poses and jabbing at anyone who comes near.

"Stab me, will you!" he glowers at the Chinese physicians with their needles. "I'll show you puncture!"

Later, when he falls asleep, only Lady Kiyomori dares to slip the sword from his grasp.

"Anyone else who brings him a weapon will suffer instant death," she threatens.

The old warrior would have wanted to go down fighting, and in a sense he did.

The next day he is prostrate, his skin so hot and his breathing so labored I do not think he will ever rise again. But the day after that he orders the servants to raise him to his feet and once again resumes his battle, though this time the sword in his hand is as imaginary as his enemies. He keeps falling to one knee and rising, but he is still strong enough to hurl a stool at a servant and drop the fellow unconscious. I stand in the doorway and attempt to reason with him. He turns, shaking his head as if he cannot believe his eyes.

"No women on the battlefield!" he roars. Seeing how fixed he is in his delusion, I suggest that Kiyomori's sons, trusted friends, and the male physicians should dress in battle garb, go in and pretend to fight alongside him for a bit, then announce that the enemy was vanquished, running away, and it was time to rest, since the battle was over. The physicians deride that as a ridiculous idea, but Munemori orders it done, and, comforted by the delusion of victory, Kiyomori falls into an exhausted sleep.

Even during the worst of his illness, he remains obsessed with Yoritomo, the child he spared twenty years ago who now spreads rebellion. Over and over Kiyomori awakes from his broken sleep demanding, "Where is he? Who is hiding him? Show me his head!"

At last his family admits that all seems lost. Lady Kiyomori, shaking, in tears, far more vulnerable than I have ever seen her, asks if there is anything they can do that will ease him. Munemori chimes in, "We will build a hall, erect a golden Buddha, commission a thousand prayers..."

"No halls..." Kiyomori rasps hoarsely.

"Of course not, Father, a golden pagoda on Itkushima..." Shigehira corrects, knowing his father's preference for the old ways over the Buddhist.

"No pagodas!" Kiyomori snarls, wild-eyed.

Lady Kiyomori kneels, grasping his hand. "Just tell us what you want, it shall be accomplished."

Kiyomori struggles, fighting his way through the fire of fever as he had fought his way through a thousand battles.

"I want...give me Yoritomo's head. Cut off...that traitor's head and lay it on my grave. His skull...will be my pagoda...that...is my memorial."

Some thought he was raving as he said that, but I saw it as his one lucid moment.

A dozen times, Kiyomori teeters on death's precipice; a dozen times he fights his way back from that brink. Machiko brews me the herbs to increase wakefulness again and again, but soon I am so exhausted I feel like I'm staggering through Kiyomori's fever-dream battlefields with him. Finally, one night, with most of his family gathered in semi-circles around his bed, he exhales one long, shuddering gasp, and is still.

Our cries and sobs alert the nobles camped outside Kiyomori's doorway to his passing. Bedlam erupts in the hall, travels throughout the mansion and spreads out into the streets. People later claimed they heard the demons in ox-carts coming to fetch Kiyomori's soul, but in reality it was all the carriages tearing up and down the streets as worried people ran hither and thither like a hive of bees that has been disturbed. Everyone knew that the real power and stability in the kingdom had just been lost and no one knew what would happen next, but with the eastern rebels growing more provocative every day, everyone feared the worst.

In keeping with Kiyomori's request, the time normally spent in prayers for the dead is devoted to battle plans. After one brief flash of tears, Lady Kiyomori becomes a rock for the family, the way her taloned fingers grow white at the knuckles as she grasps her own arms during discussions the only sign of her distress. Many times I wish that she could head the troops: her iron resolve would be far more inspiring than Munemori's posturing and excess; he is known for bringing two or three young concubines, his personal chef and an elaborate tent which requires a dozen people more than an hour to erect to every engagement. To avoid quarreling among his sons, Kiyomori had made clear that Shigemori, the eldest, was heir to his power, and concentrated all his teaching about politics and warfare to that eldest son. The others he did not challenge to learn as much, thinking to eliminate competitiveness and bickering. But then, when Shigemori died, there was no other fit to fill his place. Tomomori is fearless, but too hotheaded to be much of a strategist. Shigehira is the son most like Kiyomori, but while dogged and relentless, he is not a man who thinks much beyond the next battle. Kiyomori's brother, Tadanori, would be best suited to lead, but Lady Kiyomori will never let the reins pass from her family while she still has a son to hold them.

I was never close to Kiyomori--I doubt if there are many, even among his children, who could say they were. But he was Tokushi's father, and in some way, the father of the whole Heike clan and all associated with them. I felt sorry that he died so hard, and at only sixty-four, when his strength of body and character would have dictated that he live longer. But most of all, I am sorry and afraid for all of us who remain. When Lord Kiyomori died, it was as if a cold wind blew through the halls of the palace. It moved through with the dry death sound of autumn leaves; it knocked over shoji screens and extinguished lamps. Many said it was the soul of Lord Kiyomori being harried and hounded to the Buddhist hell. But what I felt was this: Lord Kiyomori had been a huge dragon, curled protectively around the palace, around the influence and the power he had won with his victories. Now the dragon was dead; and the gates he had protected swung open, leaving us defenseless against the harsh northern wind. The palace soothsayers all warn that, with the Heike clan in disarray, the Genji will come swooping down on the capital. That prediction does not require the genius of second sight, however. Anyone with half an eye could see that it would take a far more foolish leader than Yoritomo to resist an opportunity like this.

If one hears that it is raining two days north of Kyoto, and there is a south-moving wind, one expects to get wet. But although for years there have been signs and portents of the storm brewing in the north and east of the country-- the dissatisfaction of the nobles whose families had not had a significant court appointment in generations, the peasant rebellions which required increasing amounts of violence to put down, the rumors that the Genji clan was rising like a phoenix--no one in the court seemed to think the storm would ever come. The men must have known more than we did, and dissembled to preserve our feminine innocence and peace of mind. But with few exceptions, I believe the men lied to themselves, as well as to us, about the seriousness of the changes. The more everyone laughed and joked and flirted about the upcoming conflict, the more they painted it in gay colors of conquest and glory, the more frightened I became. They were like children, posing and posturing with their painted faces. But this was not a child's pretend war, with painted wooden swords. And the men they were going to fight were not just simple country bumpkins. I remembered the visits of the northern nobles all too well; their sunburnt, unpainted faces, the taut, muscular, animal way they moved, the slow, flickering flames of resentment held back just behind their eyes.

I voice my concerns to Tokushi, but she simply shrugs. "Amaterasu will protect her own. I pity the northerners if they attempt to violate the will of heaven." Well, it is true that nothing can touch Tokushi and her son: they are deity; to harm them would be sacrilege. The line of the Emperor is always preserved, regardless of clan warfare and political shifts. But what of Sessho and his family, far from the protective walls and soldiers of Kyoto? What of my daughter Tsubame whose family home lies in the east, close by the area of the rebellions?

The northerners who had visited the court over the years seemed bumbling and inept, out of their depth with poetry games and banter. Even their clothes were hopelessly out of date. How could we know that a race of people so inadequate at wordplay and the complexities of court intrigue would be so brilliant with swordplay and military strategy? That while our men were studying flute and literature and art, and could wield a brush so adeptly, theirs were making arrows and spears their art? There is a Chinese saying; "Words last longer than wars." But while war is being waged, take a man with a brush, and a man with a sword, and it is the man with the sword who carves the last word with blood.

Chapter Eighteen
Spring 1181

"Thank you for receiving me." Atsumori bows. We are having a simple supper in my room, silver strings of rain hissing into the garden beyond the open door. The braziers keep the room warm despite the spring chill.

"I am very relieved to have you back safe once again," I say.

He and Kiyosune have just returned from harrying the Genji. The Genji forces had taken over the Owari road and were blocking all commercial traffic from proceeding. No one could go further north than a certain pass without declaring their allegiance to the Yoritomo, which in the case of merchants meant surrendering their goods for the Genji cause. Normally it would be inappropriate to engage in warfare so soon after the death of a leader like Kiyomori, but obviously Kiyomori himself would have greatly urged it.

"I could barely sleep while you were gone," I say. "My heart was in my throat the whole time."

He smiles, pleased that I care enough for him to make me worry. He puts a hand to his throat, touching the talismans I have made for him.

"Have you so little faith in your own work? And so little in me?"

"No amount of magic and skill…immortality is for the gods."

"Yes," he says, gazing out into the rain, "all life is temporary." He grasps my hand firmly. "All the more reason to spend each moment living fully, neh?"

"Yes," I nod. "I see you are wearing--" I nod towards his violet outer robe embroidered with silver. Lavender is the color of mourning. "Did you lose a friend in the engagement?"

"Just honoring all those who were lost," Atsumori says. "It's not that I lost anyone close."

"Did you know Saikiyo?" I ask, mentioning a young noble who perished in the battles in Echizen province.

Atsumori nods. "Yes, he was young and foolish. It was his first battle. You get smarter as you go along. If you live long enough."

"I'm glad to hear that," I say, marveling at such a young man adopting the role of the world-weary warrior. "Tell me about it," I say. It's not that I really want to hear about battles and bloodshed, but I imagine anyone who has been through something so dreadful would need to talk about it.

"It was almost embarrassingly easy. Yoritomo sent out such a small force against us. We had four times as many soldiers, but they attacked us anyway. They must have believed all those stories of us being weak, dissolute nobles. We had stopped on one side of the river, and they charged across the river to meet us. Our commander shouted that their armor and horses would be wet, and we could distinguish who the enemy was that way. That's one of the biggest dangers, you know, telling friend from foe in the melee. You're just hacking and shouting in close quarters--you don't want to hurt your own people, but with everybody wearing different colors of armor and helmets, none of us can keep track of what all of our compatriots might look like. But if you hesitate, the enemy may get under your sword arm before you know it. They made it so ridiculously easy for us," he shakes his head.

"Having just crossed the water--we knew we just had to kill all the wet ones. Once they realized how over-matched they were, they tried to retreat, but with the river at their back, their horses were stumbling in the mud--I don't believe more than two or three of them escaped. It was almost shameful. One of their men would be surrounded by three or four of ours. Actually, I would never stab anyone in the back," he assures me, "only face to face. But sometimes in the excitement of a battle, not everyone is so particular about how they take a head. There were a few more skirmishes here and there--I swear these Genji are nothing more than a bunch of brigands, launching a few cowardly arrows from the bushes, then scuttling off down a steep arroyo where the horses can't follow. They're no better than us at fighting. Your fears have been for nothing."

I had shared with him my concerns that the Genji had been practicing warfare for generations, because of their role in the northern provinces, fighting incursions of the savage Ainu and putting down peasant rebellions.

"I mean, face it, they've been fighting peasants! Who can't win against people armed with hoes and rakes?" he laughs. "Yes, they found out it wasn't like fighting peasants to go up against Koremori. He's a splendid leader.

Shigemori would be very proud of him. I feel honored to have grown up with him."

"I'm sure he is honored to have you at his side. So how many battles were there?"

He shrugs. I put some more ginger chicken on his plate.

"Oh, thank you so much for having chicken. When you're fighting like we are, you really need meat."

"I know. I want you to be strong."

He puts my hand on his arm and tightens his bicep so I can feel the muscle bulging.

"Every battle makes me stronger. And your love makes me stronger."

I am amazed at how much more muscular he has grown in this last year. The slender boy is gone.

"I told my father I needed new armor. I've gotten too broad for what I have. I had blisters in the strangest places during this campaign."

"Is he having it made for you?" I ask.

"Of course. It's already done. It's just drying."

"Do you think the Genji will slink off now with their tails between their legs?" I ask hopefully.

"We gathered a lot more allies," he says as the maidservant refills his sake cup. "Men from Echizen don't want to side with the Genji; they're loyal to the crown. Thousands of new soldiers flocked to us. It's just so unfortunate that Tomomori became ill, forcing our return. We could have made a clean sweep through the northland otherwise. Have you seen him?"

I nod. "Yes, I've been tending to him. He'll be all right."

"Was it a magical attack?" he asks warily. "It came on him so suddenly, we felt certain that it was sorcery."

"It's quite possible," I agree. Tomomori had come back vomiting and losing his bowels, sweating with a very high fever, carried in a litter, too sick to ride. But only a few days of my ministrations and those of the palace physicians have brought him around. He is still weak and pale, but his fever is gone and he is keeping down fluids. "He is recovering well," I say.

"And you worry about me! I have the love of the most miraculous woman in court!"

"No one's power rivals that of the gods, and of karma," I caution. "None of us can understand the weavings of our karmic path that bring us from one event to the next. Even the best warrior, and the best sorceress are only mortal."

"You are entirely too modest. Fortunately, that is a virtue in which I am completely lacking. Would you like to see how some of my other muscles have grown?" he smiles, adjusting his kimono.

"Indeed, I don't know why I worry about you at all!" I laugh.

Machiko scurries over and smoothes down the bedding. We retire behind the curtains.

"Ah, I love the smell of the fresh air," he says, breathing in the scents arising from the wet garden. He catches me to him. "But not as much as I love your scent!"

We sink into the quilts. He knows well that it takes minimal stimulation to arouse me, and quickly ascertains that my garden is as wet as the one beyond the doors. He pulls me onto his cock, me on my back, legs wrapped around his waist, him kneeling, pulling on my wrists, pressing me tight against his belly.

Later, I hear him gasp, "I love making you scream like that." I am only vaguely aware of my own sounds, but now I hear myself as he continues to thrust deeper and faster, and know anyone along this hall who has left the doors open to the garden will be able to hear me, but I don't care. He rolls under me, pulls me on top of him. "Let me be your stallion," he whispers. He rolls with me so fiercely that when I come back to myself, one of my arms is extended over the doorsill, the sleeve of my kimono soaked with rain.

"You have conquered me, my young warrior," I pant.

"Are you conquered?" he asks, pressing his forehead against mine. "Body and soul?"

"Body and soul," I concede.

"How did we get over here?" he laughs.

"I don't know."

"You are soaked," he says. He strips off my underlayer, laughing, drags me back over to the pile of pillows and quilts tossed helter-skelter.

"Looks more like a hurricane than a spring storm," I pant, surveying the damage.

"You are a force of nature," he marvels. "I am the luckiest man in the world to possess the key to unleashing your taifun."

"And a very fine key it is," I say, stroking his now limp cock.

"I can be hard again in another few minutes," he offers.

We collapse on the tangled mound of kimonos. "Then I'll have to call you a maidservant," I say. "Mercy, my lord. Do you not see my flag of surrender?"

"Are you quite sure you are satisfied?

"Beyond all previous imaginings of what satisfied can be," I laugh.

"Shall we fetch some fresh bedclothes, mistress?" Machiko and another maidservant bow.

"Yes, please." She helps me into a transparent light silk garment. Atsumori and I lie spent in each other's arms until they have fixed a fresh dry nest for us. Then we crawl weakly into the center of the bed.

"I think I am more likely to die of excess with you than on the battlefield," he says, draping his arm limply across me. And without another word, both of us die into sleep.

Strangled cries and a heavy blow to my hip awake me. I bolt upright, heart hammering. Atsumori thrashes and cries out beside me, then leaps to his feet, knees bent in a crouch. His hand darts to his hip, as if searching for his sword. "Get away!" he cries. His eyes snap open and he glances wildly around the room.

"Are you all right?" I cry.

"Oh!" He folds back onto his knees. "It was a nightmare." He collapses on to his back, breathing as if he had just galloped through enemy lines. I roll tentatively onto my knees and shuffle to his side, cradling my right hip. He must have hit me with a knee; my hip will be badly bruised.

"Are you all right, my lord?"

His hand is splayed across his forehead, his chest heaving up and down as if he had just galloped an enormous distance.

"It's nothing," he says, trembling. "I am ashamed for you to see my weakness like that."

"There is no weakness in succumbing to one's dreams. Tell me about it."

He shakes his head, his hand still covering his face. I look up to see Machiko standing silently at a distance, waiting to see if there is anything she might offer.

"Some mint cloths and tea," I mouth to her. Mint is a powerful remedy against nightmare. She quickly returns with cotton cloths soaking in cool mint water, which I drape across his brow. "You always boast of my sorcery. Will you allow me to help you?"

"Thank you. Truly, it's not worth all your trouble."

"It's no trouble at all."

"Fetch some sake," he orders Machiko. She nods and brings it.

"Just take some of the tea as well," I coax. "The sake is more likely to lead to dreams. The mint will calm and cool them."

"The sake will steady me. I'm so ashamed."

"Please. There is nothing to be ashamed of. Anyone who has gone--I can't imagine the horrors you have been through." After he finishes the tea and sake we lie beside each other again. His eyes still appear dark and haunted. I know without his speaking it that he is afraid to close them.

"Tell me about it," I urge. "The power of a dream dissipates with the telling of it."

"It's ridiculous," he sighs.

"It's just me."

"I don't want you to be disturbed as well."

"I'll be all right. Let me share the burden with you. Surely it is the least service I can perform for your great bravery."

"All right. I took two heads in the first battle. I had them fastened by their topknots to my saddle. Kiyosune had one. You ride with them, you know, and it frightens the enemy when they see us galloping into battle with those heads. You leave your armor bloody--Yoritomo's forces kept retreating before us after that first battle. It's just…after…the heads start to stink. The way they rot, the way they decay…" he shudders. "It's like those men you killed are with you; you can't leave them behind. The jaws sag open, showing the teeth, like they want to bite." He lies back on the pillows. I can feel his belly shaking. "In my dream, it was those heads…coming at me with their mouths wide open like that. They were saying, 'One day it will be your head.'"

Horror freezes my blood. I knew they brought back heads from battle, and displayed them on stakes, but we ladies are never allowed to catch sight of them. Not that I ever wanted to. I try to pull my brain out of paralysis, to find something comforting to say.

"I will purify you with some incense. That will banish those spirits and lay them to rest," I say, rising and clapping my hands for Machiko to bring a censer.

"That would be wonderful."

I give Machiko a list of the ingredients we need to concoct a banishing incense and she sets to work crumbling the necessary resins and dried plants together. I scatter the mixture on the glowing coals of the censer, and Machiko and I fan it around him with large rattan fans until the room is roiling with billows of aromatic smoke. We cleanse the room, ourselves, and Atsumori's page sleeping by the hall doorway as well. Throughout, I chant to Inari and Nakisawame-no-Mikoto, asking them to remove all vengeful ghosts, and invoke Kishi-Mujin, purifying goddess of pines and water, to banish any remaining negativity and darkness. Then I place bowls of salt water by two corners of the bed, bowls of earth at the other two.

"These will absorb all the negative influences," I assure him. "I should have thought of it before."

"Just as well you didn't. It would have looked like a mud slide in here," he smiles.

I am happy to see him restored to his flirtatious, bantering self.

"Thank you, Murasaki. I feel completely better now," he says. He lies back down. I encourage him to turn with his back towards me so I can lay on my left hip with my arms around him. My right hip will be too bruised to lie on for a time, but I don't want him to see that. He would be greatly remorseful to have accidentally hurt me. It seems we have only closed our eyes for a moment before the pale golden light of daybreak shimmers through our gauzy curtains. He turns towards me.

"Thank you so much for last night. You won't tell anyone, will you?"

"Of course not," I promise.

He puts a hand on my belly. "You know," he says huskily, "if you became pregnant, I would marry you in a moment. Even not knowing if it was mine or Kiyosune's. Even without my father's permission. You know that."

"Thank you," I reply, touched by his gallantry. "I will continue to take my teas. I'm sure your father will want you to make a better political alliance than what I can bring. But, I hope not for a long time yet."

"Not for a long time yet," he agrees. "I'll never give you up. Marriage or no marriage--I'll never give you up. Not until you throw me out--or they take my head."

"Hush," I say, placing my hands on either side of his neck. "With all those charms around your neck, how could that happen?"

"It couldn't," he asserts cheerfully. He kisses my hands and rolls out of bed.

Chapter Nineteen
Spring, 1182

There has been a terrible famine resulting from the drought. The crops have completely failed in most of the fiefs near Kyoto and far away, though there are some, like Sessho and Seishan's properties in Tanba, which are still producing well. The dry spells were followed by crushing hailstorms which obliterated the young rice stalks. Then people began getting sick, with a plague that does not respond well to medicine or exorcism. There is much sickness and death in the capital and in the outlying areas as well. People are panicking, abandoning their fields and shops and fleeing into the mountains or the seashore or wherever they think they will be safe, spreading the plague as they travel.

The only blessing in this situation is that hostilities between the Genji and the Heike have ceased. There is not enough rice to keep the warriors in fighting condition, and they must be used to regain control of the frightened peasants. The Imperial Army is organizing groups of men to gather and burn the bodies; we hear horrifying tales of huts being burned with whole families, the sick and the well, the living and the dead, trapped inside them.

Throughout the capital, people are chattering about how we must be entering into 'the last days of the Law', referring to various Buddhist scriptures prophesying the end of civilized times and the beginning of an age of lawlessness and war. Tokushi suggested to Munemori that I perform divination using the technique of kama-oroshi; causing the deity to descend and speak through me. "Since it is Inari who is withholding her bounty and her harvest, one who grew up on Inari's mountain should attempt to divine the source of Inari's anger with us, to determine how the imbalances may be rectified," she said. I expressed the thought that it might be better to pilgrimage to the Shrine of Inari and ask the High Priestess there to do it, but Tokushi insisted that only I could be completely trusted. "We can't

161

risk gossip and betrayal, and we can't be certain every single person on Inari's mountain is loyal to us." Munemori agreed, so an auspicious time was set for the divination, to take place in the closely guarded privacy of the Rokuhara Mansion.

I approach the brazier wearing a headdress and extremely heavy and stiff outer robes, dressed as an Inari Priestess; though I was never initiated, Tokushi has the utmost confidence that I can speak with the voice of Inari.

Slow dance of drugs in my blood, I enter that state of dual consciousness where a part of my mind is watching me move towards the brazier, feeling the descent of the Inari kami into my being. The Inari kami has the essence of both male and female; I usually think of her as female, but tonight I feel the presence of both, the sacred marriage settling within me. I sense the presence of the fox aspect of Inari as well, the soft fur of a fox's tail brushing up against my ankles as it curls up at my feet. Though I know it is spirit presence only, it is very vivid. I sway like rice plants in the wind. My body adopts a certain rigid posture as the dancing of the flames in the brazier starts to penetrate my consciousness. The flames ripple and unfold into images. Tokushi is here, as are Tsunemasa, Koremori, Shigehira and Michinori. Munemori was unable to attend but has sent one of his pages to transcribe the trance. Scribes are perched unobtrusively all around, ready to take notes on whatever I say. Suddenly all the people recede, leaving only the fire and this force pushing down into me, so much larger than anything a human can hold that I feel nauseous, as if the palm of a giant hand is pushing me into the ground, so heavy it crushes all the individual consciousness out of me. Just before my mind winks out I wonder if I can survive this channeling again.

When I regain consciousness I am lying on my back, taking deep breaths of cool air. Machiko's moon-like face ripples into being above me. She seems very far away, almost as distant as the moon itself. I smile, thinking of Machiko as the Moon Goddess, or the woman in Chinese myth, Chang-o, who stole the vial of immortality and fled to the moon with her rabbit. The flicker of torches makes for a strange, undulating patchwork of light. My first impression is that I am in a cave; then I realize it is just the fantastic pattern of shadows being cast over a meditation room in the gardens of the Rokuhara Mansion, which is where we started out. A female voice, familiar but unidentifiable, asks if I am all right. Sound ripples out of Machiko, replying that my breathing is good, and that my heart is still skipping occasionally but mostly steady. I wonder, if my breathing and heart are so good, why I still feel so disembodied. Something cold is pressing into my right hand. I slowly turn my head to that side. It is as if my head must pass through six different universes before it can turn far enough for me to see a ghostly, elongated version of Tokushi kneeling beside me. She has pressed a dark green jade rabbit belonging to Antoku into my hand. "Remember how he said the rabbit would bring you back?" she says in that eerie, far-off voice. I am taken back to the time, shortly before going on this journey, when Antoku heard that I was going to be channeling, and gave me this rabbit, saying, "Don't worry, you can always come back on the rabbit." He had overheard me saying to Tokushi that I did not know whether I could survive going on another trance journey. I never would have said it if I had known he was listening; he appeared to be playing far across the room. But I should know by now that there is not much that child misses; though he is only five, he is preternaturally aware. There is something about the heavy stone cold solidity of the object in my hand that does seem to be helping; at least now my hand feels real.

Black Dragon tea is brought and put to my lips. My body feels impossibly cold, heavy, and huge, as if the oversized presence of the kami still lingered. The tea vanishes down my throat, each swallow leaving my mouth as dry as it was before. My mother said that too much of the trance-inducing drugs can weaken a person's life force, and that trance mediums do not tend to live long as a result. I remind myself to breathe into my body, though there is still so much of it I cannot feel. Eventually I vomit black bile into a bowl and they give me some ginger mint water. The heavy feeling begins to pass.

By the time I am recovered, all the men who had been in attendance are gone. Tokushi is across the room having her hair brushed, getting ready for bed.

"Are you feeling better?" she asks.

I nod. "What did I say?"

Tokushi nods for one of the female scribes to read from her notes.

The female scribe reads: "The duty of the stag is to protect the herd. If the stag goes mad, goring the does and fawns under his care, hope is lost. The sacred sword is cut from the tail of the serpent. The serpent is angry and comes to reclaim it." These words must refer to the magical sword that is one of the three sacred pieces of regalia that have been with the monarchy from the beginning. It sounds ominous, but what does it mean? There have been earthquakes, and that often drives serpents out of their holes.

163

The scribe continues at my signal. "The child holds the sword; the Naga King has called for it. Battle between the white and the red; white as bone, red as blood. The earth breaks apart from the heavens. Imbalance and unrest in the hearts of men, imbalance and unrest in the heart of nature. One side withholds life-giving waters, the other destroys through flooding and hail. Wa is abandoned."

I hold up my hand, needing time to think. Wa means harmony, but is also an ancient word for Japan, the Japan at the time of the sorceress queens. I nod, and the scribe continues. "The crescent moon becomes a bow; the hail becomes arrows. The power of Inari is both mother and father, the power of the sacred lovers. Love fertilizes the earth. Where is the sacred marriage? Where is the union of north and south, of east and west? Without the fertilizing rains of love, no child can grow in the belly. Without love between brothers and sisters of the realm, no grain can grow in the belly of the earth. The serpent writhes in a thousand pieces. Restore peace, and health will be restored. Restore peace, and prosperity will be restored. Marriages and alliances are required. It is the smallest creatures that steal the grain. It is the smallest minds that steal the prosperity of the nation. The Priestesses of Ise and Inari must meet and hold council. The sky and the earth pull away from each other. The sun and moon darken apart from each other. This is a sign of destruction."

It is unfortunate that the kami have such a habit of talking in riddles. But certainly the body of the message, that peace is required, is clear. However, I don't imagine that this is a message Munemori or any of his compatriots want to hear. What can they do to restore peace as long as Yoritomo, Yoshitsune and Yoshinaka are pressing their case against us?

"How did the others react when they heard this message?" I ask.

Tokushi shrugs. Her maids are getting her undressed.

"Oh...you know men. Talk about a ban on war, you might as well be talking about a ban on penises."

I laugh, coming fully into my body. It is so unlike Tokushi to make such an irreverent and bawdy comment, particularly concerning her own relatives.

"Of course," she says, "you also mentioned, towards the end of your trance, that you needed to go to Tanba to be in the presence of the sacred marriage as exemplified by Sessho and Seishan. Rather self-serving," she sniffs.

"We had an agreement before I did the trance that you would allow me to go there in recompense for risking my life again," I remind her.

"As if Inari would allow anything to happen to you," she chides me. "But yes, I agreed, and yes, you shall be allowed to go. And perhaps you will find out something about why their province is thriving while so many are failing."

"They did not exactly say 'thriving,'" I caution, referring to their last letter. "They said they had enough to feed their own people, but not as much as they usually have to tithe to the crown."

"Well, they are close to the only ones who have anything at all to send to the crown right now. So yes, you may go and find out if they have secrets which they have not chosen to share with us, or perhaps even secrets of which they are unaware." She pats her futon, and I crawl over to collapse exhaustedly beside her. She nods to her maids who arrange curtains all around the bed to give us privacy. She strokes my cheek and kisses my eyebrows, lips and eyelids.

"Now, that wasn't so bad, was it?" she asks.

There is no way I can express to her how difficult it is to make that journey into spirit, and how exhausting it is to return.

"My life is yours," I say. "You may throw it away on a visioning if you wish."

"Hush! I will not hear that talk," she says, continuing to caress me. "You always come back fine and you always will." Though I can see that she is aroused and wanting loving tonight, there is simply no way I can oblige her. I fall asleep in her arms.

Chapter Twenty
Spring/Summer 1182

Four days later Machiko and the maids pack everything we need for a trip to Sessho and Seishan's. We ride in a palanquin rather than a carriage--the famine has left little fodder for the horses, and the Kiyomoris' are reluctant to let any horses leave the palace stables in any case. The value of horses has soared due to the war. We are accompanied by a phalanx of soldiers. Tokushi grumbles some about how much rice is required to feed all the men needed. I argue that there have been no hostilities anywhere near Tanba in months, and that I need only a few soldiers, but she insists on sending them anyway. In spite of her protestations, however, I rather suspect she is sending them so that Sessho and Seishan will have to feed them. The court will actually be saving rice rather than spending it. But perhaps she is genuinely concerned about my safety as well; desperate times make for desperate men and the incidence of theft has grown.

Machiko and I are happy to be returning to our respective beloveds, and the journey is without incident. Morning glories and moonflowers tendril over the casements of the Tanba mansions, white and indigo disks swaying in the breeze. The courtyard is lined with posts tied together to dry fish; it is the time of year when the sea trout come up the streams. Racks and racks of fish are drying out in the back as well. Machiko trips off to the kitchen to meet Yanagi. Seishan reaches for me, but Kikuko gets there first, wrapping her arms around me fiercely, pressing her head against my belly. A soft golden glow radiates from my womb, recognizing the one she carried.

"Finally! You are back," she exclaims, nuzzling against my diaphragm as I stroke her shiny hair. "I didn't think I could live without you another day!"

Just then, six boys come rushing by--Matsu and his two cousins, wearing red bands around their foreheads, chasing three servant boys wearing white ones. "Catch the traitors!" Matsu cries. "Don't let them escape!"

"Matsu!" Seishan exclaims as a cloud of dust kicked up by the boys settles on our garments, but they race on, brandishing wooden swords, caught in the drama of their game. With a sharp clacking of clashing swords, the boys in white turn and desperately try to stave off their pursuers.

"You'll die now, Yoritomo!" yells Matsu.

"Cursed traitors!" shouts one of his cousins. He whacks a servant boy on the arm with his sword, causing the boy to yelp and stagger back. The boys collide with one of the drying racks, cascading the fish into the dust. A grim-faced guard stalks over, grabs the serving boys by their collars, and shakes them.

"But they made us do it," one of the boys pleads. The servant boys yip as he administers stinging cuffs, then slink off. The guard glares at Matsu and his cousins. "Your fathers will not be pleased," he says curtly.

Seishan shakes her head. "Boys." She puts a hand on Kikuko's head. "Girls are so much easier. Although," she says, leading us into the house, "honestly, Nori is as bad as her brothers. Kikuko is my only child with any sense these days."

My daughter smiles, looking pleased at the praise, raising first my hand, then Seishan's to brush up against her face. "I don't like to play war," she says. "I like to be peaceful."

"Peace is much better," I agree.

"Can we put on some smocks and do some painting?" she asks hopefully.

"Let your Auntie get some rest first," Seishan says. "Why don't you come in the bath with us and then we'll see about painting."

"All right." Kiku skips down the hall, calling for her nurse to get her ready for the bathhouse.

Matsu and his cousins are disciplined by not having any dinner that night, the strictest punishment I have ever seen Sessho mete out to one of his children. I am so glad that Kikuko was holding tightly to me at the time and therefore not deprived of her meal. Sometimes parents must be strict to raise good children, but I am grateful I do not have to be the one to make such decisions, though I agree if the children ruin food so carelessly it is only fair they should experience the consequences of going without. I feel a pang whenever I look at Matsu's empty place, but Sessho and Seishan seem completely relaxed. I wonder if Antoku will be as wild as Matsu in a few years.

I chat with Nori and Tomomori about how war has been set aside because of the drought and plague.

"It's dry here, too," Tomomori says, "much drier than usual. Father is going to hire some shamans to chant for the rain. Perhaps you could help."

"I'd be happy to do anything I can."

Sessho raises his eyebrows at me when no one else is looking, and I stop eating so no one will notice how my chopsticks tremble. I can never remember, when I am away, just how handsome he is, how his hawk nose and deep-set eyes and the light suffusing them turn me inside out in a way that none of the pretty painted men at court can do. Atsumori and Kiyosune charm me, making me feel girlish and playful. Sessho makes me feel like a priestess, as if I were channeling Inari, but without the drugs or the sickness. With my young men, I am a tree in flower, they the breeze, ruffling my blossoms. Sessho ripens me, heavy with fruit; his roots twine with mine, weaving me deep into the earth.

His outer robes tonight are forest green, slender capillaries of gold thread glinting in the lamplight. I try hard to respond equally to everyone at the table, politely answering questions from his brothers and their wives, concealing how badly I want to dissolve into the warmth of Sessho's strong arms.

Blessedly, the dinner ends early. "I did not provide entertainment for tonight, thinking you might be tired," Sessho says. He nods to his siblings and their families. "Please excuse us while we escort our guest to her rooms."

As we glide down the highly polished cherry-wood hall, Sessho says, "We have made some improvements to our pleasure garden. I hope you are not too tired..."

"I'm never too tired for the pleasure garden," I respond, touching the bicep beneath his sleeve.

"Wait 'til you see," Seishan says.

A kneeling servant slides open the door at the end of the hall and we lift our robes as we walk down the steps. The crushed quartz path ahead of us has been lined with stone lanterns bearing the sun on one side and the crescent moon on the other.

"What a wonderful idea," I whisper.

"Yes, well, they are sacred lanterns," Sessho boasts. "We had to get special permission to put them to this use."

"We added a shrine to the back of the garden, so we could have the lanterns," Seishan beams, "although--for devotional purposes also," she hastens to add.

"No one is more devoted to Inari and Benten than I am," Sessho grins rakishly. As the path winds up behind the hedge, I see they have also installed twinkling paper lanterns, red, yellow, green and peach, strung between the trees and the hedge.

"Oh, it's magical," I breathe, gazing at the ivory and flower patterned comforters that have been arranged for us.

"The Priestess approves?" Sessho smiles, taking my hands and pulling me down beside him. Seishan curls up to me on my other side. Pulling a strand of my hair towards her face, she sniffs. "Ooh, did you add something to your scent?"

"Our main purveyor of pine and musk no longer sends his wares to court, having joined the traitors. We have switched to a different perfumer. I'm afraid the quality may be slightly inferior."

"Mmmm--not inferior," Seishan says, "just different, slightly different."

"You have always had the most sensitive nostrils," I say, kissing her on the tip of her tiny nose.

"It's true, she always knows what will smell best on me," Sessho smiles fondly, reaching across me to run an appreciative finger along his wife's jaw line. "Ever since she amended my perfumes, I have been quite irresistible."

"Mmmm, quite," Seishan agrees, "though I wasn't doing such a good job of resisting you in the first place."

"And lucky you did not," I say. "In the trance I performed shortly before leaving the Capital, I saw that it was the perfection of your marriage that has protected the crops here in your district."

Seishan has perched herself in Sessho's lap, and he is expertly peeling off her layers of kimonos.

"We hear that Yoritomo has laid waste to the Province of Izu and that the peasants have been burned out of their homes, crops trampled and destroyed by invading horsemen. No wonder the earth has turned her back on them," Sessho says, running a finger over the jade necklace resting on my collarbone.

"Sometimes I fear our own clan, the Heike, have done as much harm as the Genji. Did the gods say anything of this in your trance?" Seishan asks.

"Inari said that the destructive passions of warriors have translated into unruly weather. But when men are so stubborn and warlike, what can we do?"

Sessho shrugs off his outer layers of robes like a snake sliding off his skin. "Who can know why a man would prefer to wield a sword of a mere thousand beatings," he queries, referring to samurai swords, which are said to be melted, forged and reforged a thousand times to make the strongest steel, "when he could be enjoying the sword of ten thousand throbbings that Inari gave him?" He illustrates this comment by placing both of his ladies' hands upon the sword of which he speaks, and political discourse ceases for some while. Indeed if all men were like Sessho, we should have no war; all the men would be busy contenting their women with love-makings and rice and all the silks and jewels that rice can buy.

I do believe it is the sacred marriage between Sessho and Seishan that keeps their land healthy, since they are living the example of Inari. Sessho rules so justly, refraining from the brutal taxes that so often equal luxury for the ruling class and starvation for the farmers, that even the poorest peasants have both hope and food for their bellies. I put that in my report to Tokushi, though I know that many nobles at court who would never think of starving their horses will find it an amusing 'woman's soft foolishness' to be concerned with the fate of the peasants.

One day, Sessho organizes turtle races. Servants catch a number of turtles in a nearby stream. They make a circle outlined with stones in the courtyard while the children mark the turtles' shells with paint, naming them and claiming them for their own. The turtles are placed in the center of the circle; whichever turtle crawls to the perimeter of stones first is the winner and its 'owner' gets a prize for its efforts. We adults join in too, naming our turtles and marking them. Sessho's turtle is almost always reliably last.

"Alas, that is me!" he cries in mock distress. "So slow! So lazy! I shall have to keep giving my regrets to Munemori and Shigehira. They keep wanting me to raise up armies and join them in battle. I shall have to explain to them that mine is the slowest turtle of all, and that is why I am so slow to respond."

"It's our rice that is feeding their armies," Seishan says. "We can't send soldiers and rice both. I don't want to hear about you leading armies in any case. One of your brothers can go. There are plenty of retainers we can trust to take troops if they insist."

"You don't think much of my war-like capabilities, do you?" he says, catching her in an embrace that leaves her invisible under his swooping sleeves. She pushes away, flushed. "You'll have to make war with me before you go anywhere," she says scowling. "I shall nail your feet to the floor if I have to."

"You are so much more frightening than the Genji," Tomomori says. "Perhaps you and that warrior woman, Tomoe, should go at it head to head! A duel to the death! Whichever side wins, wins the country!"

"Your mother would certainly win. Soon Tomoe would be heading for the hills, I am confident about that," Sessho agrees. Nori bridles. "If anyone should be fighting Tomoe, it should be me! I'm just as good with a bow as you are!" she snaps at her brother.

"Not on horse you aren't," he retorts.

"Standing still I am."

"Well, people don't stand still during battle," he says.

"I could lead the armies!" Nori insists.

"That is the most ridiculous thing I have ever heard! A fourteen-year-old girl leading an army!" Seishan shakes her head and looks at me. "The fevers of adolescence have addled her mind."

"My passion for justice, no fevers!" Nori cries. "If you go, I am going with you," she says to her father.

"No one from our household will be going as long as I can help it," he says. "Like my turtle, I am a master of delay. I still have many excuses up my sleeves, and right now my excuse is that I need to stay here and grow rice."

"Tomoe is as good a fighter as any of them, and she's not that much older than me," Nori persists. "They say Yoshinaka never goes anywhere without her and Yamabuki. He is one of the fiercest warriors, and women are his bodyguards. That's the problem with the Heike, they're all so old-fashioned!" she shouts, stomping her foot, barely missing a turtle that has finally made its way to the periphery.

"Hey, watch out, you almost hit my turtle!" Matsu cries, grabbing the creature up protectively.

"My turtle wins again!" he yelps cheerfully. "Some warrior you are! Your turtle is still standing in the middle!" he taunts his oldest sister.

171

"Turtles have nothing to do with warfare," she retorts. "This is a game. War is not a game."

"Neither is it a maiden's hobby," her mother snipes. At that, Nori stalks off. But later, when the servants set up archery targets, she comes back dressed in a man's costume and stands thudding arrow after arrow into the center of the targets. She does have very good aim.

"I told you all this learning would be bad for her," Seishan complains to her husband. "She doesn't know if she is a boy or a girl." Sessho simply stands there, beaming proudly at his eldest.

"How will we ever get this girl married?" Seishan turns to me pleadingly.

"She is only fourteen. We still have a couple of years. Many of the girls at court find the stories of Tomoe, Yamabuki and Yoshinaka to be very romantic."

"Are they out shooting bows and arrows like Nori-chan?"

"Well, no, the Empress would never agree to that," I admit.

"Maybe she should come here and try to talk some sense into my daughter."

"Maybe I should take Nori-chan to court. She is of an age, and it would give her something to do"

"I know what men at court are like," Sessho chimes in darkly. "I am not sending my beautiful daughter there."

Beautiful is a bit of a stretch. Nori is broad-shouldered and strong for a girl, and not just strong in her arms, but headstrong as well. Though I love her wildness and freedom of spirit, finding a man who is strong enough to tame that wildness without breaking it will be challenging. Unlike Seishan, I do not find it difficult to imagine her at the head of a column of soldiers. Certainly she is bossy enough. But I do not wish to raise Seishan's ire by saying so.

"Marriage is crucial for a girl, and the court would provide a feminizing influence," I say, thinking how much I would enjoy having Nori at court with me.

"With things so unsettled, it's out of the question. No, we are keeping her safe here," Sessho says firmly. "It is pleasant to think that the rebels will soon be starved into submission, but our side has been starving too, so I fear this is an intermission only, and not an end to this war. I do not want my daughter in the center of a city that combatants will soon be wrestling for. I don't want you there, either," he says to me. "But loyalty and obligation forbid me to try to keep you here as well."

"True, only two weeks this time," I say.

"Perhaps a well-timed illness," Seishan suggests imploringly.

"I really dare not," I say. "The Empress will feel abandoned if I stay too long in this time of crises. We must preserve her good-will so that another visit may happen."

"Of course," Seishan agrees. "I did not mean to be disloyal. I sound like a rebel myself, don't I?"

"Not at all. Only a loving woman with a big heart," Sessho says, patting her on the top of the head.

The twins come over to each side of her and hug her. Though not quite six, they almost come up to her shoulders. "It is clear I shall be the shortest one in the whole family when these two grow a bit more," Seishan says. "Look how much bigger than I the other two are already! Heavens, Nori is almost as tall as her father. I'm glad she waited until after she was born to turn into a giant."

"I remember you thought she was a giant at the time," I say.

"It's lucky we forget these things," Seishan agrees.

Meanwhile, Nori and her brother have been firing at the targets, insulting each other the whole time. Frustrated that his sister is outstripping him, Tomomori orders the servants to get his horse from the stables and set up the riding targets. You would think they were both boys, the way they carry on. One does not expect a girl and a boy to have such rivalry between them, but Nori is no ordinary girl. My own daughter is far more feminine, always dressing up and having her servant arrange her hair in different ways. Playing with her dolls and telling elaborate stories about them gives her great joy. She has absolutely no interest in weaponry or war, although her 'twin' follows his older brother like a worshipful shadow and wants to do everything he does. He and the other younger boys in the compound race around on their wooden stick horses, shouting, and having all manner of wild battles with their wooden swords, which results in not a few skinned knees and elbows and split lips which they show off proudly as war wounds. Kikuko prefers quiet games. She shares Seishan's love of birds and delights in coaxing them to her finger or peering into their nests. She is especially fond of the baby birds.

"They're so ugly!" Sessho teases her. "Why do you like them so much?"

"I like them *because* they are ugly," she replies firmly.

One of the few games she and her brother both enjoy is hide and seek. That game they play very frequently, and they are quite good at it. Where most children would giggle and give themselves away, they rarely do. Once they have secreted themselves wherever they are going, we find them less than half the time. They place themselves in areas where we would never think to look--somehow getting up into the rafters with the help of a servant, curling themselves under cushions in such a way that the cushions seem not to have been disturbed. They have such a passion for invisibility I think that not only my daughter, but my adopted twin son, have inherited my fox-like characteristics. Seishan says, "Next thing you know, they will be climbing over the wall of the palace," referring to my exploit of allegedly making myself invisible so I could climb over the palace wall and find Tokushi, many years ago.

"Hopefully they will have no such necessity," I say.

During one such game of hide-and-seek I ask to hide with the twins, and they show me a remarkable secret. They usher me through a trapdoor in Sessho's study, which leads underneath the house. We crouch among the stored grain and jars of foodstuffs, and then they show me how to run through the maze of support beams and storage jars to another trapdoor leading to yet another room. Now I understand how they have been able to appear under cushions that we had searched just moments before. A system of trapdoors and passageways runs underneath the house, all of them invisible to the untutored eye. I ask who showed them this and they say they discovered it by themselves. They seem enormously pleased at their own cleverness. I promise to keep their secret.

The chanting and water-sprinkling rituals performed by the shamans have done their work. An orchestra of rain plays across the tile roof, drips from the gutters. A chorus of frogs from the garden ponds shouts their gratitude. Sessho and I are in his study making love on a futon arranged for that purpose. A brazier burning nearby flutters its warmth towards us; another smolders with heady scents of pine and copal. The dry parchment scent of the scrolls tucked neatly into their cubbyholes adds an interesting undertone.

"It's raining so hard," I pant, as he rolls me onto my back, slinging one of my legs over his shoulder.

"That's not rain, it's rice."

It is true: the drops of rain clattering against the tiles sound as if the gods are casting rice on the roof.

"Oh! Plow my field!" I call out as he strokes deeply into me.

"It shall be plowed and watered," he promises. "Keep thinking of the rice."

We have dedicated this love-making to the summer rice. Each time we kiss, mouths swirling into liquid, I close my eyes and see the rice, heavy and verdant, paddies stretching green as lily pads, up into the hills.

We shift positions again, and my legs twine with his as he arches his back, pressing my hands deep into the silks with his. We are wearing nothing except for the matching green robes that he had made for us, making love in them so I can carry our mingled scent back with me to Kyoto. I scream, releasing my own torrential waters.

"Favor us, Inari, favor us. Bless us with a good crop," Sessho conjures. Sensations rise up through me like a fountain: I hear my own cries, as if from a distance; see white birds, circling. Our panting is like the sweet moaning of doves. His eyes are deep as night, and bright as day.

"I love you. I'll always love you."

"I'll find you," he promises. "In the next life, I'll find you. Marry me."

"I marry you. I marry you." The boundaries of our ribs dissolve, our hearts meld and merge. Saltwater streams flow from my eyes. "Come with me now," I whisper. My brain dissolves into light.

Unfortunately, the fortnight I have been allowed passes as quickly as if it had been two days. The Empress made very clear that I could have a fortnight and no more. What if the plague should reach the palace? What if war should suddenly resume? She was of no mind to once again have me stuck for months in Tanba.

They send me back with a couple of robes that have been made for me--the green one, which matches Sessho's, and an indigo one with patterns of dark branches bearing a few cherries which will be perfect for the gloomy mood at court.

Though I hate leaving, this time when I go back to the Empress, I return peaceful about my decision to leave Kikuko here, seeing how happy she is. I hope that all of them will stay forever in Tanba, unthreatened by war, famine or pestilence; that the magic of their love will keep the circle inviolate.

Chapter Twenty-One
Summer 1182

A year has passed since Tokushi promised to send for Tsubame. Finally, with Shigehira's troops posted everywhere, Tokushi agreed it was safe to send a carriage to fetch Tsubame. But the men came back without her, saying that she was ill with the sweating sickness, and could not be moved. Finally a letter arrives:

"Grandmother says to tell you I have recovered from my illness. I am sorry to trouble you, but I have grown over the last year and need more robes, so that when it is time for me to marry, I shall have a suitable dowry. I miss you and hope to be with you soon."

I read over and over the first line. 'Grandmother says to tell you.' Tsubame never states that she was ill. Could her grandmother have locked her up and concocted the story of the sweating sickness, which is highly contagious, to frighten the soldiers into going back without her?

I write back, "No need to worry about the dowry yet, since first you must come to court and choose from among the gentlemen the Empress selects for you. I am sending you some more cloth; the white and black pattern may seem plain, but it is very sophisticated and suitable for a girl at court. I have also sent silks in that washed, yellowy green that you favor, and a coral outer robe, to embroider as you please, with a selection of madders and pinks for inner garments, now that you are old enough to wear such."

There is enough cloth in the package to make sixteen to twenty robes. Even if she has grown some, her old things can be used for inner robes. I don't want to send too much, thinking that her grandmother is more likely to send her to court if she knows that is the only way to get the material goods she craves.

I pen a separate letter to her grandmother, telling her I have procured a necklace of biwa pearls I shall be sending her as soon as Tsubame is sent to court.

"It will be difficult for your grandmother's heart to part with such a pearl, but we must consider her future, and she is at an age to be seeking a husband. Awesomely, the Empress herself has taken an interest, taking it upon herself to make a list of men at court she believes to be suitable. She will see to it that Tsubame has properly supervised visits with all of them, and that one parallel to Tsubame's temperament and the ambitions of your family will be chosen. Naturally, she may return to visit you on occasion."

Weeks pass, with no answer from Tsubame or her grandmother. Finally I cajole the Empress into lending me a phalanx of soldiers to be sent with a palanquin, under strict orders not to return without Tsubame.

When they return, the palanquin is empty. Tokushi's eyes flash, and the leader of the regiment's face goes quite gray as he kneels and offers her a letter. She inclines her chin towards me, indicating I may read over her shoulder. I sway, bumping Tokushi's shoulder slightly. Machiko's strong hand grips my sash, holding me up.

"Please tell the Empress, most exalted one, I am most grateful for her participation in finding a suitable husband for my granddaughter, Tsubame. If only I had known sooner! However, there are several fine lords closer by who have shown an interest. Having been raised in the country, I believe she would be most happy with a country lord. While city men are often lost in other distractions, a country lord relies upon his wife, and values her the more for it. Our family line, humble, without distinction, and nearly extinguished, is not worthy of the honor shown us by her Eminence, yet we shall always remember it."

"Prepare the screens so we may have a private audience," Tokushi orders her servants. In a few moments we are sequestered behind screens in a private room.

"How insulting!" she says. "*Thank* the Empress? As if my choices would not be a thousand times more elevated than hers! Why...they are so far to the north...you don't think she could be interviewing *traitors* for your daughter's hand, do you?"

Chills race through my body, leaving me shivering. "May it not be so!"

"This borders on treason," Tokushi says, and the way she narrows her eyes makes her look, for a moment, much like her mother.

"My lady, I beg your permission to leave immediately, so that I may bring Tsubame back myself. The soldiers will not fail if I am with them. Lady

Harima has been countering your will for over a year now. Your direct order, Madam!"

"This in no way can be countenanced," Tokushi agrees. "I am tempted to go there myself, and demand that she be handed over immediately. It will be very difficult for the soldiers to be spared at this time, however. If it is not the monks, it's the easterners, if it is not the easterners, it's the northerners, and if it's not them, it's traitors within our own ranks. I simply don't know what Munemori will say when I ask for soldiers to make the journey again. Shigehira is assembling a vast army to take back the province of Echizen."

"I believe Taira Sessho would spare some of his soldiers for the purpose, and--"

She doesn't allow me to finish. "That would hardly carry the weight of sending soldiers with my insignia. It's just distracting. We can't leave the country homes undefended, what with armies of thieves and thieving armies striking so unpredictably...as soon as soldiers can be spared...I will send my order right away. Why can't things go right again?" she frets. "I just know my brother is so preoccupied with the rebels now, he is going to consider this a very trivial matter. Though I assure you," she says, laying her hand over mine, "that *I* do not consider it a trivial matter, that we should be thwarted in this way. The insult! We can have her married to one of the highest ranking men in the kingdom! A country lord!"

I am happy to see her so agitated. At least I know that she is fully on my side in this.

"This is intolerable. You were right about that woman. I have given her every respect due her age and what I imagine to be her tremendous loneliness, but this is simply not to be borne. I shall write a reply myself and command her in no uncertain terms that your daughter must be sent immediately. As soon as we can spare the soldiers to guard her, it shall be done. If Munemori had not specified that the troops be returned to active duty immediately, I should do it at once."

"Thank you, my lady." I press my head to the floor. " I promise that Tsubame will be as loyal and devoted to you as I am myself."

"Well, of course," Tokushi smiles, "how could it be otherwise?"

Naturally, since Kiyomori died, Munemori, Shigehira and the other Taira are constantly plotting strategy against Yoritomo and his allies. For me, nothing is more important than rescuing Tsubame, but even I can see that from the perspective of the kingdom, this is a very small concern.

Weeks pass. Finally a small battalion of soldiers is released for the purpose, and sent to fetch Tsubame.

Five days later, a messenger appears and is ushered into our presence in the Empress' quarters. My heart leaps, knowing that he is the one to announce my daughter's arrival so that we may be waiting for her in the courtyard. He prostrates himself. The other women look up from their sewing and writing. It is always exciting when a messenger arrives, even though this one is expected, and everyone knows he has come to announce Tsubame's arrival. Some of the women smile and nod, happy for me to be reunited with my daughter.

"My lady," he says, after the Empress has signaled for him to rise, "if I may be permitted." Tokushi has been seated behind a screen for propriety's sake, but I am seated outside the screen, wanting to be able to leap to my feet and rush to the courtyard immediately. Machiko edges over to me on her knees, beaming with delight, and grasps my hand. "You may share your message now," Tokushi says.

He bows again, bumping his head on the floor.

"My lady, I am sorry to be the bringer of tidings you may find less than desirable."

My heart stops. I hear Tokushi's sharp intake of breath.

"Convey your message immediately," she says.

"We have failed to bring back the Lady Tsubame. I bear a letter of explanation from her grandmother."

Sotsu-ko snatches the letter from his hand and passes it behind the kicho. Machiko and I slide behind the curtains towards Tokushi as quickly as possible, giving no thought to appearances.

"What does it say?" I cry anxiously.

Tokushi is trembling, the scroll in her hand shaking. All I can think is that my daughter must be dead.

"Don't keep me in agony," I beg, "is she still alive?"

Tokushi hands me the letter. It reads;

"Salutations to the Empress, and also to the mother of my Grandchild.

I hope you will join me in celebrating the marriage of my grand-daughter, Tsubame..."

I cry out, unable to help myself. Through a blaze of tears, the characters quiver and swim.

"...to the Lord Setsu-no-kanawara of Owari province. His wife recently died bearing him an heir, and he wed Tsubame on a most auspicious date. I shall miss her terribly, of course, and I deeply regret she could not have spent some of her youth serving so magnificent an Empress, with such a spotless reputation. But, of course, she was mine to give away, and as things have been so unsettled, I am certain you will be as happy as I to know that, whatever happens, she is safe in the countryside."

Whatever happens! That is tantamount to saying the northerners have a chance of winning! It is sheer treason even to allude to such a thing.

"It is entirely possible I shall have to have her executed," the Empress says coldly.

I re-read the missive in disbelief. That she would dare to defy the Empress in this way. Have I met this lord? What is he like?

"What do you know of this lord?"

"He has not declared for one side or another, but our recent requests for additional rice were met with insolence. He has sent only a trickle of rice, claiming that Yoritomo's soldiers have stolen everything from his fields, but we have recent information indicating that he has given much of the yield of his fields willingly to the rebel leaders. If not a member of the rebellion, he is certainly a part of the hidden alliance supporting them."

"Is he a good man, a kind man? How old is he?"

Tokushi frowns. "I hardly think that is what is most important here."

"Please, I need to know who has my daughter."

"I think he is about thirty-five. Neither especially handsome, nor outstandingly ugly--it hardly matters, Lady Fujiwara!"

I always know she is upset if she calls me by my formal name.

"What matters is that our will has been utterly flouted!"

What matters to me is that my daughter has been given to some man who she may not like, possibly without her consent. Surely I would have had a letter from her if she were permitted to write. She may be essentially a captive.

Some of the women sidle over, their robes making shushing sounds along the floor. I feel several hands press sympathetically against my back. Although they do not yet know the exact contents of the letter, they can tell from our expressions that the news is not good.

180

"I have not finished the letter," Tokushi says, "please hand it back."

"I have not finished it either. May we read it together?"

We kneel with our heads touching and read:

"I appreciate all Lady Fujiwara has done to support us in these paltry conditions. Lord Setsu-no-kanawara has kindly agreed that I shall join him and my granddaughter shortly, as he is having a mansion built for me, close to theirs. When it is complete, I shall be leaving this place. No doubt you shall wish to install the new lieutenant governor of the area here. I am sure Tsubame will write you when she is settled.

Yours with the greatest loyalty and respect--"

"Loyalty and respect!" Tokushi throws the letter across the room. She addresses the messenger.

"Regrettably, I must order you to ride back with all haste and intercept the returning soldiers. They must return to the Hokita mansion and place Lady Harima under arrest at once. She is not to leave her mansion, nor is she to be allowed to receive messengers or visitors."

"It shall be as you wish." We hear the messenger sliding back towards the door, and then running down the hall.

Immediately all the ladies start babbling, "Oh, what has happened, what has happened?"

"Tsubame's grandmother has had her married off without our permission!" the Empress says angrily.

Exclamations of shock follow her announcement.

"Oh, Lady Fujiwara, I am so sorry." A young woman looks so beseechingly into my face, I have to look away. She is scarcely any older than my daughter.

"Can we cancel the marriage?" I plead, "Get her back?"

"Everything is totally lawless in the northern lands! We can't even get them to send the kokus of rice that they owe us. I hardly think they are going to send back a desirable bride. When this rebellion is crushed," Tokushi says, "we shall recover Tsubame, and she will have a chance at a second marriage better than her first."

"If only we had kept her on her last visit," she mourns. "We should never have sent her back. I never imagined Lady Harima would defy me in this way. What a pity the possessions she has are mostly the gifts of your good graces! If I strip her of her possessions, she has little to lose. I am sorely tempted to have her executed for her impertinence."

I have wished for Lady Harima's death many times, but now remember how Tsubame felt that she was all alone. How would she feel if I had her only relative beside myself executed?

"Stay your hand for now," I ask. "We should not rush to judgment. Perhaps Tsubame herself consented. We do not know."

"You are correct, of course." Tokushi fans herself angrily. "Still, this insubordination is not to be borne. There must be a suitable punishment. But you are right; I shall consider the matter when I am less agitated. A decision made in haste may lead to many sutras later on."

She whispers to Sotsu-no-suke to fetch a scribe.

"I will write a letter to Lord Kanawara and let him know that Tsubame was not to be married without our express permission. Unfortunately, she has been in his possession, so it is unlikely the marriage has not been consummated. Few of our nobles will want a girl who has been tainted by intercourse with a northerner."

Machiko's strong arm around me contains my trembling. Please let this be some horrible nightmare.

"Impossible woman!" Tokushi fumes. "Take a letter immediately," she snaps at the scribe swirling his ink. "To Lord Setsu-no-kanawara."

"It has come to my attention that, unfortunately, and no doubt unbeknownst to you, a marriage has been agreed upon that is not valid. The Lady Tsubame was contracted to become my lady-in-waiting. Her mother, Lady Fujiwara Seiko, is my oldest and dearest friend. I have looked forward to having the service of her daughter as well. As she has been under my protection, no marriage arranged without my express permission can be considered valid, regardless of what other parties may have agreed to. Obviously, you were not in possession of all the necessary information. Therefore I hold your actions blameless, provided that you return the Lady Tsubame immediately upon receipt of this letter.

I do hope this does not cause you too much consternation. She is a lovely young lady. However, numerous other men have consulted with me as to a court-approved marriage, and it is I, and only I, who can make that final decision. If you wish to file a formal request, your suit will be considered as well, and you may trust that I will arrive at the most beneficial decision for the lady in question. I am well aware of your holdings, and your sterling personal qualities, and I shall consider your suit. However, as of this time, I must insist that you relinquish possession of her, and understand that this marriage is not contractually legal."

She signs the letter with her titles and seals it with the Imperial insignia.

"Have this sent immediately, with the fastest messengers and horses that can be obtained."

"Will there be a phalanx of soldiers to accompany the messengers through enemy territory?" gulps the first messenger to arrive.

"Make three copies of the message; send it with three different messengers. At least one will arrive safely. One man on a horse may more easily penetrate enemy territory than a troop of soldiers. Send them under flag of truce. If Yoritomo dares to interfere with messengers on an Imperial errand, he shall pay a price. Add to the message that Tsubame should be escorted back to Kyoto by some of Kanawara's soldiers. Assure him we will grant them safe passage, and provide the necessary documents to make it so."

After the messengers and scribes have left, Tokushi instructs her servants to arrange the dividing curtains around us. She shoos the other women away and takes me in her arms.

"Oh, Seiko, I'm so sorry."

I start to weep. Surely Lord Kanawara will not set his will against the Imperial Mother. It would be a flagrant act of rebellion.

"My little girl...my little girl...my swallow...so young...I hope he is being gentle with her."

"I hope so. Never fear, Seiko. She may be returning with the messenger."

I keep to my quarters in the week following, barely able to eat or drink. After a few days, I develop a fever. Scenes of my first marriage keep playing in my mind. I pray my former mother-in-law has not succeeded in finding a man as heartless as her son to be Tsubame's husband. If he is a rebel, what does that say for him? They have such bad manners in the north, an obvious sign of insensitivity.

Tsubame is already so accomplished in her music and her writing, how would it be for her being with some northerner who spends all his time running his fief and can barely string three words together? The northerners and easterners who have attended our banquets generally seem quite thick-headed compared to the men of the Capital. Only a coarsened man could spend his days putting down peasant rebellions, overseeing the harvesting of rice and the production of silk. Many of them seem less educated than merchants. My swallow, my little swallow in a cage. It's everything I never wanted for her. If her husband joins the rebels, she will be placed in danger, but if he refuses to join the rebels, that could put her in danger also…

My moon arrives out of course, so I am banished to the Rodukai mansion to wait out my bleeding time. I send two or three letters a day to the Empress, begging her to let me know as soon as word comes. The week passes, and I am back at court, still no response.

Finally, two of the messengers return. One messenger was killed by an over-eager soldier convinced that there was some secret message being conveyed, but the other two made it safely. Tokushi takes me into her formal audience room, where we sit behind royal screens. Lady Daigon-no-suke and Ben-no-taishi are with us, and Tokushi's sister Sotsu-no-suke, who gazes at me lovingly with her calm, owl-like eyes, and presses a supportive hand into the small of my back.

"Are the messengers alone, or are they accompanied by Lady Tsubame?" Tokushi asks as we settle ourselves on the cushions.

"Alas, they seem to have returned alone," the gentleman of the chamber says, conveying his deep regret with a cringing bow. I press my sleeve up against my face.

"Have them sent in as soon as they have changed into proper attire," Tokushi urges. "Tell them they can bathe later."

I am weak from having eaten so lightly, coupled with my illness. Sotsu-no-suke and Machiko edge close to each side of me, holding me up.

The only sounds are sighs and the near silent shuttle of fans stirring the air. It seems to take an eternity for the messengers to arrive.

"State your news," Lady Daigon-no-suke says brusquely. "The Empress is waiting."

"Most regretfully, Lady Tsubame was not permitted to accompany us hither," one says.

"We did our best," the other quavers. I imagine they are afraid that their heads will depart their shoulders as a consequence of having failed the task assigned them.

"We bear messages from Lord Kanawara and Lady Tsubame."

Lady Daigon-no-suke takes the messages and passes them to the Empress. One of the scrolls is clearly on a feminine-looking paper. Tokushi hands that one to me and unrolls the other. I want desperately to read Tsubame's missive, but first look over Tokushi's shoulder to read what Lord Kanawara has sent us.

"August One, Supreme Mother of the Sovereign,

It is an honor 'above the clouds' to receive your message. One such as I cannot expect to see the perfection of the royal hand in this lifetime. I shall preserve this scroll to be passed down through my lineage; my great-grandchildren shall cherish it. Alas, how I wish it were simple to sever the bond between husband and wife, as you suggest. Naturally, I had no idea that the girl was your ward at the time that I made arrangements for her. I cannot understand the oversight that led Lady Harima to fail to mention this. However, in the short time that I have known Lady Tsubame, I have come to love her dearly, and I believe those sentiments to be mutual. It would be too cruel to countenance a separation between my 'little bird' and myself that only the Bridge of Birds could cross. Also, it is possible that she is already with my child. Although it has only been my privilege to glimpse your Eminence once, across a room, and there was no reason whatsoever that you should have taken notice of me, I hope that you will ask of others as to my character, for my reputation and my loyalty to the throne are spotless. Despite my deficiencies, I believe I am a fit husband for your former ward. Please convey my utmost loyalty and devotion to the Sovereign, your son, and know that though my physical distance from the throne is great, the loyalty of my heart knows no distance whatsoever.
Your devoted subject--"

Tokushi tosses it to the ground angrily and motions for me to unroll the second scroll. Petals of dried flowers slide out as I open it. There is also a token, a carved mother-of-pearl bead on a cord with a sutra carved on it that I had given Tsubame when she was a child. I press it to my lips.

"Supreme Empress, Lady of the Realm,

Thank you so much for your efforts on my behalf. Truly I am not worthy of the trouble it must have taken you. Though I had looked forward with all my heart to being in your service, devoting myself to your every need as my mother has done, it seems that my karma wills it not to be so. Lord Kanawara is a great lord and a true gentleman, and I would be ungrateful to reject all he has done for me. It be unfitting for me to bring such a cloud and stain into any subsequent marriage, whereas if I adhere to my grandmother's choice, I can be held blameless. While I appreciate your elevated sense of my worthiness, I am certain this is the best match that can be made for me at this time."

It is true. Though the Empress' word would carry great weight, Tsubame could not make as fine a marriage now as she could have made had she arrived here as a maiden.

"Perhaps when things are less unsettled, I can be permitted a visit. To see your face again is the most glorious honor I could imagine."

Several of her signature ink swallows decorate the bottom of the page.

Choking back tears, I hand Tokushi her letter and gaze at the one addressed to me which had been rolled beneath it. A wisteria pod rolls out onto my lap.

"Dearest Mother,

I appreciate your concern over my rather sudden marriage. I am certain Grandmother meant what was best for me, but I was not allowed to write to you during the time I was receiving suitors to explain what was happening. The choice was made for me, but I am well content in the personality of my husband."

I know that her protestations of happiness mean absolutely nothing, having been forced to write false letters to Tokushi during my marriage. Lord Kanawara is not foolish enough to allow Tsubame to send a letter without his review of it. He could be beating and raping her every night and I would never know.

She continues, "I think we must assume that some greater force than ours has seen fit to thwart us. As you are blameless, it must be some unknown karma of mine from a past life which keeps us apart."

This pierces me to the heart. If karma is responsible, it is doubtless my own role in her father's death that is to blame.

"I do hope you shall be permitted to visit me some time, and I you. But as my lord points out, times are troubled, and safe passage is difficult to guarantee for anyone. But he vows that he will put a messenger at my disposal once a week so that we may be in constant communication. Naturally, he very much looks forward to the time when he can meet you. I am being treated well and adjusting to my new surroundings and responsibilities. Lord Kanawara's mother is a very efficient manager of his grounds and properties. She has taken me under her wing and is training me in all the skills I shall need to become the same one day. Please be happy for me. If you would be kind enough to send herbs for my health, I would much appreciate it.

Your loving daughter—"

Herbs for her health. I think she must mean contraceptive teas and ungents. I have often warned her that it is better for a woman not to attempt to bear a child before she is seventeen or eighteen, to give her pelvis time to grow large enough for the child to safely exit.

"Have the messengers rest for a night and then go back," I ask Tokushi. "I must send herbs," I whisper into her ear, "to prevent conception. She's too young."

Tokushi nods. "We shall send new messengers. These will be weary. I shall get the fastest ones we can obtain."

After Tokushi dismisses the messengers and orders two others to be prepared to return to Owari with our replies tomorrow, we all weep until our sleeves are drenched. All of the ladies press so tightly around me it is like being in the center of a soft, fragrant flower. But there is no comfort to be had in their murmured condolences and strokings. Finally I gather myself together and tell Machiko to put together a large box of herbs, both for conception and for other health issues. Who knows what these ignorant northerners know about medicine. I also ask her to pack some of the robes I had waiting for Tsubame as wedding gifts. Tokushi and the other girls donate some of their robes as well, and On'na Mari, on hearing the news, sends two of her favorite pillow books. It ends up being two large chests, one of herbs, and one of robes and books. The messengers will need to travel by ox-cart. Doubtless they shall be thoroughly examined for weapons at every check-point, and will have to take money to bribe the guards at each juncture if even half of it is to reach Tsubame. We do not send jewelry, for that is almost certain to be stolen. I label each bundle of herbs as to their uses. The ones to prevent conception I label 'to regulate your courses and reduce menstrual pain'. She is a clever girl and will understand what I mean by that. At least she shall be able to keep her womb empty until she is older.

That night Tokushi summons me to have supper with her.

"I must insist that you eat supper with me each night for the next fortnight at least," Tokushi says. "Do you think I have not noticed how your ribs are sticking out? It will not serve Tsubame for you to die of starvation."

"You are quite right," I stammer. "It is only that I am finding everything so difficult to swallow, not a deliberate plan to starve myself, I assure you. I would never betray my obligations to you in that way."

"Of course, I know that. But somehow you must manage to choke it down. Are you taking some of your own remedies for grief?"

I nod. "Yes, Machiko is preparing the teas for me. But in a situation like this, no herb has sufficient power."

"It is not as if she were dead, Seiko. She is alive, and married to a lord of some property. A northern lord, granted, but a lord nonetheless. His family is not of the highest quality, but it is far from the lowest. Her father's family was of an equal status to this lord's, and you married him. It does not sound as if she is madly in love, but she does not sound miserable either. Love can grow. The Emperor was only a child when I married him, but I came to love him dearly. She at least has an older man to unravel her virgin's knot and teach her the ways of husband and wife."

I try to stop it, but can't help a sharp sob escaping.

"I'm sorry, I am truly not fit for your table at this time."

"No matter. But I must insist that you nourish yourself. You have many responsibilities, Seiko, and you must be well enough to perform them." Machiko sits beside me and pushes the food into my mouth like a mother bird. Somehow I will get through this meal. And the one after that. And the day after that. In the past, I somehow endured our long absences, knowing that the day would come that I would see Tsubame again. But now, in spite of all the comforting words Tokushi and the others utter, I despair that I shall be daughterless all my days.

Chapter Twenty-Two
Spring, 1183

Tokushi's ladies are sitting on the graduated steps of a raised wooden platform, watching the horse races at the Iris Festival. We have iris braided into our hair and are wearing cloaks patterned with iris and inner robes dyed in various shades ranging from deep purple to yellows and browns, the purples and blues being by far the most popular. Tokushi is wearing an incredible robe that features a life-size peacock standing in a cluster of blue iris, with one yellow iris, representing the sun, embroidered above the peacock's neck. Real peacock feathers are woven into the design, and she wears a tall headdress of peacock feathers and iris. The drought, with its accompanying plagues, has passed and the early rice is coming in strongly. No expense was spared for the Hollyhock Festival last month, and the Iris Festival promises to be equally lavish.

The Capital is brimming with clouds of warriors who have poured in from all over the country in response to a joint edict issued by Munemori and Go-Shirakawa. All the southern and western provinces are well represented, and from as far north as Echizen. But none from any farther north than Wakasa, whose Lords have all sided with the Genji. The last couple of months have been filled with rumors of conflict between Yoritomo and Yoshinaka, the two most prominent Genji commanders. But Yoshinaka surrendered his oldest son and heir into Yoritomo's keeping as a sign of his loyalty, so once again they have turned a united front against us. Now with so many allies gathered under the red flag of the Taira, and with the rice harvest successful, the conflict will resume.

I want to concentrate on the pleasures of the Iris Festival, but the throngs of warriors stretching along the Kamo river renders the illusion of normalcy impossible.

My costume features layers of bright yellow alternating with blues and purples, with matching iris woven throughout my hair and the edges of my costume. The ensemble draws many appreciative glances from the assembled nobles. The ones I am wearing it for, Atsumori and Kiyosune, are both scheduled to take part in the next race. Kiyosune is mounted on his mare, Mistress of Demons, Atsumori on his stallion, Midnight Battle. Midnight Battle is glossy from having been oiled. Mistress of Demons stamps her foot and rolls her eyes, as if she believes the upcoming race will be a skirmish. Five other men on fine-looking horses wait for the signal at the starting line. The scarf leaves the official's hand and flutters to the ground. The instant a corner touches the earth, the horses surge forward. The women cheer, some rising to their feet in their excitement. Four of the horses are running so close together, I can't make out who has swept first over the finish line. In a moment the scarlet-clad official walks out leading Kiyosune's mare. The official reaches towards the mare's bridle and she slashes her teeth towards his hand, which he withdraws hastily as Kiyosune yanks on her reins. Mistress of Demons is as fierce as her name would imply. Only Kiyosune can make her seem gentle and docile. Kiyosune and his fierce mare are awarded with garlands of iris. Mistress of Demons restrains herself sweetly as the wreath is placed around her neck and stretches her neck out proudly to the applause of the crowd, knowing that she has won.

We watch two more races before I notice that Kiyosune and Atsumori are hovering by our platform, having given their horses' reins to their pages, who have led them off to the stables.

"I must congratulate the victor, and commiserate with the loser," I murmur to Tokushi, who nods briefly, shining eyes fixed on the line of horses preparing for the next race. Machiko helps me down the steps. I am wearing my full complement of twelve robes, so movement is tricky.

"You look like the very Goddess of the Iris herself," Kiyosune smiles.

"Magnificent," Atsumori agrees. "He cheated," he says plaintively, indicating Kiyosune with his chin.

"Did not!"

"He's lighter. And the other horses are afraid to get close to that nag of his because she bites."

"You're such a sore loser," Kiyosune laughs. He bows to me, eyes twinkling. "We had an agreement that whoever won the race, or placed higher, would be the one to spend the evening with you. With your permission, of course. It is that which inspired me to win."

"I was just as inspired," Atsumori protests. "Midnight Battle is in love with that bitch horse of yours. He let her win. She really *is* a demon," he grumbles.

"Maybe you'll outdo me in the archery contest."

"Maybe! *Maybe!* I'll *trounce* you in the archery contest! Why didn't I think to place our bet on that!"

"Kiyosune tonight, you tomorrow night," I promise.

"If I can get out of guard duty tomorrow," Atsumori grumbles.

"A man of your station doesn't perform guard duty," I laugh.

"It's all these warriors from every stinking backwater--some are more civilized than others. We have to post so many guards to make sure they don't set fire to the pleasure quarters or go rifling through the merchants' belongings, stealing from the market stalls, insulting women--someone has to be in charge…"

"And you have the better political prospects," Kiyosune gibes with a self-satisfied smirk. "Tadanori's son has to shoulder more responsibilities."

Atsumori glares at Kiyosune.

"He can't stand losing," Kiyosune says smugly.

"See if I watch your back in the next battle," Atsumori threatens darkly. Seeing my look of dismay, Kiyosune smiles and stage-whispers, "He's just joking!" He slaps Atsumori on the back. "Come on, let's get ready for the archery contest. If you're very, very good, and your father gives his permission, maybe I'll take your place tomorrow."

"I so regret pleading your case with her," Atsumori remarks to Kiyosune as they walk off. "I must have been out of my mind at the time."

Reassured that their rivalry remains a friendly one, I return to my seat. Later, during the archery contest, Atsumori does place higher than Kiyosune, but he does not win first place, much to his obvious aggravation.

"Poor Atsumori," I whisper to Tokushi and Ben-no-taishi, "he wants to be the best in everything."

"All men are like that," Ben-no-taishi shrugs.

"Some more than others. Our whole family is competitive like that," Tokushi says. "All my brothers are constantly trying to outdo each other. Tadanori's sons are the same. You see how hard Atsumori has worked to play the flute as well as his older brother Tsunemasa. Outshining Tsunemasa, however, is an impossible task, even if Tadanori did give Atsumori Little Branch, their hereditary flute. With such a renowned warrior for his eldest brother, how can he help but want to outstrip the others at the arts of war? He's had the finest teachers, so what excuse can he have to do otherwise?"

"That is true. He was most unhappy that Kiyosune beat him in the horse races."

"Did you happen to be part of the reward?" Tokushi asks knowingly.

"Yes…with your permission."

"Of course. They're going off to war again soon. We'll have plenty of time to console each other once they are gone."

"You did promise I could visit Tanba."

"Yes, of course," she sighs. "You want to lend your support to Seishan as her husband goes off to war. But not until the ninth: it's the first good travel day."

"The ninth then," I agree. Today is the fifth. That will give me four nights to alternate between Atsumori and Kiyosune before traveling to Tanba.

The festival ends with thousands of warriors twanging their bowstrings together, raining imaginary arrows at unseen demonic forces. The fifth month is said to have an unlucky quality, and all the activities of the Iris Festival are thought to banish ill fortune. It is a remarkably ill-starred time to resume a war.

"It's a pity iris don't smell as lovely as they look," Ben-no-taishi says, sniffing a blossom in the hope it will have miraculously developed an enchanting scent.

"Yes, but all things are perfect in their way," Tokushi reminds us. She's been feeling very cheerful about the quantities of warriors who have flocked to join us.

"You see, Seiko, you were so worried about those northern warriors. Do you really think they can stand up to these numbers? And I told you Go-Shirakawa was on our side. Didn't he send out the edict ordering these men from every corner of the kingdom to join us?"

"You are quite right my lady," I concede. But there is still a gnawing fear in me. At least Kiyosune and Atsumori have experience with war. Sessho is such a gentle man, I can hardly imagine him raising his sword against another being. He, his eldest son Tomomori, and his two brothers will be joining the Taira forces as they progress towards the Eastern Road. I have barely been able to sleep since receiving his letter a fortnight ago. Tokushi can afford to be cheerful; she doesn't know what it is like to have her lovers exposed to the sharp swords and spears of the enemy. Of course, her brothers are commanders in every battle, but they are surrounded by cordons of men who would wish no greater honor than to die defending them. Tomonori, her youngest and favorite brother, is known for his daring and valor. Having never had a brother, I suppose I don't know what that is like.

Kiyosune and many of the other men dine with us that evening, though Atsumori is conspicuous by his absence. "Atsumori and some of the other losers," Kiyosune informs me with a small smirk, "are consoling themselves with copious amounts of sake in the pleasure quarters."

"Is he really upset?" I ask.

"He'll get over it. He's very competitive. He likes to think of himself as my protector--just because he's a few months older--it's annoying to him to realize I'm just as skilled as he is."

Later, in the privacy of my room, he looks me up and down, shaking his head. "You look dazzling. I can hardly bear to undress you. Leave all the flowers in your hair, neh?"

"Yes, and you must leave your victory crown on, of course."

"Of course. Although," he whispers, "when my jade stalk is crowned with your silken garland, that will be my true victory."

We peel off our outer robes and rearrange our translucent inner robes of yellow and blue to the greatest erotic advantage. We gaze into each other's eyes, sharing a shallow bowl of wine steeped with iris leaves as we rock almost imperceptibly together until our breathing becomes too ragged for us to swallow, and he sets the wine down. The sweet scent of mugwort, strewn throughout the bed and twined with iris around the room, entices us into the territory of dreams. I cry out, drenching him with my juices; he arches his back and ejaculates into me with deep groans.

We lie back on the quilts. He takes his iris crown off, sets it encircling my sacred triangle. "That…is a reward," he sighs. "If I die during this next series of battles, at least I'll die happy."

"Don't say that," I plead, "don't ever ever say that!" I beckon Machiko over and tell her to purify the room with pine. "How can they even think about war at such an inauspicious moment?"

"It's not as if we have a lot of choice," he says. "Yoritomo and Yoshinaka have gone from being fighting cocks to two oxen pulling the same yoke. They obstinately refuse to bow their heads to Go-Shirakawa's edict ordering all those loyal to the throne to report to Kyoto immediately. Not a grain of rice has trickled through their barricades on the eastern and northern roads. The nation is at a standstill. We have no choice but to go yank the serpents out of their dens. We must put down the rebellion before it grows any worse. And we've gathered all these warriors--we have to use them. Don't worry about me," he says, patting my head reassuringly. "I'll be all right. Atsumori is sulking now, but when we are in battle together, we are like two arms on the same body, I promise you. All our information says we have twice as many men as they do. Koremori, Michimori and Tomonori will be leading the battles, so you needn't worry," he says, alluding to Munemori's lack of competence in the field. "They're strong leaders, and the men will follow them all the way to the Shide mountains, if necessary."

"If you see Taira Sessho, from Tanba, and his son--their shields carry both the Taira butterfly and the black dragon--if you could watch over them-- they're completely inexperienced."

"If I see them, I will, Lady. Is Taira Seishan much distressed?"

"Of course she is," I say. Neither Kiyosune nor Atsumori know of my relationship with Sessho, though like everyone else at court, they know my friendship with Seishan is legendary.

"Your heart's beating quickly," he observes, one hand on my chest. "I must not have satisfied you."

My heart is beating quickly at the thought of the upcoming battles, but I smile and embrace him. After another two rounds of lovemaking, Kiyosune curls drowsily to my back while Machiko's quick and clever fingers remove the crushed iris from my hair.

"I'm sorry I ruined your beautiful hair decorations," Kiyosune whispers, his tongue tracing the contours of my ear, sounding not a bit sorry.

"It can't be helped. Flowers can't last." I press my lips together, wishing I could take back that ill-omened speech.

"Are you still worried? Have I failed to relax you?"

"I can't relax when the battles are so close. Do you know when you are going?"

"Not exactly. It depends on the travel auguries. Probably within the week. We won't leave until there's an auspicious travel date. Not until Munemori's diviners receive the proper portents. Some say we shouldn't leave until the new moon, others say dark of the moon is the best time for battles. I leave that to those wiser than myself. I simply ride when they tell me to ride and kill who they tell me to kill, and make sure Atsumori comes back safe. Neither of us has ever even been really hurt," he reminds me. "I had that one tiny cut on my knuckle, and Atsumori had some bad headaches after that first battle when he got hit so hard in the head. It does seem we are under divine protection. Pity the wisteria is gone. I should feel so confident, riding into battle with a sprig of wisteria that you yourself had placed in my hair. I have perfect confidence in the new charms you gave us."

I had recently woven new charms for them that include braids of hair from the tails of their horses mixed with their hair and mine.

"I like that I have your hair in my pouch," he says. "It makes me feel very safe."

"May it be so."

"Anyway, the war will be over soon. A few months at most, though I may not see you for all that time. If I can send a page back with letters, I will."

"I know. Meanwhile, I will have a whole stack of letters and poems to send as soon as your page reaches me. Do you know what the strategy is?"

"I've been going to the meetings. There's another one planned for the day after tomorrow. Of course, everything planned in those meetings is quite secret. Much depends on the Easterners, where they choose to engage us. We'll be entering their territory, so we will have to proceed with caution. Koremori and Tomonori are fearless, Michimori is more cautious. The army may divide into two or three sections, come up around the enemy pincer-wise--it depends on their defensive strategy and their numbers, whether they divide their own forces, fight us on the plains or in the mountains--we won't know until we're there. None of these soldiers from the coast have any experience fighting in the mountains--well, none of us do; usually battles take place on the plains. That will be something we will have to learn as we go. Remember, the Sun Goddess is on our side, and Inari as well."

"Yoritomo claims to be the son of Hachiman," I say. Hachiman is the war god.

"Yoritomo claims a lot of things," Kiyosune says. "Who believes him?"

"Thousands of Genji."

"Do you think even Hachiman can stand up to the Lady of the Golden Sunlight?"

"Of course not."

"Anyway, we had all our games in honor of Hachiman today, and we will be making offerings at every shrine and temple along the way. Truly my lady, you have nothing to fear."

"Do you have nightmares?" I ask, turning to face him.

"Every warrior has a few. I'm not as troubled as Atsumori. He said he had some when he was with you."

I nod.

"As you may have noticed, once I fall asleep, I'm dead to the world. My greatest danger is being attacked at night. Luckily, Atsumori wakes up at the smallest sound. If there's a night attack, he'll wake me. My conscience is clear, Lady. I fight the enemies of the crown. If I didn't kill them, they would kill me. I dreaded war, and I cannot tell you that I like it--for me it is a duty, an unpleasant duty. I have been promoted for my efforts, which has brought honor and a higher standard of living to my family. I am the only man left in my family, as you know. It is up to me to keep my family's honor unstained. I have you to protect, my mother and sisters to protect.

I find myself surprisingly calm during battle. It is as if everything slows down for me. I can see what the man fighting me is going to do before he does it. I know how he will turn his sword arm the moment before it turns. I know how he will try to position his horse between my blade and his body. I can see how he's going to adjust his shield. Perhaps it is your gift of prophecy that rides with me.

I have a tempering effect on Atsumori. He's more of a hothead, you know that. But be assured, Lady. During battle, we remain glued to each other's sides. He thinks about my wellbeing as much as his own, and it keeps him from being foolish. All these warriors from the Kyushu and Shikoku are just itching for battle, having had no opportunity to cover themselves with glory. Our leaders plan to use these eager untried warriors as a buffer to protect the more valuable and skilled ones. Anyway, I don't believe this is the last time I will be lying in your arms. Don't you believe it either."

"I have the utmost confidence in you," I smile. But after he falls asleep, I lie awake, listening to his even breathing and the beating of his heart, as if by listening to the flow of blood through his chest, I could keep it from ever spilling.

Chapter Twenty-Three
April 1183

Machiko and I depart for Tanba on the morning of the ninth, and arrive the following day. The first things we see when we come into view of Sessho's mansion are the bushes around the edge of the outer walls of the compound, trained into diamond patterns. But only the plants are serene and in their usual positions. The place is an anthill of activity. The normally peaceful fiefdom has rarely been the scene of uncalm faces or echoed with the sound of hurrying feet. Now servants run willy-nilly gathering, fetching, packing, preparing. Peasant farmers who have never wielded any weapon sharper than a plow are now practicing spear thrusts under the tutelage of a heavy-set guard who looks as though he has never stabbed anything fiercer than an egg in his donburi. Some of the male servants look on. Though they will not be expected to fight, being along to prepare meals, wash their masters' clothes, clean weapons, dig trenches and such, they clearly feel that a little knowledge of how to use the weapons they will be cleaning could prove useful.

As we come through the gates of the outer wall, there are ponds on either side of the path, then the large courtyard in which the men are practicing the arts of war. Gardens surround the main residences. Part of the activity involves lashing acres of bamboo and thatch to the inside of the outer walls to create walkways and protected areas where archers can shoot, in addition to the lookout towers which already exist. Do they think the rebels will actually make it this far? In Kyoto, all the men speak in an off-hand way of how quickly the rebellion will be crushed, all seeming eager to 'take a head' before it is all over. Can Sessho possibly be afraid? But I trust Sessho's judgment above all men's. Frost settles along my core, and by the time I enter the house, I am shivering. Seishan comes to greet me. I feel like running to her and holding her tight, but instead I clasp her hands decorously, seeing a haunted, strained look around her normally serene eyes.

"What is all this ridiculous hammering?" I exclaim.

"It is driving me mad!" she whispers in my ear. "Come to the back of the house. It is somewhat better there."

"Did Sessho really authorize all this?" I ask as we walk along the hallway.

"Yes, he's worried about us being protected while he is gone."

"Protected from what? They're nowhere near here. They'll never be near here. This will be over in a couple of weeks. Everyone at court says so."

"The men? They think so too?" she asks, trying to mask her anxiety. I make a dismissive gesture.

"Oh, if you could only see them, the peacocks. Strutting around showing off their new armor, designing helmets so heavy a horse's neck would break under them. They're like a bunch of fighting roosters. If battles were won by bragging, the war would be over now! All day long they practice archery, sword-play, shooting from horseback. At night they do it by torchlight! There hasn't been a poetry competition or dancing in weeks! I think this whole war is just about men wanting to show off."

She laughs, faintly. "Isn't everything in life about men wanting to show off?"

We step out into the back garden, but there is no peace to be had there. Why it is necessary for the men loading food and other supplies into the wagons to shout constantly during this activity is not clear. We close the screen and retire to the quietest room. Sessho is overseeing the preparations for his departure. I know he is too wise to need to test himself in this way. Why can he not just send his servants and soldiers to the effort? I had thought to escape the insanity at the court, that it would be different here--as always, a haven. But the madness is here too.

"Tell me the news from court," she says, obviously wanting to be distracted.

"The same as here, only more so. The men are completely insufferable. They make sad allusions to their glorious upcoming deaths and every woman in court, from highest to lowest, spreads her legs for them. Mark my words, there will be more babies nine months from now than have ever been born at court." I do not mention my own two young lovers.

"I suppose all the maids will have illegitimate children and become useless and have to be sent home," Seishan speculates. I nod and sigh, both of us trying to pretend a shortage of maids is the worst inconvenience facing us.

"Even Machiko?" she asks.

"Oh no, Machiko is as sensible and devoted as ever. But as for the others...I am leaving birth control charms and packets of contraceptive teas under all the maid's pillows, as it would seem like an accusation to talk directly to them about it. I can hardly get anyone to brush my hair in the morning, they are all so exhausted from the exertions of comforting young warriors!" We laugh, but the laughter dies quickly, leaving us sipping our tea in silence.

"Did you ask him again?" I question. I have been imploring Sessho in my letters to let his younger brothers go and cover themselves with glory while he stays home to manage the land and people who are under his care. But he writes back that he must attend to a higher duty and Seishan will manage admirably in his absence. We both agree that Sessho is no warrior; it is impossible to imagine his gentleness and refinement put to such a use. She nods, bowing her head to conceal her trembling lips.

"Why can't he be sick? Why can't he just be home in bed?"

She shakes her head, brushing away tears.

"He won't."

I take some packets out of my sleeves and fan them out on the table. "Each of these has enough bitter herb to make a man lose everything in his belly and bowels for three, four days. We could let him recover a couple days after that, then dose him again--keep him weak until the war is over. What do you think? We'll give it to Tomomori too, of course."

"He'd know."

"We could make ourselves sick too. Machiko could do the dosing."

"Seiko--do you think I haven't tried? We don't understand it, but honor is everything to men. If we make them sick, they'll go sick, in palanquins if they have to. And then they'll be in worse danger, too weak to defend themselves. We can't Seiko; it's just not right."

"I would have thought Sessho was beyond all that nonsense about honor."

Tomomori enters the room. He takes after his mother's side of the family; he is almost pretty, though nearly as tall as his father. He has black snapping eyes, highly arched eyebrows, shining skin. He is radiant with his own fourteen-year-old confidence. "Father bids me greet you and inform you he regrets his necessary preoccupation with matters of state. He will join you for dinner and trusts my mother will show you the greatest of hospitality until then." The sleeves on his green and gold robes are held out with wooden supports, making him look far more broad-shouldered and mature than he is. I want to scream at him that this is no game he is going off to, but I only nod and murmur thanks. He bows and returns to his own preparations, two servants of his own age racing down the hall with him, exactly as if they were all still boys playing at war. Those tender young bodies threatened with arrows, with swords? No. I won't allow myself to think of it. Sessho will surely keep his son in the rear, behind the crush of idiots seeking glory. He wouldn't let Tomomori attend at all if he thought there were real danger. No. Of course not. I want to say something reassuring to Seishan who is wringing the sleeves of her kimono with anxiety, but I realize I am twisting my own sleeves so mercilessly the borders have begun to unravel.

Nori-chan comes in, clouds of anger darkening her face. "Why don't they let women go to war? The other side has women warriors. I'm as brave as Tomomori, and I'm better with a bow!"

"Because the other side is nothing but barbarians!" Seishan snaps at her daughter. "And because I can say no to you. I can't tell your father and your brother what to do, but I can tell you what to do, and you're not going! Women are not built to fight."

"Tomoe is as strong and tough as any of the men! And she's beautiful..."

Nori, like many young women, is enchanted with rumors of Tomoe and other warrior women reputed to fight with the Genji, said to be as skillful and ruthless as any man.

"How dare you raise that name in our house as if it were one to be spoken with honor?" Seishan cries.

I put my hand on Nori's arm, hoping to calm the situation.

"It's true, aunt," she insists, "I am every bit as good with the bow as Tomomori."

"Yes, but your arms aren't as long. Suppose you had to fight with a sword? It is too dreadful to even contemplate," her mother responds, and I see this is not the first time this argument has occurred.

Nori bursts into angry tears and cries, "It will all be over and I'll never get to see anything. I'll never get to do anything that matters!"

"Be glad you'll never get to see anything. You'll have your fill of blood and suffering bringing your children into the world. That is a woman's war," Seishan says.

"Nothing ever happens here. Everything is so boring. I'm dying of boredom and no one even cares!" Nori wails.

Well, I had predicted this. I had suggested that they send Nori-chan to court, offering to take her under my wing. But Sessho feared that all the artifice and superficiality at court would alter her. Of course, I also suspect he simply couldn't bear to be parted from his oldest child.

"Tomomori will come back with all sorts of exciting stories to tell, and I'll never have any exciting stories to tell."

"Well, I hope that's true. Life is better without that sort of excitement." Seishan shakes her head in exasperation. "Maybe you'll have a daughter like you. Then you'll have plenty of excitement."

"You just don't understand!" Nori wails and flounces out of the room just as Kikuko enters.

"Sit closer together," she commands, and when we comply, she curls up in both of our laps simultaneously. She is normally a high-spirited girl but today she seems withdrawn and morose.

"Matsu never wants to play with me any more. He just plays war with the other boys and they say I can't play because I'm a girl." She puts her hands over her ears. "When is all the noise going to stop?" she complains.

"Things will be quiet again soon," Seishan promises.

"I told my maid to hold my ears so I could read without all the noise, but she only did it for a little while."

"Well, she can't hold your ears all day."

"Come paint with me," Kiku coaxes me. "We're making uikyoe paintings now."

Painting with the wood blocks is a good meditation. Except for the muffled sounds of hammering and men's voices it is almost like a normal visit. Kiku is like a small version of my mother. I keep glancing surreptitiously at her through my hair, drinking in her beauty.

"When are you going to teach me about herbs?" she asks, daubing pink and white blossoms onto her cherry tree.

"Soon. As soon as this silly war is over. Probably the next time I visit. That will be fun," I reply.

She nods, still concentrating on her art efforts. "I want to know everything you know. I feel like the plants whisper to me. Like I almost know their language, but not quite."

I take a deep breath, remembering my mother saying that if I sat near them quietly, the plants would speak to me.

At times, my daughter's voice and mannerisms are so like my mother's it is as if I were back in my childhood, only with our positions reversed--I the mother, and she the child.

At dinner Nori is still sulking, her face blotchy from crying. Kiku is plastered to Seishan's side. I wish she were clinging to me, hugging me as tightly as an obi sash.

Matsu is watching Tomomori, eyes wide, doing exactly what he does-- eating each food his brother eats, imitating the manner in which he eats it. It is as if he thought he could will himself to be the older one, the one with his own armor and swords and helmet, the one who gets to do everything.

Sessho says, "It's a terrible inconvenience, I know, what with all these fortifications going up. But it is so noisy because I ordered that everything be completed quickly, so it will be over soon."

Nori looks up from pushing the food around on her plate. "Why do you even bother? You know they won't come here. Nothing ever comes here."

Sessho looks kindly at her. "I know. I know. All the men who are staying behind--I have to give them a sense that they have something important to do. Otherwise they will chafe themselves to death with not being able to go out and prove their honor. They need to feel a part of it all."

"Father," Matsu says, "Kai (a servant boy of about eleven) says when he accompanies you, he's just going to be polishing your helmet. I could do that! I could polish your helmet!"

"But Matsu, if you come with us, who will be left to protect the family? Someone must do that job," his father explains.

Nori soundlessly mimics her father's words, clearly enraged at the suggestion that she is under her seven-year-old brother's protection.

The younger boy, oblivious, stares at his father and older brother as worshipfully as if they had turned into gods. It's like a disease, mostly infecting the males, mostly infecting the young. Sessho is not contaminated; his disease is honor, not war. Before, I respected his sense of honor completely. But now...

Seishan is beginning to get a little pink around the nose, a sign that she is on the edge of crying. Sessho takes her hand, reassuring her that they will be back in a few weeks.

"The war cannot possibly last more than a month. All the spies report they have less than half the men we will. And as for you," he admonishes his eldest son, "there is no use getting excited, for we will see no more action than those at home. I promised your mother we would stay well in the rear, out of harm's way, and so we shall. But we'll make up some fine tales to tell. Besides, Dr. Chiu has given us some wondrous powders, some for us, some for our horses, which are so strong in their powers of protection as to make us well-nigh invincible. That, and the talismans Seiko and Seishan have made for us--why, I almost pity the Genji, whose karma and magic are so inferior to ours."

The next morning, Tomomori ties a scarf around his arm, given by his lady-love, a girl his age from another high-born family who conspired to send it to him by messenger. He's very proud and self-conscious about it. Sessho has one from both Seishan and me, decorating each arm. The night before, we did a ritual to bless their swords, bows, helmets, armor, and all other weaponry. Tomomori is so proud of his first sword. He takes it out of its scabbard to show me. I trace the swirling patterns of gray and silver metal. He warns me not to test the edge. I assure him that no one in the court has a better one, though in truth I have not inspected any other swords at close range like this.

"Really? You're not just saying that?" he asks.

"Truly, this is the best sword I have seen yet," I reply. "Have you been practicing very much?"

"Enough, enough," he says modestly. In addition to various general protection charms, I have woven their talismans with charms specifically to ward off injury from iron or metal. It should be proof against sword, spear, and arrow equally. Still, no charm is completely effective; all depends upon the confluence of karma and kami, one's destiny and one's allies. No one had more charms of protection than my mother, and they did not save her.

"The Genji think themselves warriors because they have put down a few peasant uprisings. When confronted with men of quality, armed with better than hoes and scythes, they will melt away like the mist," Sessho reassures me. But in that instant, a tiny crack opens in his facade, no wider than an edge of paper, and I know that for all his outer assurance, inwardly he is not confident, and his fear blows through me like a chill wind.

Encased in black armor, he is an impressive and forbidding presence. The edges of his helmet scroll into wings; his brow is circled with antlers. A rampant dragon on the helmet's crest raises a threatening claw. His son's helmet is a smaller rendition of his own. I pray that the power of the dragon protects them, believing, as everyone does, that those powers exist, even though sightings are rare. As I pray to the dragon spirits, their menacing power seems to fill the room. I also feel Sessho's father leaning in from that other dimension, and I ask my mother's spirit to lend her power also. Surely so much help from the unseen world will keep them safe.

I try to have no bad thoughts, so that no negative forces may cross through the hidden realms with mischief in mind. It is hard, when confronted with the sharpness of swords and the thickness of armor, not to imagine violence and to feel fear at the imaginng. I concentrate fiercely, visualizing sword, arrow and spear bouncing harmlessly away from them, unable to reach them.

I watch the intensity with which Seishan moves her beads and know that she is concentrating on positive prayers as fiercely as I am. She is dressed in a fine robe featuring two geese in a pond, the image of conjugal loyalty, but she is very pale, as if carved from ivory. Nori is weeping soundlessly, except for the occasional gasp, but the neck of her kimono is wet. Her clothing and hair are disheveled, as though she were grieving; I am disturbed at the ill-omened feel of it. Seishan has complained in recent letters that Nori is flouting her by dressing in mismatched robes and taking no care with her appearance, so this is a common habit, speaking more of rebellion than of grief. Still, she might have been more considerate and thoughtful of symbolism at this time of danger and leave-taking. I am almost surprised that she didn't twist her hair into a warrior's knot and try to sneak into the entourage, but I guess she realized that would never work.

Sessho appeared relaxed at dinner the night before, but today I can see the stress. We have all gotten up long before dawn, after little sleep. It is gray and cold and I know he wishes he were back in his warm bed with two soft and willing women, far from the unyielding textures of war.

I look in his eyes. "Promise me you'll stay out of harm's way."

"I'll try. But I have this boy to look after; we all know how hot-headed these young men can be."

"He's a good boy. He'll do what you say." Unlike his sister, Tomomori evinces no interest in rebellion. I have no doubt he will look to Sessho for his wisdom and honor his decisions.

The dawn of the departure there is a morning fog starting to burn off. The column of men stretches halfway around the compound: musicians, drummers with huge Taiko drums, some so big they must have their own carriage, a story-teller to record noble exploits, a physician, scribes, servants of every description, tents and furnishings, bathing tubs, rugs, bedding, tables, screens,

Sessho has his favorite nightingale and his musicians to soothe his ears after the dust of travel. It seems he believes their encampments will be safe and wonderful places to relax. I hope he is right.

One hundred of his soldiers are being left behind to guard his home. Some of them appear secretly relieved, others appear absolutely miserable. He is leaving behind many of his most experienced and competent soldiers. This gives me the uneasy sense he is expecting things to be worse than he is letting on.

At last Sessho gives the order and the long line of soldiers and servants winds off like an immense dragon. We watch for a very long time, seeing the red banners representing the Heike grow smaller and smaller until they are no larger than the scales of a carp.

Our servants bring tea out to us. I take the tea; Seishan simply waves them away. Nori has gone weeping back to her bed. The two younger children stand quietly with us, waving long after no one could possibly see them. Finally Matsu runs off with some of the other boys to play at war. Kiku stays with us. As the column begins to smudge and blend into the horizon like an ink painting, she asks softly, "Are they going to come back?"

"Of course they are!" Seishan says, shocked. "They have the finest magic powders! And Seiko made them the finest talismans possible. Of course they will come back. You mustn't think bad thoughts! It is unlucky! A couple of weeks..."

"A month at most," I interject.

When the company has vanished, Seishan goes inside to lie down all day with cold compresses on her forehead. She gives orders that she is not to be disturbed. She does not even want me around, as I discover when I go to check on her and a servant bars my path. "So sorry. The mistress is too ill to see you."

"Well, I am good with illness. I can probably help her."

"Not with this illness you can't."

So I realize that Seishan prefers to grieve alone. I hope she comes out of this before bedtime, so we can take some comfort in each other's presence, though we have not slept alone together, except during our moontimes, since her days in court. I do my best to appear as if all is well for the children's sake, though by suppertime I notice that all of us, even the children, are walking around as if some vital organ had been removed from our bodies.

Chapter Twenty-four
May, 1183

Tokushi draws back from my embrace.

"Really, Seiko, you seem completely distracted! Your body has returned from Tanba, but your mind has not. Is Seishan still so much more beautiful than I?"

"It's not that my lady--I am so worried--about the upcoming battles--"

Tokushi calls Naniwa to come into the chodai and fan her.

"Ah, so it's Atsumori and Kiyosune who claim your attention then," she huffs. "Perhaps you should retire to your own quarters, since you have so little interest in mine."

She brushes away my apologies and sends me back to my room.

Once there, I pace back and forth, finally sliding open the door and stepping into the garden. The leaves rustle enchantingly under a delicate breeze; the tantalizing scents of early summer jasmine caress my nostrils. Word has it that Koremori's forces have swept through Echizen province, and that joyful warriors once bowed under Yoritomo's yoke have flocked to our side. Why am I trembling like the last leaf on a November maple?

Machiko appears by my side. "I've prepared a sleeping draught for you, Mistress."

I gulp the bitter tea and lie on the bed Machiko has arranged for me. Soon her strong fingers prying the stiffness out of my shoulders, and the stupefying effect of the herbs takes hold, and I shudder into an uneasy sleep.

The horse dances under me, whinnies nervously, puffs of steam coming from his nostrils. Something heavy on my head: the dragon helmet. Brocade shirt against my skin, damp with sweat, armor black as my horse rubbing here and there against the skin. I put a hand to my throat, touching the talismans for reassurance.

"We should attack, father," Tomomori says. his face pale beneath his helmet in the gathering gloom.

"Wait for the command." A deep voice not mine but Sessho's, comes from my throat. Muffled clink of bridle and stirrup, my legs opening and closing with the panting of the Shadow Dancer's flanks beneath me. The night is moonless, the fog obliterating even the stars.

Suddenly, thousands of ghostly white banners are raised from the hills to our rear and our sides. A cacophony of panicked shouts:

"How did they get to our rear?"

"There must be thousands of them!"

"They're coming from behind!"

"Attack!"

"Retreat!"

All around a babble of confused voices, and battle yells coming from the surrounding Genji so loud the earth seems to shake with them.

"We should turn and fight!" Tomomori yells, but the surge of men and horses pushes forward, retreating towards the one route not blocked by Genji flags. All I can think of is Tomomori, getting him out of this safely, but the press of men and horses is carrying him away from me. Spurring my horse hard, "Wait, wait for me!" I call but my voice is lost in the shouting, shrieking din. Legs crushed against the close-pressed flanks of horses, air thick with the scent of fear, yells of "Come back, come back," clashing with, "Flee, flee, we're outnumbered."

Leaning low over the Shadow Dancer's neck, urging him on, eyes on the white tail of Tomomori's horse up ahead. Moonless night, impossible to see more than a few rows of horses and soldiers beyond Tomomori, but the air is shrill with screams ahead and I catch a few desperate voices calling, "Go back, it's a trap!"

I kick my horse, Shadow Dancer, mercilessly, finally close enough to grab Star Face's tail. Tomomori turns and as he turns a row of riders up ahead disappears, screaming, over an unseen brink.

"Stop! Stop! Turn! It's a trap!" I yell at Tomomori.

The horses churning forward in their panic, the momentum of riders behind pressing like an inexorable wave, row after row of riders wash over the edge. I finally grab Tomomori, pull him onto my horse, turn Shadow Dancer's head, the horses behind hit him broadside, nothing beneath his churning hooves but air, impact against rock, against flesh, the crush, the rolling, the breaking and more and

207

more falling on top until all are pulp and the river at the ravine's bottom runs red with blood.

Screaming and screaming and screaming…somewhere underneath the screams Machiko shouting, "Mistress, mistress, mistress, wake up! Come out of this evil dream!" Door slammed aside, guards brandishing spears and lanterns burst into the room glancing wildly about. Tokushi's servant Naniwa scampers in.

"The Empress has sent me to find out what is happening!"

"My mistress has just had a nightmare," Machiko says, holding a piece of silk up to my mouth to try to stifle my outcries.

Smell of fresh blood in my nostrils, screams of men and horses and the clang of metal against stone throbbing in my ears. I push her hand away. "No nightmare, a vision!" I sob.

"The Empress's sorceress has received ill-omens! Fetch the priests for purification!" the women gathered at the door babble. The crowd parts, collapsing to the floor to make way for Tokushi, who shuffles in uncharacteristically rumpled.

"There had better be good reason for this commotion in my quarters," she grumbles. "Seiko, get a hold of yourself, you are creating a panic."

Lady Daigon-no-suke pushes her way in, barking for the other ladies to return to their sleeping mats.

"Even a sorceress is entitled to a bad dream now and then. Go back to bed! You'd think the palace was on fire!"

I close my eyes and put my hands over my ears, trying to return to the bodies crushed against the rocks, to die with my Sessho.

Servants kneel before me, placing wine and nightmare banishing teas on a low table, pressing a cup into my hand. I overturn the table, throw the cup through a screen, keening. The talismans I made to protect them from sword, arrow and spear swimming uselessly in their blood. I did not make talismans to protect them from falling from a cliff, from being crushed by hundreds of horses and riders. The amulets, all the love that went into the making of them, are meaningless. Gagging, I vomit into a bowl someone puts in front of me.

"Seiko. We're alone now. Did you have a vision? Have our battles gone badly? Speak," Tokushi urges.

"We have lost a great battle."

"Are my brothers all right? What of Koremori and Tsunemasa? Who has died?"

"Everyone that matters." As more questions gush from her I throw up again.

"My lady, I do not know who lives. Only that many of our side have been killed by trickery. Please, I beg you, leave me to grieve."

Two days later, messengers arrive, half-dead from having traveled so quickly, informing us that the vision I saw came true at the pass at Kurikara, where only ten thousand of the forty thousand men Koremori and Michimori had taken with them survived. Shortly after that word arrives that we have lost another battle at Shio-no-yama; few survived that battle either, and Tokushi's youngest brother, Tomonori perished with the rest. What remains of our forces limps back to the Capital. There is no one left at court who is not plunged into the deepest mourning.

Each day messengers come bearing tales of their masters' last heroic hours, carrying scrolls inscribed with death poems. The literature of flirtation gives way to the literature of tragedy. Many of the death poems must be forgeries, since their 'authors' could have had no time during an ambush or surprise attack to scribble their final thoughts. Or if they were setting brush to paper at such a time, perhaps that explains our dismal record in battle. However, many of the poems were said to have been written on the night before an anticipated battle, and in that case they may be authentic.

The Empress asks me to memorialize the dead with my poetry, but I cannot. The language of poetry has died in my mouth. The Heike are crushed, and my beloved Sessho has been crushed with them. Inside, I am as crushed as if I too lay beneath that tomb of armor, soldiers and horses. As far as I am concerned, the war is over, and we have lost. My one wish is to travel to Sessho's country house and comfort his widow and remaining children.

"Impossible!" Tokushi responds when I beg permission. "The danger of travel makes such a plan untenable."

"If the messengers can get through, I can. I'll ride a horse instead of taking a carriage or palanquin."

"I said it's too dangerous."

"The Genji are said to be gathering for an attack on Kyoto. Traveling away from Kyoto will put me farther from danger."

Tokushi glares at me, the cords in her neck taut as bowstrings: the thought of losing me to Seishan makes her tremble. "It is taking everything I have to keep this court from sliding into hysteria," she says through clenched teeth. "I need your help, and I need you to not add to my burdens by asking for impossible things."

I bow my head. "You can see that I am too broken to be of use."

"In the last two years I have lost my beloved husband, my father, Shigemori, Mori-ko, and now Tomonori, my youngest brother. Think less of your losses and more of your duties. I will spare a messenger to take our condolences to Seishan." She dismisses me with an abrupt wave of her hand. I lean heavily on Machiko on the way back to my room. After a fruitless attempt to get me to eat, she brings my writing desk and mixes me some fresh ink.

"Beloved Seishan,

We were privileged to share the most beautiful of men. My only desire is to return to you and the children, but the Empress cannot spare me at this difficult time. When this war is over I will request to be released from the Empress' services so I can spend the rest of my days with you raising the younger children and enjoying our grandchildren together. I am shattered to lose Tomomori; I know what it is to be separated from a child, but not in such a permanent way. 'Fleeting as dew on the grasses.' My sleeves are drenched. Forgive the brevity of this letter. My eyes are so clouded with tears I cannot see to write. You know, as no one else can, what is in my heart."

A messenger takes that letter, along with missives from the Empress and other ladies who knew Seishan that same day. Within the week I have a reply.

"Beloved Seiko,

Thank you for your letter. I feel as if a lost piece of my heart has been restored to me. I do wish you could be here, with all my heart, but I understand the constraints of the time make it impossible. Naturally, the children are devastated. Nori is taking it the hardest. She has renewed her begging to let her put her hair in a warrior's knot and join the army to avenge her father and her brother. Needless to say, I have not wavered on this point. I told her that if she tried to ride off I would have her bound and gagged for the rest of the war. "I told you I would never marry!" she cried, "Now there will be no one left to marry!" I order her to her room so often, I almost never see her. I wish you were here, as you are always so much better with her fiery temper than I. The younger children do not really understand. If it were not for the sight of their smiles and the sound of their laughter I think I would go mad. Kiku asks about you often, as does her twin. Just yesterday, Matsu asked if his father and Seiko were off somewhere together and would they be back soon? I explained again that his father and brother were dead and he became angry and cried, "Nothing could kill my father!" Alas, I had thought the same myself, that the laws of karma would have kept such a good and beautiful soul from any harm. If this is a divine punishment, it must be for my sins, for he had none."

I put the scroll down, blinking away tears of rage that Seishan should blame herself, who has been the gentlest person, for this tragedy. When an earthquake comes, are only the bad trees knocked down? When lightning strikes a forest, do only the bad trees burn? Oh how I wish Matsu was right-- how I wish I was with Sessho in the windy lands. But I cannot inflict another loss on the children, who have lost so much. When I contemplate suicide, I see Sessho's eyes looking at me reproachfully. I must live the life he can no longer live, and provide his children with some of the love he can no longer embody.

The Heike had seemed invincible when seventy thousand riders with plumed armor, carrying red flags had departed the Capital. But when only twenty thousand returned, their red flags seemed limp and colorless. In only a month, the glory of Kiyomori has washed away as utterly as high tide takes a sand palace. It is like burning a whole forest in order to catch all the game within it. There is nothing left the following year. That is the sort of pride and gluttony which caused Munemori and the others not to save any forces for the future, but to squander them all while they were yet inexperienced and green.

The Capital is plunged into mourning; everywhere you look, people are wearing white as if the city now existed only in the spirit realm. The sound of bells from the temples, ringing with prayers for the dead, never ceases, day or night. Those lucky enough to have had their bodies returned to their families are cremated outside the city, and the smoke creates a pall that reddens everyone's impossibly red eyes even further.

Tokushi frets over whether she should take Antoku to the Great Shrine for Amaterasu at Ise to pray for a Heike victory. She believes the Sun Goddess could not deny the prayers of her own descendant at her principle shrine. But the roads north are full of Genji soldiers, and they have shown a lack of character profound enough to disrespect an Imperial truce. All we can do is

211

visit nearby shrines in Kyoto and promise to make pilgrimage to Ise as soon as the rebels have been safely routed.

Tokushi gently urges some of the younger girls to return to their families, as there is no possibility of arranging marriages and the gentle pursuits of well-bred ladies are no longer possible at court. Most of the families are only too happy to send carriages to fetch their daughters, seeing that their daughters might soon be in more danger under Heike protection that not. A few send missives to their daughters entreating them to remain and make their families proud by 'doing their duty.' Many of the remaining women have lost their husbands and are useless for anything, as I am myself. Some days there is such sobbing in our quarters that if you had combined all our tears you could have cast fishing nets in them, for the result would be an ocean.

I throw up almost everything I eat. I bat away anyone who comes near me with words of comfort. Only On'na Mari knows of my relationship with Sessho and his son. The others assume I grieve for the loss of all the Heike, or for Tokushi's brother Tomonori. The others who are widowed, or have lost sons, are put in seclusion and treated tenderly. No one knows that I am widowed. No one knows I have lost a son. Tokushi grieves piteously and acts as if my loss is no greater than hers. She has never had a husband of her heart. And On'na Mari's husband, Tsunemasa, has returned unhurt. She still has fits of weeping and faints dramatically--but only if an attractive young man is there to catch her. Only Seishan would understand, but because no guards can be spared, and because Tokushi needs me by her side, I cannot be where I long to be, with the broken remains of my family.

Chapter Twenty-Five
June 1183

A couple of days after I received confirmation of Sessho's death, Atsumori and Kiyosune arrive back from a separate campaign. Their campaign had not gone well either, but most of the soldiers in their battalion had been able to retreat. Both of them send notes stating that they are unharmed, expressing their eagerness to see me as soon as possible.

The thought of making love to anyone, ever again, is unbearable. They did not know that I had a husband in Tanba. It is hard to know what to say. I write identical notes to each of them, saying that I have suffered a great loss in the Kurikara mountains, and can see no one. I am grateful they have returned safely, and I hope they will receive everything they so richly deserve elsewhere. In this way I give them permission to seek other lovers. I know that when a man returns from battle, he needs a woman's soft arms around him, and her silken voice in his ear, to take away some of the horror of battle and restore him to the gentle prince he truly is. I cannot serve that function for them ever again. The pain is so huge, I consider plunging a knife in my breast and being done with it, but that would be the depth of selfishness.

Within a few hours of sending the letters, the messenger returns with notes of condolence from each of them. Both of them mention the death of their friend Arimori in this last engagement, and acknowledge that they are grieving, for him and all the men who were lost. Apparently Arimori was struck down near them, with an arrow through the neck. Kiyosune writes, "Atsumori stood over us, firing arrows as quick as lightning, while I knelt by Arimori and cut through the shaft of the arrow so I could remove it. He died while I was working, eyes looking into mine. Words cannot express the uselessness and loss I felt. Atsumori's ribs were bruised badly when he was struck by an arrow at close range, but it did not penetrate his armor, and thanks to your wonder-working talismans, both of us have once again returned safely."

Water spatters the edge of the scroll, spurting from my eyes as I think how useless my talismans were for Sessho and Tomomori. It probably puts those I love in more danger, thinking that my talismans will protect them. Certainly I know what Kiyosune means when he talks of being useless.

Machiko persuades me to eat a little gruel and rice cake. I have no appetite, but if I am not to fall ill and become a burden, I must eat something, though it tastes like ashes.

Kiyosune and Atsumori send letters every day. I ask a scribe to send formal thank you notes in response. Their long missives continue unabated, so I write a note to each in my own hand, asking them to please feel free to seek comfort elsewhere. But still the stream of letters and gifts continues. After the normal period of mourning is over, Machiko says, "Mistress, there is no way for them to comprehend. You must tell them the true nature of your loss."

She is right, of course. I send messages suggesting they both come together and visit, warning that I am not up to anything but conversation, writing, "I fear I have sad news to convey."

The gauzy white and lavender mourning robes I have inhabited for the last month hang from my thin frame. A glance in the mirror before they arrive shows my face is ghost white without any need for cosmetics to make it so. Perhaps when they see my haggard appearance, they will not feel disappointed that I am no longer available to them.

Atsumori enters wearing crimson and gold robes, with gold and carnelian bracelets, his hair freshly oiled and coiffed. His own make-up has not been neglected. Kiyosune, as usual, is far more subdued, garbed in a subtle symphony of whites, lavenders, and grays which seems entirely more suitable. I thought of sitting behind a formal curtain, but due to the intimate nature of our relationships, I feel it is only fair that they should see my face, while I tell them it is for the last time. Machiko pours them tea. I decided against offering them sake. Considering that Atsumori may be angry, given his passionate disposition, fueling it with sake could prove unwise. That is one reason I invited them together, trusting that Kiyosune's nature will be cooling water to Atsumori's fire.

"We are terribly sorry to hear of your loss," Kiyosune begins.

"But during war, loss is inevitable," Atsumori says. "But as for me," he continues after taking a sip of tea, "it makes me more determined to live each day as though it were my last, and to enjoy it thoroughly."

Kiyosune nods.

"That is a brave philosophy," I say, "I wish you all the pleasures and joys possible. Both of you deserve...everything." I set my cup down, as my hands have started to shake a bit.

"Was it a relative of yours who perished?" Kiyosune asks.

"Or another lover?" Atsumori suggests, cutting to the heart of it.

"As you know, I made trips several times each year to Tanba, to visit my friend Lady Taira Seishan."

They both nod. Though neither knows Seishan very well, they both know of my trips, and that Seishan is my best friend other than the Empress.

"We offered to escort you many times, but you declined," Atsumori reminds me.

"The reason I declined is that I was also very close to her husband, Taira Sessho, and to their children."

They nod. Then the light dawns on Atsumori's face. But he says nothing.

"Sessho and his son were killed. In the Kurikara mountains."

"We are very sorry for that," Kiyosune sympathizes.

"Yes, very sorry," Atsumori agrees. "So many brave men perished. It would take the rest of our lives to properly acknowledge all who were lost."

"I shall be grieving the rest of my life for what has been lost," I say.

"I am so sorry you lost your friend, and your friend's son," Kiyosune says.

"Am I right in guessing he was also your lover?" Atsumori asks huskily. Kiyosune looks at his friend in shock.

"Yes, you are correct," I say.

"Vanquished lover, do not sit,
Staring at the empty night.
The crescent arms of the moon,
Can bring you no comfort.
Only the arms of another,
Can do that." Atsumori quotes a still-popular poem from a century ago.

"I have loved you both, deeply," I say. "I rely on your discretion now, not to let this go any further than this room: Taira Sessho was the husband of my heart, but circumstances dictated that we could not be wed. But in every other respect, he was my husband. I bore him a daughter."

Kiyosune's eyes widen and his mouth gapes. I look down at my hands without seeing Atsumori's expression. "My shock and grief are such that...I cannot take your advice," I say to Atsumori.

"You plan to become a nun?" Kiyosune whispers.

"No. My place is here, with the Empress. But essentially, what I am saying is the same thing."

"How can you say that?" Atsumori demands. "You don't love me? You don't love Kiyosune? You don't love us?"

Kiyosune puts a restraining hand on his friend, but the sadness on his face is harder to bear than the anger on Atsumori's.

"Because we're just boys? No one that you take seriously?" Atsumori grimaces bitterly.

"He...he died..." Kiyosune cautions, patting Atsumori's arm.

"So you'll only love me--or Kiyosune--if we die?" Atsumori demands. He stands up arranging his robes angrily.

"I would be devastated if you died. I pray you will keep each other as safe as you can."

"For how long!" Atsumori sits back down. "For how long! How long do you expect us to wait?"

"You need to look elsewhere. Sometimes a broken cup can be put back together. Sometimes not."

"Meanwhile, we could die any day!" Atsumori spits. "Do we have time to go courting now? Home for a few days, then off again to fight."

"I am sorry."

"Give her some time," Kiyosune murmurs.

"We have. We have. And now we'll be leaving soon...who knows what awaits any of us. Are we to be denied what little comfort there is in this world?"

"One cannot drink from a broken cup. I am sorry. Imagine that I am dead."

"Don't say that," Kiyosune pleads.

"No, *you* imagine that *we're* dead!" Atsumori rejoins bitterly.

I put my hands over my face and turn away, unable to restrain my tears. "Please forgive me. I said I was sorry."

"Do you want them to leave, mistress?" Machiko queries in a barely audible tone.

"Yes please."

"If we're not wanted then..." Atsumori stands up. I can tell from the rough timbre of his voice that he is close to tears, but using his anger to conceal it.

"We did not mean to disturb you," Kiyosune apologizes. "We are very sorry."

"Please don't take offense. My mistress grieves terribly," Machiko says in a conciliatory tone.

"No offense is taken," Kiyosune replies in a shaky voice. I hear them stepping away, over the threshold.

"They are gone now, mistress." Machiko puts her hands on my shoulders. I curl up in a ball, covered with my robes and my hair, feeling more alone and desolate than ever. Machiko curls up next to me. "Such a cruel world, mistress," she snuffles. That night she does not urge me to eat anything. We drift in and out of crying and sleep and wake early the next morning, our eyelashes spiky with salt.

Chapter Twenty-Six
1183

Writing is pointless. Like everything else.

Chapter Twenty-Seven
1183

Everyone knows that ghosts cause havoc, wreak mayhem, take possession of bodies, and even cause those bodies to die. But few people know why. It is because they are still there, still conscious, yet invisible. They want to be loved, feared, acknowleged in some way. They exist, but no one sees them.

Now I have become a ghost in reverse.

Everyone sees me.

But I no longer exist.

Chapter Twenty-Eight
1183

Machiko says the Empress has ordered me to write. For at least three hours every day. And to eat. All of what is sent to me.

Eating is easy. I ask for fruit, mochi buns, and rice balls. Then I send Machiko on an errand and hide them in my sleeves. Later, I set them out in the garden for the birds.

It seems like a million lifetimes ago when I sat out here between the willows and the maples with a girl who knew how to hold still long enough to have the birds eating out of her hand.

As I watch the birds feast, I pluck long strands of my hair and wind it in the bushes for them to find and weave into their nests.

Some people believe that if the birds nest in your hair, it will make you crazy. But how could it make one crazy, to be part of a house of the sky?

Birds are never crazy. They have the perfect intelligence they need for each of their tasks.

It is only humans--and human ghosts--who work apart from nature, who break the sacred web of the kami.

Who make wars.

Who go insane.

Chapter Twenty-Nine
August 1183

One of the guards comes and kneels before Tokushi. "Honorable Kenrei'mon'in, there is a messenger from Lord Munemori demanding immediate entrance."

"Show him right in."

The messenger collapses in front of her, banging his head against the floor so hard I am amazed he remains conscious.

"Lord Taira Munemori is on his way and requests an audience with you immediately."

"I am always happy to receive my brother at any time. How long before his arrival?"

"Fifteen minutes."

"Fifteen minutes!" She waves him away. "I don't have time to change," she frets.

"We can just go to the audience hall as is. He is your brother, after all," Lady Daigon-no-suke points out.

"Yes, I just hate to appear so disheveled in front of him."

"You are never disheveled, my lady," Ben-no-taishi says.

Tokushi beckons to the three of us to accompany her into her audience room. Since it is Munemori we will dispense with the audience screens placed between the Empress and her petitioners.

We barely have time to settle on our cushions before a servant announces Munemori's arrival. He seems to fill up the room when he comes in. He has his father's imposing bulk, doubled by his own eating habits. He is wearing poles across his shoulders making his shoulders look twice as large as they are, giving him the impression of a giant. He can barely fit through the entryway.

"My lady," he nods towards Tokushi. He makes no effort to kneel, so servants help Tokushi rise so she can greet him standing.

"The tidings that I bring are not good."

Tokushi clutches her heart, wondering which of her family has been lost now.

"The rebels are nearing the outskirts of the Capital. Our soldiers can only hold them back for so long. I propose to take yourself and the young Emperor and make our way to Fukuhara. This is not a *retreat*," he emphasizes, "only a way of gathering more supporters from Shikoku and the coastal areas."

"Whatever you suggest, brother. We are in your hands." He looks away from her, eyes almost hidden behind his puffy cheeks, adjusts his jaw. He has trouble with his teeth and is often in pain from them. I think much of his overuse of alcohol and poppy syrups is for this reason.

"You will only be able to take the most important members of your court. We cannot take everyone. I am afraid you must dismiss most of your ladies, and take only those who cannot be spared. I have discussed the situation with Shigehira," he nods at Lady Daigon-no-suke, "and Noritsune and Koremori. We are all in agreement. Most of the wives and children must be left behind in the Capital. We cannot transport large numbers of delicate ladies, as the accommodations and conditions will be quite spartan. Also, the ladies who do come with us must be limited to one maidservant each. We are limited by how many mouths we can feed. It is hard enough to provision our soldiers; every town we arrive in, it is like locusts stripping the fields clean. The poor people are starving in our wake as it is."

"What of Takakura's other sons? And the Retired Emperor?"

"The Retired Emperor will accompany us. He is in full agreement that departure from the Capital is wise, as the Genji have formed a pincer attack, coming at us from two sides. After our recent defeats, we simply don't have the manpower to hold them off. I spoke to him myself earlier this morning. His household is packing. We will take Morisada, the Crown Prince. The other two we can leave with their nursemaids. Their mothers are of no account. With both the Emperor and the Crown Prince in our possession, no one can dispute our right to the throne."

"You do not plan to torch the palace, do you?" Tokushi asks anxiously.

"My lady, I have no wish to upset you, but the palace, the Roduhara Mansion and our families' other holdings must be put to the torch. Otherwise they will become spoils of war."

"Then we must have many carriages to take the most precious objects from the palace."

"Pack no more than what you can carry on your persons. We are leaving at dawn."

"Tomorrow! We can't possibly leave that quickly!"

"There is no choice. Travel light. Some of the lesser nobles have volunteered to take some of the hangings and scrolls from the library to their own homes. They may or may not be safe there. Servants will bury much of the statuary in the hopes of preserving it."

"The rebels are relentless," Tokushi says despairingly.

"If you have no more questions, I have much to do."

"Oh, please, brother, forgive me, I did not mean to keep you...all shall be done as you wish."

He leaves.

Tokushi stands for a moment in shock, then gathers herself.

"We have no time to waste, ladies." We return to the main rooms and she calls all the ladies to gather. When everyone is assembled, she kneels on her dais that elevates her slightly above the others, with me on one side and Lady Daigon-no-suke and Ben-no-taishi on the other. The other ladies sit in a series of crescents, filling the entire room. All are still wearing whites and lavenders and the pale pastels of mourning. Except for our dark hair, we look like so many statues of ivory and alabaster.

"Ladies," Tokushi says, "I wish to thank all of you for your service to me and my family, and the young Emperor. It seems that we must relocate the court once again to Fukuhara." She hesitates. None of the ladies raise their heads, and there is no break in the silence. "I shall only be able to take a few of you with me. It seems the rebels are nearing the city." A few stifled gasps and cries of fear greet this announcement. "Most of you will be returned to your families. Ben-no-taishi and Lady Daigon-no-suke are now going to circulate among you. If they place a jewel in your hands, you are dismissed to return to your families. Those of you who do not receive a jewel, please remain while the others begin to pack their things. We shall then discuss how many of you wish to accompany me, since I have no intention to lead any of you into hardships you are unwilling to assume. It may be an arduous journey."

Ben-no-taishi and Lady Daigon-no-suke give a jewel as a parting gift to each of the women on their lists. Most of them seem relieved and bow, taking their handmaidens with them to gather their posseions. Three come up to Tokushi. "Please Lady," one entreats, "I could never leave your side. I beg you to take me with you. I will follow you to the ends of the earth."

"Do you not wish to return to your uncle?" Tokushi says.

"I should prefer to die in your service, right here and now if necessary," the woman responds passionately.

"Very well. Ashashi-ko. You may remain."

"Oh, thank you, thank you," she says, kissing the hem of Tokushi's robe.

"And you, Imaimi?" Tokushi says.

"I also beg to be allowed to remain," Imaimi says with her lips quivering. "My family would be greatly shamed if it were to be said that I ran away."

"No one is running away. I am sending people back to their homes. There is no shame attached to it"

"Nonetheless," Imaimi says, tears beginning to streak her face, "I implore you to allow me to remain."

"Very well," Tokushi says, touching the top of Imaimi's head.

"I am just a simple country girl," volunteers the last of the three, a heavy-set girl named Hiroki-ko. "But I know how to dye cloth and make candles and cook. My family lives too far away for me to return to them safely in any case. It may be that my small talents will be useful."

"Yes, of course, I should have thought that your family is too far away for a safe return," Tokushi says. "This list was assembled in haste. Naturally, you may stay."

There are perhaps twenty women remaining in the room. Tokushi says, "Now, if any of you do not wish to accompany me, let me know. I will not be angry with you. My brother wishes for me to take only a few, but I could not choose among those remaining. Some of you will wish to accompany me because your husbands will be going," she nods at Lady Daigon-no-suke, "and others of you it will be hard for me to part with. If you do not wish to accompany us, let me know now."

One girl raises her hand and Tokushi beckons her over.

"I could think of no greater honor than to accompany you anywhere, even to the Shide Mountains," the girl chokes, "but I have recently received a letter from my mother saying that she is ill. I cannot leave her in this condition."

"I am sorry to hear of your mother's illness. Please pack your things at once and return to her."

Another girl comes forward. "A thousand apologies, but my sister has been widowed and left alone to raise her three children. I feel I should go and stay with her."

"You have my permission, Shinseise," Tokushi nods.

No one else comes forward.

"All right ladies, each of us is to be allowed only one chest of jewels and robes. Everything else you must wear. This is not to say that you may not wear many layers."

Lady Daigon-no-suke says, "Take your jewelry and sew it into the hems of your robes."

"Each of us will have only one maidservant." Tokushi continues.

"One maidservant!" one of the ladies gasps. "Oh, please, both mine have been with me since we were children."

"Even I will only be taking Naniwa," Tokushi says. "We must all make sacrifices. Lord Munemori says that wherever the soldiers pass through, peasants starve in their wake. We must not add unduly to the burden of the common people by bringing too many mouths to feed. This is my order, and it is inflexible. Your maidservant may wear several of your robes. Nothing must be left in the palace. All your other possessions must be sent back to your families, or given to others remaining in the Capital for safekeeping. Go now, and hurry!"

Everyone scatters, running hither and thither.

Tokushi kneels before her altar, stroking a red and gold enameled vase, one of so many things that will have to be left behind.

"If the soldiers will not fight to preserve the palace, what will they fight for?" she murmurs.

"It is not that they will not fight," Lady Daigon-no-suke says, "it is that they cannot win. There are simply not enough of them. We have many allies in the southern part of this land. Once we have gathered our allies we shall come back, stronger than ever. Shigehira told me last night, in our pillow talk, of the men's discussions." She quotes the old adage: "A well timed retreat prevents a defeat."

"Of course," Tokushi wipes the tears from her face. "My weakness is a disgrace to the family."

"You are strong as steel," Ben-no-taishi protests.

I kneel behind Tokushi and place my hand on her back.

"The willow bends, but does not break. We will bend before this wind, and survive the storm."

"Thank you, ladies," Tokushi sniffs. "Naniwa, get my clothing and jewelry all laid out. There are many hard decisions to be made."

Sotsu-no-suke, Tokushi's half-sister and Antoku's primary nurse since their sister Mori-ko died, enters. She kneels beside Tokushi and they embrace tightly.

"Antoku is insisting on bringing his rabbits. What shall I tell him?"

"It is impossible for him to bring his rabbits. Queen of the heavens, we must see that they are protected. Where can we take them where they will not end up in a Genji stewpot?"

"They could be released into the wild," Ben-no-taishi suggests.

"They would never survive in the wild," Sotsu-no-suke says. "They have lived in comfortable cages all their lives. They would come hopping over to the first person they saw, hoping for burdock or carrots. Is there any chance we could take one or two rabbits to mollify him?"

"No, there is no way we can take rabbits in a carriage!" Lady Daigon-no-suke says with exasperation.

"I told the children that the Emperor must see the lands and the people under his care, and that this journey is a sort of Imperial inspection," Sotsu-no-suke says.

"Yes, we don't want the children to be afraid," Tokushi says. "I still think we should take the other two."

"They are the children of merchant-born concubines," Lady Daigon-no-suke scoffs. "Who even knows if their father was Takakura? Besides, Go-Shirakawa will be with us. The younger children and their mothers have already been sent home to their families. Morisada is his favorite anyway. The other two are too young for him to play with. Trust me, Lady, the other two are as insignificant as the girls."

"He can take his rabbit toys to play with," Tokushi suggests.

"All right," Sotsu-no-suke says, looking miserable. "What shall I do if he *orders* the rabbits are to come?"

Lady Kiyomori appears suddenly. "I shall come with you and explain to him. I have ordered the carriages to be brought into the courtyard." They depart, followed by Ben-no-taishi and Daigon-no-suke.

I sidle closer to Tokushi. "Lady, in view of the fact that Munemori has insisted that we take as few people as possible...if you wish it, I can return to Tanba," I offer, hoping against hope that she will let me rejoin my family.

"How can you say such a thing!" she replies in a distraught tone. "Leave without my sorceress? I am certainly not leaving without you, however much you might wish to abandon me in my hour of need."

I flatten myself on the floor. "I have absolutely no wish to move an inch from your side," I vow. "Only, if the sacrifice should be required, I thought I should be the first to volunteer."

"Go help Machiko pack your things."

Back in my room, I stop, staggered by the rainbow explosion of silks and jewels strewn in layers and heaps so that not a sliver of floor is visible. I kneel at my writing desk and scribble a quick letter to Seishan to let her know that the court is relocating to Fukuhara, possibly beyond. "My duty calls me to follow the Empress. I have no idea what may happen in the time to come, but please know that there will never be a moment when all of you are not in my heart's deepest thoughts. I know you hold me in yours as well. If we do not see each other again in this life..." I cross out that line. "I will pray to be reunited with you in each moment," I write instead. Then I take another scroll and write a quick note to On'na Mari, asking if she is coming with us. I send that one with a messenger right away.

My jewels are the most valuable. I will send all the jewels I can't take with me to Seishan. I will divide them up between two or three messengers and hope they aren't killed by marauding bandits or simply abscond with the gems themselves. I put together a list of things I want Nori-chan to have, including a pearl-handled dagger, and set aside the tiny ivory animals my father gave me for Kikuko, along with a pearl headdress her father had made for me. Seishan will look lovely in a necklace of cool green jade leaves. To Matsu I send the Go set that his father gave me, and a carved jade horse that someone gave me in exchange for a healing. I add to Seishan's pile one of the necklaces Sessho gave me, but most of the gifts he gave me I cannot part with. I wear one necklace with its carved jade symbol for the lovers and a hairpiece with the Bridge of Birds carved from ivory and mother-of pearl. These things I will not part with until someone takes them from my body. I can't give up the more valuable things the Empress has given me, as she would doubtless take offense. I put a selection of jade butterflies aside for Kiku. I then compose another list of

227

valuables to be sent to Tsubame when it is again safe for messengers to travel that far north, asking Seishan to make sure she gets them should anything happen to me. I want to send them part of my wardrobe as well, but the silks are bulky. If my messengers are obviously burdened with valuables it will be a death sentence for them. Seishan would have to shorten my robes so much to wear them it would ruin the patterns anyway, though Nori could wear them, if she would take off the men's attire she prefers.

"If anything happens to me," I say to Machiko, "I want you to save yourself if you possibly can and take as many of my things as you can carry to Tanba."

"I would die before I would ever leave your side," she says loyally.

"What if I order you to escape?" I say, squeezing her hand. "It is likely that if an ill fate betides me, it shall encompass us both, but if it is possible, it is my wish that you survive."

"Let us not talk of such things, mistress. The Sun Goddess is on our side. The rebels will be defeated."

"Of course; you are correct." We go back to sorting my possessions. I had always thought I was not as enamored of pretty things as most, but now every robe I look at makes me think of the occasions when I wore it. I think of how Kiyosune kissed this one off my shoulder, how Atsumori slipped his first message into the sleeve of that one. How can I part from a single robe woven for me at Sessho's house, the ones that lay on top of both of us, gathering our scents as we made love beneath them?

I set aside a pile of silks and jewels and jade carvings given to me by women of the court seeking my healings and favors.

"Send this pile to your family," I say to Machiko.

"My lady, it is too much."

"What else shall we do with it?"

"We can bury the jewels in the garden."

"Just send it. It is the least I can do for taking you into danger with me."

"You are far too generous, mistress." Tears fill her eyes.

"Would you like me to send them a letter?"

"Yes please."

"What would you like to say?"

"Tell them that my all-gracious, incomparable mistress has sent these robes and jewels for their comfort, and to use them to obtain an education for my nephews. Tell them to remain loyal to the Heike, even if it should cost them their lives..."

"I'm not going to write that! I don't want it to cost them their lives!"

"Just tell them to remain loyal then...oh mistress, it seems so wrong for me...."

She stops, but I know that she means it seems she is giving me orders as I take her dictation.

"It is just this once, Machiko."

"You do me too much honor," she whispers. "Tell them to hold us in their prayers. That is all," she finishes simply. I complete the letter and set it aside to be sent with that pile of goods. After great agonizing, I pick twelve robes each for us to wear when we leave, and fill the one chest allotted to me with a few extra garments and the jewels that I am keeping. Several maidservants get to work sewing jewels into the hems and sleeves of each garment we shall wear, and it occurs to me that were we to fall into the water thus encumbered we would sink like the many stones we carry. Most of Seishan's letters I return to her, keeping my favorite. I cannot part with most of my children's letters nor those from Sessho, so my trunk ends up being half-full of old letters.

A messenger arrives. "The Empress says to be sure and bring as many chests of herbs as will be necessary." I nod, having expected that room would be made for those. I manage to sneak a few of my other jewels into the bottoms of those chests.

A messenger returns from On'na Mari, bearing a letter. I would recognize her perfume anywhere; the scent wafting up from the scroll is so dear, so familiar. I unroll it.

"My dearest Seiko,

I am utterly distraught to hear that you too are among those abandoning the city, leaving those of us who remain to their fates. Tsunemasa informed me that he does not believe that I am capable of withstanding the rigors of the flight to Fukuhara, for he says there is the possibility the Taira may have to travel farther than that, and he cannot think of myself and Akoyo in danger near the front lines. I agree with him wholeheartedly"--I smile imagining her delicate shudder as she writes this--"and am determined to return to my father's family with Akoyo. Though I have no wish to abandon our lovely home, Tsunemasa is doubtless quite right in fearing it may be made a target. Fortunately my father can keep our belongings in one of his warehouses, so if our home is put to the torch, we will not lose everything. My servants are scurrying about like ants carting everything across the city now. It is chaos out there! If only Japan was still ruled by Empresses, this never would have happened. What *is* the matter with men that they cannot resolve their differences peacefully? I shall miss you dreadfully, but Tsunemasa assures me it is only a matter of time before the tide turns and the Heike sweep triumphantly back into the Capital. I shall be holding you and our common cause in my prayers. Please give my regards to the Empress—"

Tears speckle the front of my gown. I shall certainly miss On'na Mari's sense of humor. But the thought of On'na Mari setting forth on a long journey with only one servant and twenty-four layers of garments between them is indeed laughable. I am glad she and Akoyo will be staying with her family. She has bemoaned her humble origins in the past, but she must be grateful now to return to a merchant's home which will not be targeted by the invaders. Doubtless her father will make himself as indispensable to the Genji as he did to the Heike, insinuating himself into their graces with fawning overtures and priceless gifts. I only hope On'na Mari does not become one of the priceless gifts.

The sound of footsteps running up and down the halls mingles with weeping as women fall into each other's arms, sobbing their goodbyes. A young woman named Benten-no-suke asks permission to enter. She had been one of my lovers before Sessho died and I had no heart for love any longer. She bows.

"Excuse me for disturbing you. I wanted to let you know--before I depart-- that I shall pray for you every night. I am so grateful for everything you taught me. You have been a far greater influence than you realize."

I kiss her smooth, flawless cheek. "Be safe," I say, clasping her hand. "And you," she returns, hugging me tightly. I pray she will not be forced into marriage with one of the Genji conquerors. Hopefully we shall be keeping them too busy making war to be making marriages with these ladies we must leave behind.

I go back to packing and sorting, then take a walk in the garden to clear my mind. It may be the last time I see it. Surely the garden will survive even if the palace is burned. It is the height of summer, my herbs are flourishing. I breathe in the scent of the pines, finger the feathery green growth at the end of each branch. I wonder what will happen to the koi. I hope someone will remember to feed them. There are probably too many of them to obtain their food naturally from the few insects foolish enough to land on the streams winding through the garden. The bush with the hummingbird nest tugs at my heart. I kneel and say goodbye to the fresh stands of herbs, potent with their summer saps. There is no point in gathering any, as we shall have nowhere to dry them. I wish I had known sooner so I could have harvested and dried from this year's crop. I walk up to the moon bridge where we once surveyed the burning of Kyoto, knowing that it will soon be burning again. From this vantage point I can see that the streets are thronged with people trying to leave the city. Ox-carts are jammed axle to axle, unable to move, and people are shouting and shrieking at each other. People on foot carrying enormous bundles on their backs are clambering over stalled carriages to escape. I climb down the bridge, retire to one of my favorite hidden bowers and meditate for a while, breathing in the scent of the jasmine. I rub my face against the soft star-shaped blossoms, then tie a few in my hair and return to my room.

"Ah! Lady Wisteria!" Machiko greets me, "what of this pile?" She gestures towards a waist-high heap of clothing and gems.

"We'll send those to On'na Mari."

I write a note to accompany the goods: "Any of these robes or skeins of silk that are not fine enough for you, please just give them to your sisters or your servants, as you prefer. If we meet again, I may ask for some of these jewels back, in the meantime it would please me if you would consider them yours. I will be praying for your safety."

I wish I could make up some protective amulets for her and Akoyo, but there is simply no time. They have talismans I have made for them in the past, and though it has been awhile since I consecrated them, there is no reason to think they will not still be effective. Tsunemasa is a nephew of Kiyomori's, so I fear his family could be in danger for that reason. Hopefully they will be able to blend back into her merchant father's household. But if there is anything On'na Mari is not, it is unobtrusive. If any Genji should spy her beauty, he would be inspired to possess it.

Finally almost everything has been cleared away. Male servants arrive to carry our remaining luggage to the courtyard. Tokushi has designated the pomegranate carriage for our use. Ruby red with gold finials and scrollwork, it is a vehicle designed to impress when drawing up at a party. I hope it will be sturdy enough for the use to which we are putting it. We line the entire interior with mulberry scrolls, as the worst hardship I can imagine would be to be without writing materials.

Gradually all the ladies drift out into the garden that evening to gaze at the moon.

"As the moon grows, so will our hopes and successes," one says boldly.
All of us nod and murmur in agreement, and pray to Tsukiyuki, the Moon Goddess, to protect us.

"She gave us the gifts of wind and fire and paper," one of the girls says, "so She will give us victory as well."

"We shall stop at the Hachiman shrine and pray on our way out of Kyoto," Lady Daigon-no-suke says. "All the kamis support the Emperor. Don't forget that, girls." We all nod, hair ornaments shivering together like the chittering of metallic birds. Then we kneel and write farewell poems to the palace and to the Capital.

"Extinguished by the wind,
The passing of the candle
Leaves the lantern dark," I write, thinking that after the Emperor's court leaves, Kyoto will be like an empty lantern.

"Try to write something less ill-omened," Tokushi chides me. She reads her poem:

"It only takes a moment
For a retreat to become
A glorious victory.
The snake sheds its skin
And emerges more brightly than ever."

She shoots me a reproving glance, letting me know that this is the sort of poem she expects.

Lady Daigon-no-suke recites.

"As sad as leaving,
The return will be twice as glorious.
The white of winter
Makes us appreciate
The colors of spring."

"The sun is traveling with us," one of the ladies writes, referring to the young Emperor,

"Therefore, darkness and defeat

232

Are impossible."

Tokushi exclaims approvingly and all the ladies clap.

Tsunemasa arrives and kneels near Tokushi.

"How go the preparations, my lord?"

"All is going well," he says, smiling bravely.

"Will you be bringing On'na Mari and Akoyo?"

"No," he says, looking like his heart would break. "On'na Mari could never withstand such hardships. They will be returning to her father's house in the morning. They will be safe there."

Tokushi puts a sympathetic hand on his arm. "We will be back soon."

"Yes, of course. It will only be a matter of a few weeks before we have gathered enough supporters to trounce the Genji. A month at most."

"There, girls, no reason to be melancholy. A month at most," Tokushi repeats confidently.

The girls try to hide their tear-streaked faces behind sleeves and fans.

"We are writing our farewell poems to the Capital. Will you write one with us?"

"If you wish it, Lady."

"Will you play us a song on your flute?"

Tsunemasa nods, takes the flute from his waistband and plays a song that has hopeful soaring melodies twining counterpoint with the melancholic strains. Hardly a dry sleeve is left among us when he finishes. He himself seems to be holding back his tears only with great effort. He then turns his attention to the paper proffered him by a servant, and soon produces the following;

"The same moon will shine on us
As shines on Kyoto
Wherever we go,
And the moon will be here
When we return."

We all sigh and nod with agreement. "I ask leave to spend the rest of this last evening with my family."

"Of course," says Tokushi. "Everything is under control in our household, is it not, Lady Daigon-no-suke?"

"Yes, and since I am not facing separation from Lord Shigehira, I shall remain here to address any issues, should they arise. I shall stay up all night if necessary to ensure a smooth departure at first light. You should go," she nods to Tsunemasa.

"Thank you." He bows to all of us. "Take heart, ladies, we shall think of it as a pilgrimage."

He leaves. A few other poems are presented, most of a rather melancholy nature.

"The times are dark;

But the sun and the moon

Always return from being eclipsed," Lady Ben-no-taishi says bravely. This thought pleases Tokushi, and she hands Ben-no-taishi a pearl from her sleeve.

"Though young, her spirit is wise," Tokushi admonishes the rest of us. "We must maintain a positive attitude. I'll not have people sulking in my retinue. The young Emperor must"--she hesitates,--"must never have the slightest cause to concern himself."

"It is an honor beyond imagining to be in the Emperor's presence," one of the young ladies chokes. "Better to live one day in such noble proximity than a thousand years without it."

"Well I daresay we shall all be alive much longer than a day!" Lady Daigon-no-suke responds tartly. "Enough of the long faces, girls. Let's get some sleep; we shall have a long journey tomorrow."

We hang our poems on the now nearly bare walls of the palace.

Machiko cleans my inkstone and replaces it in its case. We take it out to the carriage with my writing table, which I simply cannot do without. Back in our room, a young servant girl who looks no older than twelve holds poppy syrup infused sake out to us to help us sleep. It works so quickly I barely have time to brush my teeth and kiss Machiko on the forehead before, like the candle of my poem, my consciousness is extinguished.

Chapter Thirty
1183

The Emperor's primary attendants--Tokitada, the Director of the Palace Storehouse, and his son, the Middle Captain Tokizane--help Antoku and his brother into the carriage. The boys rub their eyes sleepily. It is a beautiful dawn, clouds turning from rose to ivory over the Eastern Mountains, swirling in eddies; the moon shines faintly, fading paler and paler as the sun rises, until it is transparent as paper. The crowing of roosters sounds like triumphal horns, as if it were the beginning of something wonderful, instead of the end of everything. The Regent Motomichi and several of our other attendants abandon us shortly after we traverse the center of the Capital. They excuse themselves saying, "We must return for several precious objects we carelessly left." But they never rejoin us. Most of the men are leaving their wives and children in the Capital, hoping they will be safer here than facing the perils of rough travel, eastern warriors, and the all too uncertain fate which awaits us. Peering outside the curtains of our carriage, I see battle-hardened warriors riding with tears streaming down their faces.

My robes are so heavy with jewelry I might as well be wearing a full suit of armor, and I am sure most of the other ladies feel the same way. Although Machiko and I have our own carriage, Tokushi grasps my arm and asks me to ride with her. So we enter the royal carriage, joining her and her servant Naniwa, Antoku, the young Crown Prince, Morisada, and their nurses. Of course we are crowded and immediately unbearably hot, even though we are leaving before sunrise. Our many layers of robes laden with trinkets insure that. Machiko, clothed in a full complement of my robes, looks flushed.

"Are you sure you would not rather have us ride in our own carriage?" I ask, fanning myself.

"No, no, unthinkable! You have to stay here with me. Besides, you need to play with the children and keep their spirits up," Tokushi insists.

The boys have been told that we are going on a holiday. I cannot think that they believe that, but they are only six and five years old, and they seem excited and cheerful rather than perturbed, so perhaps they do believe it. How do they know how many warriors are likely to accompany them on a holiday? Still, Antoku is like a hawk in his sharpness; he doesn't miss much. He is already accomplished at the game of Go, while his younger brother cannot sit still long enough to puzzle out a single intelligent move. Antoku will be a strategist, like Kiyomori. I only hope the clan survives long enough for his wits to mature. Privately I call him Kitsune-ko, little fox, a pet name I call my twins as well. People call me Kitsune-Majo, fox sorceress, because of my association with Inari. However much ordinary people fear foxes as harbingers of the supernatural, with their ability to seemingly appear and disappear into insubstantial air, I love the fox and wish all its cunning and shape-shifting abilities for the children I love. They will need that power of kitsune now more than ever.

The other child, Crown Prince Morisada, is more like a normal boy, full of giggles and mischief. He has the Sun Goddess' blood in his veins, but the way he carries on he seems more related to Uzume, Goddess of Laughter. Fortunately, just as the boys are becoming rowdy, Tokitada and Tokizane take the boys out of the carriage to ride with them on their horses. The Crown Prince is a nice boy, a charming and well brought up boy. But he is all boy, and it is a relief to have him off chattering with the young men whom he and Antoku both adore. They return to us feeling very manly indeed. Tokushi has been kind to the Emperor's other children: she oversaw their education and deportment, and kept their mothers, Takakura's concubines, under her thumb, seducing them with her myriad little kindnesses while her mother, Lady Kiyomori, terrorized them with implied threats.

As we ride, our maidservants massage our feet and perform acupressure to help us relax. It is almost impossible not to tense one's muscles in response to the jouncing of the carriage. Add to that the fear and uncertainty riding with us, and the lack of air inside, and it is no wonder we are soon miserable. We shall be traveling straight through to Fukuhara. But in only a few hours, our backs are incredibly sore from all the jolting. One of the ladies is sobbing uncontrollably, missing her family and her sweetheart, who died in the same battle that killed mine. She tries to smother her sobs in a pillow. The children look somber, and I try to cheer them up with the adventures of Tsuki Usagi, also known as Habo, the Moon Rabbit. I make a rabbit with the inner sleeves of my kimono and have it poke out of its hole (my sleeve), entertaining them with stories and singing and a hopping sort of dance. I have them put their fingers upright beside their ears so they can be rabbits too.

"Why is Habo yellow today?" Antoku wants to know. "He looks like a sun rabbit today!"

"Ah, yes," Tsuki Usagi replies, "I am dressed in Amaterasu's colors for I am traveling with her great-great-grandson, the Emperor Antoku. What a lucky rabbit!"

Finally we stop for lunch. A pavilion of gaily flowered silks is erected, and a selection of cold delicacies laid out before us.

"Where can Go-Shirakawa be?" muses Tokushi. "I sent Tokizane to invite him to join us." She claps her hands and orders a servant to find them. The children pick at their food, having gobbled far too many crackers in the carriage. I keep finding sharp crumbs in the lining of my robes.

At last, Tokizane appears, almost as white as the background of the tent.

"I hope the Retired Emperor is right behind you," says Tokushi.

"I...have dreadful news, my lady," Tokizane replies. He glances at the children, bites his lip and gestures with his eyebrows that perhaps we should talk privately. I rise with the Empress and we step over to the edge of the pavilion, which is billowing gently in a breeze scented with crushed grasses.

"The Retired Emperor did not accompany us this morning. Soldiers who went to see why his entourage was so delayed found that he had abandoned his mansion. Even when his servants were threatened by the sword, none could say where he had gone, only that he had left precipitously, in the middle of the night, with his consorts."

"But...but why?" Tokushi asks, bewildered. "Did he leave a note?"

"We fear...he may have...formed an alliance...with..."

"That's not possible! Abandon his own grandchildren? He just sent me a letter saying he looked forward to seeing Antoku more--" she staggers, then sinks to her knees, fainting, despite Naniwa and my best efforts to hold her up.

"What's wrong with mother?" Antoku cries out.

"She's tired. Napping. Say, are you boys done with lunch? Let's go feed the horses some of this fresh spring grass!" Tokitada says, and taking them each by the hand, leads them from the pavilion. No further lunch is enjoyed by anyone. Soon, the boys are again seated at the front of Tokizane and

Tokitada's saddles, while I apply aromatic herbs to the Empress's temples as she lies limply on my lap in the carriage.

At first, I too am surprised that Go-Shirakawa would abandon his grandchildren and the Empress, of whom he seemed fonder than most fathers of a true daughter. To desert us in this way, he must be convinced that our cause is lost, and the Genji will win. I wonder how long he has been parlaying with the Genji, trying to work out the most favorable deal for himself. He had long resented that Kiyomori wielded most of the actual power at the court, with himself 'no more than autumn leaves,' as he used to complain. Perhaps the Genji have promised him far more in the way of prominence and influence. Takakura had been content to play with the trappings of wealth, but Go-Shirakawa obviously longed for his hands on the reins.

Tokushi is distraught, and cannot be consoled.

"How can he leave us, how can he leave us?" she keeps crying in the bewildered tone of an abandoned child.

"He said he would always be there to protect me when Takakura died. It was a deathbed promise!" she says, as if such a thing could never be broken. I ask Machiko to tell a servant to heat some water so I can prepare a sleeping draught for her majesty. Finally, with the help of the potion, she falls asleep, her face swollen and blotchy. Naniwa applies a cucumber paste so Tokushi will awake looking calm, no matter how she feels.

My heart aches. Tokushi is simply incapable of understanding or accepting what has happened. Because of her nobility of heart, she always sees everyone as being as good and pure and noble as she is. Unfortunately, that is almost never the case. Perhaps it is better to be a schemer like Lady Kiyomori, like On'na Mari. Then one is never surprised by others' intrigues. Descendant of the Sun Goddess Go-Shirakawa may be, but he is more like Susanowo, her Storm-God twin, full of rough passions and ever bringing his will to bear in every situation, manipulating as masterfully as a magician with a sleeve full of magic tricks. Like the ninja assassins who are said to be able to battle with anything, a fan, a tea cup, a slipper, so Go-Shirakawa was never without some improbable weapon, some convoluted plot.

Around Tokushi he was a model of gentlemanly propriety though, with just the right grandfatherly twinkle. He concealed his duplicitous nature from her by simply showing her what she wanted to see: a great and noble descendant of Amaterasu, shining with her light. Perhaps it is best that the

Emperors remain children, each deposed almost as soon as the next is born. As adults, that power to obtain whatever is desired, at any bitter cost to others, is too corrupting. Ah, but Antoku is so bright, so shining--more than Go-Shirakawa, more than Takakura--because he is Tokushi's boy. Because he is Shigemori's nephew. There must be a fitting bottle to hold the wine of the sun, and Antoku's combination of lineages provides the perfect container for his ancestress' divine essence.

The old capital site at Fukuhara is a melancholy sight: the palaces and mansions and servants quarters alike all decked with mosses and climbing vines gone wild, the roof tiles broken, rain pooling on the floors, mice scrabbling everywhere, birds' nests under the eaves. But the bay is packed with Heike allies who have arrived by ship, a flotilla decked with red banners floating on the harbor like an autumn forest. It is an ill-omened thought, but I wonder how long it will be before these red flags, like the autumn leaves, should fall. We spend a melancholy night at the old palace, hearing the dismal croakings of frogs and the harsh grieving sounds of loons in the marsh. The smell of mildew is strong and it is hard to breathe, hard not to think that this blatant deterioration, this rot and decay of one of Kiyomori's dreams does not presage the moldering of all of his clan's fondest hopes.

Chapter Thirty-One
August 1183

We spend only one night at Fukuhara. It is late August, just past Obon, the Festival of the Dead. A crescent moon glimmers in the early morning hours like a spilled cup, waning and dwindling, like our power. Though it has only been two years since this was briefly the Capital, most of the buildings Kiyomori had commissioned are in a state of disrepair. The palace for Spring Blossom Viewing, the Beach Palace for Autumn Moon Viewing, the Bubbling Springs Hall, the Pine Tree Hall, the Snow-Viewing Palace, the temporary Imperial Palace with its pavement tiles shaped like mandarin ducks, all droop with decay. Moss covers the roads, and the gates are drooping with opportunistic vines. Ferns sprout from the roof tiles, and the fences have become fences of living green, overtaken by ivy and morning glories. It is like trying to sleep in a ghost world.

Even that tattered glory ends the next morning when Munemori orders the warriors to set fire to all the remaining structures and palaces so they will not fall to the onslaught of the pursuing Genji, so that these buildings will not give them any shelter, nor their destruction any victory. The waves lapping against the beach are hardly more salty than our sleeves with sorrow.

Common folk in their woven conical hats are burning seaweed. The smoke from their fires, blurring the shoreline to a blue smudge, is soon over shadowed with black billows mounting up from the city as men on horses ride through, throwing torches into every building.

Antoku pulls on Lady Kiyomori's sleeve. "Won't Grandfather be angry that those men are burning everything he built?"

Lady Kiyomori draws a somewhat shaky sigh. "No," she says, "he will understand. We are burning those things to send them to the other world, where he and your father dwell now. They will be very happy to see them again."

"Oh," Antoku exclaims, "it's a present then."

"Yes. It is a present. To the kami, especially the kami of your father and grandfather. They will be very pleased."

"They were all fusty and musty anyway," Antoku shrugs. "I could hardly breathe last night."

The boys soon turn their attention to the hundreds of boats waiting for us to board, debating the merits of this or that one.

"That one will go like the wind!"

"No, like a seagull in the wind!"

They have been told that we are on a trip to acquaint Antoku with the other lands which will be under his care. "An Emperor must know the land and the peoples of his realm, so he may care wisely and justly for all," Lady Kiyomori explains. The boys are eager to get on the boat and set off on this fine adventure they have been promised. They are allowed to board while the boatmen and warriors are preparing for departure, and they run all over the deck, examining the oars and the sails, asking which rope does what and can they help pull on them. Tokizane takes turns carrying them up the mast so they can see what it is like from up high. Tokushi did not want to permit it, but Lady Kiyomori silences her concern.

"He will need to be strong to win back his kingdom. Amaterasu will not allow anything to happen to him in Her sky."

When our ships depart, the boys sit with Tokizane and Tokitada fishing from the back of the boat. They put the fish they catch in a great bucket of water with a lid. Antoku assigns them posts before plopping them into the bucket, which he has designated the court--which makes us all laugh since it seems even a child can intuit what a fishbowl the court is at times. "You will be my Minister of the Left," he officiously tells one fish. "And you will be my Minister of the Right," he dubs the next. "And you will be Master of the Stables...horses don't eat fish, do they?"

"No," Tokizane assures him, "never."

"Good. Oh look, you got another--bring him in."

Tokizane reels the sable codfish in, unhooks it and holds its squirming silver up to the young ruler.

"You will be my scribe...oh, what will he write with?"

"He can write with squid ink," I suggest helpfully.

"Oh, good--can he use one of your writing brushes? He can hold it in his mouth."

"Certainly," I reply. "He will probably handle that pen better than many I have seen at court."

"Wisdom found...at the bottom of a deep pool," says Antoku, reciting a bit from a poem using the wisdom of carp as a metaphor. I am constantly reading and reciting poems to him, but I am amazed how much of it he retains. My twins are nearly two years older and I can hardly get them to sit still for a poem's worth of time.

"I shall recite poetry to him all the time and challenge him to poetry contests. He will be the wisest carp scribe of them all," Antoku says excitedly.

"A boat is not a palace.

A fish is not a scribe.

White-birds are not the Capital." (He refers to a type of sea bird known as a Capital Bird.)

But the Emperor Sun shines everywhere."

The maturity of the poem is stunning. After a moment of silence, everyone takes a deep breath. It seems like a sign from the Sun Goddess that all will be well.

Later, by fish-oil light, his tutor persuades Antoku to write his poem down and practice his calligraphy. Of course, Antoku does not really even know his characters yet, but he copies what his tutor has written and then declines to do it over, maintaining that the waviness of the characters is right because it "looks like a fish drew them."

"That is what I was *trying* to do," he insists, and it is all so amusing no one has the heart to coax him to try harder.

The first thing one notices about being on a boat is how cramped everything is. Our ship is most elegant, however, with beautiful polished wood decks, golden like the sunlight. The inner cabins are decorated with scrolls and vases containing chrysanthemums and peonies. When our personal altars and writing tables are set up, it looks very home-like and our spirits are lifted. I am glad not to be prone to sea-sickness; many of the ladies become ill, and no matter how much incense we burn, the smell of sickness lingers. I make compression bandages with pearls in them to press on the proper points on their wrists, and brew ginger tea. Eventually we all adjust to the wave-borne life. Tokushi vomits several times in those first few days. Her face is white as paper, but she does not complain, though I see her fingers moving across her prayer beads incessantly.

Fortunately, neither of the boys gets sick, and they dash about the boat happily as if this were the greatest adventure they have ever had. Out of the cloister of the palace, they grow brown in the sun and seem healthier and more robust than ever. The sailors help the boys put in fishing lines to drag behind the boat. They thrive under the attention of men who know all about boats and fighting and fish, and preen in their new-found manliness. I am convinced that if we all survive this conflict, these travails will make Antoku stronger, make him a better king.

Sometimes they proudly offer their fish to the cooks and sit puffed with ridiculous but endearing pride as we all praise them for catching our dinner. Other times they let them go, as Antoku practices being a magnanimous Emperor who grants felons (being a fish the apparent crime) their freedom. Sometimes he names them Yoritomo or Yoshinaka or other names he has overheard as belonging to our enemies. The leaders of the rebellion are invariably grilled or marinated, but often their smaller "followers" are lectured and released. "Will you be loyal to your Emperor from now on?" he sternly questions a small bream, which nods its head vigorously. "Then you shall be pardoned. But do not get caught in such a web of deceit again!" he admonishes, slipping the gasping fish back into the water. Perhaps one day soon he will be pardoning the lesser of the actual traitors, though I hope he will not make the mistakes Kiyomori made in allowing the sons of his enemies to thrive far from his watchful eye.

In spite of the excitement of waking up on a boat every day, the boys are expected to keep up with their studies, which consists mostly of simply sitting and listening to historical tales (largely now of war, I notice), and being cajoled to recite passages from noble poems. When we are docked on land they practice their archery and sword-play, though no one would ever expect an emperor to engage in battle. I am happier to see them practicing their dances. They are happier when fantasizing about their prowess as renowned warriors. How is it that even a boy emperor imagines himself as a dauntless hero?

Sometimes dolphins swim beside the boat, and that is a cheering omen. They seem like such happy creatures, with their perpetual smiles. We always feel protected by the kami when we are escorted by the dolphins.

We stop briefly at Itsukushima Shrine. The island is so sacred only royalty can walk on it, but the Shrine itself is on piers over the water so that attendants may also participate in the ceremonies. We write our prayers on rice paper and put them in the prayer fire, asking for what has been lost to be restored to us. The oracles we receive from the priestess there could be interpreted in any one of a thousand ways. Their vagueness makes me certain that they either do not know the answers, or felt the truth would not be acceptable. Tokushi entreats me to take one of the sacred braziers and perform an oracle fire myself, as my mother had done for the Taira in their dark days during the previous war with the Genji.

"My eyes are too veiled with tears and grief to see clearly. My feelings would be certain to distort everything for the worse." My own future seems impossibly bleak without Sessho. He was my heart, and without him I am like the burnt-out shell of a palace--the illusion of wholeness from without, nothing but black barren ash within.

Outside the Shrine I can hear the deer call desire to each other. It is such a mournful sound, you would not think they were calling each other for love. Perhaps they know, better than we, how love always leads to mourning. Here the deer are safe from hunting, and if I could turn doe I would seek my stag on this dark mountain. The doe calls her stag, the wave seeks the shore, but only the Bridge of Birds can reunite me with my Sessho. Weaver and Herdsman are separated, and only once a year, when all the birds whirl between them and form a bridge, can they cross it and be together for a night. But for mortals, only in death can we cross the star bridge to be reunited with our lover.

Every night I see one of the young courtiers sitting on the deck of his adjacent craft, piping soft, mournful notes into the night air with his flute. Each note is so lovely it is like a pearl, staining the night with its plaintiveness like the moon stains the waves with its silver. One night he slips silently off the deck into the silver-black sea, leaving his death-poem behind him, wrapped around his flute. Everyone grieves, and I weep also, envying the young man his sojourn under the sea with his throne of coral, consorting with the dolphins and water dragons. But unlike this young man, I cannot leave those who depend on me, even though those I love most are now so far away. Still, I must believe that one day we will be reunited, or if I must precede them into the windy land of death, they will at least have the comfort of knowing I did not choose to abandon them.

244

We are far from the wild lovemakings which preceded the battles of the last two years. Now, everyone sleeps alone, wrapped in their long black hair and their melancholy. The few lucky married couples, like Michimori and Kozaisho, who are traveling together try to muffle the joy of their passion so as not to deepen the despair of the rest.

Chapter Thirty-Two
September 1183

It takes forever to receive messages from the Capital when we are on the move like this. I can only imagine the frustration and exhaustion of the messengers trying to find us while avoiding being found by the Genji. At last we hear that Retired Emperor Go-Shirakawa has established a new court and preens like a parrot under the patronage of Yoritomo's cousin Yoshinaka, whom Go-Shirakawa now favors with the epithet, Defender of the Throne. He seems to have forgotten that Antoku, not he, now occupies that throne. The traitors who abandoned us during our flight from Kyoto now swill the Retired Emperor's sake and inflate themselves like puffer fish with their new titles. So we now have a Minister of the Left who barely knows left from right, and a Master of the Stables with no more intelligence than a stable boy. It is all so unimaginable, like snow falling upwards, like foxes caught and devoured by hares.

Tokushi will not hear a word against Go-Shirakawa; she still believes he is being somehow forced or coerced into betraying us. The only thing 'coercing' the Retired Emperor is his pride. He always resented Kiyomori for wielding actual power while his, the Emperor's power, remained largely symbolic. Now he sees his opportunity to match wits with a lesser man, Yoshinaka, and hopes to wangle his way back into the center of things. But the worst news of all, so bad the messenger trembles for his life in the telling of it, is that Go-Shirakawa has taken Antoku's other half-brothers, who stood third and fourth in line for the throne, and has dubbed the youngest one the Emperor and the third youngest the Crown Prince! Tokushi blanches at this and then hides her face behind her sleeve. Lady Kiyomori's nostrils flare, and her dragon talons tighten around the railing of the ship until they are white as bone.

How can there be two Emperors? Never in the history of Japan has it been so! The messenger quails before Lady Kiyomori, but in a moment she gathers herself and says, "Do not fear. We punish the makers of ill tidings, not the bearers of them. You will be paid in gold and jade for your efforts in finding us, and given safe passage as far back as is practical."

The idea that Antoku, born to the Empress, could be displaced by his youngest half-brother, born to a concubine--well, as one of the other women said later, "Might as well make his favorite cat the Emperor." The third son did not resemble his father, or the Emperor's line, so Go-Shirakawa must have chosen the fourth because he resembles Takakura. Though if it is a means of regaining some of his lost power, I doubt that even the question of whether the Sun Goddess' sacred blood flows in the child's veins matters to Go-Shirakawa. I cannot bear to think of how Antoku will feel if he hears that his beloved grandfather has utterly betrayed him by choosing his younger brother. As if it were his to choose. Anyone with half an eye can see how the divine light shines through Antoku in a way it does not with any of his brothers. *If the Imperial line does not pass through Tokushi's womb, Japan will be devoured by an age of darkness and warfare.* My mother's ominous prediction beats in my head like the tolling of the great bronze bells at the temples of Nara. Darkness descends, the relentless tattoo of war drums shadows our footsteps. *It is your responsibility…you must make sure…*How, Mother? How can I protect Antoku and help him retake his throne? How?

When we arrive at the southern island of Kyushu we journey in palanquins to Dazaifu. Many Heike supporters greet our arrival, cheering wildly and waving red banners. Astrologers and architects immediately set about finding the ideal place for a new palace.

Huge trees are dragged in from the surrounding woods to serve as pillars for the palace. The sound of hammering and sawing and the smell of fresh pine chips fills the air as the new Capital takes shape in Dazaifu. But just as the palace corridors are being roofed, Tsunemasa and several of Tokushi's brothers arrive at our mansion with the Lieutenant Governor of the Bungo province, Lord Koreyoshi. I kneel behind a wall of kichos with Tokushi and Daigon-no-suke, listening as he addresses Munemori.

"Regretfully, construction of a new Capital here at Dazaifu is no longer possible."

"No longer possible?" Munemori rumbles.

"Governor Yorisuke has ordered me to notify you that the Retired Emperor has ordered him to expel the Heike from his province. Since his orders are the Divine mandate of She Who Shines on High, Yorisuke believes it only prudent to respond. However, it is his intention to allow you to leave peacefully."

"So, old Big Nose has decided to join with the traitors? Isn't his son allied with those Genji scoundrels?" Munemori says derisively. "But what of you, Koreyoshi? At one time you were Shigemori's friend and retainer--it is only through him that you enjoy your position here. May I presume your loyalties are still with us?"

"It is true that the House of Taira has been my patron in the past, and therefore it would be fitting of me, as your former vassal, to doff my helmet, unstring my bow, and place myself at your disposal. But alas, only a fool behaves in a manner contrary to divine will, and since Retired Emperor Go-Shirakawa is the mouthpiece for Her Augustness, the Great Light Herself, I can do no other than to obey his edicts. I hope you will choose to leave peaceably, but if not, the next time we meet, it will be on the battlefield."

Chapter Thirty-Three
September 1183

Koreyoshi's forces attacked with such vehemence, cutting off escape from so many sides, we were forced to retreat through the mountains, following such a narrow, tortuous route that palanquins had to be abandoned. The wooden clogs we women normally wear outside were worse than useless for scrambling over rocks and around precipices, and by the time we reached the vast flat sands of Hakozaki Harbor, our feet were cut to pieces.

The roar of the surf sounds melancholy as we queue up to board the boats that have been donated by the lords of Yamaga to help us travel from Kyushu to Shikoku. Though loyal to us, the warriors of Yamaga have made clear they cannot protect us from Koreyoshi's pursuit. The lords of Kyushu should have owed us the fealty we hope to find in Shikoku, so there is a great dread that we shall simply be at sea forever, like the albatross which almost never comes to land. Some of the ladies wear scarves over their heads to conceal their tear-swollen eyes and running noses. In spite of having been cared for by some of the ladies at this coastal fiefdom, we are looking bedraggled in the light rain. We don't much resemble the cloud people we once were. Now we look more like the mud people.

Antoku and his brother are happily chirping at a cage containing several finches that have been given to them. Morisada breaks away, rushes to the sea's edge and throws rocks in the water. He is trying to skim them, but the rocks here are not flat, like they were at the lake where Atsumori showed the boys how to make the stones hop across the surface. Here they are all corners and points, and they just sink, plop, plop, plop. He strains for the effect he wants, an intense grimace on his face. I walk over, trailing his nurse. As we get closer, I hear him muttering through clenched teeth:

"Send a shower of arrows! Kill a thousand enemies! He shoots his arrows, and the enemies fall!" A small hand squeezes my heart, thinking of Seishan's youngest, Matsu, who so wanted to go to war with his father and older brother. Are they born thinking of war? How can a five-year old child have such war-like thoughts? Then again, with all we have gone through, how can they not have such thoughts?

Antoku stays behind, murmuring at his birds. Tokizane walks over and throws some rocks with Morisada, joining in his imagined battle. When it is time to board, he says;

"Quick! On to your horse's back! We shall gallop aboard!"

Morisada clambers onto Tokizane's back like a monkey and Tokizane gallops towards the gangplank, making snorting noises.

"I want to ride too," Antoku says, handing his cage of birds to Sotsu-no-suke. Tokitada scoops him up and carries him aboard the ship, Antoku shrieking with laughter. Machiko and I board with more decorum and sit beside the cage of cheeping finches as the boat pulls away from shore. Unlike when we left Fukuhara, no one gazes wistfully back. Everyone turns their backs on this island which has been such an unlucky place for us.

We cross the straits to the southern shores of the main island, and some remain on the vessel while others go ashore to seek provisions. Later I see a rowboat coming towards our vessel and recognize Kiyosune and Atsumori along with six or eight other men bringing cages of chickens. They take them to the hold where some of the horses are kept so we can have eggs again.

"Look! Look at the big birds! What do you think of the big birds?" Antoku says, holding up his cage of finches so that they can view the chickens being brought on board. They cheep and hop about, agitated by the swinging of the cage. I doubt the chickens are making any real impression on them. They probably have no more sense of relationship with those brown squawking balls of feathers than a koi would feel upon encountering a shark. That gets me to musing: it seems these warriors from the east and the north are virtually a different species as well, seeming so much coarser and harder than the men we are used to. I wonder what their women are like, if they are equally coarse and sturdy. My own daughter is one of those women now. Tsubame. I wanted her to fly free, like a swallow, but instead she is caged like these finches. I have no way of knowing if she is even dead or alive, but I believe I would know in every cell of my body if anything had happened to her.
I wonder if I have a grandchild by now. It seems impossible that her womb would bear fruit and my womb would not feel the pang.

My reverie is interrupted when Kiyosune comes and kneels before me. He unwraps a large bundle of mint he has brought.

"I hoped this would help the ladies heal their feet. I remember a mint poultice you gave me once, when I twisted my ankle, and see..." he unwraps another bundle, revealing the herb we call bruise-heal.

"Oh, thank you," I say, breathing the herbs' strong scents. "This is perfect. We have such need of it. Thank you so much." I take his hands in mine. He drops his eyes.

"We have failed you in so many ways. It is the least I can do."

"It is not you who have failed us. It is the loyalty of cowards that has failed us."

He withdraws his hands and bows. He and Atsumori have apparently been assigned to our boat.

Machiko and I crush the herbs and make a paste. Soon the women are feeling some relief, with their feet freshly bandaged with the cooling poultice. Tokushi and Lady Kiyomori, having been carried, are the only ones whose feet are unscathed. My own feet are bony and felt the rocks most keenly, so I am grateful to bathe them in the herbs and have Machiko wrap them with the salve. Machiko has such tough, muscular feet the rocks seem to have hardly bothered her at all. Her bruising is already healed, and she had not a single cut. Perhaps the northern women are more like peasants, stronger, able to deal with any eventuality. They must be tough, to ride as warriors beside their men. I am still removing stones from the feet of some of the women, as the gravel was pushed so deep into the lacerations that it is taking time for it to work its way to the surface. Everyone is drinking ginseng and goldenseal to keep up their strength so the wounds do not become infected.

After dinner, I go out on the deck. We have fewer ships, so there are more men on each. I see Atsumori and Kiyosune sitting together at the stern. Kiyosune has his arm around Atsumori's shoulders. Both are looking out over the dark sea. They look bleak and exhausted. My heart cringes at the way they are huddled together, seventeen-year old boys who have already fought in so many battles. I sink down into the shadows so they will not turn and see me. I realize how selfish I have been, grieving for my beloved Sessho. For me to love with my heart so crushed would be like trying to write with a shattered hand. But the least I can do for these young men who are daily risking their lives for me is to welcome them back to my body. Even if my heart has perished, my body is still alive, and it would provide them with comfort. I cannot ride into battle with them, as a northern woman would do, but I can welcome them home from battle.

Tokushi is right. I have become so selfish, caring only for my own wounds.

There are too many other men, arranging their robes around them, preparing for sleep on the deck, to approach Kiyosune and Atsumori now, but the next time I see either one of them alone, I shall ask their forgiveness for having stayed apart, and welcome them back.

The next morning, Tokitada and Tokizane are fishing with Antoku and Morisada. Atsumori has joined them. They are all laughing in a way that makes it clear that Atsumori is really only ten years older than the boys, taking that same boyish delight in their ability to capture a fish. Suddenly, Kiyosune is at my elbow.

"I wonder if I might borrow your writing desk and inkstone. I want to write a letter to my mother. Only the gods know if she will ever see it, but I am a dutiful son, nonetheless."

"Of course." I clap my hands together to get Machiko's attention and relay Kiyosune's request. She and another servant bring all the materials to the deck. Kiyosune kneels. The tips of his fingers graze my inkstone wistfully. I kneel beside him. He smiles.

"How fondly I remember all our writing lessons," he says softly.

"I also. Perhaps it is time for the lessons to begin again."

A look of relief and gratitude washes over his face. "Really? Lady Fujiwara--that would be--" he swallows and looks towards the back of the boat. "Atsumori too?"

"Of course."

"He will be so grateful to hear!" Having gotten no farther than the salutations to his mother, his brush sits, abandoned in its pool of ink.

"No privacy here," he says, looking around the boat.

"We will have to wait until we arrive at Shikoku and a place can be found or built for us."

"Our soldiers will work night and day on the building!" Kiyosune says breathlessly. "And Atsumori and I will hold off a thousand Genji each if necessary."

"I pray it will not be necessary. The Genji have not managed to land on Shikoku yet. Kiyomori's vassals and his many relatives in Shikoku have far greater stake in our success. Hopefully they will prove more loyal."

"They will be. They will be." He begins to write.

"It is a beautiful day. The sun is shining, the air is crisp. The inland sea is as flat as glass. I miss you terribly, but it is more like being on holiday than being at war. It has been quite educational to see Kyushu and the smaller islands in the realm. Lady Fujiwara sits beside me and lends her encouraging presence. Atsumori is well, and asks to be remembered to you. At this very moment he is helping Tokizane and Tokitada catch fish for our supper and for the entertainment of the young sovereign and his brother. I miss Kyoto, but it is like a long pilgrimage; the longer I stay away, the sweeter the return. If only you and my sisters could be here, and I knew you were safe, I should be content with my lot.

Your faithful son,

Kiyosune."

"Will there be messengers who can deliver this?"

"I hope so," he sighs. "The last messenger I sent never came back. If he were slain, or crossed over to the other side, or simply returned to his own family, unwilling to risk his life further on my behalf--if he delivered my letter first--one never knows. It has been over two months--no, almost three-- since I heard from them. They live a little south of the Capital--but nothing is safe with those brutes of Yoshinaka's roaming about. When I think of the household of women I have left behind, I cannot help but be uneasy."

"I know how you feel. I have not heard anything of Taira Seishan, who is as close to me as you are to Atsumori, or her children, who are like my own, since we left the Capital. Nor have I heard anything from Tsubame since we left."

He asks a servant to remove the writing materials and prepare his letter to be sent, puts his hand on mine. "I am so sorry for how much you have suffered," he says simply.

"And I for you. I can only ask you to forgive me for how selfishly I have held myself apart during my grieving."

"It was probably necessary. When my father died, I felt as if I were lost on a cloudy night, wandering without direction."

Later that evening, Atsumori and Kiyosune send a young boy servant into our cabin to ask if I will join them on deck. The ladies of Yamaga were kind enough to give us a stack of privacy screens to replace those we had been forced to abandon in our flight. Machiko sets three of them up, forming an enclosure by the railing, giving us a small cubicle of privacy on a crowded boat. Atsumori is glowing. His hair is freshly oiled, tied in a warrior's knot. His outer robe shows black silhouettes of pine boughs against a teal green background, with red and white robes beneath it. Kiyosune looks rather shabby beside him, wearing a worn blue robe that has seen better days. Atsumori rises and bows to greet me, then grabs my hands after I sit down.

"I knew you could not stay away from us for long!"

I am happy to have the power to light that lantern behind his eyes.

I bow. "I humbly ask your pardon for any offense I may have caused you. I was heartsick, but that is no excuse for my selfishness."

"Not at all. We are warriors," he says, indicating himself and Kiyosune. "You are a woman, and all the hardships we have endured are triply hard for you. All of us have lost friends and relatives who are dear to us since this conflict began. We know what it is to grieve. It is also true that life is short, and we must enjoy it to the hilt."

Kiyosune notes the worried expression on my face.

"But *our* lives won't be short," he reassures me. "Atsumori and I protect each other. Neither of us will ever abandon each other. So you need have no fears. No amount of Genji can stand against the two of us."

"No, indeed! As has been proven!" Atsumori laughs. "We are like the immortals, Kiyosune and I. We shall be tripping over our gray beards, one of these days."

"But we will still be coming to see you," Kiyosune asserts. "Even if we trip on our gray beards on our way to get there."

I laugh at the image of them ancient, stumbling over their beards as they hobble towards me with their staffs.

"May it be so," I say, toasting them with the sake Machiko has poured for us. "May it be so!"

"And faithful Machiko will be there as well," Kiyosune says, "sliding open the door to your room, keeping everything perfect, as always."

Machiko blushes with pleasure at having been honored with his notice.

We eat together for a couple of nights before reaching Shikoku. Then I must remain on the boat while they go off with Tsunemasa and others of the Taira clan to negotiate with the Shikoku gentry. There are many members of the extended Taira family on Shikoku, whose fortunes are more intimately tied to ours than the Kyushu nobles confused by Go-Shirakawa's betrayals.

Still, that night I cannot sleep, switching from side to side, anxious that some danger may have found them.

The next day they return, all smiles, accompanied by soldiers bearing the red and black flags of a prominent Shikoku family.

"Is it good news then?" I ask when they have boarded the boat.

"The best, Lady," Atsumori beams.

Later that night, when we are having dinner together, I say, "Now I must hear all about it."

"Everything is perfect," Atsumori says. Kiyosune nods.

"The Shikoku nobles will never give in to the Genji," Atsumori asserts. "They hate the upstarts as much as we do. And they are bound to us by blood, not just obligation."

"Blood is the thread that weaves the immortal tapestry," Kiyosune quotes.

"Indeed. Within a fortnight we'll have thousands of men at our backs. Tomorrow we sail for Yashima, to build a new palace and make a new settlement there. It's directly across from Fukuhara. It will only take a couple of days to cross when we are ready to thrash the Genji."

"Is it possible more battles could happen so soon?" I ask.

"As soon as we have the men for it," Kiyosune nods. "These scallops are incredible!" He places one on my plate. The seared scallop is very sweet.

"Delicious," I agree.

"Last of the green beans from Kyushu?" he asks. "Sesame buns? The Shikoku lords have sent boatloads of provisions for us."

"We were well provisioned before we left Kyushu," Atsumori says.

"Yes, but Shikoku sesame is better because it's loyal sesame." We laugh at the pun, the word for sesame leading to similar words for false friends.

After dinner, Machiko fetches some male servants to help her remove the plates, table, and serving containers. I whisper to her when she comes back to bring bedding. I am not thinking of making love to my young men, only that we might lie together and drift off to sleep looking at the stars.

Atsumori grins when the bedding material arrives.

"Are we not to wait until we have a place on land, then?"

"We shall sleep together only, looking at the stars."

"The stars are not what *I* will be looking at," he says, giving me a hot look that seems to penetrate my clothing.

"We must not cause the lady any shame," Kiyosune cautions.

255

"It is quite private behind the screens," Atsumori coaxes.

"No privacy with this one," Kiyosune says, settling beside me while Machiko tucks the layers of kimono around us.

"We could stuff a sleeve in her mouth," Atsumori suggests, waving a lime-green sleeve over my face with mock threat.

"You are dreadful! Where are your manners?" I demand.

"Maybe you should look for them," Atsumori says, taking my hand and putting it under his robes beneath the sash. I snatch my hand back and give him a light slap on his cheek.

"Kiyosune--perhaps you should sleep next to Atsumori!"

"Kiyosune is indeed a wonderful bed partner," Atsumori says, pulling me close so I can feel the hardness beneath his silks. "But that fox cannot compare with this one."

"Leave her alone," Kiyosune cautions, cuddling up to my other side, placing a hand on my belly. "If we offend her, she'll send us away again."

"Never. I'll never send you away again."

"Do you regret treating us so unkindly?" Atsumori says.

"I do."

"Then surely you should make it up to us," he says, relentlessly pressing his erection against my hip.

"As soon as there is a convenient place."

"It will take at least a month for a palace to be built. I simply cannot wait that long. I could be dead a thousand times by then," he says, taking my chin, and turning me to face him.

"Don't say that."

"Brother..." Kiyosune says, patting Atsumori on the arm.

"I have been perishing for lack of you," Atsumori persists. "And so has Kiyosune, for all that he is trying to be a gentleman. Fine, he is a better gentleman than I." He buries his face in my hair, whispering in my ear, "I need to be inside you." A trickle of moisture escapes my cleft and puddles beneath me.

"You're trembling," Kiyosune says, stroking my face, looking into my eyes.

Atsumori starts gently biting my neck and ear. My capacity to say no is spinning away from me quickly.

"It's just so...improper," I gasp.

Kiyosune kisses my eyebrows, my eyes.

"I can't possibly choose between you," I protest.

"We're brothers. There's no jealousy between us." Kiyosune says.

"None," Atsumori murmurs, his tongue flicking along the edge of my jaw. Kiyosune running his hand up and down the center of my body. "I'll keep my mouth over yours if you cry out," he says.

"Did you two plan this?"

"You're the one who called for the bedding," Atsumori says. "We're young men. We've been without you so long. We can't be without you for another moment," he says, rolling partway on top of me. I put my hands feebly against his chest, as if to push him away, but my arms have no strength.

"Be quiet," Kiyosune whispers.

Atsumori puts his hand behind my head and starts kissing me deeply. His hand slides down, pulling up my robes. Another hand helps him. Each of them pushes one of my thighs apart. Atsumori keeps his mouth on mine to stifle my groans as he rolls on top of me. My heart may be dead, but my passion is not. Red and yellow explosions, brighter than any fireworks, flower behind my eyelids. Atsumori rolls off on his back beside me, gasping. Kiyosune's face is over mine. "Are you all right, fox priestess?"

"Alive again--most unexpectedly," I whisper back.

"Are you ready for another?"

"I think so."

He rolls me over sideways, facing him, drapes my leg around his hip as he penetrates me. Atsumori turns on his side, supporting my back, kissing my neck. He reaches a hand over to feel the pulsing of Kiyosune's hips, then slides his hand to feel Kiyosune's jade stalk sliding into the gate that he has left so wet and open. Kiyosune's eyes flow into mine like an impossibly wide river. A lotus opens its blossoms at the top of my head into a great throbbing silence. The three of us lie, spent and panting, I wrapped tightly between the two of them, I the heart pulsing, they the lungs, breathing.

"Is this really all right?" I ask.

"The right arm does not become jealous of the left arm," Kiyosune whispers. It is true; I cannot tell their hands apart as they caress my body. I frequently have made love to two or more women at once, or one man and another woman, as with Sessho and Seishan, but everyone says that men are so much more jealous than women.

Atsumori is again hard. I put a restraining hand on him, more firmly this time. "I can do no more tonight."

"All right. All right. Thank you for this. We'll wait."

"Yes, thank you," Kiyosune says. "Don't make us wait too long."

Was the night clear, or cloudy? Were the stars sparkling and beautiful, or hidden behind a veil of mist? Truly, I could not tell you, for I never looked up. The vastness of the sky, incalculably dark, embroidered with light, unfurled within me. Rocked on the sea, rocked between my two lovers, I fell asleep, awaking only when the day star shimmered its vermilion under our eyelids.

Chapter Thirty-Four
September 1183

The next morning, I stand in a porcelain tub, shivering, as Machiko scrubs off the night's exertions with a large sea sponge.

"How did you ever choose, mistress?" she asks archly.

"I didn't."

"Oh, mistress..." she titters. "Truly, you are a tigress of Inari."

"Yes I am. And shameless about it. What was I thinking, keeping my gate to the heaven realms closed all this time?"

"My loyal mistress. But of course, it is Inari to whom you owe your highest allegiances. And to the Empress," she adds hurriedly.

"Yes. We must all make ourselves useful in this battle for the land of the rising sun. And love is my weapon."

"The weapon of the gods, my lady."

I stagger as she helps me out of the tub, almost knocking it over.

"A little saddle-sore this morning?" she says wickedly.

"Yes, a little." And yet, as she towels briskly up my legs, already burning with thoughts of tonight. She dries off my back, kissing my shoulders as she releases the fall of my pinned-up hair.

"Oh, mistress, you are the flame of Inari. Those two young men are so lucky to have you."

As she says this, I realize it has been a very long time since I have asked Machiko to make love with me. Perhaps she misses it as well.

"I regret if I have neglected you, Machiko."

"Nonsense, my lady. I exist only to serve you. One cannot neglect a servant."

"You are much more than a servant. You are a part of me."

"If you should die first, they will burn us on one pyre," Machiko says, giving me a rare, direct look. "I am your faithful shadow, lady. Nothing more."

We arrive at Yashima later that afternoon. Some of the ladies mutter that the sea strand here will be a dismal place for a palace, and old poems are whispered about the forlorn wisps of smoke rising from fisherman's fires of dried tulse. But for me, this long curve of beach glows golden, hopeful, its emptiness cradling the promise of new beginnings, of starting over.

Chapter Thirty-five
October 1183

As Atsumori predicted, the people of Shikoku prove far more loyal than those of Kyushu, and soon the beach is swarming with men erecting a palace and other domiciles for the court to dwell in.

Atsumori and Kiyosune leave our boat every day to help with directing the building and securing the perimeter. Every night they return, and we all pillow together behind screens arranged on the deck.

Huge pines are severed from the forested ridges high above the water and dragged to the beach to make pillars for the new palace. All the local woodcutters are engaged in this hard work, reinforced by our common soldiers. Munemori, Shigehira and other noblemen are quartered in fisherman's huts along the beach. It is very strange to see the former lords of Kyoto living in such trifling dwellings. Those of us in the Emperor's court must remain on the boat until the palace is constructed.

We are eating a meal of cockles and seaweed, with peppers and onion on the side. Cucumber and shrimp salad provides a cool counterpoint. Word arrives that the palace is completed. Once the priests have finished blessing the structure it will be ready to move in. Antoku is almost beside himself with joy.

"Hooray, hooray! My palace is done! My palace is done!"

"We can finally get off this boat!" his brother cries. They rush to the side of the boat as if expecting the plain wooden structure we have watched going up on the beach to have suddenly transformed into something they would recognize as a palace. The outside has been painted red with gold paint here and there for accents. The roof is tiled with thin wafers of slate that have not been cut into any interesting patterns.

"Probably the inside is very nice," Morisada finally says.

After lunch, we all get into rowboats and are transported to shore. There we are placed in palanquins and chairs to be carried to the palace. When we get out of the chairs onto the portico, all the ladies, including myself, commence to swaying and grabbing onto the pillars. The very ground seems to be heaving and sighing beneath us. The little boys giggle as they stagger and fall up against each other.

"What's wrong?" Morisada asks.

"It's because we've been aboard boat for so long," Antoku reminds him. "Don't you remember, when we first got to Kyushu after a long trip we felt like this?"

"Oh, yes, I remember now. It's called sea legs."

We enter through the cloth curtains that have been strung across the doorways and stare in dismay. It's more like a huge, cavernous barn or stable than a palace. It smells like the ocean. A few hanging censers burning cedar from the mountains help, but all the fat lamps are burning fish oil, and the sea is close by. At least there are numerous moveable walls draped with fabric so the space can be arranged in different ways, but there are no sliding doors or paper windows to give access to the outdoors and relieve the dark interior. The great doors at the front of the building offer a view only of the forbidding, churning sea.

In the old palace, statues of gold and jade and paintings from every era adorned each niche and wall. Here the chief decoration consists of rafts of fishing nets hung with fishing floats webbing the ceiling. The men who have labored to construct the palace for us bow with their heads touching the floor. Munemori strides down the aisleway made with their bodies, swathed in glittering green and silver, resplendent as a dragon.

"It is simple and rustic," he says, "but, of course, we do not plan to be here very long, since we shall soon be retaking the Capital."

"Thank you, Uncle," Antoku says. "This will do very nicely. It is astonishing that you were able to build it in such a short amount of time."

"Yes, thank you brother," Tokushi says, bowing to Munemori. "It is certainly more than we could expect, under the circumstances."

In the past a structure like this would have been considered too shabby for the Emperor to even visit. Now it is his home, and ours, for who knows how long. Still, it is considerably more spacious than the boat. All of the ladies smile brightly, though they must feel as heavy-hearted as I as we gaze about at our reduced surroundings.

Tokushi immediately starts making the decisions about who shall sleep where, and how the moveable walls should be arranged. She first specifies where the thrones should be placed--near the back and center of the structure. Munemori bellows to the craftsmen to begin work immediately on the new thrones and they scurry off to cut and polish the cedar wood required for the task. She places her quarters nearest the doorway where there is the most fresh air and light. Antoku and his brother, her sister Sotsu-no-suke and the children's nursemaids are situated beside her. Tokushi then walks up and down, musing to herself about where various people should be. Lady Daigon-no-suke and Ben-no-taishi she locates close to herself. She puts a hand on my arm and leads me to the back of the structure.

"Given how very busy you seem to be at night," she whispers to me, "I think it would be best if you were here in this back corner, where you may have the most privacy."

"Oh, thank you, how thoughtful of you," I reply, inwardly dismayed that she has placed me so far away from herself. She must be displeased with me for having so blatantly entertained my lovers on the boat. But she has not asked to make love with me since we left Kyoto, nor indicated much desire for my company. She leaves me staring at the space she has indicated with Machiko and our belongings while she goes off to distribute the other ladies where she sees fit. Beside me she places Kozaisho, who will be receiving visits from her husband, Michimori. They are young and ardent and have kept all of us up with their ecstasies on more than one occasion. I am glad to have her next to me. We will not be bothered by each other's romantic activities. Machiko bustles around marshalling the servants to bring in our possessions. Except for the implied insult of being so far from the Empress, I am quite happy to have this corner spot. It will be more private. It is dark, but the whole structure is dark, except for the section nearest the doors. One can't expect gardens on a wind-swept beach, and paper-screened doors would be ripped to pieces during the first storm. I take out my paintings--swirling sea scapes and craggy mountains, blossoming cherries framing a pair of ducks preening in the water. Machiko arranges them on the walls, stopping here and there to ask for instructions.

"Oh, do as you like, your eye is better than mine."

After the obligatory, "Oh, you do me too much honor," on her part, she begins to decorate. She knows my tastes better than I do. She tells the servants where to place my writing table, positioning the chests with letters and scrolls near it, situating the chests containing herbs and charms in another area, folding our bedding neatly by the back wall. Such a small quantity of possessions does not require much time to organize. There are fresh reed mats laid all over the floors. I love the fresh smell of new reed tatamis.

Munemori, Koremori, and the other clan leaders will not be living here. They will be staying in a large hall near the barracks. Another cavernous building will serve as the council hall.

The next morning, we take a walk out on the beach. The earth is not heaving under our feet nearly as much as yesterday. The boys are leaping with excitement, loading their servants' arms with shells and pungently dead starfish, digging where they see bubbles in the sand to capture the sand crabs burrowing beneath. Tokizane constructs a ring of damp sand bordered with seaweed and they hold sand crab races, which tend to be short, as the crabs prefer to dig frantically down rather than race across. The boys chortle with glee as their crabs scamper about. We ladies stand by under our parasols, laughing and applauding the entertainment the boys have provided for us. They name the sand crabs as their elders name their horses.

"Ha! Morisada! I'm going to race my crab, 'Swift as the Wind'. What have you got to put up against that?" Antoku challenges.

"'Sharp Legs' can beat him! Wait and see!" Morisada boasts gleefully.

Somehow everything seems possible now. Although our encampment is primitive, rows and rows and rows of Shikoku warriors keep arriving. The lords of Shikoku arrive bearing gifts for the young Emperor, and soon the palace contains several Buddha statues, a pair of beautifully carved thrones and other furniture carved of ebony wood. One lord arrives with a jade and jasper carving of two dolphins that the boys love, claiming that it represents them in dolphin form. Running my hand along the smooth, cool backs of the dolphins, I can imagine myself back among the treasures of Kyoto and Tanba. Several small carvings of the Buddha and other deities in jade and other precious stones are brought, and niches are installed for them. Antique scrolls are also offered, and piles of silks for new robes, so that in a couple of weeks the palace evolves into a crude esthetic that is not unpleasing to the eye.

There are no homely women at court now. There are so many more men than women that all the unmarried women each have twenty suitors or more. I receive many passionate love-notes and gifts myself, but I cannot imagine entertaining more than the two I have, so I return the gifts with kind notes to that effect. Since our time as a threesome on the boat, unless one of my lovers is placed on guard, I always see both of them together. I have a fear that I might choose to sleep with one and the other might be killed the next day. I can't bear to think of sending either of them out into danger without having been loved and nurtured beforehand.

Tokushi may have hoped that by placing Kozaisho and myself far away from her, she might spend her nights undisturbed, but most nights the entire palace seems to sigh and breathe with the barely stifled sounds of lovers coming together, for there is no greater aphrodisiac than lack of a future. Fortunately there is plenty of pennyroyal and cohosh in the nearby marshes, and during the day I am kept busy making contraceptive and abortive ointments and teas.

Not for Tokushi though. I try to ingratiate myself with her, brushing her hair, massaging her shoulders. Occasionally she permits me to spend the night with her, but we never make love. My great despondency after Sessho's death seems to have created a coolness between us. "A spider weaves only for herself," she had sniffed when my days of endless weeping and depression kept me from anticipating and meeting her needs. But perhaps her coolness extends to everyone; perhaps it is merely a way of surviving, as a frog will let itself freeze solid in the winter muck in order to wake whole and happy, free to hop away in the spring.

Chapter Thirty-Six
November 1183

We have only been esconced in our palace for about a month when word arrives that Yoshinaka has sent two of his best warriors, Yukihiro and Yoshikiyo, to attack our encampment, and that they have arrived at Mizushima Bay, directly across the inland sea from us. Immediately the camp is abuzz with warriors drilling and preparing, and a huge fleet of ships is assembled. I do not sleep that night, as the prospect of the next day's battle drives my lovers and me into frenzied love-making. Indeed, there are so many lovers thrashing in the palace all night that the fishing floats sway over our heads as if from continual earthquakes, and the smell of human musk drowns the scents of sea salt and cedar.

A couple of days later, our boats return across the inland sea, decked with rice straw weavings honoring Hachiman, the God of War. After the fleet docks, a messenger arrives for me, bearing letters from Atsumori and Kiyosune assuring me that they are uninjured and quite safe. I begin breathing again.

That night, I open my curtains to the scents of pine and tulip, cinnamon and sandalwood. Atsumori and Kiyosune stand before me, decked in their best finery, glowing in triumph.

"Sorry we're late--we had to wait our turns for the bath," Kiyosune apologizes.

"I was beginning to think you had gone to the brothel instead," I tease. A makeshift brothel has sprung up a discreet distance from the palace, though on a still night the occasional tinkle of the samisen or lilt of laughter floats to us.

"Well brought up boys like us don't frequent such places," Kiyosune sniffs.

"And there's a hundred warriors for every lotus--and they're just peasants. It's not exactly the willow world over there," Atsumori smiles. We enjoy a kettle of seafood soup together, both of them eating the tender insides of the clams and making the typically roguish comments invoked by such fare. Having them safe beside me makes everything taste so good.

"Those poor fools," Kiyosune says. "If they're all this stupid, we should be able to retake Kyoto with no further troubles."

"What happened?" I ask.

"Well," Atsumori recounts, "they had almost five hundred boats they had ordered constructed, all laying bottom side up on the beach, having been newly caulked and sealed with fir sap to waterproof them--"

"But they hadn't had time to dry," Kiyosune adds.

"No, they were freshly painted. Any fool knows that if you put a boat like that in the water it is going to sink. We sent over a boat to challenge them and launch insults."

"Oh, you should have seen Michimori," Kiyosune laughs.

"Oh yes, he's the best with insults," Atsumori says. "He came up with some creative ones. Once he started insulting their mothers, they all ran for their boats, turned them over and pushed them towards us. Just like a badger will drag a dog into its burrow and dispatch it there, so Michimori lured those silly Genji, who know nothing of the sea, into a watery grave."

"So did their boats sink?" I ask.

"Many of them quickly became saturated and sank. And of course those poor Genji don't know how to swim--well, they're too weighted down by their armor anyway. We tied our boats together," Atsumori continues, "and layered them with planking to make battle platforms. Our archers killed most of them before they got close enough to engage with. The ones that did board our vessels found that we were ready for them."

"You had to feel sorry for them," Kiyosune says. "We threw them overboard to their deaths as fast as they could clamber up. Yukihiro was killed by arrows--at least one of them Atsumori's--and Yoshikiyio drowned when his boat swamped. Munemori was in charge of our ships--we had twice as many boats and men as they did. Half our army flanked around, landing below their encampment, and took the rest of their warriors by surprise. Only a few were able to flee back to Kyoto, and when they get there, Yoshinaka will probably have their heads for being so stupid,"

"I hear he's quite ruthless," Atsumori agrees, "but all the best commanders are. Anyway, Noritsune is a commander worth a thousand. He's inherited all of Kiyomori's stealth and strategy and more."

"And his courage too. He's like a tiger," Kiyosune says admiringly. " I feel confident that as long as he is making the plans, undoubtedly we shall prevail."

"*Undoubtedly!*" Atsumori exclaims. He slides over and puts his arm around me. "It was easy to win victory. It was, after all, two against one."

"Mmmm. You like those odds?" I purr.

Atsumori grins. "Definitely."

Kiyosune smiles and nods for Machiko to take away the dining table. She and a couple other servants clear away the food and spread out the sleeping mats, where I give my lovers the heroes' welcome they deserve.

Chapter Thirty-Seven
December 1183

Soon after that battle, word came that Yoshinaka sent his foster-brother Kanehira with thousands of Genji warriors down the Mountain Sun road to battle Heike supporters in Bizen province, across the straits from us. Shigemori's old friend Seno Kaneyasu, originally from Bitchu province, had been captured by Yoshinaka during a previous battle. Yoshinaka had spared his life, and Kaneyasu vowed that in return he had given over his loyalty to the Heike, and thus won the trust of his Genji captor, Nariugi. He offered to take his captors to his holdings in Bitchu, where they might find fresh fodder for their horses, and Nariugi and thirty of his cohort took him up on his offer. Once at his mansion, he secretly told his sons and servants to give his guests wine laced with sleep-inducing herbs. When the Genji all nodded off, Kaneyasu and his sons stabbed them as they slept. Advancing under the white flag of the Genji, they marched to Bizen and killed the Deputy Governor and his Genji supporters there, having gained entrance to his mansion by that ruse. Kaneyasu then set about rousing the countryside to join him and throw off the Genji oppressors. His loyal vassals rallied around, and neighbors came as well. Ultimately, two thousand men from Bizen, Bitchu, and Bingo provinces flocked to his fief.

Tokushi asks that one of the survivors of the subsequent battle, who had made it across the straits in a fishing boat, be brought to an audience with herself and Antoku.

In the space of half an hour, a thin old man with wispy hair and missing teeth is brought before the thrones, where he prostrates himself. He looks more like a kindly grandfather than a warrior. His arm rests in a sling. Antoku sits quietly beside his mother as we all listen to Kaneyasu's retainer describe what had happened.

"My gracious lord, a thousand thanks for letting me behold the brilliance of the divine ancestress once before I die. I am unworthy of the honor." The old man bows deeply, tears streaming down his cheeks.

Tokushi makes an almost imperceptible nod. "Continue. We wish to hear of Lord Kaneyasu's last days."

"My family has served Lord Kaneyasu's for seven generations. When word came that he had given his allegiance to his Genji captors, I knew it to be a deceit, for I knew the unshakeable loyalty of his heart. After he succeeded in regaining his estate and killing Nariugi, we all knew it would not be long before Lord Kiso Yoshinaka retaliated. Throughout the province, men flocked to Lord Kaneyasu's side. Old men like myself, and boys as young as ten whose mothers came with them to cook for the army. Women who had lost husbands to the Genji put on their husbands' armor and came to fight. Only one warrior in three had so much as a metal corselet, and there were not enough arrows and swords to go around, most having been confiscated by the Genji to prevent just such an uprising. Many young boys had only sharpened stakes; many old farmers who had never fought anything more savage than gophers came armed with sharpened hoes and pitchforks. Fishermen came with their tridents."

"How many warriors total?" asks Antoku.

"I overheard one of the Buddhist priests say they had blessed two thousand and twenty seven, with more still arriving. Many of the horses bearing them were lame when they arrived. Most came on foot. One boy arrived riding a goat, with the little bow and arrow he used for hunting sparrows in his father's rice paddy. The people of Bitchu and Bizen provinces are loyal, my lord."

"Pray continue," Antoku says, looking white but very calm.

"Every forge in the countryside was fired up day and night making weapons out of plows and pots. Trees were stripped and arrows made from the green wood of their branches. We heard that Lord Yoshinaka gave Lord Kanehira three thousand warriors and sent him to subdue us. Lord Kaneyasu led us to Fukuryuji Nawate and positioned us on a long strip of dry land barely wide enough for our horses. We built archery platforms there, surrounded by rice paddies, a position impossible to assail by horseback, and dug a ditch twenty feet long and twenty feet deep outside of the paddies, covered over with straw mats and dirt. Just beyond that we erected a barricade of thorny branches no horse could leap. The mothers of the young boys and the other women refused to leave, though Lord Kaneyasu urged them to do so. I myself was crouched behind the archery platforms with a woman who was armed only with a cooking knife.

"It seemed like days, but it was only a matter of hours after we had completed the last of our preparations before the white flags appeared, fluttering over a long column of horses. As they got closer, their riders dismounted, leading their horses on foot through the maze of rice paddies. Because of this, only a few tumbled into the trap we had laid for them to be impaled on the spikes below. Lord Kaneyasu and four hundred archers rose from the archery platforms, shouted insults and sent a hail of arrows into the opposing army. Soon there was a pile of Genji dead so high they could not shoot over it and our side was cheering, *'Kaneyasu! Kaneyasu! The Crown, the Crown!'*

"We were certain we would win. But then we heard Kanehira urging his troops to push the dead men and horses into the pit. When enough bodies filled the pit, the Genji threw down their shields to make a flat surface and crossed on the bodies of their own dead. As we hoped, their horses foundered chest deep in the rice paddies, so the first wave of attackers were all killed by our marksmen. But Kanehira was relentless: just as a column of ants will keep entering a rivulet until the bodies of their dead form a bridge they can cross, so the Genji heartlessly rode and crawled over their dying kinsmen. The battle lasted all day. There were just so many of them..." the old man bows his head and sobs loudly. I feel pain in my palms and look down to see I am clenching my hands so tightly the nails have pierced my flesh.

"Forgive me my lord, forgive me," the old man gasps, trying to gain control of himself. Antoku's lips are pressed together. His chin is trembling, but he keeps it raised.

"You may continue," Tokushi says gently.

"Kaneyasu still would have prevailed if we had not run out of arrows. But once the battle became hand-to-hand, we were no match for their warriors. All fought bravely, even the women fighting beside their sons fought like demons. But our makeshift weapons bounced harmlessly off their armor and we were crushed into the mud. I was wounded, and as I fell, the woman next to me lunged at my attacker with her knife. Her headless body collapsed on top of mine, nearly drowning me in her blood. More bodies covered ours, and so my worthless self survived to bear you these sad tidings."

271

"And Kaneyasu himself?" prompts Tokushi.

"I saw no further fighting, but I understand he and a few of his finest warriors managed to flee the scene and make a stand elsewhere. But all died in that engagement, save for the unlucky few who were captured and tortured before being executed. When all was quiet, I struggled out from under the bodies covering me. The marshes were red with blood. Crows feasted on the dead. Strands of long hair pulled from the heads of women and warriors alike fluttered from the surviving stands of rice like black banners. Birds will be nesting in the hair of the Bitchu warriors for years to come. A few boys who had hidden unnoticed in clumps of rice emerged. A dozen of us, out of the two thousand, made our way to the coast where a loyal fisherman ferried us here."

"Forgive us our failure my Sovereign. No one expected the Genji to be so ruthless. They do not fight like men, they fight like demons with no human feelings. They are like empty suits of armor. To defeat them, we will have to become like ghosts ourselves."

"Your loyalty is commendable," Tokushi says.

"We are saddened to hear of the death of Seno and his retainers," Antoku says forcefully. "But their loyalty and willingness to fight to the death casts a light of nobility brighter than a thousand suns. I will pray for all who died, and for those of you yet living. Your sacrifices will not be in vain, for all of you will be incarnated into nobler forms as a result of your bravery and loyalty."

The old man shakes like a willow in a taifun, his awestruck face bathed in tears. He prostrates himself, arms outstretched. I am probably one of the few close enough to hear him gasp, "Only to behold your miraculous countenance," over and over. Those of us fortunate enough to dwell in Antoku's court have come to expect such adult pronouncements from him, but for such a one as this to be in such close proximity to the voice of Amaterasu must be an unimaginable honor.

After the survivor of the Bitchu massacre is escorted away with his pile of gifts, I retreat to my corner with Atsumori and Kiyosune.

"How are the men responding to this news?" I ask, once Machiko has erected a discreet wall of screens and curtains.

"Naturally, all are moved by Seno's cleverness and heroism," Atsumori says, gazing at the floor pensively.

"Exactly the kind of warrior we could not spare," Kiyosune adds gloomily.

"Here in the Empress' court, everyone has an anecdote of some conversation they enjoyed with Seno. He has become, in memory, a man with many intimate friends," I note.

"He never stopped grieving for Shigemori," Atsumori says, "his highest praise of me, always, was that I reminded him of Shigemori in some way."

"It proves that everyone, from nobles to commoners, are all chafing under the Genji rule and just waiting for an opportunity to wrest the power away from them, as the brave people of Binzen and Bitchu provinces tried to do," Kiyosune says hopefully.

"That's true!" Atsumori says, brightening, "Mass rebellion is probably only weeks away."

"Anyway, their alliance is about to fall apart. Yoritomo thinks he's on top, but he is far from the action in the northern provinces. Yoshinaka's forces are kept busy with his uncle Yukiiye's betrayals..."

"Like sharks which start eating each other as soon as they are born!" Atsumori interrupts.

"Men without honor like that cannot last." Kiyosune finishes.

"No," I agree, "they can't last."

Chapter Thirty-Eight
December 1183

Atsumori, Kiyosune and I are sitting on the beach around a crackling driftwood fire. In exchange for going into a predictive trance, I had asked Tokushi for two things: one, that I could have a messenger to send a missive to Seishan, and two, that I could take some time away from the encampment with Atsumori and Kiyosune. She granted both requests, although this one has taken awhile to be fulfilled, since the battle and victory against the Genji warlord Yukiiye I predicted in my trance happened shortly afterwards. Though soundly defeated, Yukiiye himself escaped with thirty of his closest retainers. The remainder of his five hundred troops died on the field of battle, outnumbered by our far superior forces. Fortunately, both Atsumori and Kiyosune returned unhurt from that skirmish.

After being purified at the shrine on the plateau above Yashima, we have three horses saddled and are permitted to gallop down the beach, just past a spit of land that put us out of sight and earshot of the rest of the encampment. As we urge our horses to sprint across the hard-packed sand near the edge of the waves, I try not to look at all the Genji heads mounted on stakes lining the beach. I hate this custom. I fail to see how the men can take any pleasure in it. The dead should be honored with decent funeral pyres, not with ravens and seagulls pecking them to bone. Clouds of both white and black wings rise as we breeze past, uttering the harsh guttural caws and cries that sound like curses in bird language. I breathe shallowly, trying not to inhale the stench of decay. Once we pass the end of the row of stakes, I breathe easier. The scent of the salt mixed with crushed herbs and decaying seaweed is far more palatable. The wind streaming through my hair feels like freedom.

We find a place to make an encampment. The servants who have trailed us at a discreet distance put up a cloth pavilion and take care of the horses while we walk up and down the beach talking and laughing. We come upon a woman with her divided skirts pulled up to her thighs in the water, hauling in a small net. She looks up anxiously as we approach and keeps bobbing her head humbly as she pulls her meager catch to shore. It would appear from the uneasy way she glances up at us, that she is not entirely sure if we are human or kami.

"May we buy some of your fish?" Kiyosune asks.

"Of course, my lord," she stutters.

He hands her a couple of coins and points out the three fish he wants. She looks astonished at her good fortune, earning so much for her catch. He tells her to deliver it to the men who are making our encampment.

The sand dabs cooked over a fire are delicious. I like the crisp, burnt edges. After we have supped, the men accompanying us fade out into the brush, fanning out to form an unobtrusive guard. We walk along the beach, enjoying the red sunset tinting the waters, then return to our driftwood fire. Many of flames are blue, green and lavender, colored by the salts embedded in the wood. I almost feel myself drifting off into trance as I watch them.

"Those dragons that you saw," Atsumori says, referring to the chanelling I performed a fortnight ago, "remember when you said the red and gold dragons would pull down the bronze one?"

"Vaguely. I remember being told that is what I said."

"Well," Atsumori says, "I saw Yukiiye during the battle, and he was wearing bronze armor. What do you think of that?"

"I think he was the bronze dragon," I reply. "As the priests said, the red and gold dragons must represent our forces, the red for the Heike, the gold for the Sun Goddess and her line."

"What you predicted came true," says Kiyosune, "you said the bronze dragon would disappear under the claws and teeth of the red and gold."

I nod.

"We totally took Yukiiye by surprise," Atsumori relates.

"He never knew what hit him," Kiyosune agrees.

"Noritsune pretended to send out just a small force--"

"And we were part of that," Kiyosune interjects.

"As he charged us, we simply opened up, letting him penetrate to the middle of our cluster, while men around the edges pretended to start fleeing. But then at a signal, we all turned, the rest of our forces came thundering over a hill, and he was trapped," Atsumori says.

"He never had a chance," Kiyosune smiles.

"There were so few of them, and so many of us, I never even got close enough to strike a blow," Atsumori says.

"No, me either," Kiyosune says. "That was the one problem: our horses were packed so close together that Yukiiye and some of his relatives and bodyguards managed to push to the edge and flee. No one was able to pursue them quickly enough, as their vanguard put up a terrific fight defending their rear in a rocky bottleneck."

"Well, he's done for now," Atsumori says cheerfully. "Yoritomo will gobble him up in one bite after this debacle."

"Good riddance," says Kiyosune.

"What do you think it means," Kiyosune persists, "the white dragon you saw prevailing over the green and bronze dragons, devouring them?"

"I think the green dragon was Yoshinaka; the bronze, as you say, must be Yukiiye," I say.

"But what about the last part, where you saw the red and gold dragons twine together and dive to the bottom of the sea, while the white dragon was in the sky, flying, like a huge cloud, and the cloud got bigger and bigger until it cast a shadow over all of Japan?" Kiyosune asks worriedly.

"I don't know," I reply quietly. Silence, except for the pop and hiss of flames, and the roar of the sea polishing pebbles and tossing them up on shore.

"What's it like, being in battle?" I ask, eager to shift the discussion away from my trance, which has been endlessly discussed and analyzed since it occurred.

"It's impossible to describe," Kiyosune says. "Atsumori, what would you say?"

Atsumori looks out over the sea and his eyes glaze as if he himself were going into a trance. "Like riding in the windy lands between the worlds," he says, taking a sideways glance at me. "You don't know if you are alive or dead, and all the other men--partly because of their armor with the horns and spikes and huge helmets--it's like fighting demons, like being a demon yourself."

"Are you very frightened?"

"Beforehand, very much so," Kiyosune admits.

"Yes, at first your mouth is dry. But once you start fighting there's this exaltation. Fear just changes into this...I can't really describe it. There is so much blood, it floods the barriers between the world of flesh and the land of spirit, and the gate between the worlds stands wide open. You go into a mad, drunken state," Atsumori continues, "you can't tell what is real and what is not, whether you still live or are already among the dead. All I really care about is that Kiyosune is still beside me. As long as we are together, it seems like nothing can touch us."

"I'm sure that's due to your talismans as well," Kiyosune says reverently putting a hand to his throat where he wears the talismans I have given him. "Neither of us has been hurt, except for a bruise or two, and thanks to Atsumori, we are always in the thick of it. We are fortunate to be under your protection, Lady."

It sounds to me as if the battlefield resembles the birthing chamber, when the gates between the worlds are pushed open by the laboring woman's agonies. The blood attracts both divine kami and wrathful ghosts; the world swirls away, and we mothers and midwives fight unseen forces on the windy plain between the worlds for the lives of the mother and her unborn child. That too can be a place of terrors, but I am always calm there, and I like to think I could carry that calm with me into the place of battle as well.

"What are you thinking?" Kiyosune asks.

"I am thinking I wish I could be out there fighting with you."

"Oh, you don't wish that," Atsumori says. "Leave that to Tomoe and Yamabuki and the other eastern warrior women. We like our women soft."

"It's bad enough worrying about Atsumori," Kiyosune agrees, "without having to worry about you too."

"Well, how do you think I feel whenever you two go off to battle? Anything would be better than being trapped day after day with a bunch of helpless, terrified women. I wish we did have warrior women on our side. I have seen the warrior spirit arise in countless gentle women during labor, and I believe they might do better than men."

Atsumori and Kiyosune both laugh unbelievingly.

"Have you seen them? The Genji women warriors?" I ask.

"It's impossible to tell," Atsumori replies. "They wear the same armor as the men. Under those helmets, who could possibly say?"

"For all we know, they don't even exist," Kiyosune says.

"Oh, they exist all right. Our spies have seen them. It will be the end of civilization if things persist like that. Women warriors! Completely unnatural! Women are naturally healers and lovers like yourself." Atsumori kisses my hand gallantly.

"Who would comfort us after battle if you went into battle with us?" Kiyosune asks.

"In nature it is the mothers who are the fiercest fighters. The males struggle and display during courtship season, but those battles look like mere bickering compared to the fight even a mother mouse will put up if her pups are threatened. When a woman fights, it is always with the fierceness of a mother defending her child, whereas men fight like stags, to see who will control the herd. *They* don't usually kill each other, do they?"

Atsumori shakes his head, looking nonplussed. Kiyosune appears not to have given this matter any thought either.

"Don't you remember the survivor who said the women fought too, under Kaneyasu?" I persist.

"Well, there's no question women will fight if they absolutely have to," Atsumori says. "But any man worth his salt wants to protect a woman. It just shows what beasts those Genji are, to strike down women and boys still children. A real man protects women."

"In nature, females don't *choose* to fight, though, do they? Even women mice, as you say, or foxes, or any example," Kiyosune says. "The males, they fight at the drop of a hat."

"Yes, they fight to impress the females," I say.

"Are you impressed?" Atsumori asks hopefully.

"No, I'm depressed. I hate all this fighting, All the women hate it. Maybe it works for mares and does. I think men fight for their own reasons now, not for us."

"We are fighting to protect everything we hold dear," Atsumori says heatedly. "We are fighting to restore the Emperor to his throne, to restore our place in Kyoto...those aren't noble reasons, those aren't good reasons to be fighting?"

"Of course they are. I'm sorry. I didn't mean it. I'm just so afraid and worried for you all the time." Tears spill from my eyes, and immediately both men cuddle up, one on each side of me, each of them daubing at my tears with their sleeves.

"Oh, now then, I didn't mean to be angry," Atsumori says. "It's just that we're fighting so hard..."

"And we want to be appreciated," Kiyosune finishes.

"I know...I just wish I could fight too. I feel so useless. If I'd spent all these useless hours practicing with a needle practicing with a sword..."

"We don't want your beautiful hands callused by swordplay," Kiyosune says, kissing my palm.

"The easterners are monsters to allow their women to fight. No decent man would think of such a thing."

I stop arguing, but secretly think that I am right. A woman does not fight for show. A man who is seeking to displace another man at court embarks on a campaign of slander. A woman seeking to displace a rival sends a philter of poison. How anyone could look at Lady Kiyomori or Lady Daigon-no-suke and think that women are inherently gentle is laughable. I do not want to challenge their illusions however. My young men are only eighteen years old, but these last years of war have made them much older, with a far deeper strain of melancholy than anyone that age should know. Judging from the way they snuggle up to me, perhaps the best thing I have to offer is this: being all silk and softness and comfort. Perhaps the gentleness of my hands and mouth on their bodies takes away the pinch of the armor, the rubbing of the saddle. By seeing me as beautiful and pure and above the fray, when they return to my arms they restore themselves to a certain purity also. I remember how I felt about my mother, who seemed to be not only herself, but the embodiment of all goodness, whose every touch was a benediction. I know that when my young men come back from battle, what they get from me is not just about being accepted into the body of a woman, but about being accepted into the heart of the world in some way. I put aside my sorrow and fear for them, and soon the three of us are twining together like serpents. They pick me up and carry me between them into the bower that has been made for us, and I give them the purification and cleansing a woman's love can offer.

Chapter Thirty-Nine
February 1184

During the chaos caused by the clash between Yoshinaka and Kaneyasu's forces, an enterprising messenger caught a ride back with some of our spies. The Empress calls me over. "There is a messenger here from On'na Mari. He has scrolls for both of us."

I am quivering with excitement, but look to Tokushi to see if she wants to read hers first. She nods to the messenger.

"How does my Lady Taira On'na Mari fare?"

"It is not for me to say...but she appears well."

"And her son, Akoyo?"

"Seems well also. Missing his father dreadfully, I imagine--pardon me, it is not up to me to imagine such things."

"I assume she sent a message to Lord Taira Tsunemasa?"

"Indeed, Lady. But naturally I delivered her message to you first."

"You are excused. Make all haste to deliver your message to Lord Tsunemasa. I am certain he shall find you food and drink and a place to rest. Do not attempt to cross the straits until you have messages from all of us in return."

The messenger bows and leaves. Tokushi nods to a scribe, who breaks the seal and reads:

"Most Exalted Lady Who Dwells Above the Clouds,

I have sent other letters, but so far none of my messengers have returned to assure me that they have reached their destination. I am offering prayers to the rainbow kami that this message she will speed through the storms of war to fall, humbly and undeservingly, at your feet. Not a day goes by that I do not pray constantly for the safe return of yourself and His Royal Highness, the Emperor. I wish to assure you that, however things might appear on the

280

surface, my heart has remained utterly loyal to you throughout this wretched occupation. I am fortunate that the Genji lord who is quartered at my home, Mira-no-suke Jiro Yoshizumi, is a gentleman who has treated myself and my family well, and prevented my home from being looted. It is painful to be forced to give refuge to one of our enemies, but considering how badly most of the Capital is faring, I feel blessed. All of the Capital laments this evil turn of fate that has placed the Genji foot upon our necks, and I can assure you that there is no one in the Capital who does not long for the return of the Taira, and our rightful Emperor, though none so longingly as I."

I smile. Without me to smooth her prose, On'na Mari gets tangled up in language rather easily.

"Akoyo is well, but misses his playmates dearly," she continues, referring to Antoku and Morisada.

"I have occasionally visited the palace, as I cannot refuse an invitation from Lord Yoshinaka. Things are much changed from when you were there. The parts of the structure that were burned have been rebuilt. You will be glad to know servants put out the fires as soon as the Taira left the Capital, so much of the structure was preserved. While the exteriors are therefore intact, courtly life was utterly lost with your departure, as if all of us left in the Capital were plunged into eternal night with the leave-taking of our lord, the Sun King, Antoku, and that night has not even the moon to light it with the departure of your luminescent self. Everything has been turned upside down since that horrid day..."

Presumably she means the day when we left the Capital.

"The Retired Emperor attempted to depose Yoshinaka, but Yoshinaka's forces killed the Retired Emperor's forces. Arrows were even fired at Go-Shirakawa's carriage, and at the boat that was rowing little Go-Toba to safety. Both of them are now virtually imprisoned at the Kan'nin mansion. I attended a celebration banquet--much against my will, of course--in which Yoshinaka preened himself, saying that perhaps since he had defeated an Emperor, he should become an Emperor. He then had the gall to say that he had no fancy for either a monk's robes or a boy's loops, therefore he declared that he should have to become Regent instead, and forced Motofusa's daughter, Motochiko to marry him, much against her will, poor lady. She tried to poison herself before the ceremony, but while it made her ill, it did not kill her, so the marriage took place a few days later, and at a most inauspicious time! Now he says that he has inherited Motofusa's position through that marriage! I am sorry to say that it is true that Go-Shirakawa sent a message to Yoritomo naming him 'Royal Barbarian-Subduing Conqueror of the Realm.' I cannot imagine what would have led to this, but it is not my place to criticize one as elevated as the Retired Emperor.

Everyone in the Capital was given much hope by your recent victory, and I assure you that we are all hoping and praying and longing for your glorious return. I am hoping that, when you return, you will forgive me for any appearance of impropriety and understand that all of us who were left behind have had to make many unwilling concessions to the invaders in order to save our lives and the lives of our children. Naturally, I would give my life to see Antoku re-installed on his proper throne.

Your Devoted Servant,
On'na Mari."

Tokushi sits for a moment in contemplation, then motions for the scribe to hand her the letter. She reads it to herself silently.

"I hardly know what to think of this. Perhaps you should unroll your own letter and read it to me." She motions to most of the others to leave our presence in case the contents are private. We draw the curtains around ourselves, with only Naniwa and Machiko attending us.

"It is more likely she will have spoken frankly to you," Tokushi says, "What do you suppose she means by these 'concessions'?"

"I imagine she means simply having to allow a Genji commander to lodge in her home--having to attend banquets and such..."

"She is only a woman. She cannot help such things. Anyway, what does she say to you?"

I unfurl my scroll, hoping that On'na Mari has not written anything indiscreet. Surely she knows anything she sends me will be viewed by the Empress.

"My beloved Seiko, Star-of-the Sea,

I send out letters, but never a word back. Perhaps you have forgotten about your old friend, On'na Mari, left in this Capital made dismal by your departure, but I have not forgotten about you, and I pray for your well-being daily. I have received a couple of letters from my beloved husband, Lord Tsunemasa, but I suppose he has more soldiers at his disposal and can send letters with them. Still, it seems that you could have sent me a small note

282

to let me know that you are all right. Things have been most difficult here, but as you have no doubt heard from my letter to the Empress, the young man stationed here, Mira-no-suke Jiro Yoshizune, has been kind, and is more elegant in his manner and deportment than one expects from someone raised so far from the Capital. He has been generous to Akoyo and myself, and has made sure nothing is stolen from my home, and I am most grateful for that. I am living in my home again, having persuaded my father to allow me to return here, but I can assure you that as least as long as Yoshizune is in charge of my household, I shall be safe.

"Yoshinaka is a wild man, but a cunning one. He has a sarcastic sense of humor I believe you would like. People chalk up his outrageous remarks to ignorance, but the fact is, he always knows exactly what he is saying, and says things to deliberately shock people. I rather think he cultivates the image of a boor so that others will underestimate his intelligence. I would caution the Taira not to do the same. He has developed insulting nicknames for all the nobles left in the Capital, and they must swallow their pride and smile when he addresses them as such. He seems always to be in the company of Lady Tomoe and Lady Yamabuki. Although women, they seem to function as his body guards, one on either side of him. Yamabuki is rather homely, but Tomoe has white skin, in spite of her campaigns out in the sun, and her face is a perfect oval. I caught a glimpse of Yamabuki's forearm as she reached for something at our table, and I was astonished at how strong and muscular it was!

"Most men would have quailed at an edict against them from the Retired Emperor, but Yoshinaka was completely unruffled, and did not scruple in the slightest in defeating Go-Shirakawa's forces and locking him and little Go-Toba in the Kan'nin mansion. When he commented about the boys' loops and the monks' robes, he was being deliberately insulting, I assure you. He is said to be a godless man, with no respect for the kami or the Buddhas. It is my impression that he believes in nothing but himself. Still, the word is that Yoritomo is quite threatened by Yoshinaka, and these two may eventually come to blows. There are rumors to the effect that Yoritomo will soon be coming to take over the Capital himself. Yukiiye, having suffered such a resounding defeat, is no longer seen as a threat to anyone.

"Please do your best to reassure my Lord Tsunemasa that I am loyal to him. I fear he may have heard that I am occupying the house with a Genji lord and come to the wrong conclusions. It is true that Yoshizune is a young and handsome gentleman. I fear he will be quite angry, and regret that he heeded my pleas not to burn down our mansion when he left. Please assure him that everything I am doing is for his sake and the sake of our son, and that if any one has said that I attend Genji parties, and appear to have a good time, well, you yourself know how I am one to put a brave face on things, regardless of how I may feel inside.

"People here in the Capital are heartily sick of the Genji. Yoshinaka essentially gives his soldiers permission to rage about in the most lawless fashion. They cut green rice, yes, even that growing on temple properties, to feed their horses, leaving the people to starve when there is nothing to harvest later. Travelers are not only robbed, but stripped naked, and left to die of cold or shame. Girls, even of high born families, are ravished, and no settlement is offered even when they get with child as a result. So you can see how grateful I am to Yoshizune, who has spared me and my household from such an evil fate. Everyone who ever complained of Lord Kiyomori's high-handed ways now regrets their words. At least if one is devoured by a tiger, it is a noble end, they lament, but to be pecked to death by a gander--that is most undignified!

"At any rate, things are rather boring without you around. I hardly think I am going to become friends with these stirring women warriors who have come down from the north. I see the way they look at me. They look scornfully at me, dressed in their plain clothes that would look fine under a suit of armor. At least Yoshizune is appreciative that he is sharing a house with a lady who knows how to look like a lady. Please do your utmost to assure the Empress and my Lord Tsunemasa that though I am forced to blend with my circumstances, like a moth whose wings are the same color as the bark of the tree on which she must rest, naturally I reserve my true colors for their return.

All my love,
On'na Mari"

"It is hard to imagine what she is going through," Tokushi says. "And poor Motomochiko! Oh!" she shudders, "can you imagine such shame and horror! It makes our travails on the wind-tossed waves look very minor indeed."

"Yes," I agree, shivering at the thought of a forced marriage with a brutal captor. "Death certainly would be preferable. How fortunate that On'na Mari seems to have one of the more decent lords looking after her interests. Of course, On'na Mari could take a tiger and turn it into a pussycat inside of a week."

Tokushi laughs. It's been awhile since I've seen her laugh. "Ah, I miss her," she says, "always so cheerful, and full of the best gossip. I wish her letters had been longer! There must be so many interesting things happening!"

"Yes," I agree, heart pounding. Tokushi seems to have missed the subtext, but knowing On'na Mari, I know she will do absolutely anything to protect herself and Akoyo. The loyalty she expresses towards Tsunemasa is, no doubt, highly theoretical in nature. If this Yoshizune is protecting her, he probably has every stake in doing so. I do not blame her. I would do anything to protect my child as well. But I tremble, thinking what this news is likely to do to Tsunemasa.

Chapter Forty
February 1184

Late in the afternoon, as the sinking sun paints our rustic buildings in gold, I receive a message from Tsunemasa stating:

"I received a message from On'na Mari today. The messenger informed me he had delivered letters to yourself and the Empress as well. If you would do me the kindness of joining me for supper, perhaps we could share our messages and discuss the lady that each of us loves and misses so much."

I leave the portico where I have been gazing at the sea, trying to write, and ask Tokushi's permission, which she readily grants.

I decide to wear some of my more understated clothing, as I fear Tsunemasa will be in a somber mood.

When I arrive, he walks over to greet me. He is wearing black with indigo threading. He looks as brooding, handsome and mysterious as the Storm God, and I immediately regret having not dressed more beautifully. He ushers me to the table, and we exchange pleasantries while we eat.

"I know better than to ask you anything serious before you have eaten," he says.

My nervousness and the early hour have actually vanquished my appetite. But the fern fronds in black sesame are very good, and the clean, fresh smell of the sea arising from the udon noodle with seafood soup restores my interest.

"And is all well with the Empress' household?"

"Yes, for the most part. We don't get much sleep when Michimori is here," I say, referring to the fact that Kozaisho's sleeping arrangements are right next to mine and that she and Michimori are famous for being two of the more demonstrative lovers in the court.

"Oh, I imagine not. How fortunate he is to have Kozaisho with him."

I could bite my tongue. What a foolish thing to have said.

"Still," Tsunemasa says sadly, "I can't really imagine On'na Mari having adapted to all this perilous journeying we've been subjected to, can you?"

"No. You did right to leave her and Akoyo behind, though I know it was a tremendous sacrifice."

"Yes. More of a sacrifice than I realized at the time."

The silks under my armpits are damp. My appetite dwindles.

"Perhaps we should talk first and eat later. I am concerned..."

"About what?" he asks, placing a piece of shrimp in his mouth.

"You seem...upset."

"Do you think I have reason to be?" he says, helping himself to some carrot and burdock.

"Well, all of us have reason to be."

"I insist, you must share my hospitality before we launch into any serious discussion."

I nod, taking some more of the cat-tail root and ferns. The cat-tail root takes far too much chewing.

"Some hijiki?" he offers, holding out the dish of seaweed.

"Thank you so much."

It is a relief when the servants bring some buckwheat pastries shaped like autumn leaves stuffed with plum paste, signaling the meal is nearly over.

The servants remove all the plates, and set the table back into the niche in the wall provided for it.

"Thank you for visiting me in my humble abode. Alas, it really *is* a humble abode, now. All of us have always spoken this way about our homes, but now modesty is outstripped by the facts. A house not much bigger than a commoner's cottage, and of the same quality of construction. One wonders what sins in a past life have led us to this state," he muses.

Images of the innocents who died to keep On'na Mari and myself safe after she killed Sannayo flash before me.

"They say the Gods test those they would make heroes," I say.

"Then may we pass their tests."

A servant pours a glass of sake for each of us. "Heroes," he says, toasting me.

"Heroes," I respond. "I am privileged to be sitting with one."

"There is nothing heroic in doing one's duty," he says with his characteristic modesty. "Though it takes a hero to miss someone like I miss Akoyo."

"I know how you feel."

"Yes, I know. How inconsiderate of me to mention it. At least Akoyo
seems to be safe so far...still no word of our lovely Swallow?"

I shake my head.

"It is a tragedy," he says. "May I be so bold as to enquire about the contents
of the letter On'na Mari sent you?"

"I have it right here," I say, pulling it out of my sleeve. I hand it to him. He
peruses it, eyes hooded, mouth an unmoving line. He reaches the end.

"You should *persuade* me. Well, you have persuaded me of things before,"
he says, an unmistakably bitter edge to his tone.

"Well, I suppose turnabout is fair play," he says, handing me the scroll he
had received. He nods, and I open it.

"Most Beloved Husband,

A whole year since you have been gone, and yet no Bridge of Birds has
formed for us to meet upon. What cruel fate is this, for you to be sleeping on
the wind-tossed waves, while I remain behind, grief-stricken as any widow.
I am always so gladdened to receive your letters. You must again thank the
brave messenger who brought them to me. Congratulations on your splendid
victories. Soon I expect to see you at the head of the column, returning to
Kyoto. What a happy day that shall be! Akoyo does well, though he misses
you terribly and sometimes cries himself to sleep at night. He insists that he
shall be a great warrior like you and shall come to your aid soon. Though only
seven, he shows amazing spirit for one so young. He practices his martial arts
daily, and does not complain anymore the way he used to. Now, he says, he
sees how right you were. He has slimmed down quite a bit in the last year, and
grown more strong. I only wish you could see how he is coming to resemble
you, both in his inner determination and his strength.

"In your last letter you mentioned having heard rumors of a type you
could scarcely countenance. Wise as you are, you know better than to believe
in rumors. The truth of the situation is, that our mansion like every other
one left standing in Kyoto, has been commandeered by the Genji. This, as
you know, is no fault of my own, though it is true that you wished to burn
our home and I did plead with you to leave it intact. Fortunately, a young
gentleman of the Genji clan named Miura-no-suke Jiro Yoshizune was
assigned to our home. Though from a family connected to Yoritomo's, despite
his grim lineage, he has been courteous and a gentleman and has offered me no

offense the entire time he has been here. If the rumors say anything other than that he has taken me under his protection, then the rumors are false. Like the goose that will not leave its wounded mate, I can assure you, my loyalty is beyond question. Certainly it is true that circumstances have compelled me to attend celebrations with Yoshinaka at the palace and other locations, as well as events with Retired Emperor Go-Shirakawa (before the recent turn of events which has led to him being confined without visitors to the Kan'in Mansion), but surely you must understand the delicacy of my position. I must put a brave face on matters in order to protect our son and our holdings here. Naturally, it is far more important that you are protecting the young Emperor, and I certainly understand why you cannot be here to protect your own family. I can only say that you should be grateful, and not dismayed, that I have fallen under a nobleman's protection, although his allegiances are an anathema to both of us. By returning to the mansion, I have been able to protect and preserve our property, which I hope you agree is a worthy cause. I know you wished me to remain safe with my father, but truthfully, I feel that I am more safe here.

"There is a current of excitement running through Kyoto after these latest victories of yours, and of course there is mass indignation at Yoshinaka's treatment of the Retired Emperor. You will be astonished to hear that Go-Shirakawa, perhaps regretting his all too hasty endorsement of the Genji, tried to depose Yoshinaka from his position, having received many insults from him, as, indeed, all of us have. Yoshinaka's soldiers have been running completely out of control. They are still quite loyal to him, as indeed they might be, since he never punishes them for any infractions. He gathered thousands of these warriors together and marched on the Retired Emperor at his residence at the Hojiji Mansion, defeated the Retired Emperor's forces, and burned his mansion to the ground. The Retired Emperor himself was given safe passage to another of his properties, the Kan'in Mansion, but many expensive pieces of art, and beautiful robes and scrolls of poetry that had been in his family over a hundred years were destroyed. Over six hundred men died, including the Archbishops of two Buddhist Temples, the Archbishop Mi'un and another I do not know. Many of Go-Shirakawa's favorite guards, scribes, and companions also perished. I can hardly imagine the despair of those who are left. Go-Shirakawa was placed under guard, and all of his attempts to write edicts and have them published have been rebuffed. Anything he has attempted to write, including personal correspondence, Yoshinaka has ordered burned. What can one expect? It is a rare day when a fox prevails against a tiger. Yoshinaka and his soldiers became even more outrageous as a result of this battle. The female servants at the Hojiji Mansion were defiled by his soldiers, and many of the girls chose to jump into the Uji River and sink to their deaths afterwards. Even a couple of Go-Shirakawa's concubines were treated in this manner. One of them hanged herself from the ancient plum tree growing outside the mansion.

"Yoshinaka has forced the daughter of Regent Motofusa to marry him, much against her will. She attempted suicide before the wedding, but the poison she took was ineffective. So as you can see from this tale, no one is safe here in the Capital. Therefore, I hope you will be gratified, instead of angered, at my position of comparative and enviable safety that has prevented me from being dishonored in such a manner. I know you did what you felt was best, leaving Akoyo and myself in the Capital. And you did no more than was your duty. I assure you that I am doing my duty as well, caring for your son and your property, and praying for your safe return daily.

"There is much talk that even as those in Seno Kaneyasu's district rose up to challenge the Genji, if only the Heike would make an advance towards the Capital, many of those who now appear to be the lapdogs of the Genji would remember their obligations to the Heike and rejoin your cause. Everyone says Yoshinaka has gone too far in terrorizing the people of the Capital. His soldiers are allowed to cut green rice from any property they like and feed it to their horses, leaving the people hungry. And as I have said, I never leave the mansion except under heavy guard, as no woman is safe upon the streets. The highest nobles have received the vilest insults, and they have absolutely no recourse. When complaints are brought, Yoshinaka merely sneers and says, "Do not my soldiers deserve their rations? Do not they deserve female companionship? Do not their horses need fodder? As liberators of the Capital, it is the least you can do for us." Liberators! His arrogance knows no bounds. Still, he is not the fool that many think. I do warn you not to underestimate him. It is not that he does not understand convention; he flouts it because it suits him to flout it, and because by never punishing his warriors, he gains their enduring loyalty.

I miss you dreadfully. I cannot wait until this horrible war is over, and you are restored safely to us.

Your constant, faithful, loyal and loving wife,
On'na Mari"

I look back up at Tsunemasa, who looks grim. He points to a portion of the scroll "What do you think she means here, when she says, loyal to *your* cause?" He raises an eyebrow. "Does she imply that my cause is no longer hers?"

"I am sure not. You know the dreadful secret. She can barely write by herself."

"This isn't her handwriting, it is a scribe's," he says. "You might think the scribe would have corrected her."

"Correcting On'na Mari is a tricky business. She does not tend to appreciate criticism, particularly from someone else she considers--beneath her."

"True," he nods. "I think the scribe took everything down as she uttered it, verbatim."

"Well, her loyalty seems clear."

"Does it? Ah yes, well, you have always been the one to re-write her letters. Perhaps you should rewrite this one. How would *you* have written it, to achieve the desired result?"

"I am ever sorry for that deception, Lord Taira."

"Well, no matter," he says. "On'na Mari's body was left at home, but the better part of her mind accompanied me." He is smiling, but there isn't anything that looks amused or happy in his smile.

"I notice she mentions how young and handsome this Yoshizune is in *your* letter, and that she accidentally refers to him as Miura-no-suke before having it crossed out. A rather personal way to refer to the enemy, wouldn't you say?"

"You know On'na Mari," I say, fearing that he does indeed know her well enough to guess what I have guessed myself. "She flirts with anything! Men, women, horses, flowers, a tree in blossom. But it doesn't mean anything."

"Ieyasu tried to tell me. But I wouldn't believe him."

"Tell you what?" I ask, mouth dry.

"That she was the kind that would never be faithful, to anyone."

"Surely you should give her the benefit of the doubt instead of believing whatever rumors--what *are* the rumors that you have heard?"

"Rumors? Oh, nothing much. Only that she plans to dance with Yoshizune on my grave." He gets up and walks to the entryway of his house, stands there looking out into the night sky. I put my hand on my chest, as if I could quiet the pounding of my heart. There is no real doubt in my mind that On'na Mari is sleeping with this Genji character. But really, what did Tsunemasa expect? That he could leave the most beautiful woman in the Capital alone and that she would remain chaste? I doubt she really has much say or choice in the matter.

After a prolonged period, he walks back in and sits, quite a bit farther away from me. His maidservant, observing this, brings out another small table and a carafe of sake for him. He starts drinking directly out of the ceramic container.

"That's what the Genji do. The young and handsome Genji, they drink right out of these bottles. Why bother with cups?" He throws one across the room so it smashes against the wall.

"Sire, really, no conclusions can be drawn. She is in a difficult position."

"Oh, yes indeed." He looks carefully at the other beautifully crafted cup, with its green crackled glaze, turning it over in his hand for a minute before hurling it too against the wall and taking another swig of sake out of the bottle. "Yes, On'na Mari is the mistress of difficult positions. It can't be easy, sleeping comfortably in her husband's mansion on her husband's silks with her husband's would-be assassin, can it?"

"You don't know that is what she is doing."

"Oh yes, we do." He guzzles the rest of the wine and shoves the empty bottle into the hands of the maidservant who rushes to take it from him. She hurries to refill it. I notice Machiko edging further away. She has been sitting against the wall, which has become a perilous place to sit.

"Please be kind enough not to endanger my maidservant, as she is quite blameless in this matter."

"Have you received other letters from On'na Mari?"

"No. I wish I had known you were able to get messengers through. I would have sent letters with them."

"I sent messengers from battlefields, when we were closer to Kyoto, not from here." He smiles bitterly. "How she wept when we were parted. How she wept." He takes the bottle of sake handed to the maidservant and drinks some more. The flickering oil lamps reveal tears trickling down his face. "How she wept."

"Of course, you understand," he says. "You have your young lovers, after all. I daresay you don't judge her behavior a bit."

"If she were disloyal to you, I would judge her harshly. But I do not know if that is the case. And I would urge you to admit that you do not know the truth of the matter either."

"Stop insulting me. I'm not drunk enough to believe that you don't know what these letters are saying as well as I do. They are saying she has betrayed her husband, her sovereign, her clan, and her country. But we should not mind," he says, standing up, gesticulating with bottle in hand, "we should not mind, because I left her behind. For her own good! To preserve her life! I left her behind. Her father said he would keep a watch on her. How much do you imagine his coffers have been enriched by a certain--Miura-no-suke? Is that the gentleman's name? And my son has to watch this. Has to watch his mother whoring herself--" he throws the whole bottle against the wall, so hard that shards of the clay are embedded in the wooden post. Machiko crouches down and edges further from the fray. Tsunemasa's maidservant rushes up and, coweringly, places another full bottle of sake on the table. He sits back down and takes another gulp from the new bottle that has been proffered. He mimics On'na Mari's tone.

"If you wanted poetry, you should have married the horse-face girl."

"Oh yes," he says, observing my shock, "she did refer to you that way. Her name should be Uragiri--betrayal. Mother of my only son. My son being raised by Genji." He shudders and drinks some more. "Think my son will grow up to be a loyal vassal of Yoritomo's?"

"Of course not! We'll be back in the Capital long before then. Before the end of the year. You said so yourself."

"You know what this means?" he says, indicating the scrolls. "It means I have to kill her. If I ever do get back to the Capital, the first thing I have to do is ride back to my mansion and kill her."

"You don't mean that. You're upset. And perhaps you have reason to be. I can't say. Don't ask me to choose between my loyalties," I beg. "I love you." My hand flies to my mouth. I did not mean to say that. "I love her as well," I say, deciding to finish my imprudent admission. "I am sure she has been as loyal to you as she can be. Did you not understand what she said about Regent Motofusa's daughter? She was forced into marriage--if Regent Motofusa

293

cannot protect his own daughter, how do you think a merchant can protect his? If she is in a Genji bed, it is because she has been forced there."

"No one ever forced On'na Mari into bed." He tries to laugh scornfully, but it turns into a sob. "I loved her so much. I loved her so much."

I go over and kneel beside him, put my arms around him. I am somewhat afraid that he will strike me or push me away, but instead he grabs me and pulls me to him, rocking back and forth. "I gave her everything. I knew she didn't love me like I loved her. But I thought she loved me a little. A little."

"She did, and she does...did you not see how she called you her most beloved husband? She does love you. You can't blame her for being weak and frightened and trying to protect Akoyo any way that she possibly can."

"I suppose it is expecting too much for a warrior's wife to kill herself before she is dishonored."

"Especially if it means abandoning her only child."

"If only I knew she had been forced into it," he sobs. "I could forgive her if it were that." I stroke his hair and kiss his face, tasting the salt of his tears in my mouth.

"She was right, you know," he says at last, looking into my eyes, his eyes all rimmed with red. "I should have married the horse-faced girl." He kisses me. In a moment, his servants have unobtrusively laid out futons and mattresses, forming a bed, and placed screens around it.

"Oh, Seiko," he groans into my mouth, "it was you. It was your writing I fell in love with. If only I could have seen with my heart instead of my eyes."

Though smarting from his reference to me as the horse-face girl, I kiss him anyway, tears sliding down my cheeks. If I myself could have been unfaithful to Sessho, Tsunemasa and I would have made a fine match. He is making love to me before all our clothes are removed. He comes inside me quickly and lies on top of me sobbing. I hold him and rock him. "I thought nothing could ever hurt as much as my second wife's death," he says. "Oh, how wrong I was. So wrong. So wrong."

I am awakened early the next morning, while it is still dark. Tsunemasa is lighting small lamps and gathering my garments.

"Get up. Machiko has to take you back to the palace. I'm sorry we can't talk."

I nod sleepily. Machiko pulls my clothing together and hastily arranges my hair. He kisses my hand. "If I divorce her instead of killing her--will you marry me afterwards?"

"Perhaps--if we are both still alive then."

He laughs. "I don't expect to be alive much longer."

"Don't say that. You never get hurt."

"Of course. You have a point. I have been stabbed to the heart, and still I live. Perhaps I can't be killed. Will you be my wife, if that is the case?"

"Let's see what happens when we get to Kyoto," I say, squeezing his hand. "You may feel very differently when you see her again."

He kisses me on the forehead. "I hope I have given you no cause for grief or offense."

"Never."

Machiko and I are surrounded by guards so that our identity cannot be seen, though no one is out in the dark to see it but other guards anyway. My honor thus preserved, we are escorted back to the palace.

Chapter Forty-One
March 1184

Two weeks later, I am sitting with Tokushi, brushing out her hair, soft as a waterfall of black silk. I keep hoping she will allow me to touch her intimately again, but she has not been lovers with me since we left Kyoto. At first it was I who was too devastated to come to her. But now, she has withdrawn inside herself to such a degree that it frightens me. She seems to think that she needs to be more pure, which to her Buddhist way of thinking means less sexual, for her prayers to be heard. Although food is not scarce here, she limits her eating strictly as well, and her ribs are now quite visible. Certainly when food was limited, it was just and noble that she would not take any more than what the rest of us had. But now her lack of appetite is clearly some self-purification, some expiation of sins never committed. She seems to think that a saint's tears and prayers will be heard, and will sacrifice anything to gain the ear of the immortals. The scent of her long black hair is soothing in its familiarity. I try to broach the subject delicately, touching her shoulder, sweeping back the curtain of hair I have just brushed.

"Perhaps you take too much upon yourself," I whisper, kissing the nape of her neck as she has always liked to be kissed.

"No," she says, shrugging me away, "you do not understand. I am being punished for having indulged too much. When we return to Kyoto, everything will change. My ladies' court will be as holy as a nun's quarters."

She turns to face me, though her eyes are lowered and glancing to the side. "I'm not judging you for what you are doing. You were born on Inari's mountain, and she is the Goddess who feeds everyone. She brings pleasure and abundance. As her daughter, I don't see how you can help but do the same. But my life is consecrated to the Sun Goddess, and she burns with a much fiercer and purer light. I am not strong enough for such an honor, and I never was. I am strengthening myself now, and hope the kami and the boddhisattvas forgive me my prior weakness."

I can see that there is nothing I can say that will make a difference. She is strong like her mother in this respect; when she has her will set upon a certain course, her stubbornness is unshakeable. I wish her strength were similar to her mother's, who is such a redoubtable warrior. Lady Kiyomori is now addressed as 'the nun of the second-rank', but her personality is that of a tiger, not a nun. Tokushi, with her child-like, implacable belief in the forces of spirit, is the real nun. If we all survive this conflict, I expect her to take vows immediately.

Just then, a commotion arises. Naniwa, Tokushi's maidservant, darts out to see what is happening. She hustles back through our curtains.

"Madam, Lord Noritsune is here. He brings important news." Quickly Naniwa and the other maidservants slip extra layers over Tokushi's undergarments, and Machiko helps me struggle into my outer layers as well. We move quickly out to the central part of the palace, where Tokushi assumes the throne, Naniwa frantically pinning up her hair and concealing its dishevelment under a hairpiece, pinning a spray of pearls on top of that. Antoku struggles out from behind his curtains, rubbing his eyes.

"What is happening?" he demands. He crawls onto the podium beside Tokushi and is boosted onto his throne. He yawns. "You must always wake me if it is something important, Mother," he admonishes Tokushi. "I'm the Emperor, you know."

She gazes at him fondly. His younger brother could sleep through an earthquake, but Antoku always seems to know when something vital is happening.

Soldiers bearing banners stride in and kneel, forming a pathway. Noritsune saunters in, like a cat whose careless pace belies the hunter beneath. Fortunately, he has the fighting and strategic capabilities which Munemori lacks. He has been very successful at uniting Shikoku against the Genji, whom he has been hunting down and killing in great quantity. His force of arms and charisma has been convincing chieftains who had previously been wavering to remain loyal to our side. Normally his demeanor is grave and determined, but tonight he is looking happier than I have ever seen him.

297

"All the rumors of Yoritomo and Yoshinaka struggling against each other have been confirmed," he says. "Yoritomo's forces defeated Yoshinaka, and Yoshinaka has perished."

Tokushi claps her hands together joyfully, and murmurs of 'Praise Hachiman!' and 'Thanks to all Buddhas!' and other grateful exclamations twitter through the room. The guttering torchlight shows faces lighting up with expressions of delight and relief. Tokushi puts a hand on my arm.

"The vision of the white dragon devouring the green has come true."

"Yes," says Antoku, "thank you for bringing us this news, Uncle Noritsune. This is well."

"Tomorrow, all our commanders will gather together," Noritsune says, "and discuss strategy. We may certainly expect to be back in Kyoto by autumn. We are in hopes that many more will rise up against Yoritomo once they see how dishonorably he has treated his former allies. Support is buckling out from under the Genji, while ours grows every day."

"And so much of it is due to your strength and courage," Tokushi acknowledges Noritsune warmly.

"You are too kind," he says, inclining his head. "I only do my duty. Forgive me for barging in at this late hour, but I thought you should know immediately."

"That was correct," says Antoku.

Noritsune bows and takes his leave. I start to follow Tokushi back through the curtains to her quarters, but she stops me. "Atsumori and Kiyosune were riding with Noritsune. If he is back, they will be too. Go on then." She pats my arm and indicates that I should return to my own quarters. How resentful Tokushi used to be when I would sleep with others; now she pushes me out the door to do so. If she has no further need of my love and comfort, what is the karma-tie that still keeps me here? Clearly my duty is no longer Tokushi's comfort. Now my giri concerns Antoku, protecting him and guiding him to rule wisely once this war is over.

Chapter Forty-Two
March 1184

Machiko prepares restoring teas without my having to ask. From the remedy trunk she fetches a bottle of sake containing flecks of gold and ground pearl that is peerless in reviving strength lost in the soul draining activity of battle. Soon there is a knock on the wall beyond my curtains.

"We are here," I hear Kiyosune's voice say.

Machiko pads over and pulls the curtain back. Atsumori and Kiyosune slip in.

"Did you hear the good news?" Kiyosune asks.

"Yes," I reply, "it's wonderful."

He kneels down to kiss me, and Atsumori sits at the table across from me, eyes glittering in the light like onyx. Both of them seem relaxed and pleased, not at all wearied from their last set of skirmishes.

"Have you heard any details?" I ask, knowing that they like nothing better than hashing out all the details of battles both seen and only experienced second hand.

"You'll be happy to know that Tomoe escaped," Kiyosune says.

"Really? Oh, but how shameful if she should abandon her lord in his hour of need."

"That's not what we heard," Kiyosune hastens to say. "They say Yoshinaka ordered her to save herself and she could not deny a direct order."

"Yes, one of the last of Yoshinaka's retainers was captured, and he said that was what happened," Atsumori says.

"He ordered her to escape...how noble of him," I muse. "What of his other warrior-concubine, Yamabuki?"

"Apparently she had fallen ill and remained in the Capital."

"Some say she was pregnant," Kiyosune says.

"A serious disadvantage of woman warriors," Atsumori hastens to add.

"How was it that Tomoe was able to escape if they were so heavily outnumbered? Did the opposing warriors let her go?"

"Ho! Hardly!" Kiyosune laughs. "She charged a cluster of soldiers, engaged with the most menacing warrior she could find, pulled him across her saddle and..."

"Twisted his head off!" The two young warriors chortle in unison.

"Then she galloped off and threw the head in a swamp," Atsumori relates. "Some of Yoritomo's forces followed her, but they decided they should rescue their friend's head from the mire, and therefore lost their opportunity to catch up with her. They say her horse, Moon Spindle, is the fastest mare alive."

"Yes, her opponents *said* they wanted to keep their friend's head from sinking in the marsh, but I suspect they stopped in order to keep their own heads on their shoulders," Kiyosune smirks. "They say she fled back towards the eastern provinces."

"I wonder if we shall hear more of her before this war is over," I muse. "If only she would raise an army against Yoritomo to avenge Yoshinaka! Wouldn't that be splendid?"

"An army is not likely to follow a woman," Atsumori says disparagingly.

"They might if it was Tomoe," Kiyosune says.

"Wouldn't you follow Lady Kiyomori into battle?" I tease.

Atsumori laughs. "You have a point. Naturally I would follow whoever was leading the Taira armies, to the Shide mountains if necessary. I thank the gods to be riding with Noritsune," he comments, lowering his voice. Kiyosune nods.

"Noritsune is fearless," Atsumori continues. "We'll win this war yet, and it will be because of him."

"Don't forget Shigehira. He is an amazing commander also, " reminds Kiyosune.

"Yes. We couldn't equal the Genji at first, but now our forces are as hardened and battle-seasoned as theirs. They have lost the advantage. Truly, I think we shall all see Kyoto again within the next six months."

"Yoshinaka's foster brother, Kanehira, put up a tremendous fight at the end," Kiyosune says, returning to the topic of the battle.

"Yes, they say he held off fifty pursuing riders by himself. His last eight arrows unhorsed eight men and sent them tumbling. Meanwhile, arrows were bouncing off his armor as if he were an immortal. Yoshinaka galloped towards the Awazu pine woods, intending to take his own life. But once there, his horse fell through ice into a marsh, and one of his pursuers shot him through the face-plate and took his head from where he sat, mired with his horse. When a cheer went up that Yoshinaka's head had been taken, Kanehira shouted, "I don't need to fight to protect anyone now. None of you are fit to take my life!" Then he put the tip of his sword in his mouth and dived off his horse, in effect severing his own head."

I shrink back, shuddering, appalled at the image.

"It was a very noble death," Atsumori asserts.

"Very brave. They were a pair, like Atsumori and I," Kiyosune says. "Bound together with such a powerful karma bond, it could not be broken. At one point during the battle, Yoshinaka and Kanehira were miles away from each other, yet while nine out of ten of their fellow warriors perished, those two could not be touched until they had been reunited, and then one died seeking to protect the other."

"How do you know all this? Wasn't it Yoshitsune's men against Yoshinaka's? How do our men know all these details?"

"We have spies everywhere," Atsumori shrugs. "We had eyewitness accounts coming back to us within days of the battle."

"Yoshitsune sounds like a force to be reckoned with," Kiyosune says.

"So, we'll reckon with him," Atsumori grins confidently. "He's no better a commander than Yoshinaka, he just outnumbered him six to one. Anyone can win a battle with those odds."

"They say he's clever, though. They say he sent a first contingent of men over the river to 'protect' the Retired Emperor and the little pretender," Kiyosune says, referring to Antoku's younger half-brother Go-Toba. "Which was well, because Yoshinaka had placed many men in position to kidnap the Imperial line and carry them off. But his plans were foiled by Yoshitsune. And being Yoritomo's brother, they'll probably be more loyal to each other."

I am discouraged to hear that there is a new, fierce Genji commander that must be fought off. It seems they grow back as quickly as we can cut them down. I don't say that, of course.

"It seems disloyal, but I can't help being glad that Tomoe escaped," I whisper.

"It's only natural," Kiyosune says. "I think many were delighted to hear of her escape, for all of us admire a woman of such courage, even at the same time that we deplore the Genji's cowardice in allowing their women to fight for them."

"Ah, what is the occasion?" Atsumori says as he sees the swirls of crushed pearl and gold glinting in the cup of sake Machiko has poured for him.

"When we heard word of battle, I thought you two had been involved and would need your strength restored."

"No, this one we just heard about," Kiyosune says. "The best sort of battle, the sort where the opposing forces devour each other. Just like the dragons of your vision," he says. "Now if only the red and gold dragons can take down the white one remaining."

"Surely that should be possible, now that both Yukiiye and Yoshinaka are defeated," I agree.

"Perhaps the part where you saw the red and gold dragons twining together and diving to the bottom of the sea signifies that the Heike will once again control the sea passages, as always," says Kiyosune hopefully.

"Japan can't be divided," Atsumori says. "We'll retake Kyoto and Antoku will once again be acknowledged as the one and only legitimate emperor. It's just a matter of time. Then we'll track Yoritomo to his lair and take his traitor's head."

"Will you be returning to Fukuhara soon?" While the Genji have been snapping at each other's throats, about half the warriors have relocated to Fukuhara, reclaiming the old Capital there and setting up a fortress at Ichi-no-tani.

"We ride where Noritsune rides," Kiyosune says.

"But tonight our riding is for your pleasure," Atsumori smiles mischievously.

Kozaisho's thrumming, shimmering cries of ecstasy wash through from the other side of the curtains as she embraces Michimori. We laugh softly, hearing their sounds; but soon we are galloping between the worlds ourselves, and our own sounds drown everything else out.

Chapter Forty-Three
March 1184

I kneel at my writing desk, straining my eyes to see by the light of the guttering fat lamps, recording what I have been told of the war's progress. Writing is a meditation; as a child I believed my mother's writing kept peace and order in the world. Though I know my transcriptions have no such power, there is something in the act of translating horrors into language and trapping them on paper that seems to diminish their ability to ravage my dreams.

A messenger arrives; an archway with curtains is positioned in front of me. I put my sleeve through so the visitor knows I am there. I am wearing gradations of gray and green, plum blossoms on a misty background decorate my outer sleeves. Machiko still makes every effort to see that I am properly turned out, despite the fact that nothing else in our lives is proper at all.

The shadowy figure beyond my curtains speaks. "My lord Koremori requests an audience with you." Koremori is Shigemori's oldest son. He is twenty-four, a beautiful young man resembling Tokushi, with his father's sensitivity and air of melancholy. I am intrigued, wondering if his intentions are romantic. He has drooped like a cut flower since leaving his wife and two children in the Capital.

"I am always at Lord Koremori's disposal," I reply to the messenger.

"Can you come now then?"

"Now?" It is most irregular to request a lady to leave her quarters so late at night, and though it may be facetious to refer to this simple wood building as 'the Palace', a lady-in-waiting does not leave the palace without the Empress' permission, and I cannot bear to wake Tokushi, who is only sleeping with the aid of one of my potions. "The hour is late; I cannot ask permission from my mistress. I shall ask her tomorrow if I may visit Koremori at a more suitable time."

The figure beyond the curtain bows and vanishes into the gloom and I resume my writing. Within moments, it seems, the figure has returned. "Lady Fujiwara, I must request your presence. A council has been drawn together unexpectedly. I know how much my father relied upon your wisdom. I urge you to overlook the peculiarity of the hour and to join us." I recognize Koremori's voice, and am abashed that he has found it necessary to come himself.

"I am honored, and of course I will come." Machiko runs to fetch me a warm outer robe, then quickly dons a hooded cloak herself and escorts me out from behind the curtain. Koremori and several of the other young generals are waiting for me outside the palace entrance.

"Shall I accompany you, Ladies?" asks one of the palace guards, a tough, sinewy looking man no one in his right mind would wish to cross. Koremori nods, gesturing for another guard to fall in behind us, assigning two of his personal guards to take their place until our return.

"There shall be no appearance of impropriety. My aunt shall have nothing to complain about," Koremori assures us. Flurries of snow swirl across the bleak encampment, hissing and dissolving as they waft into smoking torches. Our clogs stick in the mud with every step, and I wish they had thought to bring a palanquin, though the Meeting Hall is not a great distance. I am not happy to get the hems of my robes wet, but it can't be helped. None of the men have asked my advice in quite some while. I hope they do not want me to go into trance. I do not have the proper herbs, and I am fighting a cold that has been making its way through the court. We reach the hall.

"I am going to announce your presence," Koremori says, "so that you may be properly received." He leaves us in the outer room. We look around, struck by the dilemma of whether to kneel in a room made filthy by all the shoes and armor that have been left there. Machiko whips her cloak off and lays it down and we kneel close together for warmth, with the guards standing over us watchfully, fingering their spears. Koremori returns, pulls open the curtains and bows. "Enter."

Our guards take just one step inside and wait, flanking the entryway. The walls of the chamber are lined with the retinue of warriors that have accompanied each of the nobles. An area at the end of the hall has been curtained off. I sense Lady Kiyomori's presence behind that curtain. The nobles are gathered at a long table. Koremori motions for me to sit between him and Munemori. There is murmuring and nudging as I come in; for a woman to be asked her advice on matters of state is always cause for comment. An old man who is a well-known diviner is also present.

304

"Ah, well, you have your sorceress," Munemori lisps through his missing teeth. He passes a missive down towards me. Koremori takes it, smoothes it open and hands it to me. I incline my head towards Munemori, awaiting his specific verbal instruction to read it. He waves his hand impatiently. "Go ahead."

I open it up. It is a letter from Retired Emperor Go-Shirakawa. In it he invites the Heike to return to the Capital with the Emperor and the three Imperial treasures. He has called for a truce between the Heike and the Genji, saying he wishes to have peace, and that our Imperial claims will be acknowledged and reinstated if we return to the Capital. I bristle at his reference to Imperial 'claims', as if there could be any doubt about Antoku's right to the throne. Go-Shirakawa has placed his youngest grandson, Go-Toba, on the throne in our absence, but none can dispute that he is the illegitimate child of a concubine.

"We want to know what the Inari Priestess thinks of this," Koremori says when he sees that my eyes have scanned the last line.

I think it is a trap and we would be fools to walk right into it. The immediacy and certainty of my gut response leaves me in no doubt. But there are other traps, and having no idea who has spoken in favor of a return to the Capital, and who opposed, not knowing whose feet I shall be treading on by voicing an opinion, I take a deep breath.

"Should we believe this missive or not?" Shigehira prompts. "The words are, of course, what we all want to hear. But our spies say that Genji troops are moving towards the Capital."

"Yoshinaka is dead", asserts one of the nobles. "The rest of the Genji will be at each other's throats soon enough. They are too busy fighting each other to be any threat to us,"

Another man speaks up: "Everyone in the Capital, including the Retired Emperor, is longing for the return of the Heike, yearning for us to return and husband the city and the monarchy as we always have."

"What is your opinion, honorable one?" Koremori asks me.

I look again at the scroll, and all the characters seem to dissolve and melt together, recoalescing as a single word: LIES.

"If we respond to this offer, we will be walking into a trap," I say bluntly.

There is a sharp intake of breath throughout the room. I have not couched my language in a form that is especially feminine or particularly polite.

"Will you do a divination for us then?" asks Munemori.

"That won't be necessary." I roll the scroll back up and hand it to the page who offered it to me. "This is all lies."

A commotion of voices rises through the room like an agitated wind. "I told you so!" "How can she be so sure?" "Who does she think she is to call the Retired Emperor a liar!"

Munemori holds up a heavy hand and glares around the room, much the way his father would have done.

"Are you staking your reputation on this?" he asks me. His words are so slurred I fear he must have been drinking before this letter arrived and he convened this council.

"Yes my lord. My reputation or my life, whichever you prefer." A vision swims before me of the baskets and baffles woven by fisherman. "If we return to the Capital now, we will be like fish streaming into a trap from which there is no escape."

Munemori nods. "Thank you." He inclines his head to Koremori, who stands and bows to his uncle, then turns to escort me out of the room. Machiko rises from her place kneeling in front of the wall and follows. Koremori escorts us back to the Palace himself, though he could just as easily have left it to the guards. He droops beside me, with no attempt to recover his martial bearing. He must have wished very much that we could return to the Capital, where he could once again be restored to his wife and children.

"Have you had any word from your wife?"

"Yes, they all write, begging to be allowed to join me. Alas, I cannot expose them to the hardships and uncertainties we face here. It would be the worst sort of selfishness. At least I have the peace of knowing they are comfortable in our old home. I fear the Bridge of Birds shall be required before I see my beloved again."

"I hope not."

We arrive at the Palace. "Thank you for your insight. Hopefully it will persuade those fools who still believe the Retired Emperor can be trusted," he says. We bow to each other and he returns to the council. I resume my writing, praying that the council will act skeptically towards any overtures from Go-Shirakawa.

Munemori sends his regrets to Go-Shirakawa, stating that as soon as the Genji concede their disloyal quest and return to their home provinces, the Taira will be happy to return and take up the reins of state once more. Meanwhile, the rest of our army mobilizes to join our forces already located at Fukuhara and Ichi-no-tani, across the straits. When Kiyosune informs me of the coming move a metallic taste rises in my throat. I request an audience with Munemori, hoping to change his mind. I am informed that his schedule does not allow him to meet with me for several days. Meantime, everyone is feverishly packing the camp up and boarding ships to cross the Inland Sea. By the time I am admitted to Munemori's presence, most of the soldiers have already sailed. A screen of state is set up between us. I wonder whether this is to preserve my modesty, or because he does not want to look me in the eye.

"I haven't much time," he rumbles.

"My lordship, it seems to me that Yashima is a safer place for us."

"Is this what you wanted to talk to me about? Your womanly fears? I am a busy man, my lady. I hope you have more important reasons to have disrupted my busy afternoon."

"My lord, I do apologize if I have offended you in any way. It just seems that perhaps the Emperor and his court would be safer if left here. At least, his journey could be postponed until all defenses are in place around Fukuhara, and Yoshitsune's forces have been defeated."

"You think I have not thought of that!" he roars. "I have thought everything through! You are dismissed!"

I am escorted out. Two days later Tokushi, Antoku, and the rest of our entourage are preparing to board the Imperial ship. Munemori appears the morning of our departure, motioning for Tokushi, Lady Daigon-no-suke and myself to draw aside with him.

"Everything has been arranged at Fukuhara. However, in answer to some of your concerns," he eyes me balefully, " the Emperor, his brother, and all of you women shall be safely left aboard boats anchored at Wada Misakai harbor. I do hope this satisfies any concerns you ladies may have had!"

"We are entirely within your hands, brother," Tokushi responds quietly.

Chapter Forty-Four
March 1184

Antoku and Morisada are extremely happy to be back on the ships. It takes us two days to cross the sixty miles of sea between Yashima and Fukuhara. Atsumori and Kiyosune make hawk-eyed kites which they sail with the boys off the back of the boats in the stiff March winds, forcing me to dose the children with ginger-honey tea to stave off the ensuing sore throats. When we arrive, Atsumori, Kiyosune and the other warriors disembark, while we women and children are left on the boat that has served as our floating palace. On the shore, our warriors are swarming like a hive of ants, setting up breastworks and fortifications, restoring and rebuilding many of the buildings at Fukuhara. They are setting up barricades at the shrine at Ikuta Woods, just north of Fukuhara, and finishing a fortress at Ichi-no-tani to the south, securing the coast on both sides of Fukuhara to re-establish our foothold on the main island. Every time I look at the bustle on shore my heart starts hammering so hard I fear I will pass out. I know this is a mistake. While Munemori agreed with me that the letter from Go-Shirakawa was not to be trusted, he seems to think we are ready to reclaim this part of the coast with military might. Atsumori says that the plan is for us to build up our strength, gathering our allies from Shikoku and from the south, then to march on Kyoto, not under banner of peace, but with the determination to defeat the Minamoto once and for all.

"There are many, from commoners to nobles in Kyoto who will rise up against the Genji oppressors as soon as we near the gates of the city," Atsumori assures me. "The rebels will be crushed. It is the will of heaven." If I were analyzing the situation with my head, I might think this was a workable plan as well. I cannot point to a flaw in it. But the nausea I feel is not from the churning of the sea beneath our ship. Machiko brings me cool washcloths for my forehead and cups of calming tea. Tokushi comes and kneels beside me, eyes shining as she watches the activity on shore.

"Are you not feeling well?"

I nod.

"You are probably tired from caring for all of us when we were sick. We are back!" she exults. "My father would be so happy to see that we have returned. I feel his spirit is with us, guiding Munemori."

If Kiyomori were here in body, we probably would not be in this mess, but as there is nothing to be gained by frightening her, I smile weakly and squeeze her hand, hoping that my malaise is indeed the result of exhaustion or even illness.

"Not your time of the month, is it?"

"No."

"That's good. There's no where for you to go!" she says, meaning that there is no place a menstruating woman can be isolated from others on this boat. We have tried to maintain the tradition by putting menstruating women on one boat together when their courses coincide, but with male children, male rowers and guards underfoot it isn't really practical.

It is the sort of spring day that would seem to prohibit sadness. As I look off towards Ichi-no-tani, I see boats ferrying horses back and forth. The fortress does look impregnable. Precipitous cliffs fade into pine-studded mountains behind it. High walls of enormous boulders and entire tree trunks create a narrow entrance to the fortress, and stair-steps of archery platforms guard that entrance, manned by hundreds of archers wearing the livery of lords from Shikoku and Chinzei. Ten rows of saddled horses arc in fans below the archery platforms. There are dozens of boats anchored here, scarlet flags snapping like confident flames in the wind. Perhaps it is just the relentless tattoo of the battle drums causing my heart to race.

Kiyosune and Atsumori left our boat this morning, having been assigned to Ichi-no-tani, commanded by Atsumori's uncle, Tadanori. Our ship was too crowded for intimacies, but I had slept with Atsumori and Kiyosune the night before we left Yashima. They were excited, certain that a decisive Heike victory is now within grasp.

"We shall have cherry viewing at the Capital!" Atsumori said with a mischievous smile, reminding me of a time we made love under a cherry tree and ended up covered with blossoms. They are like cherry trees themselves, young and blooming. I am like an old, twisted plum, still brightly blossoming but gnarled with age and wind and hardship. Sessho used to call me 'willow woman', fluid in the wind. My body is no less fluid than it was, but my heart is a storm-knotted cypress. They are so beautiful, and undressed they seem perilously fragile, and my joy in our union that evening was followed by tears.

"Hey," Atsumori said gruffly. "No need for that. We're seasoned warriors now, and your charms are peerless. We always come back safe."

"Nothing can happen to either of us because we always protect each other. Neither of us will ever be left wounded on the battlefield. We'll protect each other with our last breath," Kiyosune adds.

I tried to contain myself but sobbed even harder. I wish I could have made love with them again last night, but here on our floating palace such assignations are impossible.

After we drop the warriors off at Ichi-no-tani, our boat rows slowly against the wind to our mooring site at Wada Misikai. The grooms are trotting the horses up and down the beach, giving them a chance to stretch their legs after having been confined in the ships' holds for two days. A fishing boat comes near. Guards in a small boat go out to meet it, bargaining for some fish. Dolphins leap and swirl around our boat. Antoku and Morisada laugh, tossing them small silver minnows. Dolphins are a good omen. Perhaps I am just exhausted. Perhaps Munemori is right, and it is my woman's heart that fails me. Even the thought of returning to Kyoto fails to cheer me. A Heike victory will be hollow for me with Sessho gone. It may be just the heavy shadow of my own grief causing me to be so anxious; it is nearly a year since he died at the defeat at Tonamiyama.

Nightfall finds me on the deck again, gazing towards the campfires clustered on the beach like swarms of fireflies. Antoku comes over and sits in my lap. My chin fits comfortably on top of his head.

"Don't the campfires look like fireflies?" I say.

"Oh, yes! I wish they were! Why do fireflies only come out in summer? Remember when we used to chase them in the garden and put them in those paper lanterns? You don't think the Rebels have spoiled the Imperial gardens, do you? I want to catch fireflies again this summer."

"That will be fun. We'll have light from the fireflies and music from the crickets."

He nestles more deeply into me. "My rabbits love hearing the crickets. They have very sensitive ears, you know."

That night the two little boys bring their sleeping mats out and doze on either side of me after a long discussion about whether or not fish enjoy looking at the stars. I lie awake listening to the sea slapping against the hull, the sound of men's voices carrying across the water. From inside the cabin a few tremulous notes on the koto waver like stars on the water. Kozaisho, Michimori's wife, is the only one to have brought a koto on our flight, but lately she has felt too sick from her pregnancy to play. As if in response, the mournful vibrato of a flute rises from the shore. Soon the koto hushes and Kozaisho slides open the door and moves to a kneeling position on the deck.

"Do you think that is Michimori's flute?" she asks hopefully.

"Perhaps." The song being played is somber, the high notes tremulous as the wind in dry reeds. It sounds like Little Branch, Atsumori's flute. I imagine him sitting beside one of those campfires with Kiyosune, playing, perhaps wondering if I can hear. A star falls through the sky like a tear of fire.

The next morning I wake before dawn to the sound of men's voices. A supply ship has drawn up to the royal boat, brimming with fruits and vegetables and the gabbling of live ducks and chickens. As each day passes, the boys become more and more anxious to be on land, to see the carpenters at work restoring Fukuhara and to watch the warriors bivouac and practice for the next engagement.

"An Emperor should inspect the troops," Antoku says to Lady Kiyomori, trying to sound lofty rather than wheedling.

"After the Palace has been at least partially restored," she replies. "You must have a place fit for your magnificence."

"Can't we just go to the beach for a short while? I want to look at the soldiers."

"Me too!" Morisada exclaims, leaning over the rail and bouncing up and down on the balls of his feet. "I'm tired of being on the boat!"

"Now, now," says Tokizane, coming forward. "Let's go fishing! Your mother and grandmother are counting on you to catch some fish for their lunch!" He and Tokitada take the boys by the hand and lead them to the bow of the boat where they enter into a heated discussion of what sorts of hooks and bait will work best. I wish that Atsumori and Kiyosune had been chosen to stay on board as two of our guards, but though they are so young, Atsumori's

311

bloodline dictates that he serve as a commander; therefore they must be on shore to lead a regiment. I strain my eyes, scanning the shore in search of Atsumori's black armor with the green lacing, or Kiyosune's gray armor laced with white. I catch a glimpse of Tsunemasa in his distinctive indigo armor with the red and dark blue lacing, wearing his enormous antlered helmet, riding his horse Night Quickness, shouting encouragement to clumps of men erecting defense barriers. Then I feel dizzy and have to lie down, head and heart pounding like Taiko drums.

Lady Kiyomori saunters up to me. "Is there anything you want to tell me?"

"No madam."

"I hope you are not with child."

"No, indeed I am not."

"There'd be no way to know who the father was."

Everyone knows of my attachments, but it is extremely rude for her to make reference to it. I sit up and stare away from her to the glittering veil the sun makes on the water. She comes and stands beside me.

"You have nothing to tell me?"

"It would be better if more of the men slept on the ships. Until the defenses are complete."

"My thoughts exactly," she agrees. "But Munemori will not be moved on this point. He is as stubborn and headstrong as his father," she mutters. "But he lacks his father's wisdom," she says, more to herself than to me. "He says the fortress at Ichi-no-tani is impregnable, and that he will keep most of the men safely within those walls."

"What of the cliffs behind the fortress?"

She laughs. "No one could come down those cliffs. Unless they can change themselves into birds." I stay silent, watching the gulls called Capital Birds circling our supply ship. When I look back she has gone, without so much as a swish of silk. Though in her sixties now, she is as silent and cat-like as ever in her movements.

Another sleepless night. I look over the rail of the ship towards the Heike fires on the beaches, and notice, just beyond the trees, a swath of fires so numerous they echo the sea of stars overhead. Running silently down the deck, I take the arm of Tokizane and point.

He nods. "The Genji warlord brothers. Yoshitsune and Nori Yori. We expect an attack at first light."

They do not wait until dawn. I wake from fitful sleep to the sound of screams and battle cries coming from Ikuta Woods and the area of Fukuhara. I gaze out at the two lines of campfires divided by the dark woods, looking like the lanterns of the dead floating down the rivers at Obon. Soon all the ladies are out on the deck, straining their eyes to see the battle we can hear. One by one, the fisherman's huts flare into light, having been torched to illumine the night battle. Even some of the woods themselves are set on fire and I wonder if the Ikuta shrine itself is threatened. In the flickering light cast by the fires we see some figures on horseback, and many on foot, clashing back and forth from trees to beach and back again. Arrows are whizzing everywhere. At this distance it is impossible to tell who are the defenders, who the attackers. One of our boats pulls close to shore and sends a rowboat to pick up injured men.

"This is where we beat them!" Morisada crows, bouncing up and down beside me.

"Soon we will be back at the Capital!" cries Antoku.

It appears to me that Nori Yori's men have broken through our lines. A line of fire bordering the woods makes me think our barricades have been put to the torch. Lady Kiyomori is fingering her jade prayer beads, but the prayers I hear her muttering are not to the Buddha, but to Hachiman.

"Their forces aren't as good as ours," Antoku asserts.

"Or as brave," his brother agrees. Both boys have their hands clasped tight around the railing, shooting dagger like glances towards the shore as if they could will the battle to turn out the way they wish it. Their nurses try to coax them back to bed, but both stoutly refuse.

"The least we can do is stay awake and give the warriors our prayers," says Morisada.

It is hard to argue with the logic of that. None of us will be able to sleep until the battle is resolved. Soon it becomes obvious that our line is retreating. Fukuhara is overrun, and the buildings which had been being restored, become avenues of flame mounting to the heavens. This has always been such a bad luck place for us. The guards pace back and forth on the deck like caged tigers. It becomes apparent that the Genji are prevailing, at least in the area we can see. The Heike are falling back towards the fortress at Ichi-no-tani. Some are streaming towards the boats, cutting their moorings free, taking them out into the current. Some warriors plunge their horses into the sea and swim towards the boats. At first they are winching the horses up onto the boats; later the

313

warriors are forced to turn their horses heads towards shore and clamber onto the boats without them. We see one warrior shooting his horse with his bow rather than let it be captured by the enemy.

"Not the horses. Don't shoot the horses," Antoku whispers.

Much as I strain my eyes, I cannot determine in the dusky melee any distinguishing characteristics of armor that would tell me how my dear ones fare. The ladies are wringing their hands, sobbing and praying. As hope begins to fade from the faces of the adults watching the carnage on shore, the boys' eyes mist and their lips quiver. The sky grows lighter and lighter as dawn approaches, and the battle is now unmistakably a rout and a massacre. A boat near shore takes on so many fleeing men that it capsizes; those few men who make it back to shore by clinging to their horses are soon cut down by arrows. A boat pulls up to ours. "The battle is lost! We are gravely outnumbered! We must flee!"

The anchor is hauled up, men scramble to adjust the sails, and the rowers put their backs into it. The sun rises and we see snow flurries spinning like falling blossoms through the evergreens on the mountains. We pass another swamped boat; the men clinging to it cry out to us to take mercy and stop for them.

"We've got to stop the boat and help them!" I cry.

"Yes, stop the boat!" Antoku orders.

"The Emperor cannot be jeopardized!" Lady Kiyomori glares at Tokizane.

"The Emperor commands the boat to stop." Antoku's voice is wobbly but he raises his chin bravely, defying his grandmother as few men have ever dared to do. The sailors and guards stand paralyzed, eyes darting from one to the other, not knowing whom to obey. Lady Kiyomori's face softens and she kneels down to Antoku's height. "Your word is law, of course. Only, the current is so strong here, the boat cannot be stopped. If you order the men to do something they cannot do, they must commit suicide out of shame."

The desperate cries of the men in the water begin to fade as the current carries us past. Antoku bows his head and sobs and all of us weep with him. Tokushi slides out across the deck to him on her knees, pulling him and Morisada into her embrace. "I am only a woman and cannot bear this. I need your strength with me, and all of us need your prayers. Come back into the cabin and pray with me." The boys allow themselves to be coaxed back in the cabin, and half of the weeping women accompany them. Lady Kiyomori remains, narrowing her eyes as she surveys the battle still raging on shore. So many of our men are fleeing the battle, the boats are taking only nobles back on board. We see peasant soldiers and loyal servants clinging to the boats only to have their masters on board cut off their arms, forcing them to fall shrieking back into the sea. As we approach the fortress at Ichi-no-tani we see that it is burning. There are dead men all along the beach, and corpses swaying like seaweed throughout the shallows.

Two riders break free of a cluster of fighting men and ride for the water. The hair on my neck rises as I see that the one on the black horse wears armor with green lacings and a horned helmet. Atsumori! His companion has gray armor with white lacings, and though I cannot make out the fox and badger figures on his helmet I know it must be Kiyosune. He is bent over his horse's neck, an arrow protruding from his right shoulder. They race down the beach towards one of the Heike ships, several of the Genji in hot pursuit. Atsumori smacks Kiyosune's mount with his bow, and the horse surges into the water. Atsumori sends a shower of arrows towards his attackers, so swiftly it is hard to believe they have all come from the same bow. Three of the horseman are hit; the one remaining dismounts to help a wounded friend. Atsumori gallops his horse into the water. Kiyosune is already halfway to the boat. The arrow must have penetrated where the armor joins. I can fix that! He will be all right! I look back towards Atsumori and stop breathing when I realize he has turned his horse around and is heading back towards shore. A lone Genji stands on the beach, beckoning for Atsumori to return. Though he must be bellowing, his taunts come faintly to us. "Coward! A commander never turns his back on an enemy!"

"No! Atsumori! No!" I scream but Atsumori never turns his head. His horse stumbles in the wet sand as he emerges from the waves and in an instant the Genji has leapt from his own horse, knocking Atsumori to the ground.

"Atsumori!" My head turns towards the faint cry. Though almost to the boat, Kiyosune has turned his horse and is heading for shore. He yanks the arrow out of his shoulder with a guttural scream and struggles to draw his sword with his left hand as he urges his horse towards shore. The Genji has removed Atsumori's helmet and is straddling him, dagger in hand. A regiment of Genji warriors are thundering down the sands towards them, still at a distance, but closing in.

"Kiyosune, no! It's too late!" I scream. I throw myself against Tokizane. "Save him, do something, make him stop!" His only reply is the tears streaming down his face.

The Genji stands, holding Atsumori's head. Kiyosune's screams of rage sound like a hawk as he spurs his horse out of the water. He has almost reached Atsumori's killer when an arrow from the approaching warriors strikes his mare in the chest and she skids to her knees. In one smooth motion, Kiyosune slides off his horse, sword drawn, shining in the sun. In the next instant the first wave of horsemen surround him and he disappears beneath half a dozen flashing swords.

"Shut up! Shut up! Compose yourself, Lady Fujiwara!" Lady Kiyomori keeps slapping me until the shrill sounds ripping through me stop. I stretch to look over her as she pins me against the railing. We are well beyond the scene of the battle now. I can only guess that the two dim objects raised high on spears over the triumphant Genji are my lovers' heads.

Chapter Forty-Five
March 1184

Machiko gave me a potion to make me sleep, and I did not wake until the next morning. By that time we have passed far beyond the Awaji straits and are drifting near Aki Province. No one knows whether it is safe to return to Yashima, or if we should seek refuge at Itkushima Shrine or find shelter with allies near the southern tip of Shikoku. There is no telling where the other boatloads of survivors have gone, or which of the men have survived. Having eaten nothing for a day, I try to choke down a few bites of the rice porridge Machiko keeps lifting to my mouth, but it is hard to swallow. None of the other white-faced ladies seem to be faring any better. After drifting for several days, we end up docked near an island friendly to the Heike, with several other boats carrying surviving warriors anchored around us. Messengers ferry back and forth trying to determine who has perished and who has survived, but no one knows how many boats escaped, nor where the winds and tides might have carried them all.

Tokikaza, one of Michimori's warriors, comes to our boat asking for an audience with Kozaisho. In such cramped quarters, we cannot help but overhear as he recounts to her how his master had been surrounded and killed near the mouth of the Minato River. "Before the battle, Lord Michimori told me that if he were to fall, I must not throw my life away, but instead should show my devotion by finding his wife and letting her know of his fate. That is the only reason I have kept my worthless self alive."

Kozaisho makes no reply, merely pulling a cloth over her head and sinking to the ground while her nurse rocks her prostrate body, keening.

A boat bearing Tomomori arrives. Lady Kiyomori has shown no emotion at the deaths of her nephews Atsumori and Michimori, but when Tomomori steps on board our vessel she gives a single sob and presses him to her, shuddering.

"Munemori?" she asks.

"He is well. He and Norimori have returned to Yashima, but I could not rest until I had found you."

"And the others?"

"My boy...my boy, Tomoakira is dead," he sobs. "He died saving my life."

Tokushi bursts into tears at the word that her nephew is dead. Lady Kiyomori makes no sound as she hears of the death of her grandson, but tears are dying her gray robes black.

"Kiyomune?" she asks.

"Munemori's son survived. No one knows about Shigehira or Koremori. Moromori perished."

Lady Kiyomori staggers. Servants help her sit. I lean over the side of the boat and vomit up what little I ate of my lunch. Moromori was Shigemori's youngest boy, only fourteen years old. I keep seeing his beautiful almond eyes and his sweet smile.

"Noritsune?" Lady Kiyomori gasps.

"He lives. But Norimori's youngest, Narimori, is said to be dead, though it is only a servant who has reported seeing it."

"What of Tsunemasa and Tsunetoshi?" Tokushi asks.

"Tsunetoshi, Kiyofusa, and Kiyosada perished together after a furious fight in which they killed at least fifty of the enemy."

Hearing that she has lost not just another cousin but two of her half brothers, Tokushi slumps to the deck. Lady Daigon-no-suke sits beside her wringing her hands.

"Are you certain no one knows what has become of my husband?" Lady Daigon-no-suke presses.

"Many boats are unaccounted for. It is likely Shigehira is on one of them. Forgive me for this next tiding, but Tsunemasa is also dead. He was killed at the edge of the water, acting as rearguard so that others could board the boats. He died bravely."

Bravely. As if that matters.

"It is the end of the Heike," Lady Kiyomori mutters.

"An attendant of Sukemori's and Aromori's said they made it onto a boat. A warrior claims to have seen Tadanori fall when Yoshitsune and his demons plunged down the cliffs into the back of the fortress."

Lady Kiyomori looks less stunned as she hears that two of Shigemori's other sons have survived.

"Tadanori dead. And Tsunemasa. They seemed indestructible. What of Tsunemori?"

"He lives, if surviving all three of one's sons can be called living."

If Tadanori is dead, then Tsunemori and Norimori are the last of Kiyomori's brothers, the last of the generation that defeated the Genji in the original battles between the clans.

"Is it certain about Tsunemasa?" I ask.

"Many of us saw him fall," Tomomori says miserably.

Tokitada and Tokizane bow their heads and weep unashamedly. Lady Kiyomori presses her fist into her mouth but a few deep groans escape her. Tokushi weeps as though her heart would break and I know I should go to her and comfort her, but all I can do is cling to Machiko and shake like a storm-tossed tree.

Tomomori kneels before me. "Lady Fujiwara, I hate to ask, but we have many injured men on my boat, and few physicians..."

I hear a hollow voice saying, "Of course," and watch myself rise. Machiko scurries to pack our supplies. Male servants take the wicker cases from her and we are helped onto a small craft with Tomomori to return to his ship.

It is a large ship, but it seems the entire deck is lined with wounded soldiers. A single male physician, accompanied by a servant, sinks to his knees beside one of the wounded men, looking as if he is so exhausted he will never rise again. Male servants and uninjured soldiers offer fresh water and a few words of comfort, and change the bloody bandages. Several rowers stand over a pot of steaming water, stirring bandages with an oar. Drying bandages festoon the rigging and railings, the different colored strips of cloth making the ship look as if it were decorated for a festival. Hachiman's festival, I think bitterly. I am paralyzed at the sight of so much groaning, whimpering human need. Where to start? Fortunately, Tomomori leads me over to one of his friends. I unwrap the bandage from the man's head. His ear has been sliced off, and the gash runs from the top of his head to below his jaw. Machiko has corralled some servants and is barking orders like a general, setting up pots of steaming herbs. Narukirameki looks up at me and manages a smile.

"What do you think, Lady Fujiwara? Am I ready to embark for the pure land?"

I put my hand to his forehead. He is only slightly feverish, and the edges of the wound are pulling together. "I'm afraid your sins will be keeping you in this world, Lord Naru." He kisses my sleeve. I call Machiko over to stitch the parts of the wound close enough to sew. The rest will simply have to scar as it will. I tell her to poultice the wound after sewing it, though she knows what to do as well as I, and move on to the young man lying next to him. He has an arrow wound through the place where the shoulder meets the chest, a vulnerable area where the armor is laced together to allow movement. The same place at Kiyosune's wound. I swallow the tears rising in my throat. "How are you, Kikoshi?" I ask, addressing him as a young noble though he is not a gentleman I recognize.

"I want to go home," he whispers. He cannot be more than fourteen or fifteen years old. He is hotter to the touch than Naru. I beckon a servant to bring some of the fever- reducing tea and pack the wound front and back with anti-infective powder as deeply as I dare. He thrashes and cries out as I work.

"Forgive me. I am such a coward," he gasps. Tears prick my eyes. "Not at all, my lord. Please think nothing of it," I murmur.

The next man has an arrow wound in the thigh which is healing nicely. The one after that has several sword cuts which have the stink of putrefying flesh. I tell some servants that his only hope is for them to pour boiling water over the wounds on his arms and hands, then bind everything with burn salve. They take him near the railing and stand in front of him while others work, so he will be less humiliated by his shrieking. The next man somehow took a sword thrust into the abdomen. He is white and unresponsive. I beckon over the Buddhist priest making the rounds as this man is beyond any help but prayer.

After awhile the men and injuries blur together. Some I know will die, but for most I have hope. The most severely injured men obviously never made it as far as the boats. Within hours I am low on supplies and send some of the rowers to the island with a list of herbs for them to find, hoping that remote though this place is, the local apothecaries will have a supply of the things I need. Servants bring us soup and sake and we work on through the night. The next day we return to the royal ship and sleep for several hours as if dead, then go to another ship. There are four boatloads of soldiers, and about a quarter of them are injured. Fortunately four healers have come from the island, or Machiko and I would have died from our task. Soon I feel nothing but exhaustion. We sleep about four hours of each twenty-four during four days time, and no poppy syrups are required to make our sleep deep and dreamless.

At last Tomomori decides we must return to Yashima. The Genji have not attempted to cross the straits or pursue the surviving Heike and their allies. Shikoku is still ours. Funerals are held on the island for those who have died and the pyres are still smoking as we haul anchor. I stand at the railing, watching the island dwindle behind us. Lady Kiyomori appears beside me, places her hand on my shoulder. "Thank you," she says simply. "You are indeed your mother's daughter."

Tokushi comes to the other side of me. "Can you do something for Kozaisho? She won't eat or drink, not for the last two days."

All I can think of is how badly I want to sleep, but I nod and she leads me to Kozaisho. She is collapsed in a heap, much the way I saw her last, with robes pulled over her head. Her nurse is lying beside her, looking woebegone.

"Kozaisho!" Tokushi shakes her shoulder. "Seiko is back. She has come to heal you. Sit up please."

Kozaisho sits up, her eyes vacant, face drawn and haunted.

"Enough, Kozaisho!" Tokushi snaps. "We are all devastated. We have all lost more than we can bear. I have lost half my family. Seiko has lost her lovers, but you don't see her moping around. No! She has been caring for the men who are wounded, with no thought for herself. You at least carry a child, a memento of Michimori. You think I don't grieve for my cousin? Now do whatever Seiko tells you so you don't lose this child as well!" She flounces off.

Kozaisho looks at me pitifully. "Tell the Empress I am sorry to have displeased her," she pleads.

"We are all heartbroken. The Empress does not mean to be unkind," I reply.

Kozaisho's eyes brim with tears. "The karma tie between myself and Michimori was so strong, I cannot bear to think of living without him."

I brush my hand across her abdomen. "But you carry his child who is his legacy, who will make Michimori immortal. You must eat and drink to preserve the life of your child, Kozaisho."

Tears stream down her face. "Not one woman in ten bears a living child and survives the birth. To give birth in such a public place on the storm-tossed waves--better to die with some dignity!"

I place my hands on hers. "Kozaisho, people talk such nonsense about childbirth. I will be there to tend you, and I will get you through it."

"Even if it all turned out as we wish, every time I looked at the child I would miss Michimori all the more. I cannot live without my soul, and Michimori was my soul."

"I know exactly how you feel. But once you have a child to consider, your life is no longer your own, to dispose of as you wish. When the child is born, life will again seem precious to you."

"I am certain you are right, Lady Fujiwara," she says humbly.

I indicate for Machiko to brew some restoring tea for Kozaisho and her nurse, and watch while they drink it. I should like to give her a tea to lift her spirits, but the herbs best for that purpose are not safe for a pregnant woman.

The next night I am awakened by the sound of shouting. "Ho! Help! A noblewoman has jumped into the sea from the Imperial Ship!" I pull on an outer robe and hurriedly go out on deck. Kozaisho's nurse is screaming, pointing towards the heaving sea beneath us. Immediately torches are lit and seven or eight men strip to loincloths and dive, searching for her. The sky is blanketed in thick indigo clouds and the sea seems as dark as ink. All the ladies are soon on deck, praying loudly. Finally there is a shout of triumph and we see men pulling a limp figure from the waters. They hoist her onto the deck. Ignoring propriety, one of the men pushes against her chest, and quantities of water issue from her mouth. I press my fingers to her throat, frantically searching for a pulse, but she is cold as the ocean and there is not the faintest flutter to be found.

"She's gone," I say, and Tokushi and all the ladies collapse to the deck with loud lamentations. Kozaisho's nurse tears her hair, shrieking, "Why did you not take me with you!" and tries to throw herself over the side, but the men restrain her despite her struggles. Kozaisho lies with her black hair spread out, streaming water, the thick fringe of her lashes dark against her cheeks, her translucent white outer garments rounding gently over her belly. She still looks like a beautiful ripe fruit. It is hard to believe the spirit is gone from her body. I imagine her searching the windy land for Michimori, and their reunion, and bitter tears fall from my eyes as I long to pass through the watery dragon realms myself, to be with Sessho.

Chapter Forty-Six
August 1184–March 1185

I swirl my brush in the ink, write Atsumori's name on the parchment stretched tight onto a four-sided lantern. One panel must dry before I can inscribe the next. I set it next to the lantern for Kiyosune, pick up another and set Tsunemasa's name on it. Then Tomomori, then Sessho, then my mother and father. The beach is lined with vats producing thousands of candles; all the servants are busy carving as many boats for the dead as they can. We have been preparing for this Obon, this festival of the dead, for months. Since the defeat at Ichi-no-tani five months ago, the task of honoring the dead has become vast. Michimori, Kozaisho, Koremori, Tsunetoshi, Moromori, Tomoakira. I sit surrounded by a circle of the dead. Machiko mixes my ink, brings me restoring teas. We are sitting beneath a pair of gaily flowered pink parasols protecting us from the sun. If not for the task before us, one might think we were having a lovely day at the beach. One can barely walk inside the palace, for all the women crafting their mementos for the deceased. Each of us has dozens to honor now. As Obon approaches, the spirits of the dead mass about us in such numbers, the force of the living seems puny by comparison.

When the night of Obon comes, we set up altars for the dead and feast in their memory. I put out salted plums for Sessho's boy, Tomomori, remembering how even as a child he preferred salty to sweet. I pour cups of sake laced with crushed pearl and flecks of gold for Kiyosune and Atsumori, plum wine for Tsunemasa, seared fish and sesame greens for Sessho with the last of the Green Mountain sake. I toast my glass to his, murmuring our favorite poem:

"Do not smile to yourself
Like a green mountain
With a cloud drifting across it.
People will know we are in love."

Finally all the torches outside are lit, and we follow the priests with their billowing censers down the aisle of flame. In Kyoto we would have gathered at the banks of the rivers running through the city, cradled by the mountains with their glowing bonfires of sacred script. Here, courtiers, warriors, and servants alike gather by the river dividing Yashima and our makeshift Imperial residence from the rest of Shikoku. Each person has ten, twenty, thirty, even forty boats to launch, there has been so much death; the throngs of the dead who have come to visit us overwhelm the numbers of the living left to mourn for them.

A woman next to me whispers, "I hope my father and brother will not be confused, wandering around Kyoto searching for us."

Her mother hugs her. "I'm sure not."

"Spirits always return to the hearts which love them best," I say.

I feel Sessho inside me as I speak, the light within the lantern. When I close my eyes, I see my mother's serene eyes, feel her eddying about me like warm water. They seem more real than any of my friends still living and I long to cross to the windy land to feel this communion with them always. But too soon the time of visitation is over and I, like all the rest, light my wicks one by one and sail the spirit boats containing them out upon the river, starting with the ones like Lord Kiyomori and Emperor Takakura, that I was least close to, and reluctantly parting from my closest beloved dead at the last. Atsumori's mischievous smile. Kiyosune's lopsided grin. I tie their boats together. I barely feel Tsunemasa. Perhaps his spirit is with On'na Mari and Akoyo in Kyoto.

The shuddering of the gongs, incense roiling like mist. The river is soon so thronged with the spirit boats that, except for the flames dancing from each, one could walk across the river on the memories of the dead. I set my mother's boat in the water, asking her to look after the men I have loved. Finally I tie Tomomori and Sessho's boats together, symbolizing the karma tie keeping them together in the spirit world. My hands quiver with the effort of letting them go. The river of light flows majestically to the ocean, where all the boats are capsized, the lights doused. The glittering lights representing all those lives, all those hopes, snuffed so abruptly, so brutally by the black tides engulfing them.

Machiko holds and fans me. It is a sticky, hot evening, without a pitying breeze. Several women faint and must be carried back to the palace.

324

The next day the beach is littered with the debris of boats and candles. Shinto Priests make a funeral pyre of them, and the colors of the flames that dance throughout it are supernatural in their intensity and variety.

Autumn arrives early, bringing fogs dense enough to muffle our sobs. The few trees nearby are mostly evergreens; there is no going to view the changing colors of the leaves. The dropping of those brightly colored leaves would have seemed far too personal a message anyway. Our world is gray and ghostly; then the fog turns to rain, the rain becomes sleet, the sleet turns to hail and the hail to snow. So many kinds of water in our seaside abode, all of them cold, except for the falling of hot tears, and those leave us feeling coldest of all.

New Year's Day passes without ceremony. All the things that should have been done, positions that should have been awarded, feasts that should have been held are ignored; even the drumming and chanting and ringing of bells to drive away demons seems quiet and diminished, as if all of us realized the demons we are confronting have found fleshly abodes and will not be so easily banished. Still, many more warriors have gathered for us during this respite, their tents and banners stretching down the beach and back up towards the hillside farther than the eye can see, and people begin speaking hopefully that this new year will restore the Heike to their former glory. Tomomori, with half of our remaining army, is stationed at the island of Hikoshima, controlling the sea roads. Yoritomo's brother Nori Yori and his troops are starving in Nagato Province, as Heike loyalists all along the Inland Sea deny them rice and the ships they need to pursue us. Yoshitsune, having neither the ships nor the manpower to follow up on his victory at Ichi-no-tani, guards against uprisings in Kyoto. I am too lost in my melancholy to hope.

Tokushi continues to be extremely remote. She has experienced so many losses now; brothers, uncles, cousins, so many lost at Ichi-no-tani, she seems completely unresponsive to anything except prayer. She always wants to know what the common soldiers are eating, and except for the meat, which she abhors, she will eat that and nothing more. As a result she grows thinner and more ethereal all the time.

Even Antoku and Morisada are subdued. Antoku especially is taking the losses in his family very hard, especially when he heard that Koremori had committed suicide. Koremori had been missing for a couple of months, since the battle of Ichi-no-tani. At last his servant returned saying that Koremori had escaped the slaughter, made his way to a Buddhist temple and taken vows renouncing the world; but not content with that, he and his other supporters who had taken such vows dove into the sea and never surfaced. Antoku worshipped his cousin, whose children had once been two of Antoku's closest playmates. Koremori had become like a father to Antoku after Takakura died, and Tsunemasa had been a beloved uncle, the old warrior who never showed a flicker of impatience towards the boys who idolized him.

Antoku spends many hours praying with his mother for his deceased family, taking seriously his role as the sovereign to use his prayers to intercede for them in the next life. He is far more serious than any child his age has a right to be, but with circumstances as they are, what can one expect? Even Morisada, as feisty and exuberant a child as ever lived, is subdued, clinging to his nurse and openly wailing for his mother. He seems to have lost all interest in soldiers and fighting and talks only of going home.

Now, when he builds sand castles he always kicks them down and stomps them flat.

"The castle looks so pretty with its red flags and sea-shell decorations, perhaps you should leave it?" I suggest.

"Things always get smashed anyway, whether they're pretty or not," he retorts, jumping on it. And indeed, having seen so many things left burning in our wake, how can the children have any sense of continuity? Impermanence is the law of this world, but it seems that now everything we love is as evanescent as the morning dew. A castle cannot stand, even in a child's imagination.

As the first signs of spring emerge, people talk longingly about the Capital, about how the plum blossoms would bloom, first on one side of the river, then the other, indulging in pathetic reminiscences about cherry blossom viewing parties, the poem written by this man, the dance performed by that one. The men who wrote the poems and performed the dances are gone now, their bones bleaching on the battlefields, or turning to pearl under the waves. The conversations quickly turn away from those missing to discussions of which garden was prettiest this time of year and to feasts of the past, but soon they trail off into melancholy, for the gardens and mansions of Kyoto are as much ghosts as the men who had inhabited them.

Munemori is half the size he used to be. The sacks under his eyes hang halfway down his cheeks. Tokushi, Sotso-no-suke, Antoku, and I are dining

with him and Kiyomune in their quarters. The March winds lash the
structure, making the beams moan and creak.

"I'm sending Noriyoshi with a punitive force to subdue some rebels on the
other side of Shikoku who are refusing to send us men and arms. Another
five thousand warriors sail to the mainland as soon as the weather permits, to
harass Nori Yori's forces and to take vengeance on any in those coastal districts
who are supporting them. We know that traitors from Suo province are giving
the Genji ships and teaching them how to sail."

"But there will still be plenty of soldiers to protect us here?" Tokushi asks.

"Yes, yes, of course. Nothing to fear. The Genji would never dare to attack
us here at Yashima, which is so well defended. At Noritsune's suggestion, we
have sent parties of soldiers to every beachhead throughout Shikoku so that
wherever the Genji attempt to land, they will immediately encounter resistance
and messengers will summon further troops to repel them."

"Thank you uncle. That sounds like a fine plan," Antoku nods.

All are on high alert during the soft, sparkling weather of early March, with
lookout boats patrolling the entire length of the coast. But near the equinox,
spring storms blow in, keeping every boat close to shore.

I sit bolt upright, heart pounding, hair and silks sticking sweatily to my
skin.

"Mistress?" Machiko inquires groggily, struggling to sit. Panting, pressing
my hand to my chest, I hear torrents of rain ripping at the slate tiles of the
palace roof like an infuriated beast.

"A bad dream, mistress?" Machiko asks.

*The Storm God, Susanowo driving three small boats loaded with Genji warriors
ahead of him in a thundering tempest. Hachiman himself standing in the bow of
the lead boat, lightning crackling around his antlered helmet. A sleeping garrison
on the beach slaughtered, their blood pooling into a crimson lake. And a word,
pounding in my brain: Katsuura--'hidden victory'.*

"Very bad."

"Predictive?" Machiko asks fearfully.

"I don't know."

Machiko rummages through one of the herb chests to find a remedy for
nightmare, but I push away the aromatic salve she hands me. Predictive
dream or merely nightmare? I have many nightmares now: feeling Atsumori
and Kiyosune pressed close to me, only to wake in my dream and find that

they have no heads; red-bannered ships spinning like autumn leaves in the current, crashed to splinters upon the rocks; Sessho's horse rolling over on him, cracking open the shell of his armor as if it were the husk of an almond, crushing him into pulp on claw-like boulders. I shiver miserably, chilled by my own sweat, wishing desperately one of my men were here to hold me and tell me it would be all right. They are all gone. Every man I have ever loved-- Sessho, Tsunemasa, Atsumori, Kiyosune. All.

"Get me my outer robe," I tell Machiko.

"You can't be thinking of going out in this," she pleads, helping me into a black quilted jacket. I push my curtains aside, pick my way through the silent hall, Machiko bobbing after me holding an oil lamp.

"Open the doors," I order the guards. As if in response to my request, the wind outside howls its challenge, slashing ropes of rain against the doors so hard that they quiver. The men hesitate.

"Lady Fujiwara?" Tokitada emerges from the shadows, face pale in the gloom. He draws close to me, smiling wanly.

"You *must* be a sorceress if you propose going out in this."

I glance at the guards. He motions them to stand off from us so we can speak privately.

"What is it?" he asks.

"I dreamed the Storm God helped the Genji across the straits. Hachiman was with them."

He considers this, brows furrowed. Then he gestures with his chin towards the guards. "Open the doors. Just a crack," he cautions as they spring to their task.

They push the doors open to a width of six feet, then brace themselves to keep the shuddering doors from flying apart. Rain hurtles into the columns before me like a horizontal waterfall. The encampment is dark; no torches can survive this onslaught. No colors but gray and black, and the white lines of surf exploding as they attack the beach, each impact strong enough so the shock is palpable through the floor beneath us.

Tokitada shakes his head. "Only the gods could survive out there tonight. Trust me, Lady, if the Taira cannot put to sea, the Genji cannot. They are mountain people, not sailors. Yes, they came down cliffs we thought only a bird could mount at Ichi-no-tani, but even a seabird could not dare these winds. We have watchers posted at every bay and inlet..."

328

"You're right, of course. It was only a dream."

Tokitada nods to the guards. It takes four men, heaving and grunting, to pull each door closed and bolted. Trembling, I want to throw myself into Tokitada's arms and weep, but instead I merely nod and stumble back to my dark corner. Machiko holds a poppy syrup to my lips. I shake my head, sitting with my back against the wall.

"Go to sleep," I tell her.

"Mistress…"

"I command you to go to sleep." She lies down and feigns sleep for a few minutes until exhaustion carries her off.

I stare into the darkness. Strange, how a person's absence can feel more vivid than their presence. With Kozaisho and Michimori gone, the space beyond my curtains is empty, echoing and ghostly. Without Atsumori and Kiyosune, my own quarters seem unbearably large. I still turn my head whenever someone walks by, expecting them to slip through my curtains, faces merry, bearing branches of purple plum they found for me far back in the mountains. Such huge holes in the fabric of life. The world is all holes and edges now, like a swatch of ancient silk, crumbling and falling apart in my hands.

Chapter Forty-Seven
March 1185

Two days later, Munemori's fifteen-year old son Kiyomune bursts into the palace followed by other youths and a cluster of soldiers.

"The villages on the hillside behind us are all in flame! The Genji have landed and encircled our camp from the rear! We're surrounded!" The young men shout.

"Has anyone seen the warriors? Couldn't the fires be accidental?" Tokitada queries.

"Every village as far as the eye can see, accidental? No! We're surrounded! The only escape is by sea! My father has ordered it! Gather only what you can carry! Escape to the boats! The Genji will be here at any moment!" Kiyomune yells.

Frantic screams fill the air as everyone, servants and ladies alike, races to gather their possessions. Scrolls fly through the air as people search for the letters that meant the most to them. Servants tear out to the boats bearing hastily packed chests.

"Quickly, quickly, we must get to the boats now, leave anything you don't need!" Tokushi cries.

I hand Machiko my writing kit and the letters I have saved.

"Get these on the boat first!"

Antoku staggers out the door carrying a statue of Kannon as big as he is.

"I don't care about the clothes, you idiot!" Morisada screams at a trembling servant. "I want my collection of boats and badgers! And my sword, don't forget my sword!"

Machiko rushes back to my side and the two of us struggle to lift the chest with my robes and jewelry. All around us, women are screaming, "Where are the porters! Where are the porters!" Tokitada and Tokizane dash in and scoop up the boys, carrying them out on their shoulders while Tomomori places Tokushi in a palanquin so she can be carried across the beach to the boats. Finally two men take the heavy clothing chest from us and Machiko and I feverishly pack up my herbs and salves.

"Faster, faster mistress," a young page urges, hopping from one foot to another, finally snatching the medicine chest from Machiko and running out with it at a gallop, despite the fact that it must weigh almost as much as he. Machiko grabs a bundle of her own possessions and I stagger out with a chest containing my journals. We are among the last to leave the palace and step out onto the foggy beach. Outside, the scene is like an anthill that had been kicked over; men and horses aswirl, warriors looking for the enemy, other warriors and servants leading horses onto the boats. We are nearly trampled before half a dozen foot soldiers make their way over to us and form a protective circle, escorting us through the melee to the ships. The Imperial ship has already slipped its mooring and is sliding away into the current. The soldiers bundle us into a rowboat and paddle us to the ship, where we suffer the indignity of being hoisted aboard like so much luggage.

"I thought we had lost you!" Tokushi says with great agitation. "I told you to hurry!"

"We couldn't leave the herbs," I say. "We'll need them where we are going." I am relieved to see that the servants have managed to get everything on board. "Look, I brought some of your things as well," I say, opening the chests and showing her some of Antoku's keepsakes and an ivory Buddha I had picked up, which had been dropped or abandoned in her servants' haste.

"Oh, thank you, thank you for being so brave!" she cries, stroking some of Antoku's toys and baby clothes that had been left behind in the panic. Tokushi's eyes go wide, staring over my shoulder, and I turn to see, on shore, warriors with white flags and Genji insignia galloping out of the fog, brandishing swords and torches. Emerging from the mists with their tall antlered helmets and snarling battle cries, they seem like demons ripping through the veils that divide the worlds. We are well out into the channel now and safe, but the Genji hurl their torches onto the palace, and the flames catch, despite the dampness, climbing the walls to the roof like white and yellow vines of destruction. Gasps and sobs erupt from the ladies and their servants, many of whom left precious valuables there. Several unfortunate servants who had not made it out in time run from the building, scattering jewelry and kimonos as they flee. One trips and falls, and is trampled by a warrior

331

on a dark horse. The others run screaming into the water where our warriors snatch them up, throw them across their horses and swim them out to boats closer to the shore, while warriors on the shore loose volleys of arrows towards the attackers. All the noblewomen made it onto our boat or another close by; I was the last of the sixty-five high-born women to escape.

In the mist and smoke, it is impossible to tell how many Genji there are. Groups of six to a dozen appear on the beach, weaving sinuously to dodge the arrows from the boats, calling challenges from just out of earshot, then galloping out of sight. They taunt our men to stand and fight, then dissolve in the fog. Skirmishes erupt here and there, but judging from the number of fires in the nearby villages and beyond, flickering in and out of the mist, their army must be huge, so while a contingent of our warriors mount a rear action, the majority are clambering aboard the ships, eager to avoid the fate of those surprised last year at Ichi-no-tani.

The hooting Genji set our garrisons on fire next, then the entertainment halls and fisherman's huts and makeshift residences; soon our whole settlement is ablaze. Prostitutes run shrieking out of their quarters, and peasants who had provided us with fish and rice and other services herd their howling children away as quickly as possible. A pair of women from the prostitutes' quarters emerge with robes and hair ablaze, rolling over and over in the sand, writhing and convulsing, finally still. My teeth chatter as I realize that could have been me and Machiko. The palace burns quickly, caving in on itself in a flurry of sparks and black smoke.

"They destroyed my palace!" Antoku cries.

"I wish we could have got the fishing floats," his brother says. "They were so nice. So beautiful. They wrecked everything!" he starts to cry. Antoku tries to hold back his tears, but he is only a child of eight, after all.

As the hours pass, it becomes apparent that there are not really as many attackers as we thought. We keep seeing the same helmets over and over, and it appears there may only be a hundred of them or so, though perhaps many were killed by our arrows and removed from the scene. Some of our warriors who had retreated take small boats back to the beach, form a phalanx with their shields, and try to engage the Genji. But the Genji just dart back and forth, offering no stable target. Soon the warriors on our side retreat again, signaled by those on the boats that more Genji are seen streaming down the mountainside. This group is only an advance force; others are undoubtedly behind. Our side has been fooled before into attacking what appeared to be a small force, only to be outflanked by a hidden larger one. Since all of our structures are already lost, we may as well yield the beach. Those who had been attacked from the seemingly impregnable mountains behind Ichi-no-tani must feel they are living the nightmare all over again.

"We should have stayed and fought," one of our soldiers mutters to another.

"There's no fighting against demons," the other replies. He is still walking lopsided from a wound in his side he received at Ichi-no-tani. "Besides, we had to look after the women. Anything happened to one of them, they'd be using our heads as fishing floats right now."

Yashima hadn't been much of a home compared to Kyoto, but now that the current is carrying us away from it, leaving us adrift with only the pitiful possessions we managed to save in our pell-mell rush to escape, we all sink into a quiet melancholy. Once again we are abandoned to the wind and the waves, and set sail for Hikoshima.

Chapter Forty-Eight
March-April 1185

We stop at several places along the Shikoku coast, encouraging our allies to join our flight. We arrive at Hikoshima in Kyushu with a veritable armada. Noritsune and Tomomori had established a base on Hikoshima after Ichi-no-tani, and here they have raised an impressive navy from both sides of the Dan'no'nura straits. The entire bay is crowded with red sails and banners. As we approach the harbor, the sun is setting, and the sea is ablaze with gold. Dolphins crest out of the water, leading us into the harbor. Antoku walks to the prow and bows respectfully towards the setting sun.

"Divine ancestress, I am here."

I walk over and stand beside him.

"Look how golden everything is," he murmurs. "Do you think it's a good omen?"

"Without a doubt."

Morisada skips up to the front of the boat to join his brother, looking down at the dolphins and calling to them.

"There's thousands of them!" he yelps.

"The sea kami are on our side," Antoku asserts.

I marvel at the way the boys seem able to put defeat after defeat behind them and continue to greet each new day as if this is the day our fortunes will turn and everything will be right again.

Our boat is anchored inside the harbor. A crescent of war ships is anchored across the mouth of the harbor, guarding the passage. No one offers to take us to shore, so we can only gaze longingly towards the land. This harbor is ancient; the stone steps leading from the water almost look as if they grew there. A town with shops and an open-air market with billowing squares of red and white striped cloth shimmers exotically in the dying light. Huts of fisherfolk stretch out in every direction. An ornate white palace rises on the hill in the background, looking like an enlarged pagoda with the sharp, curved hooks of its roof clawing the sky.

"Like a ghost palace," one of the young women breathes.

"Stop that inauspicious talk!" Lady Kiyomori snaps.

The young woman wilts, apologizes, and bows away from the railing, retreating to the cabin.

Her comment seems to stir up all the grief barely concealed in everyone's hearts, judging from the drooping shoulders and heavy sighs of those remaining. We are all smiling tight, frozen smiles that would fool no one looking closely.

Only the boys are genuinely thrilled to be somewhere new.

The light fades into darkness and the town disappears, save for a few brave torches lining the quay. The ladies all move inside for the evening meal. The gold light of the lamps spills from the cabin to the deck. I move past the light, into the shadows near the rear of the boat, where Machiko placed the screens almost two years ago when Antoku and Kiyosune coaxed me to be lovers with them both. I touch the railing at the place as if it were the lip of a shrine.

How could a year have passed since their deaths? I feel as if I have slept through most of it.

A small hand grasps mine. I look down into Antoku's uplifted face.

"Mother says you must come in and have some dinner now."

Chapter Forty-nine
April 1185

Machiko wakes me at dawn with a strong cup of iron dragon green tea. The morning passes with a tedious session of sewing and prayers. Finally, after lunch, I escape to the deck. The sails snap in the strong spring winds of April. Tokitada and Tokizane have taken the boys to the back of the boat to fly kites off the stern. In spite of their best efforts, one of the kites gets tangled in the rigging, and one of the sailors must shinny up a mast and along the rigging like a spider to cut it free. Once cut, at first it twirls towards the deck, but then a gust of wind takes it and spirals it into the water, where it quickly becomes a sodden mass and sinks. Morisada bursts into tears at the loss of his kite. He refuses to accept another, and cries, "I don't want the green one, I only wanted the red one!"

His nurse leads him back into the cabin. Antoku's chin droops towards his chest. Tokitada and Tokizane encourage him to keep flying, but he hands them the strings and sits on the platform on the rear of the boat, looking off to the mouth of the harbor broodingly. Tokushi puts a hand on my arm.

"Go see what's the matter with him. He'll always talk to you."

I slide quietly beside him. "Mind if I join you?"

"As you wish," he sighs dispiritedly.

"It's too bad about the kite," I venture, after we have sat in silence for a while.

Antoku nods. "Morisada is just tired of losing things. We both are."

"We all are."

"I miss Atsumori and Kiyosune," he says. "They were the best with kites."

I press my lips together, but tears spill out of my eyes anyway.

"Oh no, I made you cry," he says, and blots my tears with his own sleeve.

"The fault is never yours, my sovereign."

The boat rocks back and forth.

"Do you think the Sun Goddess still likes us?" he asks.

"Of course. You are her Imperial Grandson. So many things are out of balance--the kami can only work together properly when things are in balance, and so much is out of balance now."

He nods. "I miss Michimori too. Do you think he and Kozaisho are happy, in the spirit world? Will their baby be born there?"

"I think so," I say.

"What about Koremori? His wife is still alive, isn't she?"

"Last we heard, she was taking vows."

"What about the children?"

"I think her parents are caring for them."

"Why do people drown themselves?"

"Well, Kozaisho didn't feel she could live without Michimori. Sometimes lovers feel that way about each other."

"But what about Koremori and the other Kiyotsune, the one who drowned himself? They were young and fun and nice."

"I don't know. I don't know how they could abandon our cause like that."

"Do you think Koremori really became a monk first?"

"Yes, I think so. You probably don't remember your uncle Shigemori, but like him, Koremori had a deep love for the Buddha."

"We all have that," Antoku says impatiently. "I don't think I would like to be a monk. I wouldn't want to be bald, for one thing. Do people really think Go-Toba is the Emperor? He's just a baby."

"I am sure they are afraid to say anything. I am certain the people have not forgotten you."

Antoku takes a deep breath. "If we are defeated--by the Genji--don't tell anyone I asked--will I have to commit suicide with the others?"

"First of all, we can't possibly lose. Next--of course not, you're the Emperor. And you are a child, and children don't commit suicide."

He leans close to me and takes a shaky breath.

"I keep dreaming," he says, "that I am sinking in the cold sea. I keep kicking and trying to get to the surface, but something is holding me down. Then I breathe in the cold water and I wake up."

"Oh, darling..." I say, pulling him close. "What a dreadful dream. How long have you been having that?"

"Just since we heard about Koremori."

"It will never happen," I assure him. "I haven't had any dreams like that."

"You're the Inari sorceress, so you would know, right?" He looks up at me trustingly.

"Certainly," I say, looking into his dark, sad eyes. I kiss him on the forehead. He turned eight years old a few months ago. The way he wrinkles up his forehead when he is thinking makes him look like an old man.

Again the torches are lit along the quay and the waterfront. We can hear women laughing and the happy carousing voices of sailors lucky enough to be permitted to visit the inns, taking a much needed reward of food and drink and female companionship.

"It looks beautiful with the torches, doesn't it?" I say to Antoku, trying to distract him. He nods, lying draped across my lap, propping one elbow on the deck.

"I wish we could go over there," he says. "That's the bad thing about being the Emperor; nothing is ever good enough for me to go anywhere. To tell you the truth, I wouldn't mind so awfully much if things weren't good enough. I'd still like to see them."

"I know. But it is your karma to be the most important one of us."

He stands and leans against the railing. Tokizane sidles closer so as to be able to grab him if he leans too far. But I know Antoku well enough to know how unlikely that is, so I remain seated where I am. Torches are lit on the perimeter of our boat. The few sails not bolted down make a shuddering sound, but the wind has died to a breeze with the coming of dusk.

"Lady Fujiwara?" Antoku says.

"Yes."

"Is it true that my mother had a very hard birth with me and if it wasn't for you and my grandfather, the Retired Emperor, she would have died?"

"It was a difficult time. Through no fault of yours," I hasten to add.

"Sometimes," he says softly, "I think it might have been better if I had never been born."

I have never heard Antoku sounding so despondent. I kneel beside him, looking over the rail. Several fishermen in a boat below, having seen the Emperor peering over the rail, have prostrated themselves and are all lying face down in their boat, which wobbles past us, no one manning the oars. Antoku is so used to people prostrating themselves before him, he doesn't seem to notice how strange it looks.

338

Sotsu-no-suke emerges from the cabin. "Time for dinner, Your Highness," she calls.

"Is it eel again? I'm not having eel again."

"There is eel. But there are other things too. You don't have to eat the eel."

"Good, because I'm not going to. I'm so sick of it." He turns to me and says, "Maybe you could make me a nice potion so I won't have any more of those bad dreams. Would you?"

"Yes, of course, I'll ask Machiko to make it up right away."

I take Machiko aside and we discuss the types of herbs we might use. I have never made a sleep potion for a child before. Opium is out, as it would make his dreams more vivid than ever. We think carefully about which herbs are most likely to give him a dreamless sleep without making him groggy the next day. We decide to add cherry blossoms to the mix, to make any dreams he does have cheerful

The only way the Genji can reach us is by sea. Many of our soldiers journey out to round up all the boats and men to sail them they can find, training humble fishermen in the guiding of larger vessels, taking seasick farmers and teaching them to be rowers for the larger craft. Male servants take their positions at the oars, and every day part of the fleet may be seen drilling in the straits to the throb of the taiko drummer's commands. A huge smithy is erected and at least sixteen smiths are kept busy day and night. The clink and clank of swords being pounded becomes a constant counterpoint to the shrieks of sea birds.

The lord of the area has thrown his support to Noritsune and the Heike. We are often invited to his palace for lavish meals. He employs very skilled bakers; Antoku and Morisada brighten and chatter happily when the servants enter bearing trays laden with many styles of sweets, some of which they have not seen before. The boys find the fried mochi balls drizzled with honey, steeped in fresh blossoms of cherry and pear, to be irresistible. One night, after dining there, Morisada develops a terrible stomachache. The whispering that he has been mistaken for the Emperor and poisoned flits from boat to boat with the speed of lightning bugs flashing at the sight of lightning. Having sat close to them during dinner and observed how many of the sweets the boys devoured, I am convinced that it is nothing more than a case of over-indulgence, and the physicians taking his pulses and examining his tongue finally agree.

Indeed, the next day he eats a little rice and drinks the mint tea I brew fresh for him every hour, and listens raptly to Tokizane's ancient war tales. The day after that, he is well enough to challenge Tokitada and Tokizane to a wooden sword battle with him and his brother. He and Antoku slash and whirl about fiercely with their elegantly painted mother-of pearl inlaid swords. Tokitada and Tokizane have the unenviable task of impersonating the Genji in these battles: shuffling about on their knees they are no match for the boys' speed, and they take some hard wallops across their shoulders and heads, whereupon they must die over and over again, wriggling in not altogether feigned anguish on the decks while their young conquerors stand over them triumphantly and then pretend to saw off their heads.

"Thus fall the enemies of the Empire!" Antoku shouts.

"And all the stinking Genji!" Morisada crows.

I know it is normal for boys to play this way, but we women are so bitterly tired of war, it is hard to watch and applaud anymore. We sit under the gentian blue and pink parasols that have been brought to us, fanning ourselves and watching the activities on shore that we cannot participate in. On shore, prostitutes garbed in bright flowered robes, twirling parasols, call gaily to men, waving them into the brothels. I wonder what that would be like, to be intimate with someone that you did not know, and might not even like, to be with strangers day after day.

If I had any Buddhist inclinations at all, I would probably become a nun. All the men I have ever cared about are dead; Sessho, Tsunemasa, Atsumori, Kiyosune. Any hopeful missives I have received from lonely courtiers over the last year have gone into the braziers. I can't let myself love anyone again. It simply isn't worth it.

As April nears its end, flocks of birds swoop low over the ships, chattering together. Our boat is alive with similar chatting as Tokushi calls us together to hear the news. Her brother Tomomori, who has been in private audience with her, steps forward.

"Our spies inform us that Yoshitsune has added hundreds of vassals from Shikoku who have turned against us to his forces. They are said to be rampaging up and down both sides of the straits, commandeering every boat they can lay their hands on. Most of the Northerners are from land-locked provinces and know nothing at all about the sea. But they are learning from disloyal sailors who once served us. Naturally, the Heike will once again prevail in a naval battle, as we always have, so do not be alarmed. We expect their attack within the month."

Soldiers erect breastworks of earth and branches to prevent any enemies from coming by land from Kyushu. A boat crammed with women from the town is rowed out to a large ship anchored close by. I assume they are prostitutes until I see them strewn about the deck like colorful blossoms, sewing madly on the sails. Soldiers on another boat show new recruits how to fend off enemies attempting to board with pikes and slashing naginatas. They demonstrate fighting in various positions throughout the boat, showing how to slash with sword in one hand while grabbing hold of the rigging with the other. I watch carefully, imagining using my own dagger to such effect. Every five minutes another woman bursts into tears from all the tension, upon which everyone scurries over to pat her and comfort her until the next woman begins sobbing or faints.

"Now girls," Tokushi admonishes, "this will be the final battle. Soon we shall be back in the Capital. Think how brave the men need to be! Show them you have confidence in them with your serenity!"

"Yes, stop acting like a bunch of beaten dogs who cower when they see a stick," Lady Kiyomori says testily.

Machiko helps me unpack bales of herbs, and I enlist some of the other women to help us make salves and cut bandages. I can't imagine what it will be like to be back in the Capital with so many of the men dead. Fortunately there is too much to prepare to spend much time thinking about it. There have been so many other 'last battles'.

The rains thunder down hard, beating like war drums, forcing us all into the cabin. Lady Daigon-no-suke sits leaning with her head against a pillar. Her crumpled posture and the vacant look in her eyes tell me how much she must be missing Shigehira, who was captured a year ago. If we do win this battle, it is likely Shigehira will be executed in retaliation. I imagine she has no idea what to even hope for. The sound of pegs being pounded into place as each ship is fortified thumps through the walls. One of the girls near me is whispering prayers for Kozaisho and Michimori, fingering her prayer beads of onyx and jasper. All we can do is wait.

Chapter Fifty
April 1185

Munemori has taken the Emperor's entourage from the large and beautifully appointed Imperial Ship and crammed us on a small boat devoid of decorations. The assumption is that the Genji will focus their attack on the larger, more imposing boats, believing that the important people of the court would be housed there. The Genji, anchored in Otsu Harbor, are said to have a huge navy at their disposal. Tomomori and Noritsune have decided the best approach is for our ships to be poised in an enormous semi-circle, bridging the straits at Dan-no-nura.

I step outside the cabin into the oyster-gray light of early morning. Most of the ladies are still slumbering, but I have been unable to sleep. The huge crescent of our ships bobs at anchor, red banners hanging limp in the still before the dawn. In the distance, I can make out the sails and white banners of the enemy. Perhaps once again it is a Genji trick, pretending to have an overwhelming force when really it is much inferior to ours. Tomomori seemed confident last night when he assured us, "The Genji can fight on horseback, but on the water? It will be like fish trying to fight in the trees."

Far off, the sinister tattoo of taiko drums begins. The enemy ships that have been patrolling back and forth, perhaps to prevent our escape, fall into a line and advance, followed by more and more ships coming around the curve of the mainland, hugging the shore to avoid being caught by the powerful currents. So many--like a huge flock of seabirds! They have twice as many ships, though some of their vessels are no more than peasant fishing craft. Men stripped to their waist, oiled skin gleaming over their bulging muscles, begin pounding the drums on our ships. Tomomori stands on the prow of a nearby ship, giving an impassioned speech to his men. I can't quite hear what he is saying, but the men cheer loudly, shaking their spears and bows whenever he pauses. Near the other end of our crescent of ships I recognize Noritsune by his headdress, exhorting his men with similar fervor. All the warriors in the surrounding boats roar their approval.

The door to the cabin slides open. Lady Kiyomori slips out beside me. "It begins," she says calmly. I nod. It is impossible for me to be pregnant, but these last few mornings I have been waking up nauseous. I press a hand to my belly, swallow the metallic taste rising in my throat.

I look around at the warriors on our boat. Many of them have been with us since the beginning. They are the canniest and strongest of them all; it is the greatest of honors to protect the royal family. Their bows gleam like new moons, the eagle feathers fletching their arrows stir in the rising breeze as if they were anxious to fly. Some are armed with curving naginatas, some with four-foot long swords that could cut a man in half with a single blow. They kneel in silent rows, resolutely watching the approach of the enemy ships. I cannot detect the slightest hint of fear on a single face. I feel comforted seeing how alert and composed they are, relaxed but full of restrained power like cats watching a mouse hole. The wind rises as the sky lightens, and the current reels the Genji ships closer.

Before the advancing ships, a surge pushes up from deep below the ocean's surface. I lean over the deck, straining my eyes. Perhaps the sea kami themselves are rising to defend us. Then they jump, and I see it is ripple after ripple of dolphins, flashing in the dawn. There must be thousands of them: I have never seen so many. Perhaps frightened by the approach of so many enemy ships, they are not playing in the spray of the bows, as they are wont to do, but leaping far ahead, as if fleeing the Genji. When the dolphins reach our armada they dive, passing underneath, resurfacing behind us, then vanishing through the straits to the sea beyond.

"How read you this omen, Lady Fujiwara?" Lady Kiyomori asks, voice husky.

"They seem to be fleeing."

"But we shall not!" she says stoutly.

"Of course not."

"You will always be there to care for my daughter?"

"Yes."

The tide is drawing the Genji closer and closer; this was the plan, to utilize the treacherous currents of the straits to pull the Genji into the jaws of our fleet and then devour them. Volleys of arrows are launched from both sides.

At first, most land in the water, but as the current draws the ships closer together, increasing numbers find their mark. Two of our men grip arrows protruding from their bellies and fall forward into the water.

"Perhaps you ladies should return to the cabin." Tokitada nods respectfully, fitting an arrow into his bow. "It would be best if you were not seen."

Lady Kiyomori takes my arm, so I have no choice but to follow her back to the cabin. Everyone is awake now, fingering their beads and praying.

"I want to go out and see," Antoku says.

"Me too," chimes Morisada.

"We *have* to see. This is the biggest battle yet. This is where we win. I'm the Emperor, I need to be there. The warriors will take heart if they can see me," Antoku insists.

"Now boys," Lady Kiyomori admonishes. "Remember what your Uncle Tomomori said. We were moved from the Imperial Ship to this one so we wouldn't be seen."

The boys groan. The servants place porridge in front of us. The boys gobble theirs, but most of the women, like myself, are just stirring it with their spoons, bringing some to their lips and then setting the full spoon back in the bowl.

"Eat, ladies," Lady Kiyomori orders. "It will be a long day and we must have the strength for it." We obey, though it is like choking down paste. The thunder of the drums grows louder, punctuated with yells and screams, the thudding of arrows, the shuddering of hull scraping against hull. Most of the cries are unintelligible, but I hear one voice calling, "Get the commander, get the commander!" Another voice rises above the din, "What have we got to lose, men! Hit hard, hit hard!"

"I'll see you in the Shide Mountains!" yells another.

Some of the women begin to tremble and weep quietly.

"Just keep praying!" Antoku urges. He shakes one of the young women and presses her beads in her hand. "I'm so sorry, my Lord," she apologizes, and begins praying in a shaky voice. After an endless half hour, Lady Kiyomori nudges me and whispers, "Go see how things fare."

I slide open the back entrance to the cabin and peer over the shoulders of the kneeling bowmen. The first line of white-bannered ships has clashed with the front row of our vessels. Warriors from both sides are grappling enemy ships with rakes, pulling them close enough to board. It is impossible to tell who is who as the battles rage. An older man, teeth bared in a ferocious snarl, backs his opponent across a railing and slashes off his head, which plummets like a stone into the water. The still twitching body, arcing crimson from the neck, follows.

As I watch, a contingent of ships nearest to the mainland suddenly haul down all their red flags, mounting white ones in their stead. Then that tip of the crescent breaks away, and at least twenty-five of our ships, under the command of Shigeyoshi of Shikoku, join forces with the Genji. At first I wonder how the Genji defeated them in such unison, but then realize we have been betrayed. The men from Shikoku were some of our best sailors. Men hurl grappling hooks from the traitor boats, boarding the red-flagged boats near them with harsh yells and flashing swords, slaughtering their startled allies of moments before.

"What is happening, what is happening?" Tokushi calls anxiously.

I can't bear to tell them of Shigeyoshi's desertion and betrayal.

"Our men are fighting bravely," I say. As I watch, Taira forces board a large Genji boat and set fire to it; the warriors on board plummet over the side, sinking as soon as their heavily armored bodies hit the water. Other white-flagged boats nearby are rowing away, attempting to retreat, though their efforts are against the tide.

"A large Genji ship is burning. Some of our allies seem to have deserted us, but our side is still more skillful and may prevail," I report.

"Take the rowers! Take the rowers!" I hear the Genji shout. Arrows whiz from the Genji ships, impaling the helpless unarmed seamen rowing our boats.

"They're shooting the rowers!" I exclaim, "The Genji are shooting our rowers!" Such a thing is unheard of in a naval battle. Noblemen do not deign to shoot servants, especially unarmed ones. The cowardice of it is stunning. I see rowers sprawled over their oars or twisting in agony, clawing at the arrows skewering them. Our ships begin to swirl and turn helplessly in the current, unable to control their movements without rowers, and I see the dark genius of it.

"Cowards!" Antoku leaps up. "Shooting unarmed men who aren't even warriors! Please, Grandmother, let me go out on deck! The Genji will see their sovereign and be ashamed!"

"The risk is too great," Lady Kiyomori says, pulling him down on her lap. "Our fate is in the hands of the Gods now," she murmurs. "We must comport ourselves with dignity."

The Genji have begun shooting flaming arrows. The sails on one of our ships ignite, billowing into a sail of fire. In a matter of seconds, the deck catches and men begin leaping off the prow into the water. Most of them sink. A few manage to swim to another ship where men drag them out of the water with long rakes and ropes. On another ship, fighting is savage. I see men being thrown off, sometimes locked in combat with each other. The eerie whooing of the battle conches and the frenzied drumbeats mix with screams of triumph and agony. Row after row of our boats begin to spin and swan about drunkenly. Two boats bound together by fighting platforms are pulled into a whirlpool and smashed against rocks, drowning Genji attackers and Heike defenders together. As more and more of our ships spin out of control and are boarded, a path of turbulent water opens between the attacking Genji and our little craft. An arrow crashes into the body of the guard standing nearby. He staggers back against the cabin with a guttural cry, then rolls down the deck and off the side.

"Please go inside, Lady Fujiwara," one of our warriors calls to me as our soldiers send a volley of arrows in return.

I retreat into the cabin just as another arrow smashes into one of the upright posts of the cabin, sending splinters flying.

"Shut the door!" several women shriek at once, and I slide it closed.

Clack of prayer beads fills the cabin as frantic prayers to the Buddha and Kannon are fervently whispered. I sit by Lady Kiyomori and notice that, though she has taken the vows of a Buddhist nun, her prayers are exclusively to Hachiman and Amaterasu.

"Lady of Highest Heights, shine your impeccable brilliance, turn back the forces of darkness," she mutters. "Do not abandon your grandson."

Antoku prays in a very loud voice. Morisada joins him. "Take the Genji heads, Hachiman!" Morisada shouts.

"Give us victory, Divine Ancestress," Antoku beseeches.

Our boat twists and fishtails. They must be shooting our rowers. Many of the women retch into bowls held by their servants. All of us take a turn behind the screens emptying our fear-loosened bowels into the night-soil pots. The stench of vomit and fear saturates the cabin.

346

"Burn some incense," Tokushi nods to Naniwa. Naniwa's hands are shaking so badly she can't light it. Machiko leans over to help her.

"Forward, forward!" I hear our men yelling to our remaining rowers. "Shoot the commander!"

A horrible screaming erupts below decks as another rower is hit. The screaming goes on and on until it is abruptly cut off. Our cabin falls silent until the screaming stops. Then Antoku starts praying again, his voice shaky at first, but growing stronger. The others join in. Morisada leans across the table and tugs on my sleeve. "Pray!" he urges anxiously, "we can't lose!" I nod and move my lips silently to satisfy him. The thunder of the taiko drums is so loud now it is like the roaring of a storm-driven ocean. I strain my ears to try to make out, amidst the drums and screams, anything to let me know how the battle progresses.

Finally, Lady Kiyomori says, "Go look again, Lady Fujiwara. Be careful not to be seen."

I slide open the door, but at that moment an arrow thuds into the body of the guard standing in front of it. He falls to the deck before me, twisting around the missile like a worm on a hook, blood bubbling from his nose and mouth. His eyes, narrowed in agony, lock with mine then glaze as his thrashing body shudders to silence. Hiroshi, one of our warriors who has been with us since we left Kyoto. Half of our rowers are dead; the other half struggle to control the boat.

"Prepare to be boarded!" Tokizane shouts. "Get ready to fend off the grappling hooks, they're getting closer!" Tokitada runs forward and closes the door, leaving me in the gloom of the cabin.

The relentless hammering of the drums draws closer, until the cabin throbs with it.

"Fend them off! Fend them off! Don't forget who you are protecting!" Tokitada yells.

Light flashes like a sword as the door slides open and a fierce looking warrior pushes his way inside. The women scream before he takes off his helmet, and we realize it is Tomomori.
"Oh, Lord Middle Counselor, how fares the battle, are we victorious?" several women babble at once. The screams of battle and dying seem terribly close.

"Throw out those chamber pots and anything valuable. It would be a shame if the Imperial boat was seen to be untidy." He kneels before Antoku.

"I am sorry, but it seems that the battle is lost, Your Majesty. Our good fortune has run out. The tides and the Gods have turned against us, but I hold myself entirely to blame." Antoku blanches white as a statue of ivory. Tomomori rises and begins helping the trembling maids tidy the cabin, as if the commander of the Taira forces now was nothing more than a servant.

"What is happening, what is happening?" shrieks one of the ladies.

"What do you mean? We can't lose, we can't!" cries another. He turns towards them with a bitter smile. "It seems you will be making the acquaintance of some very fine eastern warriors," he says, using a word for acquaintance that implies that the acquaintance we will be making is sexual in nature. Some of the women kneel in stunned silence, some collapse, whimpering and begging the gods to protect them, sobbing, "We can't be losing, we can't be losing." I am proud that Machiko is calm and resolute as she and the other maids quickly clean the cabin.

"Show some courage and some pride," Tomomori admonishes. "That is all that is left to us."

Tokitada and Tokizane slip into the cabin, slide down the wall and crouch, quivering with exhaustion.

Tokushi stares vacantly, hands clasped around her prayer beads but no longer praying. Morisada clings to his nurse. "We're the good ones. Antoku's the Emperor. I'm next! We can't lose!" he whimpers. Lady Kiyomori cuts the cord binding the chest holding the Imperial regalia, slides the Sacred Sword through her sash. I stand and walk out on the deck. Most of our warriors are dead or wounded, but five or six still fire arrows furiously at the approaching Genji vessels. I look up and see one man tangled in the rigging, arms swaying with the movement of the ship. The rowers are all dead or injured, sprawled over each other in a pool of bloody water. With every movement of our boat, a foam of blood and seawater sloshes up against my robes. The iron smell of blood is everywhere.

Two ships are still between us and the Genji, attempting to block their path to us. We swing helplessly back and forth in the current, which is carrying us rapidly into the straits, already bristling with the lumber from wrecked ships. The sea is full of men struggling to stay afloat. Genji in small rowboats are paddling from one floating cluster of Taira survivors to another, sometimes pulling them on board with rakes and taking them prisoner, sometimes slicing them into pieces with naginatas. Dead men and parts of dead men are floating everywhere, so many one could almost walk on their bodies to shore. A father and son in the boat next to us jump off the prow holding hands, immediately sinking into the water. A couple of Genji play a boisterous game of catch with a young man's head before hurling it off the boat. The sea is littered with red banners, as if the leaves had fallen from an autumn forest all at once.

Lady Kiyomori steps out onto the deck, leading Antoku by one hand, holding the bead strand box containing the sacred jewels with the other.

Antoku blinks in the strong sunlight. "Where are we going? Are we going to surrender?" he asks.

"No," Lady Kiyomori replies, "we Taira never surrender." She takes him to the prow of our ship. "Bow to the East, to your Imperial Ancestress. Now to the West, to the direction of the Buddha."

Lady Daigon-no-suke clambers out of the cabin holding the jeweled jade box containing the Sacred Mirror. She sinks to her knees at the sight of the destruction of the Taira fleet. Pitched battles are still being waged on many of our ships, but vessel after vessel is being taken by the Genji, with the Heike defenders either being slaughtered or leaping off into the water. Many do not even wait to be boarded, but are jumping off in pairs or clusters: fathers and sons, brothers and comrades leap holding hands so as to journey to death together. Paralyzed at the sight, by the time I turn my gaze to the front of our ship, it is too late.

Lady Kiyomori ties Antoku's sash firmly to her own. "Up now," she coaxes, boosting him onto her hip, sliding one of his legs through her sash. I suddenly realize what she is going to do, and I stumble towards her, tripping over the body of one of our warriors, skidding on his blood.

"Grandmother," Antoku protests, his voice shrill with fear, "where are you taking me?"

She gazes at him sadly, and the look she gives him is the most loving I have ever seen her give anyone.

"Under the sea, we have a palace," she promises. Then she steps out over the railing, into the air.

Several of the other ladies burst out of the cabin and follow her, a stampede of silks and high-pitched prayers hurtling over the rail.

"Naniwa, get me my inkstone," Tokushi cries. I teeter over the body of another warrior, reaching the side door of the cabin just as Tokushi and Naniwa emerge. Tokushi stuffs the inkstone in the breast of her kimono and

349

they rush to the side of the deck and jump off together. I slip back in the cabin. Machiko hands me my inkstone. "I am going with you," she insists. "I will hold on to you so that we both sink."

"Come along then."

Back on the deck, Lady Daigon-no-suke calls, "Lady Fujiwara, come quickly! Take the mirror!"

The clunk! clunk! clunk! of grappling hooks grip claws into the railing as a Genji ship rapidly pulls alongside.

"Lady Fujiwara, quickly! The Sacred Mirror!"

I struggle towards her, seeing that an arrow has pinned her skirts to the side of the ship. No sooner do I take the mirror box from her than an arrow whistles through my sleeve, not touching my arm, but pinning me to the cabin. Machiko ducks just in time to keep a third arrow from taking off her head, and slides across the deck to me in a prostrate position.

"Oh mistress, are you all right?" she cries, looking up at me with an expression of sheer terror.

"I'm trapped!" I cry, struggling to hold the box and still rip free of my sleeves. Before I can tell her to fetch Tokitada or Tokizane, warriors are swinging from the Genji boat to ours. Our few remaining warriors spring into action, fighting and slashing. One of the attacking warriors tosses Hiroshi's body off the boat as if it was made of feathers, strides over and yanks Machiko to her feet by her hair.

"Leave her alone!" I shout.

A large man swaggers over. The other warrior drops Machiko and joins him.

"What have you got in that treasure box, ladies?" the larger one asks, taking it.

"That is the Sacred Mirror! It is death for mortals to look upon it!" Lady Daigon-no-suke spits. The Genji Commander snaps his head towards us just as the soldier opens the box. A searing light flashes from the mirror into the eyes of the two soldiers leaning over it. They scream, rearing back so suddenly one smacks the other in the nose with his elbow. Blood cascades down the wounded man's face as he shouts, "I am killed!"

"Anjiro!" the commander shouts, but before he can finish his command, another warrior slides across the bloody deck, eyes averted from the mirror, and slaps the lid back on the box. He stands. "Minamoto Uchibo, son of

Ishido, has rescued the Sacred Mirror!" he crows, holding it proudly over his head. "As you thought, this is the royal boat!" he calls over to the Genji Commander clad in purple and silver who is stepping from their ship to ours.

"Where's the Emperor? Where's the rest of the regalia?" the warrior asks us.

"In the sea. Safe from traitors forever," Lady Daigon-no-suke chokes.

"Are you the Empress?" the man asks, pulling the arrow out of my sleeve and the wood it was pinned to with one sharp jerk.

"She is with her son," I reply, trying to blink back my tears. The man starts working the arrow free from Lady Daigon-no-suke's skirts. I stagger to the side of the ship just as a young girl rushes from the cabin and throws herself into the water. One of a group of Genji in a rowboat below grabs her by the hair with his rake and pulls her, gasping and sputtering, into the small craft, hauling her in like a net of fish. Several other ladies huddle together in the boat, soaked and shivering. A nearby Genji rowboat fishes two more ladies out with long rakes, catching them by their long black hair and dragging them in.

"Ho, what a fine crop of mermaids!" one cries.

"Not so fast, ladies, we want to have some fun with you first," calls another.

Her hair is all in her face, but I recognize her robes and see that they have Tokushi in the boat. Some of the women still on our boat call over the side, "That is the Imperial Lady! Do not touch her! That is the Empress!" The men bow their heads, abashed, and make no more rude comments towards the other ladies they have captured. I crane my neck, searching for any sign of Antoku and Lady Kiyomori, but other than the Sacred Bead-strand box of jewels, which the Genji have plucked from the waves, there is none.

The closest Genji ship ties up to our boat and their warriors begin boarding. One of the last of our guards is hit by an arrow and falls, writhing briefly at my feet before expiring. The sole survivor, a man named Manatsu, heroically engages the Genji as they board our vessel. The Genji commander with the soaring helmet and beautiful silver and purple cloth beneath his armor waves his underlings away and battles Manatsu, doing him the honor of fighting with a man far above his station. Manatsu takes a slice in the arm right away, but he keeps fighting. As good as our warrior is, the Genji is the better fighter. He leans in, slashing, then slides back, parrying, just out of reach: parry, thrust, parry thrust, until somehow he slips under

Manatsu's weakening defense, cuts him on the leg, then steps back, unscathed, deliberately bleeding his opponent to death, slicing and stepping away, slicing and stepping away, playing with him the way a cat plays with a wounded bird, an icy, detached half-smile on his lips. Meanwhile the other Genji stand around, leaning on their bows, laughing and making bets on how long it will take our warrior to die. Manatsu is a huge, muscular man, and though his heritage is common, his spirit is noble. It takes a long time for him to die. Though slipping in his own blood as he parries, he never cries out or shows any weakness, until finally the Genji slides his sword under Manatsu's arm and through his chest and he crumples slowly into a pool of his own blood.

Tokitada and Tokizane kneel on the deck before a Genji noble resplendent in reds and yellows, handing him their swords. Sotsu-no-suke clings to her husband until he begs her not to shame him, but to tend to the Empress instead.

The Heike noblemen who have already surrendered are escorted to a rowboat, leaving only the women and little Morisada. Morisada's nurse clutches him to her lap, looking ready to tear anyone apart who comes near. The rowers are long since dead, lying in pools of bloody water in their rowing stations. The Genji start throwing the bodies of the dead overboard. The commander who slaughtered Manatsu so cruelly kneels for a moment by the body murmuring something I assume is a prayer, or perhaps an acknowledgement of the other man's bravery, then motions his men to throw that body in the water as well. Genji soldiers carry Tokushi and the other girls they had fished out of the water back onto our ship. The other women are shaking and crying. Tokushi stares unseeingly, obviously in shock, perhaps not even realizing yet that she is still alive.

Tokushi sits like a broken doll where they place her by the side door of the cabin. Naniwa clutches her, weeping, refusing to unclench her grip even when I ask her to fetch some dry clothes for the Empress. It is Daigon-no-suke who does that, bustling back with some towels, glaring truculently at the Genji as if daring them to touch her.

Enemy soldiers herd the maidservants to the back of the boat, naginatas flashing in the sun. A Genji rowboat skims alongside our ship and the soldiers begin handing the maidservants down to the waiting arms of the Genji in the boat below. One of the men wrestles Machiko over to the side. She struggles with the Genji lifting her over the railing. One of the men reaching up from below pushes up her skirts, exposing her legs.

"She's got some nice thick calves on her, doesn't she?" he smirks to the man next to him.

In a moment, I am at the railing. I reach out for her, leaning over the edge of our bigger vessel--our fingers almost touch. I whirl back, yank a sword from the scabbard of a warrior who had his back to me. I bring the sword over my head but two men grab me and tear it from my grasp before I can bring it down. The men push me from the side of the boat, laughing. I tip my sleeve so the dagger I carry falls, hilt first, into my left hand, then sidle towards one of the warriors, eyes downcast as if to petition him.

"I need that one back," I gesture towards Machiko. "I'll pay any price for her."

"Will you now?" the man leers, grasping my exposed right hand and pulling me closer.

I slash my dagger towards his throat. He gets his hand up in time to deflect it; it nicks a tiny piece of his flesh before scraping harmlessly along his armor. He wrenches my left wrist so hard I fear it will shatter; the dagger clatters to the deck. He grabs me by both arms, picks me up and shakes me.

The man dressed in purple laughs. "Ah, Uchibo, how careless of you! You'd think you'd know the women warriors are the worst by now!" Uchibo glowers at him, pushes me back against the cabin and helps toss Machiko down to the arms of the waiting Genji below. I run to the railing but two of the men restrain me. I can only struggle helplessly as the last of the sobbing maids is slung over the railing and the boat containing them is rowed off.

"Think your fate will be any different, Heike slut?" one of the men mutters sarcastically.

"Keep an eye on that one!" orders a glowering, officious looking Genji. "She almost slit Uchibo's throat!"

"He would have deserved it, for being careless," the commander repeats, leaning on his bow. The richness of the white, purple, and silver robes hanging out from his cuirass and the ornate design of antlers and lightening on his helmet indicate he is a person of importance. His armor is too soaked with blood for me to tell what color it was originally.

He saunters over to the men holding me. "Let her go. I'll keep an eye on her." He stands close, wide stance bringing his head to my level, hands on hips, sunlight glinting off his broad white smile. "I am Yosenabe Yasuda no Saburo Yoshisada." He continues with a description of his ancestors and their accomplishments, concluding, "You I know already: Fujiwara no Seiko, known as the Murasaki--renowned poet and sorceress, descended from Taira no Fujuri, Lord Kiyomori's sorceress."

I pick up my robes, which slap heavy and wet with blood against my ankles, and back away from the grinning warrior, away from the smell of blood and the sexual heat curling out from him, back to the cluster of women piled like crumpled flowers in the exposed central cabin.

Tokushi is sobbing heartbrokenly. Lady Daigon-no-suke and Sotsu-no-suke are draped over her, their hair mingling with her hair, their sobs mingling with her sobs.

I crouch in front of her like a cat, ready to pounce on the first Genji who dares approach her.

Another Genji boat pulls alongside ours and more warriors clamber over the rails, including a pompous, big-bellied man in straw-colored armor with a helmet so large nothing shows of his face except his mouth. "The Crown Prince, his nurse and the Empress are to be brought to Yoshitsune's ship immediately. Two or three of the Empress' older companions shall be allowed to accompany her. The younger ladies are to be divided among our valiant commanders."

The laughing Genji swaggers over to me. "I'll take this one," he avers. "I like them fiery."

Lean, tanned, creases running from his crescent eyes to his mouth-- perhaps under other circumstances I might have found him handsome. In this moment, if my eyes could have shot forth the fire in my heart that laughing braggart would have been reduced to ashes.

"I insist that you allow any of us who wish to die to find honorable death in the waters," I say in my most commanding tone.

"You want to die?" the laughing man seems incredulous. "I am Yosenabe Yasuda no Saburo Yoshisada,"--he repeats the boring litany of his lineage and accomplishments--"ready to honor you and take you as consort--you prefer the cold waves?"

"I prefer the waves."

His eyes flash, then grow cold.

"Go then!" he indicates the prow of the ship.

I crouch, facing the Empress.

"I request your permission to seek peace beneath the sea," I whisper.

"No--Seiko--someone must pray for them."

"Let me pray from under the waves."

"What of your daughters, Seiko?"

Daughters. All this time I thought she did not know about Kikuko. What will become of my fatherless daughters if I perish?

"Don't leave me," Tokushi weeps. "I forbid you to leave."

"I am at your command," I whisper, sinking numbly to my knees.

Tokushi, her maid Naniwa, Lady Daigon-no-suke, Sotsu-no-suke, Morisada and his nurse are loaded into a rowboat to be taken to Yoshitsune's ship. The rest of us are now spoils of war. Yosenabe, having already claimed me as his prize, has men under his command take me to one of the captured Heike boats, which is apparently also his prize. Placed in another of the small boats, I watch Tokushi being rowed off in another direction until they disappear around the prow of a ship. Some Heike boats still drift aimlessly, abandoned; others burn. The sea is littered with red Heike banners, like a pool cluttered with maple leaves in autumn. An arm floats by, still wearing the shred of a blue tunic. Cheering Genji skim from place to place in their small boats, dragging some survivors from the water with rakes, killing others. A group of Heike servants kneel cravenly on the deck of a large warship, prostrating themselves before a Genji lord. A lacquered chest full of my belongings that I hold tightly as if it were a child, is all that remains of my old life.

Chapter Fifty-One
April 1185

We reach the boat that is our destination. The place where the rowers sat is aslosh with crimson. Genji soldiers are washing the upper deck, however, and it is almost clean when we step onto it, the honey-colored wood wet and shining, smelling of sea salt and soaproot. Two warriors lead me inside the cabin, close the screens behind them. I hear one kneel down on each side of the doorway and know they will stay there, alert and watching, until their master returns. It does not matter. I am forbidden the cool oblivion of the sea. I kneel on the futons, staring vacantly at the screens.

Often, in meditation, it is hard for me to still my mind, to "be with what is, free of past or future", as my mother had instructed me. When my body is still, my mind grows insect wings, darting here and there. But now, though the world beyond the screens is busy with activity and shouting and the relentless rocking of the sea, here all is stopped, silent and dead. My world has ceased and my mind stops with it. Though my body rocks with the rhythm of the ship, my mind is absent: soon I am as completely unaware of life as if my spirit had taken the undersea journey it had wished.

Later, I come back to myself, a sense of dark danger washing over me. Beyond the closed screens, lights bob, lanterns signal, breaking the night into patterns of light and shadow. Again the sound, sending dark pulses of fear ripping through the quiet I had built at my core. His voice. The Genji who claimed me on the boat, outside, on the deck, talking with his men. My throat and mouth go dry. I feel in my sleeve for my dagger, curse myself for having lost it this morning. I should have held it against this moment. *The younger women are to be divided... think your fate will be any different?* The mocking voices of this morning grate into my memory, as the screen slides open and he steps in.

In an instant I am standing, facing him, my hands curling into claws beneath my sleeves. He kneels, wraps his sword ceremonially in a length of cloth, setting it by the small altar. Only then does he rise and walk the length of the cabin to face me. He looks me up and down with little expression on his face, the large blue artery in his neck pulsing strong and quick, and I imagine the knife I no longer have ripping that blue river open to a red fountain. He smiles then, a small, triumphant, savoring sort of a smile, and begins slowly taking off his armor, watching me all the while and smiling, as if he expects me to admire his body.

The unspeakable idiocy of him. Am I to desire one of the men who has destroyed my world?

"When I was only a young man relegated to the country, coming to court with my father, I admired you," he confides, boyishly pleased with himself. "Now I have earned you!"

"Stealing is not the same as earning," I retort with full contempt.

He steps closer, shows me a long seam on his forearm, an arrow wound still healing in his chest.

"I have earned you--among my other rewards," he asserts arrogantly.

His face grows hard. "Lie down and prepare to receive--and pleasure--your new master."

Hot despair fills my chest. I keep my feelings out of my face. If only the arrow had not caught my kimono, I would be at peace in the sea.

"What has begun by force must end by force. I do not intend to help you."

He grins. "I expected nothing less of you."

He grabs for me. I dart for his short dagger which he still wears, twist it half way out of its sheath; his hand grasps my wrist, I gasp and let go. He releases his grip just short of snapping the bones and throws me back against the futons. We roll about--the struggle is exciting him. My submission might thrill him less but I cannot submit meekly, though I know I have no hope of winning. As he pushes my clothes apart I rear up and manage to catch his chin between my eye-teeth; blood pours from the wound. This is more fight than he had in mind; hurt and angry, he slams me down. I bite his shoulder but he shoves my head aside before I can break the skin and pushes a kimono over my face to protect against my teeth.

Sharp tearing as he takes me roughly; I cry out and rage against the cloth. And like all the Heike today, I lose this battle. I lose this war.

When he is finished he gets up quickly. My face is still covered by the blanket. He orders one of his retainers to tie me so I cannot jump in the sea. The man binds my ankles loosely, my wrists more securely. My captor orders the servant to bring one of the futons outside; he will sleep on the deck.

Once certain I am alone I begin to cry, to grieve for Antoku and all the men who died today, for Machiko and all our serving women who must be suffering rape after rape, for Tokushi, who is beyond my comfort. As for myself, torn open and dishonored, it is well that he has me bound; all night I weep brokenly, longing for the cold purifying embrace of the sea.

Chapter Fifty-Two
April 1185

I sleep only briefly, towards dawn. A serving man wakes me, bringing a basin of water and a towel. He unbinds my wrists and ankles, leaving me with one ankle tied to an upright beam by a long section of rope. I wash up as best I can and lie down again, crushed and drained. After a time the man re-enters, bringing rice and fish. I ignore it and drift off to sleep.

I wake to the sound of oars, and men laughing and joking between the boats. "Hey, Yosenabe! Did you survive your encounter with Tomoe last night?" calls one, comparing me to the famous woman warrior.

"Hai. She's a real wildcat, that one. Look what she did to my chin!"

Burst of laughter. Sick shame suffuses me. I have been raped, and everyone knows. I put my hands over my face and shiver, cold with humiliation. Surely they did not touch Tokushi. Let Toki be safe, I plead with the powers. To be raped after what she has been through would be unsurvivable. I press my hands over my ears so I will not hear any more of their jests and jibes. And I pray for Tokushi's well-being, for it is too late to pray for my own.

Yosenabe enters the cabin with a servant bringing lunch. The servant arranges a folding table, tea, fish, rice, and seaweed, bows and returns to the deck. He kneels outside the partition, face averted. The screen and curtains are left open to the sea breeze. Bizarrely, it is a beautiful day. I sat up quickly when the screen slid open, not wanting to give him the satisfaction of seeing how completely I had been crushed. Now I edge as far back away from the table as I can, given the rope binding me to the pillar, and keep my face turned to the floor.

"If you promise not to jump into the sea, I'll take that off."

I nod slightly. I am going to stay alive for my children. For Tokushi. I feel him at my ankle, sawing the rope free with his knife.

"There!" he says, as if he has done me a tremendous favor.

359

I pull my leg away from him, close to my body.

He moves back to his side of the table. "I brought lunch. O-cha?"

Still not looking at him, I scoot closer and take the cup of tea. Its warmth is soothing. He begins eating. Finally I take some food. I can't starve myself if I am going to live. I've had nothing since porridge yesterday morning, before the battle. After a few bites I put the food back on the tray table. Everything tastes like ashes.

"Put the flap down," he calls to one of the soldiers, "Close the screen." The screen closes, leaving us in half-light. Metallic taste in my mouth. Do I not even have respite until tonight?

"Seiko--I'm sorry if I hurt you."

This surprises me so much I glance up at him startled. Then quickly look down again.

"Did I hurt you?"

I nod slightly.

He comes around to my side of the table. His hand brushes my calf.

"Is it bad? Let me see." I look at him, hard.

"Why? So you can brag to your men about how badly you tore me?"

He winces, looks away. After a moment he gets up and leaves the compartment, telling his manservant to clear away the table. I hear him ordering a small boat alongside. Then he leaves. I curl up in a ball with my face under a comforter and go to sleep.

I have no idea how long I have slept when I wake to find him kneeling over me. Involuntarily I pull away. His eyes register my fear before I am awake enough to conceal it.

"I brought you some medicine." He presses a jar of salve into my hand. Abruptly he stands and starts to leave, pauses by the partition, his silhouette outlined dark against the blue sky. It is still broad day. "Do you want me to leave the screen open?" he asks, back towards me.

"No."

He pulls it shut and again I retreat under the blankets.

He comes in again with dinner. His manservant arranges the food and leaves us alone by lamplight.

I am hungry but I cannot eat. The thought that he will soon be forcing me again makes me queasy. Under the sleeves of my kimono my hands twist and untwist.

"Are you starving yourself?" he asks

I shake my head. "I just can't eat."

"Because you're afraid?"

"No. I'm not afraid," I lie quickly

He leaves his side of the table and comes over to me. My stomach turns over.

"Listen Genji," I whisper, looking away from him. "I have decided to remain alive and submit to you--only because I hope for some chance to see my children again. But I warn you Genji," I look him in the eye. "If you fall asleep beside me, I will kill you."

He takes a deep breath. "You hate me, don't you."

"Yes Genji, I do."

"Don't call me that!" He gets up, paces a few minutes and sits back down facing me.

"My name is Yosenabe Yasuda no Saburo Yoshisada ! You are allowed to call me Hiro!"

I look away, seething. "As you wish," I whisper between clenched teeth.

"Look. I apologized. I'm sorry I hurt you. Can't you forgive me?" he asks in a tone which implies I am being totally unreasonable.

I look at the floor and say nothing.

"Look," he takes my face and lifts it, points to his chin. "You hurt me too."

"I hurt you," I respond evenly, "but I did not shame you."

He hangs his head. "With my behavior last night--I shamed myself," he admits quietly. He stares vaguely past me. "I have been at war almost two years. A warrior grows hard in order to endure. I needed--to take you--to forget what happened that day." He shakes his head wearily, his lips tighten. "I know you can't understand." He puts his hand on my arm, surprising me with his gentleness. "I won't come to you again until you have had a chance to heal. If you won't fight me so hard--I'll be tender with you. We'll start over."

Chapter Fifty-Three
April 1185

Hiro comes in to join me the next night for supper. I am more relaxed, knowing I have a few days respite to heal. I am rather surprised to notice that, cleansed of his bloody armor, and with fresh robes, he is as presentable as any man. His clothes tonight are, in fact, cleaner than mine. His outer robe is a dark blue with white crane patterns, red-orange inner sleeves, inner kosode of white which doesn't even appear stained though I can only see an inch of it bordering his outer robe.

Hiro smiles, saying something courteous about how good it is to gaze at a beautiful woman after looking at ugly soldiers all day. It seems impossible that this could be the monster who coldly hacked Manatsu to death before my eyes and raped me that first night.

"We have pickled okra and radish, grilled fish, several types, including eel--rice, miso, and burdock with sesame sauce. The villagers have been very generous today," he concludes with an ironic smile.

He picks up various tidbits with his chopsticks and places them in my bowl, inquiring, "Do you like that?" and urging, "Try some of this." I am astonished at his consideration--serving me food and tea with his own hands as if he were the servant and I the master.

I eat freely, knowing I am safe from assault tonight. His hands fascinate me. They're very large--larger than any man's hands I have ever seen except for common laborers and soldiers, and who looks closely at them? And yet they are extremely dexterous and adept. I catch myself smiling hesitantly, but my smile dies when I remember one of those hands grasping my wrist, which is purple and black, and still so sore the weight of my silks against it is oppressive. I warn myself to remember that this affable exterior I am being shown now is not all of this man; I have already seen the other side. Like my husband, who could be romantic and charming and play the biwa with such sensitivity and quote endless reams of poetry, and who also enjoyed inflicting pain.

"It is good to see you eat," he says. "You have decided to live?"

I nod.

"Of course," he notes carefully, "that is exactly what you would say and how you would behave if you were planning to find an opportunity to kill yourself, neh?"

"If it were not for my children and my loyalty to the Empress--I would find a way to die," I admit. "Truly, as they say, a woman with children is a woman without honor."

He shakes his head, smiling. "I do not think you are a woman without honor." He opens his kimono. "I came in here without even my small dagger tonight--to make sure it did not end up in my throat--or yours."

"So sorry, but that was prudent," I acknowledge.

"How many children do you have?" he asks.

"A daughter from a first marriage whom I never see--she is married now, to a man who sided with the Genji." I cannot keep the bitterness from my voice. "And"--I hesitate, unsure of how to describe a complicated situation--"twins--a boy and a girl."

"Twins! How fecund! How fortunate! How old are they?"

"They are nine now. I have not seen them since they were seven."

"It has been as long since I have seen my boys. They were only three and five when I left. I am afraid they will not recognize me when I return." A brief vulnerability appears in his eyes before disappearing behind the warrior's mask. That we share the same heaviness of heart, both missing our children, makes him more human to me.

"Where are they? Who takes care of them?" he queries.

"With--my husband's principal wife."

"His principal wife--do you fear that she mistreats them?"

"No, oh no. She loves them. I only fear for all of their safety."

He nods sympathetically. "And where are they?"

"In Tanba."

"And their father?" he asks softly.

"He and his oldest son died at Tonamiyama."

I bow my head and weep.

The Genji puts his arms around me and draws me back against him, the sleeves of his robes hanging down around me like the wings of a large, comforting bird. I fight to control my emotion, but my control is like a child's fragile wall of sand, my grief the waves that obliterate it.

Finally I sit, head down, shaking but silent, ashamed of having shown my weakness before the man who has murdered them and dishonored me.

He strokes my head, then unwraps himself from me. "Go to sleep. Don't forget to use the medicine I brought you."

Is this man truly the same as the demon who raped me? With two such different faces, which one is real? Wondering, I fall into exhausted sleep.

Chapter Fifty-Four
May 1185

The next two days I grieve, lonely and isolated, as our ships traverse the Inland Sea. While I still fear the Genji, I find myself looking forward to his presence in the evening. He is the enemy but he is someone to talk to. He is courteous, and while not sophisticated, he is not stupid. Hearing more about his wife and children reassures me that he is not a monster when he is not at war. I allow myself to hope that it was the war that made him insane that first night. That perhaps he is rough, but good-hearted. It is clear from how he speaks of his wife that he loved and respected her and longs to share his life with another woman when he returns home. He speaks with pain of how he heard that his infant son, whom his wife had died bearing, had perished soon after he left to join Yoshitsune's forces.

"The nurse said in her letter--he could not live with both his parents gone," he blinks hard, "and I thought--perhaps if I had stayed and he had felt his father's love, he would not have followed his mother into the other world."

I cover my face with my sleeve, thinking of Sessho's children, now deprived of their father's love, and of Antoku drowned beneath the waves, his beauty and promise lost forever. And Atsumori and Kiysosune, hardly more than children, their careless courage and gold-flamed passion extinguished; and all the fatherless children and childless fathers now doomed to live in a world without the comforts of kinship; loss upon loss more than any human heart can bear.

Hiro comes softly as a cat and sits behind me. The bulk of his body forms a cove containing my harbor of tears.

"When I saw our Emperor go beneath the waves," he says after a time of respectful silence, "I thought the world had come to an end. No one wanted that. All among the Genji forces wanted to be the one to rescue the Emperor and return him to the Imperial Palace. His grandmother, the Nun of the

Second Rank, was a brave woman, and ruthless. But none would have harmed a hair on the young Emperor's head. I think she made a mistake to take him beneath the waves. And what will our country be without the Sacred Sword? With one of the three sacred treasures missing, how can we exist?"

"It's a miracle the bead strand box floated to the surface and was saved," I say.

"It was my arrow," he adds pridefully, "that pinned your sleeve and saved the mirror. That oaf Uchibo had no right to pluck it from the pillar and cast it away, but his boat reached yours first. He is precisely the type of brute that makes Westerners say that Easterners have no manners."

He pulls back gently on my shoulder so that I look in his face. His somber mood is gone and he is smiling. "Do you remember seeing me at court?"

I shake my head.

"It was in the spring of 1177, before the great fire. My father wasn't feeling well and he had come to ask that the Governorship of Shinano be passed on to me. Which Emperor Takakura granted. He held a banquet for us-- and I saw you--across the room with the Empress and her other ladies--we country bumpkins weren't allowed to sit anywhere near you, of course--and I noticed you because you were so tall--and your neck was so long and white and I thought--what would it be like to kiss that neck?" He kisses my neck lingeringly with his tongue. "Then--I couldn't even talk to you. Things are different now, neh?"

Then I remember--the lad from the provinces who stared so openly at me with his wide grin. Who saw me smile back at his boldness before I managed to hide my face behind my fan. All the girls tittering behind their fans at the outrageous insolence and lack of manners of the eastern barbarians.

"Maybe you should invite him to your room," Moriko had teased me.

"Can you imagine what pillowing with a barbarian must be like?" another girl giggled.

"Much the same as pillowing an ox, I should think!" replied a third. Then Tokushi cleared her throat softly and everyone hushed.

"Girls: we are at a dinner honoring the Northerners. You are being as mannerless as they," she chided softly. "Although," she paused, smiling behind her fan, "it is most amusing. And we can laugh about it later."

"I remember now," I admit, tears pricking my eyes thinking of Tokushi, and how her manners were always so impeccable, yet she was kind to everyone, correcting them so gently that no one ever felt rebuked.

Hiro kisses the nape of my neck and begins rubbing my shoulders. It has been so long since a man's strong fingers have given me comfort. I relax back against his hands. Sessho's face appears before me; I burst into tears, shamed at my disloyalty. Hiro pulls me to him, awkwardly at first, then with more assurance, stroking my back. "It's alright. I understand. It's alright." I wipe my tears away on my sleeves. If this keeps up they will soon be as encrusted with salt as a ship's sails. Hiro takes my heavy hair in his hands, caressing it, rubbing it across his face. He kisses and lightly bites my neck again and a thrill of fear courses through me. If he becomes aroused, perhaps he will forget his promise to let me heal. I am so swollen and tender I cannot sit or move without pain. Even if I did not struggle, intercourse would be brutally painful.

He opens my robes wide at the neck and shoulders and begins massaging me. When he touches my upper arms, I wince. He pulls up my sleeve, sees the mottling of bruises around my upper arm.

"Did I do that? No, that was that ox, Uchibo, when he lifted you--or Kansai and Kasegi when they were disarming you."

He lifts off my other sleeve, sees the matching bruises on the upper arm and the bracelet of blue and purple around the wrist.

"I am responsible for that one," he says quietly, touching my wrist gently. He calls for one of his men and orders him to fetch a salve for bruises from the healer. He touches my arms wonderingly.

"So small," he murmurs. "You fought so hard for someone so small. I will always respect you for how hard you fought, Seiko."

"So I must keep trying to kill you to maintain your respect?"

"No, no," he says hastily. "Now that we respect each other--we can be--at peace."

I keep to myself the fact that this respect is not mutual.

The soldier arrives with the salve. Hiro applies it himself, smoothing it on as tenderly as a mother, and I am surprised his big, calloused hands can be so gentle. "You fought knowing that you would lose. That takes a true warrior."

Chapter Fifty-Five
May 1185

The Genji allies from Kyushu, the mainland, and surrounding islands return to their homes as we travel north along the Inland Sea. The remainder of the fleet docks in the inlet below Yashima Plateau. The bay is calm, but so crammed with ships bearing the moon-pale insignia of the Genji, it is as if the placid harbor were turbulent with foam. It is bitter to return to the place where the Shikoku Palace had been, held captive by those who defeated us here. Warriors swarm from the boat, grateful to be on dry land, and soon all the peasants in the area are employed with the manufacture of palanquins to carry the captive women and the Genji wounded up the sheer slopes of the plateau to the shrine above where all can be purified at the sacred Emerald Naga pool. The way up is so steep I am convinced the palanquin and the sweating, grunting servants who carry it will all be pitched headlong into one of the ravines. My mind doesn't consider this possibility entirely unpleasant, but my body still responds with shocks of fear each time one of the cursing bearers stumbles. As servants set up the encampment near the shrine, I see some of the other Taira women step, woozy and pale, from their palanquins. They notice me too, but look away, unable to meet my eyes. I want to shout to the young women not to be ashamed of having been raped, that it is the Genji warriors who deserve to feel disgraced, but I say nothing. Underneath my indignation, I'm ashamed too.

Dawn casts its pale light over row after row of warriors, generals and common foot soldiers, pages and servants, as well as small clusters of brightly clothed captive women and men, all kneeling by the Emerald Naga pond, watching while the soldiers of every rank take turns ceremonially washing the blood from their armor. By noon my feet have fallen asleep from remaining motionless so long and the pool is red with blood, ruby, rather than emerald. The smell of blood is so strong that the horses, tethered dozens of yards away, whicker and tug nervously against the thongs that bind them, recognizing the scent of battle.

The water purification complete, both Shinto and Buddhist Priests move through the mass of armed men, murmuring chants and incantations to banish the vengeful souls of the slain, sending great clouds of incense rolling over the crowd.

Through most of the ceremony I keep my head down. I am trembling; from the sick smell of blood permeating everything, from my grief at seeing the last physical remainder of the Heike washed away as if their life force was only dirt, only impurity. Red was our color: red were our sails, red our flags and banners, the red of the life-giving blood of the feminine. Of all the red passion and power of the Taira, only the red pool remains. Now only the white banners and flags of the Minamoto fly, white like clouds which obscure the sun, white as the piles of bones left bleaching behind them on their murderous trail north of Kyoto to the tip of the Inland Sea.

It will not be that easy, I think silently to the assembled victorious warriors, it will not be as easy to wash these stains from your karma as it is to wash this blood from your armor. It will not be that easy. No chants or prayers can change what has been done. No incantations can bring back what has been lost. Amaterasu will not smile on those who have murdered her grandson. The Sacred Sword has been taken because the victors have misused the power of the sword. Annihilation brings no triumph, I silently warn the solemn rows of men in their freshly washed armor. This ceremony does not have the power to cleanse what has happened. The blood remains.

Across the way, kneeling on white rush mats brought forth from the temple, is Tokushi. Her face is hidden behind her gold and purple fan, but I recognize the fan, and the purple, lavender, and white robes with red inner sleeves that has long been one of her favorite combinations, despite the inauspicious shade of lavender. Now, alas, the mourning color of lavender will always be appropriate. I steal glances at her throughout the ritual, but her head remains down, so she does not see me. I want to shout but instead I whisper into her mind, "Toki. Toki." She starts, as if she had physically heard my voice, looks around beside her and then across to me. Her face suffuses with light. Her eyelids are red and swollen from crying and she looks about twelve years old. "*My Toki*," I remember saying when I was seven and she was two, possessively picking her up and carrying her on my hip as if she had grown from there.

369

"Like a tree with two trunks," our mothers would say fondly. I want nothing more now than to pick her up, clasp her tight and keep her safe, as I could when I was the bigger child. "She's *my* little girl," I declared to Lady Kiyomori. The woman whose frown could make warriors and ministers of state tremble smiled indulgently at me. "Then you take good care of her, Seiko. Like your mother takes good care of me."

Tokushi gleams, transcendently beautiful in her sorrow. I gaze at her with the longing most would reserve for a vision of Kannon. She is like a snowy egret, immaculate in the marsh; nothing can touch her innocence, her purity, the essential nobility of her heart.

After the service, she beckons to a young Genji who listens, bows, and fetches Yoshitsune. She gestures towards me and says something to him. He frowns, crouches beside her for a moment, shaking his head. She pleads passionately. He shakes his head again, explaining something with an expression of inexorable patience, then rises, bows, and returns to his place. She looks over at me with an expression of utter devastation, lips trembling and eyes brimming with tears. She makes the gesture, "my heart, your heart," and I return it to her. *Be brave. They cannot keep our hearts apart*, I think to her.

Then the soldiers come and politely gesture for the ladies to rise. All stand and bow to Tokushi. She bows to me. As they lead her away she looks back over her shoulder at me, touches her fingers to her lips. I bow again, my heart breaking. When I rise from my low bow, she is gone.

As the unconcerned sky swirls with soft pink and blue pastels, heralding evening, a pageboy so young and radiant I cannot believe he is a Genji warrior appears at Hiro's tent with a letter from Tokushi. In it she writes;

"Dear Heart: I begged Yoshitsune--begged--for you to be returned to me. I told him we had been together since we were children and that I could not possibly live without you, but he refused me."

In the way she has written the character for refused, I see her shock that her request could be denied, that she no longer has any authority. She continues:

"He said that he has given my women as gifts to reward his top commanders for their valor and loyalty and that he would be disloyal to his vassals if he broke his troth with them. He said Lord Yasuda was already quite fond of you and, being a widower, would probably ask for you as his principal wife, a request that he, Yoshitsune, would certainly grant. He pointed out as delicately as possible that as Governor of Shinano Province and with extra honors and high position awaiting him, Lord Yasuda would be far better able to care for your needs than I. He assures me that you are not hurt, and are being well treated.

Please write back immediately to let me know if you are truly all right.

Your loving Tokushi."

Immediately I beckon to Hiro, who has been sitting nearby, and hand him the precious letter. "I must make answer to Her Highness immediately. Will you please send for paper and brush and ink?" He nods, barks the orders to a subordinate and sits reading the letter.

"You will say that you are being treated well." It is a statement rather than a question.

"Of course."

"You are very close to the Lady Kenreimon'in."

"Unworthy as I am, yes."

I compose a reply quickly, fearing that they will change their minds about allowing us to write.

"My dearest Tokushi, Kenreimon'in, Illustrious One,

Seeing your face today, 'the moon peeked above the clouds.' I grieve bitterly for the loss of Antoku and I grieve to find myself forcibly separated from you. I was never worthy to be in your presence, but 'all things shone in the light of the sun.' I crave that 'sunlight on a still pool' of your presence above all things but it seems 'all the leaves have fallen from the tree.'

Please do not concern yourself about my welfare.

I am being treated well.

I love you and miss you above all things.

It is natural for us to grieve. We can only hope that our 'tears will become pearls.'

Like a pearl

The moon

Disappeared into the waves.

Blue all around us

This ocean of tears.

I pray for you hourly, my Lady, my sovereign, my love, my life.

Your Seiko"

Tears streaming down my face, I search through my belongings, find a green and white jade flower pin which Tokushi always liked. I press it and the letter to my heart and gesture to Hiro to give it to the messenger.
He unravels it first, reads it, scowls, rolls it back up and gives it to the messenger. He waves the man away, looks at me quizzically.

"Are you lovers then? With the Empress?"

"Certainly not!" I flare. "How dare you! Remember who you speak of!"

"I know who I speak of. I know how these letters sound," he returns, unabashed.

"There is more to love than pillowing," I retort, "Though I do not expect a northern barbarian to understand that!"

He reclines, propping himself up by the elbows, unperturbed by my outburst.

"Hai. I'm a barbarian. Pillowing is all I know about. Speaking of which--" he looks significantly at my groin, then back to my face. "How are you feeling?"

I press my lips together and blush, but for the moment I am saved from answering. The messenger returns almost immediately, bearing a cedar wood box. Inside are three matching hairpins with drooping pearls--some of Tokushi's most stunning formal jewelry.
With it is a poem written in a most refined hand.

"For my pearl
Who still shines
In the sun-has-set
Sky of my heart."

I realize by the magnitude of the gift that she fears she may never see me again. I cover my face with my sleeve and sit motionless, lost in sorrow.

After a time, I feel Hiro's sleeve, then his hand brushing my hair and the back of my neck. I look up. We are alone. The tent flaps are closed and lanterns cast a soft golden glow, making it look as if we are inside a magic gourd. A brazier of incense is smoking, unleashing an intoxicating mix of sandalwood, musk, and lotus.

He sits down cross-legged and gestures for me to sit facing him. He looks in my eyes. "I have been purified today. The blood has been cleansed from me."

He looks as if he would like to go on but does not know what to say. Finally he reaches over and strokes the side of my face.

372

"I could find prettier girls. Or younger. Certainly more co-operative. But there's something about you...that fascinates me." He raises his eyebrows speculatively. "They say you can turn yourself into a fox. Is that true?"

I smile ruefully. "If it was, I wouldn't be here."

He laughs, equally ruefully. "You'd bite me and run out that door," he agrees. He touches his hand to his chin, remembering. "If you're going to bite me--could you do it a little more gently this time?"

I cover my face with my sleeve and laugh nervously. How strange that he should begin by raping me and progress to courting me. Truly barbarians are beyond understanding.

Hiro pulls over a small table and an iron stand shaped like three black dragons supporting a copper pot of warm sake and pours us each a cup. I should be doing the pouring, so he does me honor by offering it to me. I drain the first cup with unladylike speed. He raises one eyebrow but says nothing as he refills it. I sip the second cup gratefully, feeling the hot wine start to illumine my bones. It will be much easier to submit if I get drunk. Mentally I praise him for thinking of it.

I hand out my cup to be filled again. He is still sipping his first as daintily as a cat. He refills it.

"You like this stuff, eh?"

I nod and sip this one more slowly, realizing that nothing can happen while we are still drinking. I have seen men drink until they pass out, but I have never been close to it myself. Surely that would be ideal. The less I am aware of what is happening, the better. He pours himself a second cup, me a fourth. He regards me in the lamplight.

"Maybe I was wrong about being able to find someone prettier."

He sets his cup down and moves over behind me with that unnerving, cat-like quiet that is his habit. A shimmer of sake shivers over the edge of the cup into my lap. He unties my hair, takes out a comb and begins brushing it. I finish the fourth cup quickly. I fear he will turn back into the monster he was that first night, the monster Sannayo became whenever he drank.

"How much does it take to get you drunk?" Hiro croons in my ear.

"Five cups," I lie. Three will make me woozy and I am already swaying slightly as I sit.

"Then this is your last," he says, pouring it for me.

This one I sip with infinitesimal slowness. I will never finish it and therefore nothing will happen.

Hiro brushes my hair and rubs his face in it, breathing in its scent of tulip and musk. Then, ignoring the fact that my cup is still half full, he pulls my kimono down, exposing my shoulders, and begins rubbing his lips and face over them while his hands massage my back and the tops of my arms. The medicine has done its work. I am only a little sore now. But I fear being torn again, and my belly is quivering like wind-ruffled water.

"I--need to urinate," I murmur, get unsteadily to my feet, grasp his shoulder to catch my balance. I wobble over to the chamber pot. "Don' t look."

"Promise not to kill me if I turn my back?"

"Yes."

He turns from me while I pee. I am drunk enough so that everything has auras around it. The lights around his body are particularly fascinating, like the softest of colored flowers and smoke curling up from around him. Since his back is turned to me, I feel free to stare. I shuffle back over to him on my knees. It is much easier to keep my balance this way. I drain the rest of my sake cup, gaze longingly at the container holding the rest. He takes the cup from my hand, sets it on the lacquered table.

"Come," he says, gently pulling me over to the futon and pillows, "lie down."

The sake isn't helping. He reaches a hand inside my robes, feels my belly quivering. He pulls me to him. "Come on now, don't be frightened--I'm not going to hurt you. Show me your spirit, Seiko."

I breathe deeply, trying to calm myself.

"Are you cold?" he asks, pulling a comforter over us.

"No." I press my head to his collarbone. "Do what you have to. Just get it over with."

"Get it over with? Pillowing is not about 'get it over with!' You sound like I'm about to chop off your head!" He lifts my chin up, trying to get me to meet his eyes. "Haven't you--ever enjoyed pillowing, Seiko?"

"Of course I have." Tears warm as sake rush out of my eyes. I quickly wipe them away.

"Am I so bad? Am I so ugly? Other women have found me--attractive."

It seems as if I am still on board ship, that feeling of nothing solid, everything moving. I wish I were anywhere but here.

"Take off your clothes." His tone is soft, but commanding. I sit, my face averted, hot blood pounding in my throat and cheeks, and remove my clothes.

"Lie down," he says. As I slide back under the covers I see he is also naked.

"I'm just going to rub your feet Seiko." He sits up, covers me with the comforter, drapes his outermost robes over his shoulders and starts massaging my feet.

I breathe deeply, willing myself to relax, trying to get the heat from the sake to circulate throughout my shivering body.

"Does that feel good?" he asks after awhile.

"Hai," I reply faintly.

"I want to make you feel good."

His hands move up my calves, then higher up my legs, and it does feel good but I am still afraid.

Suddenly he is under the covers, rubbing his cock along my calf, up my thigh. His mouth pauses to worship for a moment at my portal, then continues kissing up my belly, fingers delicately circling my nipples. His jade stalk noses its way into my cleft--relief--I am stretching, not tearing, and it does not hurt.

"Is that alright?" he whispers

"Yes."

"Tell me if it hurts."

I nod. My eyes have been closed the whole time. I cannot bear to look at him, but being reduced to feeling intensifies the sensation of being opened. It feels so much more shameful to submit like this meekly, than to fight and lose. But I cannot continue to resist and be torn open each time. How long would it take to die of such treatment? Too long. And my children's best hope-- perhaps their only hope--lies in my acquiescing. Giving in. Giving up.

As if from a distance I notice my breathing is quick and shallow, hear his long sibilant intake of breath like one who is sinking into a hot bath. Finally, his pelvis pressed close to mine, he allows some of his weight to rest on me. A deep groan comes from his throat, vibrating through my lips, and my whole body vibrates in response. Without thinking, I kiss his throat, caress his back lightly with my fingernails. He groans and begins moving inside me. His hands caress my breasts and I feel his mouth against them, tongue circling and flicking the nipples. He plows deeper, groaning with every thrust, and I moan soft echoes.

I flush with shame. Have I forgotten that this too is rape? That this is my enemy, a Genji killer? Am I so spineless as to respond?

I hold my breath and let it out slowly, using the breath to reduce the sensations. To allow the Genji to pleasure me would be the ultimate humiliation. I clench my teeth and my fists. He thrusts harder, perhaps trying to elicit a passionate response, perhaps just riding the waves of his own feeling. But the friction reopens the tear healing in my vulva. I make a small sound, then set my teeth against the pain. I know from his breathing and the mist of sweat on his body that he is too far gone to stop now, however much it hurts me. At first he interprets my groan as arousal and pushes more passionately into me, but then he feels how my body has tightened and guesses the truth.

"Is it hurting?" he gasps.

"Yes," I say truthfully.

He stops moving inside me. Surprise makes me open my eyes. His face clenched with effort, lust warring with kindness.

He sinks onto me, his cock throbbing inside me, his heart thumping against my chest like twin drums. "I'll just--hold still--it feels so good to be inside you Seiko."

After a few moments joined like this, his voice hot in my ear; "I want to fuck you hard so much but I know I can't." He pulls out of me, jerks into his own hand in quick, savage thrusts, releasing his hot rain with a gasp and a shudder. He wipes his hand with rice paper near the bed, rolls over on his back beside me and pulls my head to his heaving chest. I ride with his breath as it slows from a gallop to a more even pace.

"Thank you Seiko. This is the best it has been for me with a woman--since my wife died." His breath slows still further and his feet and hands twitch as sleep comes over him. Suddenly he snaps awake. "Is it--safe for me to sleep here tonight?"

The tension in my body has dissolved and I feel drugged. And grateful for his restraint.

"For tonight--yes."

I am not sure which of us slept first. I wake, hours later, in the still of night, a dream about Sessho so strong I can smell his unique scent, still feel the dark enfolding warmth of his arms around me. I close my eyes, visualizing his body in an attempt to make his spirit stay.

"Please forgive me for surrendering to the barbarian," I silently plead to Sessho's spirit. "I know of no other way to care for our children now that you are gone. Forgive me if ever I take pleasure in his embrace, or bear his child. It is with your heart that my heart is forever joined. I will pray for your soul, that we be rejoined in a gentler time." Remembering Sessho's kind brown eyes and how deeply he understood me, I sob silently. Though asleep, Hiro's arm tightens around me as I weep soundlessly, wishing he could be Sessho.

Chapter Fifty-Six
May 1185

By the time I awaken in the morning, Hiro has already left my bed. Outside I hear the sound of many men's voices and flapping sounds like the wing-beats of enormous birds. Curious, I venture to stick my head out through the tent flaps. Two guards kneeling outside the doorway instantly spring to their feet. The camp is alive with activity, like a disturbed beehive. The flapping sounds are created as men fold up the tents in preparation for resuming our journey. A page materializes before me, kneeling, and proffers a length of purple, gold-patterned cloth. As I take it, thinking it must be from Tokushi, a letter falls out.

"Wait for my reply," I admonish the page, and withdraw into my tent to read the missive in private.

One glance tells me it is not from the Empress. It is a morning-after poem, from Hiro.

"Though he has rough hands
A commoner appreciates silk
More than a nobleman."

His calligraphy rustic, like a brushwood fence. The paper I am sure is whatever came first to hand. The poem is original--not a single literary allusion that I can detect. Of course, he probably has been too busy with his bow to dabble in literature. I think of Sessho, how erudite he was, how careful with his language, how exquisite his hand, finer than any woman's. Of Kiyosune's beautiful poetry. Atsumori's style. These men are gone now, replaced by men who know nothing of poetry or art or music. Men who care only for the calligraphy their sword can carve upon a living body. Men whose music is the Taiko drum stirring them to frenzied violence.

I rock, grieving, head in hands. That world is gone, the men I have cared for are all gone. The Genji will take me to his governorship in Shinano and there will be no one to talk to, to recite poetry with, to be a true companion.

But if the children could be with me--if Seishan could be with me. Ah, life would be bearable then. We will raise our twins in courtly ways. We will be happy, as happy as we can be without Sessho. Once things settle I will be able to visit Tokushi, or at least, to write letters. Living closer to Tsubame, I will see her again, watch her children grow.

I ask a guard crouching unobtrusively at the entryway to the tent to bring ink and paper immediately. The paper is coarse but it cannot be helped. Re-reading Hiro's poem, I am quickly inspired.

"Noble silk

Is spun from a lowly worm.

Who knows what brocades

May flow from a common heart?"

I sign it simply Seiko and send it off.

The messenger returns in a while with a flowering branch.

On it is tied a note:

"The bare branches of winter

Always surprise us

Blossoming in spring."

The phrasing is awkward, the sentiment common, but it touches me. Hard to believe I could blossom again, but I take the branch and hope stirs faintly in my heart.

The messenger bows. "My Lord says so sorry but he is busy with the troops. You must prepare to leave; someone will arrive shortly to help you pack." It is terrible to have nothing to give a messenger but a kind word. And I cannot yet utter a kind word to a Genji warrior, even one so young and beautiful as this boy. Then I think of Tokushi. She would be polite and kind no matter what happened. "It was--" the words of gratitude stick in my throat, but I persist, "...kind of you to bring me the branch," I tell the messenger, inclining my head slightly. He bows deeply. A servant arrives to help me pack. He is so rough and clumsy compared with Machiko. None of the maidservants they took from us are among the captives I have seen. Is Machiko alive? Where is she now?

The nights we spend sailing across the Inland Sea, Hiro is occupied meeting with the other commanders of the huge army; but when we set up camp at Akashi Beach in Harima, he makes sure the tent is once more enchanting with lanterns and blossoming boughs, and I know what to expect. Outwardly I am compliant; but inwardly I resist. Refusing to let him pleasure me is the only control I have; it gives me back a shred of my dignity to keep that much of myself to myself. My body is almost entirely healed. My spirit is still torn and hemorrhaging. I miss Tokushi, Machiko, and all the other women desperately. The thought of Antoku's small body struggling for air in the cold water, his terror, how I promised him it would not happen, keeps me awake at night, afraid to fall into dream.

For the next several days things continue in this way. Hiro falls upon me as if I were clear water and he a man dying of thirst. Physically I open to receive him while remaining emotionally inviolate. Starved for female tenderness, he soaks it up from me and each day seems more relaxed; the harshness in his face softens as he remembers that he is not just a warrior but also a man. He does not seem to notice my inner absence. Then, one night after pillowing, he lays his hand on my belly.

"You submit but you don't surrender," he observes. "There is still a hard stone in your belly against me, neh?"

I nod.

"Are you still afraid?"

"No."

"Then why?"

I don't answer.

He leans over me, running his hands aggressively up my flanks, over my breasts, down to my cleft.

"Do you need me to take you?" he hisses. "If I force you without pain will you let down your waters for me?"

"It will make me hate you," I reply in a flat, hard voice.

"More than you do already," he returns, his face darkening with anger.

I am too confused to respond. I realize I no longer know how I feel about this man. Respect and contempt, revulsion and desire, sympathy and hatred all swirl together.

"Is that right?" A blue cord pulses in his throat. "More than you do already?"

380

My lips tremble and tears spill from my eyes. "I don't know. I don't know how I feel about you anymore."

His face is still intent, but not angry. "I want to pleasure you. I want you to let down your hot rains to me."

I slide out from under him and push him away, anger filling me like wind pulsing in a ship's sails.

"Why do you want to pleasure me, Hiro? It's because then the conquest is complete, neh?"

"No. NO!" he exclaims emphatically. "If pleasuring is conquering then-- you've already conquered me. You conquer me every time I look at you." He looks off in the distance for a moment, then continues, his voice serious and intense. "It's true that first night--I wanted to conquer you. I wanted you to acknowledge that I was your master. I wanted that. Now--I want you to love me. We can make a good team, Seiko. You're what I want in a woman- -intelligent, strong-willed, and passionate. I know you're passionate under that wall you've put up between us. I can protect you and provide for you--and whatever children we have between us. You can help me--with politics--with insight--with sorcery if indeed you have that art."

He smiles, nudges me playfully. "How many other men will risk being with a notorious fox woman?"

The old calumny no longer hurts but my mind is swirling.

He sighs at my blank look and the playfulness leaves him.

"You're here. You're not in this situation of your own choosing, but you're here, so make the best of it. Like me going to war. It was not what I wanted but I gave it everything. None of us can escape our karma, neh?"

I am still too bewildered by my mix of emotions to respond.

Hiro looks down and away, his face is impassive, but the slight droop of his shoulders expresses everything.

"I can't go on like this with you. If you can't... I don't know. I can't go on like this."

He gets up and picks up a futon. "I'll sleep by the campfires tonight. Think about what I've said, Seiko."

The next day, alone in my palanquin, I consider the implied offer, and threat, of Hiro's monologue. At one time, for such a one to woo me for marriage would have been considered outrageous. But now, everything is different. The barbarians will rule now, bizarre as it is to think of a court where ruffians set the standards and mimic the ways of 'the good people' they have destroyed and displaced. The unimaginable is here now. And my children need protection. Otherwise they shall surely be banished or reduced to beggarhood. I have no choice but to please him. Otherwise he may choose to give me to another captor and take some other prize. To be passed from one to another like a common whore--not even my obligation to the Empress will keep me from taking my life under those circumstances. For the sake of my children, I must give myself fully to the Genji. I cover my head with a length of cloth and rock. Black despair swirls like mist from my core and spreads throughout my body, and I long for death as deeply as I have ever longed for love.

At last the gray day coalesces into flurries of rain pattering on the roof of the palanquin. I fight against the gloom in my heart, take sword against despair. Hiro is right. No one can conquer karma. Who am I to judge him, when my own hands are not free from blood? Of all the Genji, surely he is the best. He truly believes he was fighting to restore order to the threatened monarchy, to right injustices perpetrated by the court against the rural nobility. Who can say these injustices did not exist? But he has the flaw of the noble-hearted. He believes the intentions of his allies mirror his own. He is going to be disappointed.

I drop into meditation, imagining myself as Kannon, all merciful, opening my heart in compassion to Hiro. Again and again my thoughts turn to Sessho, and my eyes brim over with tears. For hours, I pray to his spirit for forgiveness, and to Kannon, to comfort my heart. At last my heart opens, like the blackness of a crow stretching its wings into flight. And as my heart opens, I feel what I have been longing to deny: that under my hatred and repulsion and fear of Hiro--there is desire. Was I not attracted--in spite of our differences--that evening in court? If he had managed to send me a letter that night, might I not have invited Tokushi's wrath and dared to meet with him?

When Hiro comes in that night through the folds of the tent, he looks tired and drained. He does not seem to notice the incense I have lit, or the flowers I had one of his men fetch and arrange. He speaks little during the meal and seems of low spirits. I pour him tea.

"You seem weary, my lord. Are you not well?"

He rubs the place between his eyes. "One of my friends and retainers died of his wounds today. He was my father's age and had known me since before

I was born." His mouth twists. "I suppose that makes you happy," he says hollowly.

"How could I be happy that you have lost a friend?"

"He was a Genji, like me," he laughs bitterly. "Don't you wish we were all dead?"

"Not all," I whisper, almost inaudibly. I rise and sit behind him as he has so often sat cradling me. I rub his neck and put my head against his.

"What can I do that will help bring you peace?" I ask.

"I suppose you could lie there like you were dead and let me have my way with you." He roughly pushes my hand away.

Frightened, I retreat to the other side of the table.

"You don't feel any desire at all for me, do you," he states, his voice leaden.

"Actually," I admit in a small voice, "I do."

He looks up at me searchingly. "Then..."

"When I feel desire for you I feel so ashamed..." I shake my head, unable to go on, feeling shame at having to acknowledge it.

He moves the table aside so it is no longer between us.

"It's because--if you surrender to me you surrender to the enemy. That's it, neh?"

I nod, for that is part of the truth.

"But I don't want to be your enemy anymore. What will it take for that to be over between us? Suppose I were to take you as my wife, Seiko--there can be no shame in a wife making love to her husband. We could not be enemies then."

"It's not just that. It's--being disloyal--" I can't go on.

"To your husband's memory," he says softly. "If you were my wife--I would want you to grieve so for me." He sits contemplating me, knees apart, elbows on knees, chin in hands. "Hai. I understand," he says thoughtfully. "My wife died just before I left to fulfill my obligations to Yoshitsune. It was hard to leave the children without a mother, possibly soon to lose their father. What I mean is, it is hard to be bleeding inside, yet still it is necessary to honor our obligations. But when we fulfill our obligations, we become strong."

"That is true." I look in his eyes, feel the shock of wanting him course through my body, followed by the inevitable wave of shame.

He leans back, half reclining on the pillows behind him.

"Suppose I were to say I loved you?" he asks.

"If you loved me, you would cut off my head." I see the words hit him like a slap and regret them immediately.

I slide down onto the silks beside him, cradle his face. "Hiro, I'm sorry," I murmur, "I didn't mean it." Then I make wordless apology, with my tongue, my lips, then my whole body, and the lineage I carry, of a priestess of Inari, the Goddess of Love.

Chapter Fifty-Seven
June 1185

"Eeii! If you don't make your stitches closer than that, our mistress will turn you into a bat, or a turtle!"

"If she's so powerful..." a second voice drifts into a protesting murmur.

"Stupid girl! It's not for us to know how the immortals conduct their affairs! Have you not seen the way our master looks at her? He is completely bewitched! Who knows what spells she is concocting..."

Obviously the servants sewing beyond the protective petals of the paper screens that surround me believe I am still asleep. But for the last hour I have been sitting on the floor by a black lacquered table, my hands aimlessly tracing the carved curlicues swirling about the edges of it, so much like the black wind sweeping through the Capital.

Hiro has been assigned to Noritsune's old villa northwest of the city. Passing through Kyoto, I was shocked to see how much of it was still in blackened ruins. There are simply not enough mansions left in the city proper to house the Genji commanders within the city itself. The villa borders a forested area which leads up into the mountains. It is smaller than a great mansion would be, but more than ample for our needs. It has an enormous garden. Hiro favors the platform built adjacent to the rock garden as a place for contemplation. I personally find the rock garden far too austere; I prefer the koi pond with its small waterfall running over shelves of shale. Hiro has given me this room with a wisteria arbor arching just outside the sliding doors to be my own. He has taken for himself a room in the center of the house which has only one entry and does not open onto a garden. Peace may have come, but he still thinks like a warrior, choosing the most defensible space.

His men have set up an encampment surrounding the villa's enormous stables. He likes having his loyal warriors from Shinano close by. I am frequently left alone, as his duties take him to conference with Yoshitsune and the other commanders. I have taken to napping during the day so I can be fresh to greet him when he comes home in the middle of the night, though some nights he does not return at all.

It is good to have women around me again, though most of them cower at my smallest glance. I ache with missing Machiko. Did she survive the days following the last battle? Is she in a brothel, a nunnery? Will I ever know?

I am striving to make the house a comfortable retreat for Hiro. Looking after his needs is not so different from looking after Tokushi's. But it is a struggle to ascertain how to take charge of an entire household: with the Empress, I was never responsible for organizing the servants, and when I lived with my first husband, his mother managed everything. There I was even more utterly a slave than here, so I remind myself that I have experience in surviving far worse circumstances. I try to emulate Lady Daigon-no-suke's firmness when dealing with the servants, doing my best to conceal my how unsure of myself in this role I feel. I pray she is able to survive Shigehira's execution--he is such a redoubtable warrior, it is hard to imagine the Genji will continue to spare him. Tokushi would be completely lost without her. When the new government is more established, and each of the contending army leaders has received one or more of the posts that they have vied for, and all the honor and responsibility have been divided up, then I will be able to see my old friends.

I unroll a letter from On'na Mari, laying it lovingly on the table.

"My dearest Seiko,

Words cannot express how relieved I was to hear you had made it safely back to Kyoto. Miura-no-suke tells me you are under the protection of Lord Yasuda, who stands enviably close to Lord Yoshitsune himself. Miura-no-suke--who is now my husband--I grieved Tsunemasa for a year, but, as you know, grief can't go on forever--has become quite cozy with Retired Emperor Go-Shirakawa. No doubt each of us has connections which could prove quite valuable to the other. There is no point discussing our losses and sorrows. Akoyo and I wept rivers when we heard the news about Antoku. Akoyo has not been allowed to visit Morisada yet, but maybe soon. I do hope you will be staying in Kyoto! No doubt Lord Yasuda has shown you the invitation to the full moon party celebrating our marriage! You *must* come, I am *dying* to see you again. Wear pearls to celebrate the moon!

Your faithful--On'na Mari

Ah, On'na Mari. Cat-like, always landing on her feet. I used to judge her, selling her beauty for power. But now, with my children's lives at stake, I make the same choice.

I read the letter again, smiling at her relentless buoyancy. She is right. There is much to grieve for, but I can imagine life being bearable. I can imagine there even being moments of joy. I will never cease grieving for my Sessho, and all those I have loved, but there is hope of a new life, like green plants poking up in the spring after a fire from the charred hulks of trees. Where the land is scorched, the grasses take over within a year.

I failed in my quest to protect Antoku and see him rule wisely. Perhaps now my only obligation is to protect Seishan and our family. Perhaps now I can have the life of the householder I have always craved.

Beyond the sliding doors, the summer rain whispers. I fan myself, pushing away the tendrils of hair adhering damply to my throat. The moist warmth makes me think of Hiro, his passion, his ardor. The maid is right; since I surrendered fully to him, matching his heat with mine, he has behaved like a boy besotted. He has promised to offer his protection to Seishan, Nori, Kikuko, and Matsu.

"Maybe this Nori would be a good wife for Issho. With her skill at arms, she sounds like a proper Genji girl, doesn't she!" Hiro had enthused. "And my boys will be excited to have an older brother and sister."

I have come to think I can be a good wife for Hiro. I have put aside my notions of romantic love. If he will care for me and my children, I will devote myself to supporting him in any way possible. If I can rescue Sessho's family, then my life will not have been entirely wasted. Perhaps the Heike women taken captive will serve to infiltrate the Genji warlords and turn their minds to peace.

Now that I am again in Kyoto, so close to my children, each day away is unbearable. I have written letters to them--four, by now just waiting to be delivered--telling them how much I love them, how eager I am to see them again, and how I am working to bring us all back together. I mix my own ink rather than disturb the soft murmur of maids working so hard to make new robes for Hiro and myself so we may appear splendid at whatever functions might happen at the new court. I start a fifth letter.

'Dear Matsu and Kiku,

Soon you will have a new father, whom you must respect and always obey, and two younger brothers. We will always grieve what we have lost, but we will still be a family. It has always been my dream to live with you, and soon that dream shall become real. I do not know yet if we will be living in Kyoto or Shinano province. I hear Shinano is as beautiful as Tanba, but with more high mountains and waterfalls.' I draw a picture of a waterfall plunging between two mountains. 'Take care of your mother. Soon we will be together. Write to me!'

As I write my daughter's lovely, delicate face appears in my mind. Her chin is pointed like mine. Other than that, her face is so much like my mother's, I believe the soul of my mother has come back to me as my daughter. When Kiku was born and I nursed her with my own breasts, she looked up at me with that exquisite indigo gaze, that gaze from the other world, and I knew she was my mother returned, the way our hearts folded around each other, like petals from the same flower, growing around that same mysterious golden center. She was pollen and nectar to me; I rubbed my face on her belly like a bee rolling itself in drunken ecstasy in the soft yellow fronds of a flower's heart. How she wiggled with delight as I swept my hair back and forth over her body.

And Matsu, such a perfect blend of my beloved Sessho and Seishan, his skin like beaten gold and his sly sense of humor, so like his father's. I smile thinking of how close those two are, Pine and Peony, as if they were twins in fact. When they were little, they even had their own private language, and later, shared with no other children the secrets of their hiding places. These long boring days, waiting for Hiro to return, I lovingly review my carefully hoarded memories of every scrap of time I spent with them. The faces they would make to each other if they didn't like the things they were eating--or asked to eat. How they would hide the offending dried squid or radish in their sleeves and feed it to the birds later. They liked grilled rice balls the best; those never went in the sleeves. And my daughter, Kiku Botan. She liked ginger with everything. No matter what it was, she would always wrap it in ginger first. Their physician, Dr. Chiu, would laugh, "Oh, hot, hot, ginger too hot for a girl, too hot! Too much spice for a girl, too much spice!" he would tease, loving her spice, as we all loved her for it. Like my mother, her strength never shows itself in anger or spite, but only in that strength of will that, through her very beauty and gentleness, causes everything to be given to her. I keep thinking of them as I saw them last, at seven. What will they be like at nine?

Hiro comes home late from the day's meetings. I have waited up for him, making sure that the servants offer him refreshment promptly. I am trying to take control of the household, to make things comfortable for Hiro.

"How kind of you to wait up for me," he smiles. Beneath his smile, he looks exhausted. The meetings seem to be wearing more heavily on him than warfare.

"You look weary, my lord."

He shakes his head. "I would rather fight a force two-thirds greater than my own--things are straightforward enough when I have a sword in my hand. These endless meetings--having to be so careful never to offend anyone..." he shakes his head.

"Does it seem you will be denied the rank and position you deserve?" I ask.

"I'm a simple country lord. If I can just go back to my governorship in Shinano, to be left in peace to raise my sons and govern my people, I'll be happy."

"Have you no ambition, then?" I tease, hoping to lighten his mood.

"My ambition is to stay alive and to make no enemies who would later seek to destroy my sons," he replies grimly. "Is that not enough ambition for this day and age?"

"Shall I order the servants to bring you something to eat?" I ask, pouring him some more tea.

"No thank you. There's always refreshments circulating around."

"What has the council decided about the lives of the surviving Taira commanders?"

"Yoshitsune would like to spare them," he says, shrugging off his outer robes with the help of a servant. "But it's up to Yoritomo. Yoshitsune will be taking Munemori, Kiyomune, and Shigehira to Kamakura soon. Yoritomo will make the final decision. I'm sorry to report that the Retired Emperor Go-Shirakawa, seems very anxious to see their heads--not attached to their bodies."

I place my hands over my solar plexus, feeling like I'd been kicked.

"I thought he was offering shelter to Tokushi."

"He is. But I understand he doesn't visit her often. I don't imagine he has mentioned to her that he is doing everything he can to destroy her remaining brothers."

I hope she never hears of it.

"I don't suppose there's any hope of saving Kiyomune?"

"I doubt it. After all, that was the mistake Kiyomori made, letting Yoritomo, NoriYori and Yoshitsune live. I can't imagine Yoritomo will make the same mistake with the sons of his enemies."

"But he owes Kiyomori a debt for his life," I say.

"Well, Yoritomo is not much of one for debts, unless they're debts owed to him, at least that's what I hear," he says, almost inaudibly.

"Tokitada and Tokizane?" I ask.

Hiro brightens. "Ah, they're in better shape. Tokitada being the brother of Go-Shirakawa's beloved Empress Kenshumon'in, the Retired Emperor has argued stridently in their favor. And Tokitada has offered one of his daughters as a wife for Yoshitsune, and he seems quite taken with her--he has the hero's appetite for pleasure, that's certain. If any of the Taira survive this, it will be them."

"How soon can we send for Seishan and the children?" I ask. He has already promised to do this.

"You seem very eager for me to have another concubine," he smiles, referring to my plan for Seishan and myself to share him, as we had once shared Sessho.

"I am very anxious to see my children."

"I am anxious to see mine too. Don't you think I would like to send for my children as well? I haven't seen them in two years, as you have not seen yours. Things are so unsettled now in the Capital--both of our children are safer where they are."

"What do you mean by that?"

He nudges his cup towards me; I pour more sake into it. One of his fingers makes a nervous tapping motion against the table. Disciplined as he is, it's a nervous mannerism I've never seen him exhibit.

"What is it? Is there bad news? Is Tokushi alright?"

"The former Empress is as content as she may be. I understand she is planning to enter a nunnery, which surprises no one."

"Tell me," I plead.

"I'll be quite busy, what with Yoshitsune taking the prisoners to Kamakura. It's up to me and Yoshitsune's other most trusted commanders to keep order in the Capital while he is gone."

"Is there fear of an uprising? Are the monks causing trouble?"

"No, it's not that...your friend, the former Lady Taira Tsunemasa..."

"You said she had married Miura-no-suke, the Genji who was quartered at her home."

"Yes: they were married, less than a month ago, after the Taira defeat. She's dead."

"We have an invitation to their home--for a full moon party--" I protest helplessly.

"We won't be going now. It seems one of Tsunemasa's retainers, left behind to watch over her and her son--considered her remarriage an act of disloyalty-- he entered her bath and killed her, then himself."

How could any man raise a sword against that beautiful face?

"What of her son, Akoyo? Is Miura going to adopt him, is her family taking him?"

Hiro turns his shoulders slightly away from me, looking uncomfortable.

"I believe--he is also dead."

"You believe, or you know?"

"He is also dead."

"By the same guard?"

"No. Yoshitsune didn't want this--none of us did--but Yoritomo has ordered--ah--ordered--"

"Ordered what?"

"Yoritomo--doesn't believe we should leave any of the sons of the Taira alive."

"Any of the sons? How old was Akoyo? He was barely eight!"

"None of us wanted this," Hiro repeats.

"Killing boys of eight?"

"Munemori's eight-year old son, Fukusho, was killed today," he says miserably.

"Then what will become of Matsu? This is insane...are they going to kill anyone outside of Kyoto?" Suddenly I understand why Hiro doesn't want my children coming to the Capital. I grasp his forearm. "Will they be safe in Tanba?"

"I hope so. It is far. Best if they stay away from the madness of the city now."

"How old do they consider..."

"All the children," he says flatly. "All the Heike boys. Down to the infants."

"You're killing children?" I whisper, withdrawing my hand from his arm as if it had been scorched. "You're killing children?"

"I'm as unhappy about this as you are. I won't do it myself--don't you think I've tried? I've talked until I am blue in the face--what do you think I've been doing, every night, meeting after meeting? Several of us arguing, there's no honor in it...but with both Yoritomo and Go-Shirakawa insisting on it--you should have seen how Yoshitsune wept when they brought him the heads of some of those boys...it's not what any of us fought for."

"But you're letting it happen."

"My head rolling around in the dust beside theirs isn't going to change anything!" he rasps through gritted teeth.

"You're monsters."

"They're arguing it's what's necessary for a lasting peace."

"It's your disgrace that will last," I choke bitterly. "Go-Toba is the son of a Taira concubine. Is he to die also?"

"Of course not. He's the Emperor. His mother was only a concubine. His father was not Taira. Mothers don't matter. It's the children of Taira fathers."

"Will you send soldiers to protect my family in Tanba? Or just bring them here--I'm Fujiwara--no one has to know--"

"How do I explain my interest in a couple of Taira children? Trust me, it is better they stay outside of the city. They'll be safer there. Hopefully the governor of Tanba isn't high enough on their list of important Taira nobles..." he leaves the sentence unfinished.

"You promised you'd take care of my family," I plead, grabbing his arm again. "Hiro, please, you promised me..."

"I will keep my promise," he grunts, still not looking at me. "There is nothing I can do at this time. There's more...things are complicated right now...there's rumors that Yoritomo and Yoshitsune are at odds again. It's more than rumors--Yoritomo fears that since Yoshitsune is the one who won the battles, and all the men who fought under him worship him--Yoritomo is afraid he will lose power to his younger brother. Yoshitsune doesn't want that. He just wanted to avenge his father's death, he wanted to bring justice to the land. As do I." He rubs the place where the bridge of his nose joins his forehead. "They'll talk at Kamakura, and all this will blow over," he mutters, sounding anything but confident.

"Are you presiding over this? While Yoshitsune is gone--is it you who will be hunting these children?"

"No! I said no! I have sons of my own--Seiko--I'm in charge of the perimeter of the city--to make sure that any sign of rebellion or resistance is crushed. Not that I expect any."

"So all the Taira men will be executed then?"

"Some will probably end up being banished. Tokitada was wise to pledge one of his daughters to Yoshitsune. He and Tokizane hope to stay in the Capital, but I imagine they will end up on an island at the end of the world. Only those few, those more distant cousins of Kiyomori, will live. The rest will die. The clan will die."

"Promise me you won't kill any children," I beg.

"I can't make my hand lift a sword against a child," he says, glancing at me before looking away again. "I'll turn it against myself first. No one of my rank is being asked to dirty his hands in that way. No, it is the lower-ranking soldiers once loyal to the Heike who are being forced to do it to demonstrate their allegiance to Yoritomo. It's the price for their lives." A bitter smile twists his face. "Our karma may be stained with their blood, but our robes will not be." He turns towards me. The grooves along the sides of his mouth are deeper; a dozen new lines trace patterns of exhaustion across his face. He cautiously touches my shoulder with a cupped hand, as if I were the thinnest of china porcelains, easily shattered. "I'm sorry about your friend. I'm sorry about her son." His large hand settles over mine, rendering it invisible.

Chapter Fifty-Eight
July 1185

A long black table has been placed outside on the platform overlooking Hiro's rock garden. The June rains have stopped. The full moon is shining down on the pebbles of the rock garden. The pebbles themselves are round and white as baby moons, raked into patterns like the froth of waves eddying about the large dark stones which represent the islands in the northern seas. Nightbirds are calling in the woods. The scene reminds me of the last two years when I spent all my time on or near the sea. As melancholy as it was, now I miss it. Beyond the rock garden, a black stream gurgles softly as it pours into a pond frosted with floating lilies. The night is remarkably peaceful, in spite of the increasingly raucous party going on inside our mansion.

Two of Hiro's closest friends, Hiyadoshi and Issho, are sitting with us. Issho is my favorite of Hiro's friends. He always talks to me as if he were genuinely interested in what I have to say, unlike most of Hiro's other allies who regard me as if I were a decorative piece of furniture. Every so often the faint lilt of samisen, a high-pitched giggle of female laughter, or a man's amused bellow drifts up to us. It took me weeks to plan this party for Hiro's friends and supporters. Fortunately Noritsune's former cooks, whom we inherited with the villa, knew what to do when I described the delicacies I had enjoyed at the Empress' table and requested them for this event. I wish I had paid more attention to how Seishan managed Sessho's household. When she joins us, I will strive hard to learn everything she knows.

Hiro had excused the four of us from the party by saying we were going to write poems under the moonlight.

"Ho, becoming a regular nobleman!" one of his friends had exclaimed drunkenly. "Poems under the moonlight! Careful! Careful, Hiro! Your noblewoman is making you soft!"

"We're beginning to wonder who the captive is," another of his friends smirked. "You've been wandering around like a love-struck puppy since Dan-no-nura!"

Hiro laughed, not seeming to mind their teasing.

"You're just jealous, gentlemen," he shrugged, flashing that white smile.

I am slowly becoming accustomed to the white teeth of the Genji. Since Yashima, I have not dyed my teeth gray myself. When I first catch a glimpse of my white teeth in the mirror I always startle. It seems fierce and animalistic to leave the teeth white, but these are fierce and animalistic people. Compared to the cataclysmic changes we have been through, it is a very small adjustment.

"See if you can write enough poems for all of us," Hiro addresses me once we are all kneeling around the table, handing me coils of paper from inside his sleeves.

A young page prepares the ink in my inkstone and kneels at a short distance. He is so quiet, it reminds me of Machiko. I feel naked without her, stripped of my shadow. As I gaze at the rock garden, all I can think of is those I love, lost under waves as white as those stones, bones bleached white as moonlight.

"She's too close," Hiyadoshi complains to Hiro. He is older than Hiro, sacks puffy as cocoons under his eyes, though the moonlight erases some of his wrinkles.

"I trust her with my life," Hiro says.

"Trust is a luxury we can't afford," Hiyadoshi insists.

"Well, she hasn't killed me yet," Hiro replies, smiling at me.

"Are you sure that's not just for lack of opportunity?" Hiyadoshi jabs, shifting irritably on his heels, his movement revealing flashes of orange and crimson under his darker robes, like a red-winged blackbird.

Issho, who obviously worships Hiro as if he were his older brother, looks towards me, then back to Hiyadoshi.

"I trust her too. We may need a sorceress on our side, in any case."

"Hmmph," Hiyadoshi purses his lips, "look what happened to her last list of clients. Fine, Hiro, put your head in the noose if you like. What did you want to talk to us about?"

"I think you know what we need to talk about, gentlemen. How do we respond to this insult?"

"We don't," Hiyadoshi states. "Get caught in the middle, between Yoshitsune and Yoritomo? 'Only a fool seeks to interfere in a quarrel between brothers,'" he says, quoting an old proverb.

"We *are* caught in the middle," Hiro says. "We've come all this way with Yoshitsune. We can't abandon him now."

"We can do whatever is necessary," Hiyadoshi asserts. "Yoritomo is the head of the clan. Yoshitsune owes him his fealty, so do we. Case closed, Hiro. This isn't our quarrel."

"What of the other matter?" Hiro persists. "I've ordered my soldiers not to kill any more children until Yoshitsune returns. We're too busy patrolling the perimeters of the city. We don't have time to go drowning babies," he growls.

Hiyadoshi shakes his head. "Hiro, what happened to the Heike when they tried to fight against the current?"

Hiro clenches his jaw.

"Remember when the fishing clans were teaching us to sail? The part that happened after you finished being green as grass and puking over the side? They showed us how you have to use the winds that are available, not resist them? If the winds don't blow in the direction that favors you, how you take down your sails? I'm taking down my sails, Hiro. I plan to wait this conflict between Yoshitsune and Yoritomo out in some nice, quiet little harbor. Whoever wins, that's my lord and master. When I see which way the wind is blowing, I'll raise my sails again."

"Hiro's right," Issho protests. "We can't abandon Yoshitsune after all we've been through together. What's Yoritomo done? He's sat in Kamakura, never risking his life once. Yoshitsune has never asked us to stick our necks out any farther than he's stuck his own. And now Yoritomo denies him entrance into Kamakura? It's a disgrace!"

"You're young and idealistic, Issho," Hiyadoshi says. "You have an excuse. I'm not sure what yours is, Hiro, unless lovesickness has addled your brain."

My poetic brain has gone completely numb. Hiro had shared the message he had received from Yoshitsune, saying he was detained in a village outside Kamakura. Tokimasa took the captives from Yoshitsune's command, stating that Yoritomo suspected Yoshitsune of plotting with Retired Emperor Go-Shirakawa against him. "First he tells me to befriend Go-Shirakawa, then he brands me as a traitor for having done so!" Yoshitsune had written.

"In the name of the Gods, what does he want?" Hiro had exploded. "The man is his brother, and the most honorable man on earth! I know he is loyal to Yoritomo! Someone must be poisoning Yoritomo's mind!" he said, pacing back and forth.

I don't understand why Hiro is so surprised at Yoritomo's behavior. He killed his cousin Yoshinaka without a second thought, and has no qualms ordering the murder of infants. Hiro believes that others of his faction are as honorable as himself. He is going to be disappointed.

"I'm not comfortable discussing this while she's here," Hiyadoshi reiterates, jerking his chin towards me.

"Who do you think she is going to tell?" Issho asks. His outer robe is a glaring yellow no Kyoto noble would have worn, even in the spring.

"I don't know," Hiyadoshi shrugs in my direction. "No offense, Lady. These are harsh times."

"I understand completely, Lord Hiyadoshi," I return. "But as Lord Issho points out, Lord Yasuda is my master now, and all my loyalties are owed to him. I hardly think I shall be making common cause with Lord Yoritomo."

"What of Go-Shirakawa? Were you close to him, back in the day?" Hiyadoshi probes.

"No, my lord. Anyone who takes the Retired Emperor as an ally..." I shrug, not finishing my sentence.

"So if Yoshitsune comes back and wants to make a stand against Yoritomo..." Hiro persists.

"Look, Hiro, I like you," Hidayoshi breaks in. "I shall be sorry to lose you. I was friends with your father. But don't kid yourself. I'm not interested in dying for some idealistic cause. I have a wife. I have five adult sons, all of whom survived the war. I'm a lucky man. And you, Hiro. You have two living sons. Look at that pretty woman over there. Is life so bad? So everything's not perfect. So everything's not the way we envisioned it to be when we signed on for this campaign. Is life so bad? Look at this villa! Look at this garden! You want to live to get back to Shinano, and so do I. Ask your woman; you brought her out here. What do you think, Lady Fujiwara? Your birth is so much more exalted than ours; you must be well-versed in court intrigue. What do you say, how do you advise your 'lord and master'?"

"I don't know either of the brothers in question," I demur.

"No one knows Yoritomo," Hidayoshi growls. "Always six deep in guards, no one can get near him. He's Yoshitomo's oldest; he's the head of the clan. Not our clan, but we fought for him and pledged our loyalty. What goes on between Genji is a Genji problem. We helped defeat the Heike for them; let's take our rewards and go home, Hiro."

"Maybe if enough of us who care about honor and dignity make a stand…" Hiro ventures.

"The killing of the children is shameful," Issho agrees. "Yoritomo's gone too far with that."

"Yoshitsune is the one who ordered it!" Hidayoshi says.

"No, Yoritomo ordered it," Issho cries passionately, "and Yoshitsune felt he had no choice because he would be accused of treason if he didn't."

"What do we care about a bunch of Heike children anyway? They're not our children. If the Heike were so concerned about their children, they should have fought harder. It's not our problem, Issho! I've made it through two years of war. I'm ready for peace. I'm ready to go home. Whoever's ass I have to kiss to get there, I'll be kissing it, then I'll be on my way. And I don't want you," he glares balefully at Hiro, "persuading those hot-headed sons of mine to join you on your mad quest. It was Yoritomo's men who came to my fief to ask for my loyalty, and I gave it, and they're the ones who came to your fief--and yours, Issho. Nothing has changed. Who rules the Genji--that's for their family to decide, not for the likes of us. We're simple country lords. The sooner we escape from this city of a thousand spies, the sooner my feet are on the Hokkaido Road, the happier I'll be. I don't understand you, Hiro. Don't you want to get home alive?"

"Of course I do. I would like to get home with my honor intact as well."

"This isn't a question of honor," Hiyadoshi argues. "We've all fought honorably. You were at the forefront of every engagement, Hiro. Now we're just talking about intelligence. We're just talking about not getting involved with things that don't really concern you. There's not enough talk about you picking the Heike sorceress for your bed? People are already saying you're bewitched. Now, you want to make a stand saying honorable men don't kill children--as if a bear cub never grew up to be a bear. It's like drowning puppies, Hiro…"

"No, it is not like drowning puppies!" Hiro smacks his hand against the table.

"Honorable men don't make war on children! I've admired you all my life, as a man of honor and wisdom…"

"It's war, Hiro. It's messy. Do you want this war to be over, or do you want your sons to have to fight it? Kiyomori spared the sons of Yoshitomo, and they rose up and destroyed his sons. Spare any of their sons, and they'll rise up and destroy yours. It's a new day, Hiro. We can't afford honor. If we want peace--lasting peace--this is how it's achieved. It makes me sick to my stomach too. Many things over the last two years have made us feel that way, neh? We've swum three-quarters of the way across an ocean of blood. There's no turning back now, Hiro," he finishes softly.

A silence falls over the table. A pair of birds break from the woods, dark wings rowing over our heads.

"I'm not going to discuss this any more," Hiyadoshi says. "Our absence will be noted. Pass me one of those scrolls, Lady. I'm going to write my moon poem and go back inside to the party." One flick of his wrist and an empty circle representing the moon appears on his page. "I don't indulge in treasonous talk, and I haven't heard any while I was out here," Hiyadoshi murmurs. He scratches out a few lines and waves his meaty hand over the page to dry the ink.

"Care to share your literary efforts with us?" Issho asks.

"The moon is fat
as the fortunes of the Genji.
Its white banner will fly forever." Hiyadoshi reads. He yawns.

"I suggest you compose something equally loyal," Hiyadoshi advises.

He gets up, grimaces as he stretches his barrel-chested bulk and saunters back into the party, his bodyguards closing in a rectangle around him as he goes.

Issho smoothes out a scroll, gazes contemplatively at the moon, presses a character or two into the paper, then squinches his eyes closed, concentrating.

"Everyone's writing poems except the poet," Hiro notes, looking at me. "Can you believe this, Issho? Can you believe Hiyadoshi?"

"He's like a horse that's getting close to the barn," Issho says.

"I'm like that too," Hiro says, "but to go through all this and return without my honor--that's a pill too bitter to swallow."

"I know how you feel," Issho says, "and I'll follow you, whatever you choose to do. You're like an older brother to me. I'll defer to your decision."

"I don't understand what Yoritomo is thinking. Yoshitsune is the most loyal man on the earth. I've trusted him with my life many a time. When we defied the storm to cross the straits and capture the garrison at Yashima, I expected my grave to be at the bottom of the sea--but he got us through it. Does Yoritomo think he truly can't trust his own brother?" Hiro agonizes.

"No honor among thieves," Issho whispers.

"Is that who we've been fighting alongside for the last two years? Thieves?"

"I never thought so until this last couple of weeks. Now I'm not so sure," Issho confesses. "You're the one who taught me that a noble enemy must be respected, that the victor must be gracious to the vanquished. 'Noble in defeat, noble in victory.' There's no nobility in throwing babies into wells or burying them alive."

"What did you write?" Hiro asks me, seeing my brush moving.

"A waterfall of light
Pours from the moon.
White pebbles ripple against
The rock islands like foam.
I can almost hear the surf," I read.

A lopsided smile twists Hiro's face. "I had hoped your brilliance at poetry would rub off on me. Instead, my ineptitude is rubbing off on you!"

"I'm sorry my lord. I'm too upset to write. Please forgive me."

"This talk is not for ladies," Issho says apologetically.

It had been Hiro's idea to have me, pretending to be drunk, urge and herd the three men out into the garden, insisting in a giggly voice that we must go write poems in honor of the moon. My presence is thought to be antidote to any rumors of plotting.

"Hiro told me about your children in Tanba," Issho whispers.

Hiro sees the look of pleading on my face before I have a chance to verbalize it.

"I can't leave Kyoto until Yoshitsune returns. I'd be abandoning my post--I'd be executed like a common criminal at the riverbed. Issho is equally committed to his duties."

"Just give me some soldiers. You don't have to go with them--I can lead them, I know the way."

"Haven't you heard anything tonight? Don't you see the position I am in?" He massages his temples with his fingers. "Write a poem for me too. One of you, both of you, I don't care. I've had too much to drink. When Yoshitsune returns, what can I say to him? 'I'm going for a little vacation to...Tanba? While your brother decides whether he's going to kill you or not?' How do I explain my interest in these Heike children? What excuse do I give for keeping a nine-year old boy alive when they are taking nine-months old infants and throwing them into wells? The son of a warrior..."

"He's not the son of a warrior! His father was the most peaceful man... he never wanted to fight. Sessho was a distant, distant, distant cousin, a third cousin, a fourth cousin--he was a governor of Tanba! If he'd been important, he would have been here in Kyoto! He fought because he was ordered to, because he had no choice. He and his older son died in the only battle they ever fought!"

"Do you think that makes a difference to Yoshitsune or Yoritomo?" Hiro sighs. "I can do nothing until Yoshitsune returns...enough, enough! Look, I need your support. You understand intrigue...I'm going to need all your help to maneuver my way through this mess between Yoritomo and Yoshitsune. Hiyadoshi's right, I can't make myself conspicuous by..."

I press my hands to my face. Somewhere in the city, doors are being kicked down, children are being ripped out of their screaming mother's arms.

"Do you still believe you are fighting for a just cause?" I ask bitterly.

"I don't know," he whispers.

401

Chapter Fifty-Nine
July 1185

Hiro is gone, as he has been most nights since Yoshitsune returned. I call a maidservant to trim the wicks of the lanterns, and the guttering light smoothes and becomes calm. I read again Lady Daigon-no-suke's letter to me.

"As perhaps you have heard by now, my beloved Shigehira was executed. Though his only crime was his love for and protection of the crown, he was executed by men so evil their names do not deserve to be written. Munemori and his son Kiyomune perished also. Shigehira's servants assured me that they all died well, and bravely, even Kiyomune, who was barely more than a child. Now to add to my grief, I hear that their heads have been hung by the prison gaol, as if they were common criminals rather than uncles of an emperor and defenders of the throne. After my dear Lord Shigehira's execution, some of his retainers managed to return his body to me for a proper funeral. Rumor has it Lord Yasuda is besotted with you. Since you have found favor with a commander who is close to Lord Yoritsune, perhaps you can help me. Please use your influence to see to it that Shigehira's head is returned to me, so it can join the rest of his body journeying to the heavens. To display heads of men who were killed with their hands tied behind their backs, rather than in battle, is shameful.

As for myself, I have obtained permission to rejoin our Lady, whom I still address as the Empress. Soon I will be leaving my sister's house to join her, as we plan to live out the rest of our lives in a nunnery, praying for the dead.

Please help me if you possibly can."

In one of the increasingly rare times I had with Hiro alone, I showed him Lady Daigon-no-suke's letter and asked him to talk to Yoshitsune about it. He promised that he would. But he has said nothing about it since.

I wonder if Atsumori and Kiyosune were ever given a proper funeral.

I set the letter beneath my desk and ask the maidservants to extinguish the lamps.

The heat of July makes it difficult to sleep; even the thinnest layer of silk clings to my sweaty skin. Tomorrow I must ask for a lighter fabric. The humid night laps against me like water, pulling me down.

Black feathers brush past my face as I tumble through a storm cloud of crows, landing in the courtyard of Sessho's mansion in Tanba. "They're coming!" The terrified maidservant's voice shakes as she clutches the hem of Seishan's robes. "They've burned three villages east of here, raping women and killing any men who resist. They're searching for...Mistress, they're killing all the boys, all the little boys. They say the sons of the Heike must all die."

"What shall we do?" a very pale Seishan cries out to Sessho's youngest brother.

"We must dress our sons in servants' clothing," he replies.

"Mistress, no," the servant blubbers. "Do you not understand me? They are killing the peasant boys also in the districts the Heike ruled to make sure none of the noble sons of the clan are successfully hidden.

"I'll take Matsu and ride," Nori offers. "How close are they?"

"Less than two leagues to the east. You can see them if you walk up on the scaffolding," the maidservant whimpers. "Oh, may the Buddha protect us, Buddha protect us."

Seishan and Nori climb up to the archer's platforms. One of the archers cries out and points to the south. Another line of warriors bearing white banners emerges from the trees.

"They're too close. It's too late. We can't get away. I'll fight to the death then," Nori vows, grabbing a bow from one of the startled archers. Seishan cuffs her daughter. "I forbid it! Come with me!"

Seishan clambers down from the platform, calls Matsu and Peony over to her.

"The soldiers are almost here," she says. "Matsu, remember how you hid from us and no one could find you? You must hide now, in a place where no one can find you, and make no sound, until you hear me calling for you, understand?"

Matsu nods. "Don't worry Mother."

"I'm going with him," Peony says. "Come on," she tugs at Matsu's sleeve. "Don't worry Mama, they'll never get us. We know a place they'll never find us."

She and Matsu run into the house.

"You too, Nori!" Seishan calls to her eldest. "Wait, take your older sister! You're going too, Nori."

"I'm not leaving you. I won't leave you, Mother."

"You and Matsu are the ones who most need to hide. Did you not hear what they are doing to the young women?"

"I'm getting my bow," Nori insists.

"I forbid you to touch it!" Seishan cries out.

"There's an emissary approaching with a flag of truce," one of the men on the archery platforms calls out.

"Shall we grant him entrance?" Seishan asks.

"It's probably a trap," Sessho's brother Kiminobu replies, nervously touching his throat.

"What other choice do we have? Did you see how many men they have?"

"Yes. You are quite right. Show him in."

The emissary, garbed in bright white and scarlet, kneels before them.

"My Lord Yoshitoshi says that amnesty will be given to those who surrender, provided they swear fealty to Lord Yoritomo."

"What are the terms?" asks Kiminobu, at the same moment Seishan blurts, "We accept your generous offer."

"Mother!" Nori hisses. "You can't believe them! You can't trust them! Better for us to fight and die nobly, like Father."

"Naturally the governorship will be given to one of Yoritomo's allies," the emissary says, "and most of your valuables will be divided. But you will be allowed to keep some of your more personal possessions."

"And our lives?" Kiminobu asks.

"Naturally."

"Then we accept your terms. Open the gates!" Kiminobu calls out.

"It's a mistake!" Nori cries out, trembling.

"Hush! Keep your chin up and behave with dignity." Seishan grasps her daughter's arm. "Many men will insult a peasant, but will treat a lady with the respect she deserves. Make sure you conduct yourself as one."

Genji soldiers pour into the courtyard. The Genji commander, bulls horns and a fletch of eagle feathers protruding from his helmet, steps forward and begins reading the names of Sessho's family members from a scroll.

"Both of my elder brothers died at Tonamiyama, and their eldest sons as well," Sessho's brother says, trying hard to hold himself rigid to quell his trembling.

"So you are Taira no Kiminobu?"

"Yes. I am prepared to swear fealty to Yoritomo, as agreed."

"Bring all the men and boys of your household out to swear their oaths," the commander orders.

Kiminobu brings his two sons and Tomo's remaining son out of the house. The chamberlains and other important male servants set their weapons down and kneel in obedient rows.

"Kneel," the commander orders. "Bow to the east. And ask the Buddha to give you a good rebirth."

He nods to his soldiers who spring forward, press the kneeling men and boys into the ground, and cut off their heads.

Seishan cries out and Kiminobu's wife runs screaming towards the soldiers. Two of the Genji lieutenants grab her and drag her into the house, stripping off her clothing as they go, her three-year old daughter running behind them, shrieking.

A volley of arrows from the Genji troops topple the men on the archery platforms before they can draw their bows.

"You lied to us," Seishan gasps. Nori grasps her by the shoulders, holding her up.

"That's close enough, Genji," Nori warns as the commander saunters back over to them, boots kicking up the yellow dust of the courtyard.

"I have another name on the list. You have another son," he states coldly.

"He's dead. Sweating sickness. Six months ago," Nori lies.

The commander gestures and men pour into the houses, mansions and peasant dwellings alike, bringing out every male child they can find, ripping off the girls' clothing to make sure no boys are concealed.

They cut the boys' throats and toss them into a pile. The yellow dirt of the courtyard turns red. A red haze descends over everything, tinting earth and sky.

The commander turns away from Seishan and Nori, placing his hands on his hips, calling instructions to the men searching and looting the main house. Nori takes a knife from her sleeve and hurls herself at him. Instantly, one of the soldiers knocks her to the ground with the blunt end of his spear. Three more fall on top of her.

"What else have you got in there?" they chortle, searching with rough hands through her robes, slapping her across the face when she struggles. "Girl needs to be taught some manners. Who do you think you are, a northern warrior girl?"

"Permission to search thoroughly?" one of the men asks the commander.

The commander nods. "She needs to be taught some manners."

They drag her off to one of the peasant huts.

405

The courtyard reverberates with women's screams, first as they struggle with the soldiers for their children, then as they are thrown to the ground and ravished.

The commander waves off the men approaching Seishan, who stands frozen.

"Leave her be. I want her to identify her son's head."

A macabre bucket brigade of soldiers forms, passing the heads of boys from hand to bloody hand, dangling each in front of Seishan's unseeing eyes.

Men grabbing servant women by the throat, raping them in the kitchen. Precious vases being hurled to the ground and broken. Art being ripped off the walls.

"Commanders get first pick of the jewelry," one soldier warns another as the first tosses Seishan's pearls and rubies into a sack. "They'll get first pick of whatever I show 'em," the soldier replies.

I slide unseen through one of the trapdoors the twins once showed me, into one of the tunnels beneath the house.

Peony and Matsu are huddled quietly in each other's arms inside one of the hidden passages, quivering to the sound of crashes and thumping above. I gesture to them, but they don't see me. Something like a disturbance of wings passes between us, and when the shimmer settles, I see my mother standing beside them, regarding me, eyes dark with sorrow.

"Mother..." I whisper.

She puts a finger to her lips, indicating the need for silence.

Then I smell it: the acrid smell of smoke. Then the tearing sound, that roaring of a ghost army, the flames.

Smoke seeps into the space like silently searching hands, winding, probing, exploring. The din of the flames grows louder and louder.

Peony and Matsu stuff their sleeves into each other's mouths so that their choking makes no sound.

"Save them," I whisper to my mother. "Save them like you saved me."

My mother moves towards the children. She is wearing a purple cloak the color of the last moments of twilight. As she moves closer to them, I see the first trembling stars emerge in its depths. She lays down over the shuddering children and holds them close. She places her head between theirs, and her hair slides down over them in ebony waves.

A high thin sound, a shrill scream, a child's scream.

Then my maidservants are standing around me, wringing their hands. "Oh mistress, please wake up mistress, it's only a bad dream." Screams rip through me, shaking the fibers and sinews of my body apart.

"Fetch some lemon water!" one servant cries to another.

Guards thunder in, blades drawn.

"Our mistress is being attacked by evil spirits! We may need an exorcism!" the head maid cries to the men.

"Get away from me!" I push the maids aside, slap the face of the guard crouching before me. "Where's Hiro? Fetch my lord!"

"He's not here, mistress. He hasn't returned from the city."

I push my way past them all, open the sliding door and stagger out into the warm July night. A jostle of soldiers forms a protective oval around me. I strain my eyes, trying to see in the moonless dark. But there is no statue of Kannon to cling to. There is nothing to hold onto at all.

Chapter Sixty
July 1185

Hiro has finally returned. He is sitting across from me, face creased with concern. He is wearing a black outer robe woven with abstract patterns of gray, white summer under robes peeking untidily through.

"I am sorry I could not get here sooner," he apologizes. "I know you're upset, but you should eat," he says, indicating my plate. The sizzled gray strips of river eel on the porcelain make me want to throw up. "I can't," I say, swallowing my nausea.

He sets his chopsticks down, and his bowl of soup as well. "Are you pregnant?" he asks, a faint smile playing around his lips.

"No. At least, I have no reason to think so...Hiro, did you get any of my letters?"

He nods. "You thought your children were in danger. I got permission. I'm going there tomorrow to fetch them. I should have told you that right away. It was not wise for you to send me such letters; neither of us knows how safe they may be from prying eyes. In the future, please do not commit anything to paper that you would not say out loud to anyone."

"Will you start tonight?"

He shakes his head. "I told the men to be ready first thing in the morning."

"I'm coming with you. I know the way."

"I have directions, and a man from Tanba to lead us. I have arranged everything."

"I'm coming too."

He finishes his miso soup and sets down the bowl again. "It's too dangerous. Lawlessness is rife out in the countryside. It's no place for a woman right now."

"Are you saying you don't think you can protect me?"

408

"No, that's not what I'm saying. I can protect you physically, but I can't protect you from seeing things a lady cannot see."

"Such as?"

"Burned villages, homeless peasants…"

"And who is burning these villages, Hiro?" I know I shouldn't be combative with him. "I'm sorry. I'm very upset. Please forgive me."

"I'm worried too. What makes you think your children are in danger? I spoke to my guards. They said you hadn't received any messengers."

"I had a dream."

"You have been through enough experiences to give you plenty of bad dreams. I've seen you have bad dreams before."

"Not like this. Hiro, people have always exaggerated my power, that is true. But I am a daughter of Inari; often my dreams are predictive. It has happened before."

"If you don't find this appetizing, what else can I ask our cooks to fix for you?"

"Hiro, please don't worry about whether I'm eating."

"Your maidservants said you have eaten nothing yesterday or today. And you wrote to me that you would kill yourself if I didn't come home immediately. Are you starving yourself?"

"No! I'm too upset to eat! Hiro! How would you feel if it were your children?"

His hand immediately makes the gesture for warding off evil.

"Seiko, I have told you, I am leaving first thing in the morning, before the break of day. Now I need to eat, and sleep, and so do you." He returns to his meal. "I don't appreciate you trying to bribe the guards while I was gone. They told me about you offering them jewels and coins to take you to Tanba. If I am to leave you in charge of the house, I need to feel I can trust you."

I pick up my plate with the offending fish and throw it over to the side where it shatters. Servants rush to clean up the mess. I put my elbows on the table, and my face in my hands.

"That's enough, Seiko," he says quietly. "I am giving you every honor due to the northern person of the household, and I intend to marry you when we reach Shinano. But you must play the part of a good wife to me."

"Bring me my children, or I will die," I whisper.

"I've asked Issho to stay here while I am gone. It is less than two days there, and two back. Nonetheless, I want you to feel that there is a man here you can rely on."

"Why couldn't you come sooner?"

"I am a man with a man's duties. You've lived a sheltered life, Seiko, and I intend to keep it that way. Politics is just a more devious form of warfare. I am doing everything to extricate myself from the tangle of alliances and betrayals closing about Kyoto like a net. Everything I am doing I am doing for you, for your benefit, for our family together. Please try and appreciate that, Seiko. I need to come home to a woman's softness and love, not harshness and judgment."

Without his help, we are all lost. But all I can do is put my head on the table and shiver into silent sobs.

After awhile I feel his hand gingerly patting my head. "You must promise to eat while I am gone. Promise me, Seiko?"

"I promise. I'm sorry, my lord. I am sorry for failing you. Fear for my children has left me undone."

"That's very understandable. You are only a woman..." he moves to my side of the table and pulls my head to his chest. "I wish I could say all of your fears were unjustified. But Seiko, your daughter will be all right. It is the daughter who is your true child, as you have told me. Little girls like that are quite safe."

Not if she stays with her brother. Not if she hides with Matsu. But I can't tell him the details of my dream. To speak it is to risk making it more real. Perhaps it is just my womanly fears.

"You need to write a letter of introduction, so that your friend knows that I come as her friend as well. Set yourself to that, Seiko. And just stay strong while I'm gone. You don't want the children to see you like this, do you?" he chides, mopping my face with his sleeves, heedless of my make-up smudging them.

"Of course not. I'm so sorry. It's hard when you are away..."

A smile lights up his face, making him look years younger than the aging warrior who sat down with me a few minutes ago.

"You miss me. I knew you would come to love me," he says happily, "You're missing me!" He rocks me against his chest. "Don't worry, soon we'll be home in Shinano and you'll see so much of me you'll get sick of me. Though naturally, I have duties there as well. Though I have trusted subordinates, I

410

like to travel to every corner of my province, to let the peasants see that I am concerned for their welfare, but also to let them know that I am watching, and that I expect every grain of rice to be accounted for. Maybe you can come with me. We can stay at inns, make pilgrimages…it will be nice having the voices of children in this house," he says dreamily. "I look forward to meeting them. Do you think your Nori would be a match for Issho?"

"I think she would eat him alive."

Hiro laughs. "Ah, you haven't seen him in battle. He is a gentle soul, but stronger than he appears. He has the courage to hold his ground, even when outnumbered. Come to bed with me. I'll hold you, and you won't have any nightmares. But first, drink your soup." I choke down the soup.

Sitting on the edge of the chodai surrounding his bed, we feed each other peach slices. I drop a piece in his lap while trying to maneuver it into his mouth.

"Ah! You're going to have to get that…no," he says, holding me by the arms, "you're going to have to get that with your mouth…"

I flavor his jade pillar with peach juice. He crushes more of the peach over my breasts. "First peaches…" he murmurs, quoting an erotic poem. Predictably, our coupling leaves me sobbing. I put my head on his chest.

"Save my babies, Hiro. Save my babies. I'll be the perfect wife, I'll do whatever you want. Just bring them safely to me."

"It'll be all right," he promises. "You just get the house ready. Issho can bring merchants, and you can pick out anything we need to make the northern suite of rooms quite comfortable for them."

He falls asleep. I try to calm myself, listening to the steady thud of his heart, and the rise and fall of his breath. But I am shaking like a dry leaf that cannot cling to the tree for long.

Chapter Sixty-One
July 1185

I am sitting behind a screen etched with cranes among the bamboo, clasping my wrists with my hands, breathing shallowly. Hiro should be back today. I have spent the last four days isolated in a cluster of screens around my altar. The altar features a carved wooden fox, seashells, and the charms for an easy birth that I made when I was pregnant with Peony. I sit with her baby clothes on my lap, closer to a state of unconsciousness than one of meditation. I sent one of the maids out to cut me a peony chrysanthemum in the garden. She came back with the yellow and white chrysanthemums typically used for a funeral instead. I knocked them out of her hands, yelling, "Stupid, stupid girl!" She ran off crying. The servants have been afraid to approach me since. They pad past my screens so quietly, like ghosts. I shiver and try to put the similarity out of my mind. This reminds me of the dim time after my mother's death--I can barely remember, but it seems there was this same unreal quality, this living in a mist outside time and feeling.

The incident with the flowers is all the contact I've had with anyone except for the servants brushing my hair and bringing me food, which I can barely touch. Issho has asked to see me each day, but I sent notes saying I was too ill for company.

Finally a messenger arrives, telling me our lord has returned from his journey. An older maid helps me to the veranda where I watch the horses and foot soldiers trudging towards us. The white banners they carry are grimy with dust, drooping under windless heat. As Hiro rides by I do not rush out to greet him but remain hidden behind the columns supporting the wisteria on the left side of the house. He does not appear to notice my absence; he does not look towards the veranda where he might expect me to be. He rides by rigid, eyes straight ahead, and seeing his posture, I know. I do not have to watch the rest of the column of soldiers ride in but I do. There is no palanquin but it is possible a child could be sitting in front of a soldier. The horses stop, seven black ones in the front--Hiro's and the six belonging to his top men. The sweaty, grassy smell of the horses wafts over me. The yellow dust rises in puffs from under their hooves, swirls in a cloud of gold, of topaz, and disperses, like my hopes. My eyes close and I feel myself sway slightly.

Then I hear a small voice and for a quick, heart-searing flash I think it is Matsu. I open my eyes. Hiro's friend Issho is kneeling before me--his voice so soft and close to the ground I thought it was my young one. He murmurs a complex and rather obsequious greeting, drenched in apologetic nuances, and hands me a packet wrapped in lavender silk. I stand holding it, noticing not the package in my hands but the wisteria growing before me; the strong coiling vines, how loaded down the plant is with heavy pods, how much of the plant's energy goes into the making of seeds, how the purple flowers we love so much are not for us but for the bats, the bees, the hummingbirds, the pollinators whose greedy tongues and swift movements will lead to this, the fruit, the harvest. How dense the pods are. How quiet the day is. The crickets that were chirping a moment ago are now quiet. The soldiers are dispersing quietly, servants leading their horses to the stables. No joking or anything of the banter one would expect from soldiers back from a mission, glad to be home.

Women fan me anxiously, chirping like crickets. One of the older maids is holding me slumped over her lap. A servant presses rice wine with an infusion of bitter herbs to my lips.

"A nice gentleman is here to see you, you mustn't sleep through his visit," wheedles another maidservant. I sit up, attempting to pull myself together, although it is like trying to gather dust into a human shape. I see Issho sitting in a dark portion of the foyer a couple of yards away, politely looking elsewhere, pretending to be caught up in his own private reveries, carefully not noticing that I have fainted.

Once I have composed myself Issho bows slightly in my direction and the servants bring in a long table, then tray after tray of delicacies--sea urchin roe, butterflies made of radishes--as if we were properly seated in a receiving room, as if everything were quite normal! I still have the packet in my hands, clutching the rectangle of cool pale silk as if being held were its sole purpose. A maid places bits of food in a shell-colored bowl, coaxing me to eat. I notice that Issho, being plied with food and wine on both sides by two of the prettier maids, is taking just one bite of each delicacy offered, saying how good it is, but leaving a rapidly accumulating mound of uneaten food on his plate, using his chopsticks to move things around like a picky child trying to convince his nursemaid he has eaten more than he has. Now and then he looks in my direction, eyeing me with a sort of wary compassion and concern. I remember the funeral of a child I attended long ago, how the child was wrapped in silk--much like this packet. One of the maids asks if I would like her to open the packet for me. I nod. She takes it from my nerveless fingers and spreads the opened scroll on my lap. It is a letter from Seishan.

"Thank you for trying to put the leaf back on the tree. Soldiers came here five days ago. We saw them winding up the hill like a malevolent serpent. I told the children to hide. Nori refused, even though I told her it was most imperative of all for her to hide. But she stood beside me holding me. Peony and Matsu hid somewhere in the house--remember how good they were at that. Then the Genji came. They promised mercy if we surrendered. But once inside the compound, they demanded that I turn over my sons. I informed them that my eldest son was dead. And they said that, according to their records, I had another son. They knew his name and age. Nori quickly lied, saying, 'he is dead also'. Then the soldiers searched the house, and all the outlying buildings. And they gathered all the male children they found, my nephews, even the servants' children. They cut their throats and they left them in a pile. Then they torched the houses: the servants' houses, the great house. They never found our children. But the flames did. I do not expect you to forgive me. It was my fault the children were hiding in the house when it burned. They took Nori to be a Genji concubine. There is nothing left for me but to become a nun. The world has seen fit to sever my attachments."

There are some amber prayer beads in the packet, along with the letter, which is on a severe white paper. Each character in the letter is as perfect as if it were copied from a children's letter book. The beads are also perfect, so round, so uniform, so cold. She must have had it in her sleeve. A white jade talisman for long life attached to the beads dangles like a mockery.

I sit in stunned silence until Issho, whose presence I had forgotten, asks, "Is there anything I can do?"

"You can lend me your knife."

He swallows. "That I cannot do."

"Would you not kill yourself if you were defeated?" I ask.

"Yes," he concedes. "And I know well you have a warrior's heart. But you also have a master who commands your loyalty. When Hiro has been purified...I am sure he will endeavor to do whatever is right." He looks at me, eyes almost pleading. "When our fathers planned this, years ago--this was not what they planned. None of us...wanted this."

"Clearly, some of you wanted this," I reply coldly, staring into his eyes.

He lowers his gaze. "Yes...but I did not, nor Hiro...nor did any of us from Shinano." He looks out the doorway. "We are like amateur gardeners, who fight to save a tree by pruning it, but through a lack of skill find we have invited boring beetles and other parasites into the tree through its wounds." He rises as if his back hurt him, goes to the door and bows. "I'm sorry," he says simply, and walks out.

I stand up--I can't really feel my body but I can hear the silk swishing along behind me. Back in my room, the screens arranged tightly around me, I ask one of the older maids to call Issho back and ask if he will deliver letters for me. Another maid brings my writing table, which is white, bone-colored, very smooth wood, not the black lacquered type. She fetches the ink and brush and an assortment of scrolls, bows and backs away, her face as pale as the table. I place Peony's baby clothes on my lap while I write, snuggle them up to me as if she was sitting there. My first letter is to the Empress. I send her the amber prayer beads and write:

"I am so sorry to add another bead to those who must be counted in your prayers, but my children, Peony and Matsu, have followed yours into the sea of forgetfulness. When the sun has descended to the depths, how can its brilliant colors long remain in the sky? I pray you to release me from my service to you, and ask for permission to 'seek another life beyond the waves.' And if possible, to send me that which is needed that I may make this journey. I will remain, as always, your devoted and faithful Seiko. I have no doubt that we will know each other again in another life.

Asking in all humbleness for this one last favor."

I roll the lavender-tinged paper up with the wisteria pods I have asked one of the maidservants to fetch for me and wrap the bundle with raven-black silk embossed with a pattern of birds and branches, choosing this piece because of how dearly Toki loved birds, perhaps because her inner wings yearned for their freedom which would never be hers. One of the maids sews it shut with a gold and purple edging of embroidery thread. As the maid sits nearby, expertly stitching up the cloth, I start another letter, this one to Seishan.

"Your letter has destroyed my heart. All is ashes. Still, if you would write and let me know something of my daughter's last years when I have been unable to see her, and your son's also, I would be so grateful. I will pray for you in the next world, as you will pray for me in this one. I pray that your prayers will bring you peace, and will open a door for me to obtain some measure of peace. If you could obtain a knife or poison to send me, I would be most grateful. Pay your messenger generously and ask him to be sure the letter falls into no hand but my own. Thank you, I love you always. Seiko."

I then add a postscript: "Do not blame yourself for the deaths of our children. This war is like a taifun: nothing can stand against it. We are like rice laid low before the wind."

I wrap this missive in white silk, have my maid sew it closed. I write instructions for Issho, asking him to have his men deliver the black one to the Empress and the white one to Seishan, imploring him to send only his most trusted men to make sure the messages arrive, and to be sure they wait for a reply and bring it directly to my hands.

Issho writes back, "I will take the one to the Empress myself, and I will send one of my most trusted envoys to take the other to the monastery at Nara where Hiro's men have given Lady Taira Sessho safe conduct."

In only three days the reply from Nara comes. The wrapping around the letter is very plain, as befits one who has renounced the world. The packet is given to me by one of the maids; I fill her hand with coins for it. It is so heavy, I have hopes that Seishan has found a blade and sent it to me. I open the package quickly. Strand after strand of long black hair slides out onto my lap—all the hair she has cut off to become a nun. I keep sifting through the hair, thinking there must be at least some small note, some word of farewell or blessing. But there is only the thick black hair, with its eloquent silence. She has repudiated the world, and me with it.

After three days of ritual seclusion, Hiro sends me a note.

"I have been purified of the deaths I witnessed. While I am clear of the contamination, I shall never be clear of the shame. If the peasants burn the rice stalks in the autumn, after the rains of winter something green comes once again. Hope is a smaller seed than rice, but perhaps, one day, it will yet sprout. Please meet with me now in the main hall."

I begin to write a reply;

"Mice are killed when the field is burnt. The mice do not grow back."

Then I crumple it. It will be better if he does not realize the extent of my despair. He will not watch me so closely. Though Seishan has failed me, perhaps Tokushi will not. Always she has been so compassionate; surely she will not try to keep me here when I can be of no comfort to her. I finally decide to join him without writing a letter.

He sits on a dais, resplendent in his gold and black robes. He might have at least worn clothing in the colors of mourning. Perhaps the Genji do not grieve. I am wearing pale lavender embroidered with silver phoenixes. I kneel opposite him on sea-green pillows embroidered with pale gold thread.

"Words cannot express how sorry I am for your loss," he says.

I nod in acknowledgement.

"Shinano province is very beautiful," he continues, after a painful silence.

"We are here," I reply.

"I have put in an application for the governorship to be mine and my sons' in perpetuity. And I have waived all further honors. I hope to return there as soon as possible. Will you return with me?"

I raise my eyebrows in surprise. "Do I have a choice?"

"If you could choose to be anywhere, now, where would that be?" he asks gently.

"With the ancestors. With my children," I murmur.

He looks away, his jaw tightening.

"If I gave you permission, would you become a nun?" he asks. "Not saying," he hastens to add, "that I will give you permission, but if . . ."

"No," I say.

"Then you prefer to be with me than to be a nun."

"The time has come*," I say, quoting from the poem by Tsurayuki:

"Seiko, I expect you to feel that way now. But we can make a new start and put all this behind us. You will love Shinano. There will be no painful memories for you there. We'll go hunting together. I'll take you to see the

*"The time has come
To till the rice fields in the hills,
Oh, do not blame the wind
For scattering the blossoms."

most incredible waterfalls on earth. There'll be eagles and hawks nesting in the trees. So many pines in Shinano. Priest-trees, elder trees. It may have changed some in the last two years, but I left it in very capable hands and I expect it will still be beautiful when we return. I have gotten favorable indications from Yoritsune and I hope to return by October. That will be a most auspicious period, according to my astrologer." He leans towards me, touching with gentle fingers the cloth over my womb. "When you have healed--perhaps a grain of rice. . ."

"I need time to grieve," I say, turning my head from him.

"Yes, I know, of course. I'm sorry I could not come to you right away. But... pollution."

"I understand," I say, though inwardly I think he is a fool to consider himself free of pollution now. If the dead can indeed pollute the living, he contaminates himself by being in my presence. But I do not say that, or anything else.

"Your maidservants tell me you have not been eating."

"The thing that one knows first of all is tears," I say, quoting another poem.

"Yes, this world is sad and fleeting," he replies, picking up the allusion. "But that is its nature. Your lack of appetite is understandable, but as your lord, I must insist that you eat. I cannot permit you to starve yourself."

I shake my head.

"Regrettably, I must kill one of your maidservants for every day you do not eat."

"Do not damage your karma in this way!"

"So sorry, but if you choose not to eat, the karma will be yours."

"I will eat." Already my karma is tainted by the death of innocents, and perhaps it is those deaths that caused my daughter to be taken from me. Only one life more am I willing to take from this world, and that is the life that is mine by right to take. Surely Tokushi will find a way to help me.

Hiro politely takes his leave, and I return to my room, where I ask for medicine to help me sleep. The syrup is black and tastes of anise, a most hated flavor, but I choke it down and rinse my mouth with water.

I am groggy throughout the next day, even into late afternoon. My servants bring word that Issho has returned--but that he has gone first to see my master, and I fear for the sanctity of my letter from Tokushi. I ask one of the maids to 'overhear' the conversation between him and Hiro, but before she

418

can return with any news I am summoned to Hiro's presence. I notice it is an order, rather than a request, and my heart sinks.

In his greeting room, Hiro stalks about like a storm cloud, clothed in black lined with a gray 'teardrop' print and angry red. "Sit," he barks at me. He straddles the pillows opposite me and with an angry flick of the wrist rolls out a soft purple piece of cloth; on it a beautiful knife with an ornate, bejeweled sheath glitters, taking possession of all the light the lanterns have to offer.

"What is this!" he demands.

"I've never seen it before," I reply honestly.

"Issho says you ordered him to take a letter to the former Empress-- and this is what he brought back!"

"I am in no position to order. It was a request."

He pounds his fist on the floor. The knife jumps. It is close enough for me to reach, if I stretch my arm all the way out. But I know well how quickly Hiro can move, and have no doubt that his great hand would be about my wrist squeezing, forcing me to drop the death I desire. My hands stay on my knees.

Warm pooling of blood in my throat, throbbing, in the place I would put the blade if I but had it in my hand.

"Is there a letter?" I ask, forcing my voice to remain reasonable.

"No! There is no letter!" he shouts. "There is no message whatsoever!" You asked for her permission to kill yourself, didn't you?"

He gets up and stalks around, then hurls the knife through the shoji screen. It clatters hollowly into another room. I gasp, shocked that he would treat something from the Empress, possibly even a part of the royal regalia, in such a disrespectful manner.

"You asked *her* for permission--she is not your mistress, *I* am your master. You want to die, it is I that you ask for permission!"

I put my hands over my eyes and slowly sink to the floor, curled on my side. His feet stomp angrily over to me. I breathe quietly, expecting one of those feet to kick me in the belly. It's what Sannayo would have done. I relax, waiting for the blow. Instead he grabs me by the hair, and pulls me up, facing him. The pain makes my eyes water.

"You're mine and you stay here as long as I want you, as long as I have need of you! You understand?" I say nothing, but I don't look away.

"Yes, cry!" he exhorts me. "Cry out your grief!" He lets go of my hair and begins shaking me by the shoulders. "Cry it!"

"You had no right!" he shouts, dropping me onto the pillows and stomping off again. "You had no right to do this and she had no right to send you this!"

He strides out of the room, retrieves the dagger and rages back in, smashing the fragile pale wood of the doorway with one hand, brandishing the knife in the other.

"She has no more power!" He smacks my face, not hard, like he smashed the doorjamb, a short, controlled cuff. The fire of blood that will congeal into a bruise dances hot in my cheek.

"Say something!" he demands.

"I don't know what to say," I murmur, looking down at my clasped hands.

"You will obey me, you will stay alive, until I give you permission to do otherwise?"

"Hai," I concede softly, head down and looking at the floor.

I surrender being able to commit seppuku in the Genji fashion. I wanted to do it in that manner to make a statement, to reproach the child-killing Genji in a way they would understand, to shame them. But I can take a woman's route. There is a pond here. In Shinano, there will be lakes and rivers. He cannot watch me forever.

Chapter Sixty-Two
August 1185

A slight breeze catches the orange-red silks billowing between four poles erected to shade us from the summer sun. We are on a hillock overlooking the mansion. From here we can see the Kamo River glittering silver as it winds towards Kyoto. Behind us, and to the right, the forest stretches. The August heat coaxes the heavy, hot scent of pine sap to waft like incense, dominating the more delicate floral scents from the garden below us. On the other side of the river, a golden pagoda glints, overlooking its own reflection in a mirror-calm lake. The city streets seem quiet: almost all commerce suspended as all prepare for Obon, making lantern boats and feasts for the dead.

I have been sitting beside Hiro as he constructs boats for his mother and father, his wife and their infant son. He begins daubing his grandfather's name and titles on another lantern. "The land had been hereditarily ours," he explains to me. "It had been lost to us for generations, and then my grandfather received the governorship, and my father inherited it from him, and of course, me from my father. I can't explain the feeling I have when I'm at my mansion, or my family's shrine. A feeling of rightness, being in one's proper place. As much as you say you loved Tanba--I'm sure you will love Shinano equally."

He has been carrying on these one-sided conversations with me for days. It's not that I am unwilling to talk with him. Only that I am surrounded by a silence so all encompassing that it seems impossible. As if I were a fish at the bottom of a pond, hearing a human speaking to me from above, his words penetrating but dully through the heavy water. I can see my hands resting on my knees, but I can't feel them; therefore I have not picked up my own brush to write the many names of my own lost ones.

Hiro begins inscribing lanterns with the names of his comrades who have perished in battle, telling me about them as if I were a recalcitrant child at a history lesson.

"I know the task must seem overwhelming," he says at last, gesturing to the mountain of lanterns the servants have made, waiting for my dedications. "You have lost so many, so recently, and so close," he whispers.

If I had a knife, I would open a vein in my wrist and paint their names with my blood.

"Let me help you," he offers. He picks up a lantern. "Ah, smell those pines," he says. Hiro sketches a picture of a pine tree on one side of the lantern. "Matsu," he murmurs, inscribing the boy's name on another side. "I'm sorry I never met him. I would have treated him as my own son."

He paints the silhouette of a peony on the next lantern, but the ink spreads, heavy and blotting. She wasn't heavy like that, my Kiku Botan. She was light, like a feather, like a faery. He writes her name on the other side, and I can't bear how thick the characters are. I find my hand reaching for a lantern, which he hands me. I write her name in my most delicate script.

"No parent wants to live to write the name of their child on an Obon lantern," he says. "But most of us do."

I start writing the names of my dead on the parchment, if only to forestall him from doing any more for me. I don't want to imagine Sessho's response to seeing, not my writing on his lantern, but the brushstrokes of the enemy who now claims me.

A maidservant pours us more of a cool herbal beverage of lemon, mint, and borage, which is supposed to keep the summer fevers at bay.

"Thank you for thinking of my children," I manage to say.

"It is good that we both have lanterns for them," he says. "They are my loss too. Children that I had hoped to raise as mine."

His loss. He knows nothing of loss. How does one make a lantern for an entire way of life?

"What do you think we should draw on the lanterns for the young Emperor?" he asks. "I suppose the Imperial Crest." He carefully begins daubing the butterfly crest of the Taira on one side of the lantern, the Imperial Crest on the other.

He never met Antoku. He has no idea what was lost when he went beneath the waves.

I remember Antoku sitting on my lap, with the top of my chin folded over his head. I know what he would like to see on his lantern. Habo, the moon rabbit.

"Why the rabbit?" Hiro asks.

"They were his favorite pets, before we left the Capital. He had dozens of them. He was very gentle and sensitive, like them."

Hiro nods. "As one would expect from a child of the Imperial Line. People are now saying that Antoku was the incarnation of one of the Naga Kings. The sword from the regalia was originally stolen from the body of a great serpent. Now many are saying Antoku was the incarnation of that serpent, come to reclaim his sword and take it back with him to his watery realm."

Of course. Leave it to the Genji to take the most undeniable message of the gods' displeasure and twist it to their advantage.

Hiro is wearing an outer robe of a dark, almost muddy, green. The Genji don't seem to have any sense of what colors are appropriate for what seasons. One imagines they simply put on whatever comes closest to hand. I have been wearing mourning shades of lavender over white summer robes, since the children's deaths.

It takes the better part of three days to inscribe all my lanterns. Such an astonishing crowd. Will the night of Obon be long enough to put them all in the water? It is almost everyone I have ever known.

The birds twitter. The young are ready to fly now. I wonder if Seishan is able to feed the birds at her nunnery at Nara. I wrote to her again, but there was no response.

I asked Hiro to find out which man had taken Nori as a concubine. He discovered it was someone who had already been given permission to return to his home in the far north. I can't imagine Nori as a prisoner. I consider inscribing lanterns for her and Seishan, and for myself. I can only think we should be counted among the dead. When I have passed, there will be no one to inscribe a lantern for me, except perhaps Hiro. I wonder if my daughter Tsubame will hear of my death. Part of me feels I should try to stay alive for Tsubame's sake, but I have always been more a mother of the imagination than of the flesh for her. It is so long since I have seen her, and I might never see her again in any case. There was no reply to the letter I sent her when I first

423

returned to Kyoto. My messenger returned saying that the lady in question was said to be well, but he had not been permitted to see her. Perhaps she considered our flight from Kyoto to be the final desertion on her mother's part.

For my last lantern, I decide to make one for myself, for the woman whose ghost can still move a brush, even if she no longer feels any sense of connection to her only surviving child. I paint a wisteria design on it.

"Who else did you know whose sigil was the wisteria?" Hiro asks, picking it up. Then he sees my name on the other side, carefully sets it back down and kneels in front of me. His hands press into my thighs, the heat throbbing through my lavender silks.

"You are not dead, Seiko," he says. "You will recover from this. Now is when you need your sorcery. How would you call a soul back from the dead, a woman who had suffered your losses? Tell me the formula, tell me the remedy, I will fetch it for you. Let us 'brush from each other's wings the frost.'" I flinch under his searching gaze, shuddering at the sensation of his hands gripping me, my flesh waking under his touch. I name some herbs that are good for melancholy. They do not have the power to revive the dead, but it cannot hurt to give him something to do. I am touched and saddened that he thinks of me as his mate, quoting from a poem about the Mandarin ducks, symbols of conjugal loyalty, brushing the frost from each other's wings. The poem he references ends, 'How sad if one is left to sleep alone!' Tiny floating notes from the wind chimes hanging under the eaves of our home drift up the hill to us.

"After tonight--we'll feast with the dead, we'll talk to the dead--and we'll say good-bye to them. Once a year, they visit. Then we go on with living. The ancestors were wise to make it so. This is a difficult time, but we can recover from it," Hiro insists.

I nod slightly, acquiescing, hoping it will make him take his hands away so I can retreat, back in the protective mists that accompany me even on the sunniest days.

That evening we travel to Kyoto and stay at an elegant inn. A deck swathed in white reed mats extends out over the river, making it easy to set our vessels onto the flowing surface of the water. I tie my boat to Sessho's with a strand of my hair and set them in the water together at a moment when Hiro has his eyes closed, praying for his infant son. I watch our two boats processing with serene dignity down the center of the river. It eases me to see myself returned to my beloved, then departing with him.

The banks of the river are six deep with weeping mourners. From our inn we have a view of the waterway as it flows through Kyoto, a river of flickering light, winding towards the distant sea like a golden dragon.

I tie Peony and Matsu's boats together with another strand of my hair. It seems suitable, since they lived and died as the twins they were claimed to be. I set my mother's boat to follow and watch over them.

Then I watch as an entire court, nobles and scholars, women and warriors, children and maidservants, flows away from us, their boats so thick on the water they jostle together, light against light, flame against flame, riding the whispering breath of the river out of the city, into history.

Chapter Sixty-Three
September 1185

Hiro, his friends, and their consorts are going to see the maple trees near the back of the property that have started to turn. The turning of the first branch is a very significant time, always honored with poetry, as is the necessary visit to see the last leaves clinging forlornly to the nearly bare branches, in the hope of watching them fall. The first turning is greeted with a sense of excitement--the air starts to get crisp and cold, especially in the mornings, and we all change our wardrobes, bringing out the padded jackets and showcasing the autumn colors.

We go deep into the forest to view one especially brilliant branch. Male servants precede us into the forest, carrying freshly cut boards cobbled together to unfold into a portable bridge. They put it over muddy areas left by the first rains and we clomp across with our wooden shoes. Where it is drier we walk on a winding path. A maidservant walks alongside, holding my arm to steady me. We stop by a slender waterfall framed by the branch which has just turned. There is always one stone bench here; for this occasion it has been augmented by several wooden benches. I'm startled that the benches have been placed as if they were just something to sit on without any regard as to how they will look like when we first see them. The benches themselves should be in a more attractive pattern, an artistic statement in themselves. It is important to make the things we can control beautiful because most of life is so completely beyond our control. Especially now, when most things are so ugly. But then I remember that the people who cared about those things are dead, and since our party is composed of Genji warriors, they probably won't notice a thing.

A slight breeze eddies through the clearing. A few wayward hairs blow across my face, teased free of their arrangements by the change of season, which dissolves all arrangements. Hiro looks very handsome, his outer robe a dark green with a red maple leaf pattern, the inner layers all browns and whites and greens.   He was overseeing some of the dyeing the other day, getting exactly the shades he wanted for our fall wardrobes. He showed a lively interest, walking among the pots, pulling, stirring with a wooden ladle, examining various pieces in progress, saying, "Yes, I want one the color of oak leaves, one the color of this bark…" When I expressed surprise at how knowledgeable he was about which barks and leaves create which colors, he said it was something his mother had taught him. Like Sessho, who so enjoyed supervising the dyeing process, making sure the colors were just right for himself, for his gifts to me, for his wife and children.

Once we are seated the servants provide us with paper, ink brushes and our inkstones. I run my hand over the coiled dragon guarding my inkwell, one of the few objects that remains from my old life. First Autumn poems. For me, the last. I write,

"In the outer world,
First leaves have just turned.
In the inner world
The branch is bare.
In between…?"

I put that one aside. One of Hiro's pages takes it as reverently as if it were a scripture.

Most of the Genji have not begun writing yet, still pondering the branch solemnly. One has brought his concubine. She's a very young girl, someone who was not all that significant, only recently come to the Empress' service before the war, certainly not part of the inner circle. I don't know her very well. She had been a shy virgin--even now she cannot be more than sixteen. She's a little plump, and very quiet, silently yearning towards me. I write another:

"Over the edge of the rock
The water is continually lost.
Soon leaves
Like Heike banners
Will also float away."

I do not think I will be able to write anything that is not of a depressing nature. I look over at Hiro, see that he is beaming, noticing that I have already finished two poems. In his smile, I read his thought that because I am writing,

I must be happy. Though perhaps it is just his pride for his prize, who was once said to be the best poet at court.

I take a third piece of paper and write;
"In the gull-plucked shell
There is nothing.
On the winter branch
There is nothing.
Inside the cage of my bones,
There is nothing."

My hand is better than usual; the characters formed clearly, with a great deal of space between each. They look as isolated as the sentiment expressed by the poems. I used to be too impatient to write gracefully. I used to scrawl quickly, so my hand could keep up with my thoughts. But now, time ripples seamlessly into timelessness, deep as the canyons of Kurikara.

The servants have brought out everything we need for picnicking under the maples, and the sake has circulated through several rounds of generous toasts and prideful boasts. Buckwheat buns with savory fillings of salmon with cucumber shreds and salted plum are passed by servants, followed by balls of sticky rice rolled around bean paste and slivers of crisp pear.

Hiro reads his poem. He is wearing his swords ceremonially, as are all the men, wanting to be reminded, perhaps, of their victor status.

"The leaves turn crimson.
Soon they will be as scattered
As the red flags.
They are gone.
But not forgotten."

As he sits down to applause, I see that he is proud of himself, thinking I will be pleased that he honors my people by remembering them. Does he think this will make me feel better? Will there be noble songs sung later, of how the Genji courageously slaughtered the Heike children, after the Heike had let the Minamoto sons live to betray their kindness?

Issho stands up and reads another military sort of poem--the autumn leaves 'crimson as the blood of the courageous'. He does not talk about the blood of children. Perhaps it is not as red as that of warriors.

"Vanquished by the cold winds
Though close to death

428

The leaves grow ever brighter,
Crimson as the blood of the courageous.
What a shining example!"
Hiyadoshi, Hiro's older friend, holds forth next.
"Leaves turn. The river rushes.
These things change, yet are unchanging.
So loyalty is unswerving,
When it follows the highest good."
Ah. That one seems to have been directed at Hiro. Well, a small poem
can carry a large agenda. It was always that way in court, too. Flattering one,
needling another.
A fourth Genji stands.
"The call of the war conch
The red of the autumn maple;
These things stir the heart."
The next Genji to rise is studious looking, quite tall, older, somewhat self-
important as men who frame themselves as scholars usually are. He doesn't
seem like a warrior but perhaps he is. He reads a poem about the melancholy
tapping of the woodpecker in autumn.

It's not his composition. It's an old poem he's presenting as if it were his,
presuming that his companions are so ill-read that no one will recognize
it. Before I can stop myself I comment, "That woodpecker tapped several
centuries ago. What a long lifetime it has!"

He darts a seething glance in my direction. But I doubt anyone else has any
idea what I am alluding to. It's like going out autumn-viewing with a bunch of
children.

"Ah, now we will hear from our very own Murasaki." Hiro says.

"No...." I shake my head demurely. "I was not able to come up with
anything."

"Oh, come now. I saw you quickly write three poems in the time it took
each of us to compose one. We will not be offended if your sun casts us in
shadow. We know you have been practicing poetry while we have been busy
with the bow," Hiro urges.

"Ukifune will be happy to share her efforts," her Genji owner boasts.

"Oh, no..." The plump girl shakes her head, blushing. "I...I...would be
embarrassed!" she stammers.

"Especially if Madame Murasaki, the poetry expert, chooses to critique it," snipes the tall man whose plagiarism I had pointed out.

"No, no, we'll have none of this shyness, the ladies shall read their poems," Hiyadoshi insists gruffly.

She finally reads, in a halting voice:
"I do not understand the power
That turns the green leaf into flame.
How can I understand my own heart?"
A good poem; it has a number of fine puns relating to transformation and fire. Yes, she is educated; what a shame it will be wasted on the Genji.

I read my three poems, one after the other. As I expected, they are followed by a deadly silence.

"Ah well," says Hiro in a jovial voice that sounds only slightly false. "Too deep for me, eh gentlemen?" The others laugh, gratefully. We traipse back through the forest to a grassy hilltop where the servants have set up targets and the men engage in an archery competition. Ukifune and I kneel, watching. Hiro has rented a couple of elegant women from the floating world for the occasion, who sit clustered together nearby like butterflies temporarily perched on a branch.

Of course they are making pretty exclamations and snapping their fans in excitement at this show of Genji military prowess. The surly thin man is not a bad archer so I suppose he was a warrior after all. Perhaps he did his warring from a distance, for he looks as if he would be far too fastidious to enjoy the prospect of blood on his clothes.

Sitting behind the men who are waiting their turns, I see Issho's small knife hanging from his purple and yellow brocade sash, the ornate handle pointing right towards me. He is sitting so close, I could snatch it right out of its sheath, but I am well aware how quickly these men move. The chances that I would be stopped before I could follow through with killing myself are too great. I do not want to risk embarrassing Hiro if I have to live to face his displeasure later. I sit quietly, allowing myself to become remote as a stone, now that I no longer have to perform.

After admiring the sunset, the party moves inside for an evening feast. The table is lavishly piled with every sort of autumn delicacy. It is good that these women Hiro has procured are here to keep up the gaiety level, to flirt with the men and make them feel good about themselves.

I am seated between Issho and Hiyadoshi. One of the other men, the one with the young Heike concubine, has gotten drunk enough to be telling off-color stories, including his exploits involving her. She cringes, blushing bright red, on the verge of tears. I brace myself as best I can, trying to harden myself so as not to care if Hiro decides to share any details of his liaison with me. But he carefully avoids any reference to me, while teasing the entertainers in convivial good humor.

Hiyadoshi boasts that he could eat a thousand of these fresh-water clams. Issho responds with an insult, laughing that what he really needs are oysters.

"If you refer to their tendency as an aphrodisiac rather than an impotence cure...then bring them on! Remember I like them hairy!" Hiyadoshi bellows. The conversation degenerates to jokes about sea cucumbers, the kind of talk men indulge in at a table where there is limitless sake to be had.

"Eat some more! You're too thin!" Issho says to me, trying to coax me to have more of a shellfish dish he claims is restorative. Hiyadoshi makes a remark equating me to the shellfish--hard on the outside, sweet on the inside, indicating he is not fooled by my cool facade, so I assume Hiro has regaled his friends in private with tales of my passion. But it does not matter. I am the picture of propriety, like the delicate white flowers of the u no hana bush that are overshadowed by their leaves, blooming in the darker recesses, portrayed in poetry as having the characteristics of the ideal women: lovely but calling no attention to themselves. I always thought I would have to be dead to be as quiet and shy as those women. It seems I was correct.

The men like the gay banter of the hired women, but they respect those who are quiet and restrained, who hold their own counsel unless asked.

Finally Hiro looks over at me with concern and says, "You must be tired. You need not stay up entertaining us."

"Yes, I will retire now, with your permission."

Later that night I hear him and the other men making love with the women that he hired. I'm just glad he didn't ask me to be there. I am a dry branch; I will bear no more of that sweet fruit. I sit with the shutters open all night feeling the moonlight, cool as bone-light pouring over me. Soon I will be a ghost, pale as this moonlight; soon I will go wandering in search of the ghosts that I have loved.

The men spend the next day hunting. When I know that they are safely gone, I walk out and beckon over one of the captains, someone I have been watching. He has an unfortunate face; his long upper lip gives him a rabbity look. He seems both brave and timid at the same time, as if he were someone who could be talked into things, perhaps, someone with ambition, but too cautious to have caught Hiro's eye. A couple of the maids follow me out, as they have been instructed not to let me out of their sight. I make impatient, shooing motions at them and say to the captain, "I need to have a word with you alone. Can this not be arranged?"

He puffs himself up, and orders the maids to leave us in a most imposing tone. "She is safe in my care!" They anxiously scramble off, still keeping us in eyeshot. I ask him to come and sit with me behind the wisteria. His concern that this may be slightly improper flickers across his face, yet his curiosity and self-importance at having been summoned prevail, and he accompanies me. I sit on the wooden bench, he kneels beside me, head bowed, awaiting my communication.

I have already secreted a vast amount of jewelry in my sleeves, and now I take it out: the large pearl headdress pins that Tokushi gave me, a jade bracelet, sapphire hair pieces, and an ivory netsuke of Kannon. His eyes grow huge.

"Listen, if you will but obtain me a sharp blade, and a moment of time in which to make use of it, all these shall be yours." At his look of shock and surprise I admonish, "Don't answer. But continue to listen. Of course, if it were found that you had helped me, your life would be forfeit. I understand that. But consider this: suppose if the blade you got me was not your own, but one of your underlings; and consider then, if you slew that underling and claimed to have found--" I take out a loose jewel that I have held back until now, "this jewel in his pocket--and if you slay him then, and say to Hiro that you killed him when you saw what had happened--you would then have all the other jewels, and Hiro's gratitude, and a promotion."

He looks at me with alarm and I pray that I have chosen the right man to approach. He appears to be astonished by the details of my plan. I take the heavy pearl headpiece and press it into his hand. "Feel this," I coax. "It is quite real. It was a gift from the Empress. It can be yours."

He swallows, and then swallows again. I decide to risk further. "Take this piece with you," I urge, closing his hand over it. Though he holds it almost as if he feared it were poisoned, I can see the temptation rising in him.

"When you bring me the knife, I will give you the rest," I promise, tucking the rest of the gems back in my sleeves. "Are we agreed?"

"I...will do my best for you, lady." He bows, touches his forehead to the ground, and disappears quickly back to his post. The maids come running quickly back to join me, but I favor them with a withering glance before they can seek to engage me in their prattle, and tell them I am going to meditate here by the wisteria. Glumly they assume kneeling positions at a discreet distance.

Hiro spends that night with his friends, and I am not invited to join them. Perhaps they have succeeded in persuading him that he can do far better. The entertainment of dancing girls who exist only to please him, who do not have to be coaxed into life must be a refreshing change.

I wake often that night, restless in the moonlight. I had hoped the captain would come and give me his answer sooner. I ponder what I will do if he attempts to steal the one piece I have given him without keeping his end of the bargain. I guess I will report him to Hiro and have Hiro execute him. Of course by then he may have sold the pearls. Moonlight leaks in through the shutters. I decide to stay awake. It may be my last night on earth, if the soldier comes to me with the blade tomorrow. I open a shutter and gaze outside at the guards Hiro has posted between my quarters and the pond. They're sitting with their heads propped on their hands, no doubt wishing they were sleeping. They may even be dozing, so motionless they sit, but I know they would wake immediately were I to make any sound.

How lovely things look, silvered by the moon. The gravel footpath sinuous with crushed silver, like a snail's track, silver on the stepping stones strung like pearls across the pond. Soon I will be traveling across a similar path of light. Perhaps, if the gods are generous, I will be able to catch up with those who have gone ahead of me. I imagine Peony and Matsu with my beloved now, and for the first time I am glad that Sessho went ahead of me so that he could be there when the children crossed over. At least they did not have to go to the windy land alone. "I'll be there soon," I whisper.

The next morning I rise to say good-bye to our guests. I manage to smile and flutter my hand and bow as they leave, all the proper things that a wife would do. My liberation is close at hand, and I have no desire to shame Hiro.

Later he calls me in to have lunch with him. Seaweed with rice and salty plums and mountain yam custard. He watches me curiously as we eat. Perhaps he expects jealous reproaches for his nights of excess.

"I have a gift for you," he says, after the eating table is taken away.

He opens his sleeve and pulls out the ornament I had given the captain. I press my lips together in dismay, try to think of something to say like, 'Oh, you found out it was stolen.' But I know that lie is not going to work so I don't try it.

"Yukinari is very loyal to me." He sets the pearls in my hand. They are cold as droplets of ice. I sit dejected, head bowed, eyes closed, shoulders slumping, watching the moonlight path spread so enticingly before me evaporate like dew, watching my loved ones recede farther and farther away.

"Why didn't you ask him for poison?" Hiro asks. "Because you thought he could find a knife more easily?"

I suppose the guard has reported our conversation verbatim. I made the wrong choice. It seems impossible that Hiro could have inspired total loyalty among his men, but perhaps he has.

"Do you really have the courage to use it?" Hiro asks.

Chapter Sixty-four
September 1185

I've begun starving myself, in spite of what Hiro said about killing the maidservants. It's his karma, not mine.

I'm still drinking beverages--water, miso broth, tea. With no food to blunt its effect, sake becomes quite potent. Interesting colors and shapes wheeling around, the sounds of the household, how they make a pattern, like music. I begin to be able to hear the ghosts of the Heike who were killed, the ones who used to live in this house. Frequently I hear footsteps, children running and laughing. It is comforting, for I must be getting closer to the land of the dead if I can hear spirits moving around. I wish Peony would come visit me. I tell the maidservants to bring me some of the special sweets that were her favorite to try to tempt her here. If I leave them out on the altar for her tonight perhaps she will come into my dreams for them. I set the sweets on a low table right beside my sleeping mat. I wake in the night just in time to see a small hand reaching through my gauzy sleeping curtains and purloining the sweets. I call out, "Kiku! Kiku Botan!" The hand disappears; sound of tiny feet running down the corridor. I get up quickly and run after them, calling for her to stop. She stops and turns, shamefaced. It is one of the shortest maids, small and young, but no longer a child. She looks at me and then away, clearly terrified.

"Those aren't for you," I say simply.

Hiro comes striding out of his sleeping quarters.

"What's happening!"

"It's nothing. I had a dream."

"I heard more than one pair of footsteps." He glares around, catching sight of the young maid who, half-swooning, cowers on the floor.

"Yes, I'm afraid I frightened one of the maids rather badly."

He holds his hand out to me. "Come."

I follow him to his room. He runs his hands up and down my arms in dismay, touches my breasts.

"You're not eating," he says. "They're lying to me, they're lying. They've been saying you've been eating, but you're not eating at all, are you?"

"Please forgive me, but no."

The anxiety vanishes from his face, replaced by hardness. "Which one of your maids do you want to die, then?"

"Do not damage your karma in this way."

"No, this is your karma. It is your choice."

We are standing close, clutching each other's sleeves. I wait until he looks at me, until I catch a glimpse of the frightened boy hiding beneath the harsh man.

"Please Hiro. Please let me go."

"You want to starve yourself? Is that really what you want to do? Is that how you want to die?"

I bow my head.

"I would prefer to commit seppuku as a formal protest against the killing of the children. That is what I would prefer. If you were to offer me any gate, that is the gate I would choose."

He winces. "Seppuku is a very painful way to die. Even the strongest warriors dread the day when they will have to cut their belly. I suppose you could cut your throat instead. That's much faster...but still...you can't imagine the pain of disembowelment," he says to me. "I've seen warriors who died that way..."

I shake my head. "I already know the pain of having the womb torn out of my body. Any pain that takes me out of this pain is a pain well worthwhile."

He looks so miserable then that what little is left of my heart goes out to him.

"*Shigata na gai*," I whisper. It can't be helped."

"Go then," he says.

I get up and bow, unsteady on my feet. I begin to leave, trailing my sleeping robes.

"Stay," he says, in a softer voice.

I turn back to him. He indicates his bed. He takes me by the arm, leads me gently to lie beside him. I am grateful for his warmth. I'm so cold all the time now, and he's as warm as a big stove. He chafes my limbs to warm them. "You're so thin," he whispers, "you're not like yourself anymore."

The next morning I wake to find him still in bed with me though normally he would rise early.

"You're too weak now to commit seppuku. It takes a lot of physical strength to do that. You have to be able to pull the knife through the muscle. I don't think you could slice a rice cake in your present condition."

"At the graveside, arguing about which doctor," I quote, expressing that the argument is meaningless, since the opportunity for seppuku is not available to me anyway.

"I can't keep you captive if you won't stay with me," he says. "You'll always be looking for a way to kill yourself. Sooner or later, you'll find one. Start eating again and get strong." Almost inaudibly he adds, "I will give you your wish."

He sits by the edge of the bed, shrugs a green and gold patterned kimono on over his muscular shoulders and back, like a dragon re-acquiring his skin.

"I'll give you what you need. You can write a letter to Yoshitsune indicating..." he swallows, "and I will see that it is delivered." His eyes are closed, his face heavy with resignation.

"I'm sure Yoshitsune will provide some other woman to take home with you." My attempt at comfort sounds hollow.

"Yes," Hiro says dully, "I'm sure he will."

He calls a manservant to bring us breakfast. I drink the rice porridge broth. Chewing the rice is exhausting.

"You have to eat more than that if you want to get strong again," he admonishes.

"Right after a fast, a person should eat small," I reply.

"Yes, that's true," he concedes.

I continue to eat over the next five days. Does he really mean to keep his word or is it just a trap to woo me back into life? I don't know. I have to trust that he will keep his word for his own reasons, his blind infatuation with his own integrity perhaps. Perhaps there is already another woman that he has in mind.

The red flags of the Heike live again on the autumn hills, brief conquering before the fall. Mischievous Tatsu Ta Hime swirls her winds, making the dried leaves dance. It would have been hard to die in the spring, but in the fall it seems like the natural thing to do, to fall like the leaves and let the wind carry me.

I pray every day for Matsu and Kiku Botan, lighting incense to carry my prayers to the invisible realms. Life is so ephemeral, so brief.

"Only a little while to be oneself,
Then to dissolve away.
Leaving a good scent
Is enough."

Hiro spends a great deal of time walking in the forest. He usually takes his bow and arrows but he never seems to come back with anything. I think it is probably his peace that he is hunting.

After a week of eating, I ask him if he thinks I am strong enough yet. He probes my arm muscles with his fingers. "No, no, it will take a while longer."

The next day he takes me to the clearing by the waterfall. He shows me a piece of animal hide stretched taut like a target. He has me put a knife through it and pull it across diagonally. It is hard, even with both hands.

He takes the knife from me as if he did not trust me with it another moment.

"Do you really think you could do that in your own body?" he asks sadly.

I bow in assent, trying not to let him see how much the exercise has shaken me.

"Will you look at the letter I have written," I request, "and see if you think it is appropriate?"

He nods miserably. I show him the letter, to be sent to Yoshitsune along with my body. He makes a few small suggestions for changes.

Later, before dinner, I see him poring over the Lotus Sutras.

"Anything interesting?" I ask.

"Not really," he says. "But I thought--I would try it."

"Don't you think," he says over dinner, "that you have a responsibility?"

"What responsibility is that?" I ask, dreading what might follow.

"To Japan. You are the last of the old ways. You die, those ways die with you. You stay alive, with your writing--perhaps with future children you might have," he says cautiously, "you might yet have quite an influence on the world."

I shake my head, holding my arms inside my sleeves.

"You cannot make a new kimono out of rags."

"Sometimes a wound makes you more powerful," he argues.

"If it is not fatal," I agree.

"I've treated you well," he states. "The only reason I haven't married you is that things have been so unsettled. But as soon as we get back to Shinano..."

I don't know why he thinks marriage will make a difference. I never cared that I was not formally married to Sessho. Will my children be less dead in Shinano?

"Is there nothing that will persuade you?" he asks hopelessly.

I sigh and look down, unable to think of anything I could say that would not hurt him further.

"The only reason I am consenting," he says in a low voice, "is that soon we will be in Shinano. I do not want the children to learn to love you, only to lose you. And I do not want you to have to die in some humiliating and dishonorable way."

After a long silence, he whispers, "If you die, everything I have fought for will be lost."

"Perhaps," he says, "I should order one of my men to commit seppuku so you can see how it is done."

"No." I say. "No more useless death."

"And what do you call your death if not useless?" he flares. "What do you prove? Do you think Yoshitsune will care? Or Yoritomo? Do you think it will make any difference to them? Or any of the child killers? Your gesture will mean nothing to them. Nothing. If they had a conscience to be stirred it would have been stirred by the cries of the children. You make the mistake that I made," he says bitterly, "You mistake them for honorable men."

"No," I sigh, "I do not make that mistake. Perhaps you are right and it will make no difference at all. But for me, I will know that I did all I could to protest what has been done. That is all a helpless captive can aspire to."

"Would you want to live if I let you go free?" he asks.

"Where would I go?"

"That is my point precisely!" he says. "I would have let you go before now if there was anywhere for you to go."

He's lying, but it's an endearing lie.

"You need children. My children need a mother," he starts again .

"Are you breaking your promise to me?" I ask.

The hard warrior mask slips over his face. "I'm just testing your resolve."

"My resolve is firm," I reply. "I would like to depart when the moon is full, eight days from now. You will be leaving not long after that to return to Shinano, is that not so?"

"Yes."

"Are we agreed then?"

He nods his head brusquely, rises and strides out.

Chapter Sixty-Five
October 1185

"Have you made notes on where you want your possessions to go?" he asks me the next day over lunch in the garden.

"Perhaps you could send my clothing and jade pieces to my eldest daughter. She has not responded to my letters, but perhaps she will find some value in them. As for the rest of it--I'd like you to keep it--perhaps you will have future daughters or grand-daughters."

"As you wish," he says in a hollow attempt at indifference.

I try to think of something, some poem or quote that would make him feel better. Finally I say, "All of the mother's careful care in the nest cannot keep the young birds from the air under their wings."

He toys with his food.

"I would make one more request," I venture.

"Speak."

"Is it possible you would assign one of your men to be my second?"

I know that in the Genji tradition it is a rare suicide in which the man cuts his belly and then waits the long hours it might take for him to die. Generally another man, a friend of his, stands beside or behind him and cuts off his head as soon as the initial cut is made.

"There is no one I would trust," he says finally, after a long silence, "to do it perfectly."

I take a deep breath, let it out shakily. I must do it alone then. I'll have to put cloth in my mouth to keep from crying out.

"I will do it myself," he says, almost inaudibly.

"You will..."

"I will be your second." he says, a remote, haunted look on his face. "Because I cannot bear to have you suffer."

He gets up and walks off towards the forest before my astonishment has dissipated enough for me to express my gratitude.

One of the maids is making a plain all-white garment for my seppuku. Hiro has been on a drunk for the last couple of days. My maids inform me that he is drinking all the time, even calling for sake in the middle of the night. I hope he will not lose his determination to help me, and I know it is wrong of me to ask it of him. The faint tap tap of workers, building a bamboo platform out back in the garden where I can perform the ritual, mingles with the hoarse autumn cry of the cuckoo.

Three days before the full moon I stop eating, taking only water and tea. I will want my stomach to be empty. And also, I remember how easy it was to think about letting go of life when I was not eating. Now that I have been eating again, my body betrays me by taking pleasure in the sweet earthiness of cat tail roots, the spongy texture of the moss growing around the garden benches, the whispering silk of Hiro's sleeve and the warmth of the arm beneath it. The way my heart beats faster in response to the way the wind ripples red through the maples, betrays that not all of me is eager for this journey to the other world. I find myself going around the garden saying farewell to the trees and the plants although I have not known them for very long. But one wishes to say good-bye to one's friends, and I have no more friends to say good-bye to, except for these.

I write to Seishan, even though I know there will be no reply, nor even time for a reply to be made. "Pray for us all. When it is your time, your family will be waiting. Thank you for being my true sister. May our different ways of renouncing the world bring us peace."

I write to Tokushi and tell her how much I love her and ask her to pray for me. "I am looking forward to seeing our kin under the sea. Perhaps I will be allowed to go to the Naga Palace where Antoku dwells; if so I will take as good care of him there as I ever did in the upper world."

Much as I yearn to be reunited with Sessho and the children and Antoku, I don't know if the Windy Land bears any resemblance to our world. Some say that when a person dies they go alone, that their spirit returns to the life force in the same way that a brook returns to a river and a river returns to the sea; that the brook is simply dissolved in the ocean, simply lost. But even if I completely forget who I have been and who they have been, there will not be the pain of missing them anymore.

"You are a wicked and selfish girl," one of the older maids dares to chide me later that evening, "the master's sleeves are wet because of you." I do not rebuke her but simply cast my eyes down, stroking my hair as it falls over my shoulder. I never asked for him to love me, I think defensively. But then, no one asks anyone to love them. It is like a magic spring that appears in the wilderness for no reason. What can a spring do, if the one it has appeared for will not drink from it?

I draw the maid aside and ask her to take a message asking if I may visit him. She returns saying a message will follow, and after awhile one of his men comes, saying that he is not well and will see me tomorrow.

I know it is cowardly to want to feel the comfort of his body next to mine. I lie alone instead. Everything about our way of life has been washed away, like a child's sand castle, obliterated by the sea. And I feel that sea tugging on my form now. I find myself touching my body, my hair. Feeling the bones under the flesh. How soft my skin is, my hair. Touching the pulse at my throat and deep along the navel.

How innocent the body is. It is so sad that for my suffering to come to an end, my body must suffer and come to an end. No, I could never be a Buddhist nun. I am far too attached to the beauty in this world, to the sensations of my own body. But just on the other side of this world, on the other side of the veil, stand my mother, and my Sessho, and my children, waiting for me, and I must shed this body to reach them.

Sitting on a bench in the garden, drying my hair in the sun, I see Hiro standing with Issho as servants tighten their horses' saddles. I walk over to them.

"Are you going for a ride?" I ask.

"Hai," Hiro says, as he swings up on his horse. "Thought I'd go out in the woods and see if I could find any innocent animals to kill," he says with a tone of forced joviality. Only his mouth smiles. The look in his eyes is of someone who's being tortured.

"Stay pure," I admonish him, patting him on the leg.

"Too late," he replies, with a grim laugh.

He turns his horse's head away from me. Issho shoots me one reproachful look, then follows. They move off towards the woods. Hiro doesn't look back at me. I know I am tormenting him, but we are both in the clasp of karma and nothing can be done.

The day before I am to die, Hiro asks me to go walking in the woods with him. We walk, breathing in the scents of decay, admiring the glory of the leaves. He asks the servants to follow far behind. It's so nice to walk, just the two of us. We go up into the hills, past the borders of his property. It reminds me of walking with Sessho, that companionable feeling when you can just walk silently beside someone and be happy in each other's company.

He breaks the silence by saying, "Soon the branches will all be bare."
It is the beginning line to an old poem, but I don't know if that means he wants me to fill in the rest of the poem or if he is simply stating what he feels. I quote the second line.

"The geese have already fled to the south."

"A dried leaf, a feather..." he shakes his head. "Spring seems so far away."

I pick up a scarlet leaf and hand it to him. "When you think of me, think of what the tree has lost," I say, intending to comfort him with the thought that the tree survives the loss of many such leaves.

"The maple loses all," he replies, "but in the spring, the tree is green again." His phrasing is awkward and unpoetic, but his meaning is clear enough.

We walk on, silent once more. A chill wind comes through the trees, penetrating our clothes. "Some trees bend with the wind," I acknowledge, "some trees break."

"Some grow old and lonely," he responds. His tone holds a note of self-pity, but I do not blame him for it. The leaves that have already fallen rustle under my robes. I wish my robes did not rustle so loudly. It is the cadence of the leaves I wish to hear, the interesting dry sound that the dead leaves make against each other, how different it is from the soft, sibilant whispering of the green leaves in full sap as they rub together in a spring breeze. In spring when the wind blows, the leaves seem to talk to each other, to conspire, to call messages from tree to tree. In autumn, the leaves are dead, talking not with each other, each to each, green to green, but sending their pale, dry echoing whispers to the land of spirit.

I remember collecting autumn leaves with Matsu and Peony, comparing them, writing poems about them, pressing them to keep their bright colors from fading so quickly. I find myself wishing I still had some of those leaves that we preserved, even though I know that they and the children who kept them are gone to ash together. Hiro thinks me more powerful than I am, saying it is my responsibility to continue the old ways. He says my death will make no difference, yet neither would my life make any difference. I would vanish into the countryside of Shinano like a stone thrown into a pool. Even if I wrote, none of my writing would be read. I have asked him to take this diary, which I had hoped to make into a book, and to bury it under the ritual platform where I commit suicide. Perhaps someone in a future generation will unearth the box, open these scrolls and remember what truly happened to the Heike. By then the Genji will have told so many stories about us--already Kiyomori is described as being inhuman--it will be said that we were a race of Tengu goblins who had to be eliminated so that Japan would survive. Already they blame Antoku's death on his grandmother--as if their ships had not been bearing down on us. Was she wrong to think them child-killers? Recent months have shown that she was not.

As Hiro bends down a flawless maple branch I notice his large, calloused hands. He is like a boy who goes butterfly hunting: all he wants is to see their beauty close up, but in his clumsiness and excitement, tears their wings. I do not blame him for those parts of myself I lost during my captivity. He was as innocent as a child who puts a cricket in a cage so it can sing him to sleep at night. A man wanting a woman's comfort and approval cannot be blamed for the fragility of the butterfly. That is a flaw of nature.

"Just before they fall...they are at their most beautiful," he says in a husky voice, regarding the branch. I put my hand on his.

"That a butterfly cannot live longer than a season is the fault of no one, not even the autumn wind," I reply.

When we come back down the hill into the garden, we pass under a willow tree trailing its yellow leaves in the water. We stand watching the ripples eddy around the branches combing the water, the leaves floating loose in the current.

"Oh, Willow Woman," he puts his arm around me, "would that like this willow, you would bend in the storms and not break."

"Would it were so."

"I wish I could turn back time to when the leaves were green. I would do things so much differently."

I try to think of something that will comfort him.

"Not even the autumn wind can change its nature. All things are as they have been made."

"Will you stay with me tonight?" he asks, under the willow.

"Yes," I return without hesitation, "it would please me."

That night as he lights the candles in the lanterns, we admire each other's autumn foliage arrangements, the short stemmed brown and gold chrysanthemums bordered with brown leaves, a few maple leaves fanning like flames, then still higher, a tangle of gold leaves and red berries, looking disheveled as if the wind had passed through.

"Yours is superior," he concedes, "but you have the greater training."

"Yours is very fine," I say, "at least the equal of mine."

He has been fasting today also, purifying himself for my ritual suicide. We drink rice tea, tasting of earth and of autumn. The autumn incense he has made spreads its scents through the room, earthy and rich, almost painful in its muskiness. My body feels raw with sorrow. I am choosing to abandon life, to destroy my body, which is innocent of wrongdoing, which has never given me anything but joy. Through the double layer of my hair and my tears, Hiro's face softens, suffused with light. I wonder why I have never really seen how deeply caring he is.

He looks at me with equal sorrow; then, holding my shoulders tightly, kisses me passionately at the base of the throat. My heart pumps wildly, the sharp intensity of being alive, pierces my body like a knife.

We start kissing intensely, then stop abruptly when he pants, "Seiko, a boon, a favor--"

"Yes?"

"Just for tonight, call me your husband."

"Yes, my husband."

We make love with abandon. I release myself completely with him, no qualms, no shame, no holding back, fully entering the fire, the red of the autumn leaves, scarlet of my extinguishing life blazing brightest in the moment before annihilation; just before it falls it is the brightest, just before it falls...

I am sobbing so hard it is like being caught in a wild October storm. The taifun catches us, a pair of autumn leaves caught in a savage whirlwind. We spin around and around with each other until the room dissolves, both of us tossed helpless as leaves in a storm of converging passion and karma.

Afterwards, he presses his hand against my belly and I start to cry because my belly feels so vulnerable, so tender, and I'm afraid of the knife.

"It's all right," he says, his voice cracking a little. "Even the fiercest warriors are afraid to put the knife in their belly. Seiko--wife--I am very strong, and my sword is very sharp. You will not suffer Seiko, I swear to you, you will not suffer."

Then he bends his head and I feel his tears hot against the back of my neck. But his body doesn't shake with sobs like mine does. His warrior's training allows no movement of his body to betray his true feelings. Only the hot wetness at my nape anointing the flesh he will sever tomorrow.

We make love again with desperate fierceness. In lovemaking he allows himself to sob and cry out. He rolls on me fiercely, almost throwing me around on the pillows, but I am not hurt, anymore than flames can be hurt by stirring the logs in the stove that carry their light. We both scream, a prolonged, endless cry and collapse, shuddering into each other's arms. He kisses my body as if he were trying to memorize me with his lips. He kisses my neck frantically, as if undoing what he must do tomorrow, as if his kisses could magically preserve my neck from his sword.

We make love again and again and while the intensity of it does not diminish, the exhaustion between increases, until finally I, at least, drift off into slumber. In my last memory, it was yet dark, yet when I wake the world is beginning to stir, little creaks throughout the house betraying the movement of servants tiptoeing around, horses whinnying outside, and then the crowing of the cock and the singing of the lark heralding the arrival of my last day.

Chapter Sixty-Six
October 1185

I take a deep breath, savoring the air in my lungs, luxuriating in the softness of the bed-clothes. I reach out to touch Hiro, who is kneeling beside the bed, writing.

"You're awake," he says. His gaze is so tender it's like his warm hands touching me wherever he looks. He puts a hand behind my head and kisses me very gently on the forehead. "Good morning, wife," he says softly.

"Good morning, husband."

"I wish I was killing you in the heat of battle, so I wouldn't have to think about it."

"You should have killed me when you first boarded the boat. Better so, perhaps."

"No," he says, "I do not regret what has been between then and now. It will be over all too soon."

"Like so many things."

He kisses my head, caresses my hair, pulls open his robe and lies down beside me. We hold each other for a while, breathing like two lungs in one body. Balanced precariously on something thinner than a blade, our breathing a threshold between life and death. I am on the edge of a high, high cliff, looking down to the river winding far below like a silver thread, seeing the forests and the fields laid out below, so far down, and soon to fall.

His hand gently encircles my throat. I am glad that my neck is so thin. I remember how quickly he cut the head off that man who insulted me; surely that neck must have been much larger than mine. It will be very quick, if he does not hesitate. We came together in violence, but now, as he cups his hand over my heart, rocking me, I feel he is my oldest friend.

"We should spend the day separately, meditating and purifying," he says finally.

"Yes," I agree. It will make it easier for both of us. If we do not have some

448

separation now, it may not even be possible for him to keep his promise when the moon rises. I start to pull on my outer kimono, but our hands keep sliding under each other's robes, touching the skin with reverence, a devotion beyond our volition. This is the last person I will touch; this is the last skin, other than mine, that I will feel. I breathe in the scent of him, the heavy sexual perfume of this night, the last time I will drink the incense of a lover's body. His strong fingers massaging the flesh of my forearms, out to the fingers and back up to my shoulders.

"You will not change your mind." He says the words as if he were strangling on them.

I run my hands over his beautiful, sorrowing face.

"No."

"Go then," he says, sliding off the bed and standing. His eyes downcast, he indicates the door.

I take his hands and kiss them.

"Thank you," I say as I walk towards the door. I keep expecting him to call me back but he doesn't and I pass over the threshold of his room for what I know is the last time.

I look back; he is standing with his back towards me, his hands clenched. *Shigata ga nai*: it can't be helped.

I return to my room, unconcerned that I am in a disheveled state and have left most of my clothes in Hiro's room. I put on a deep red cherry outer robe with soft under layers of white and green, choosing carefully, since this is my last day.

I spend the day meditating in various parts of the garden. There is no reason to have me guarded now; the solitude is exquisite. I allow myself to kiss the bark of the trees, the powdery bark of the ash tree, the somewhat rougher maple. Run my fingers along the cypress, which is too rough and shaggy to kiss. I kiss the maple leaves, which are thin and soft like an old woman's skin.

Everything sparkles after a night of love, the colors both sharp and soft; it reminds me of being a child, everything suffused with this luminous glow. I walk towards the waterfall, feeling grateful for my life. Sessho, who held the key to my every lock: how comfortable we were together, like an interlocking puzzle of monkey-pod wood, polished and smooth, fitting together with seamless grace. Peony, so much like my mother: I shake my head with wonder that a creature of such piercing perfection could come from me. My mother,

her long thick hair falling over me, holding me in her lap and telling me stories while I relaxed against her, knowing with complete assurance what every fox kit and bear cub knows: as long as mother is here, I am safe.

I close my eyes, the pour of the waterfall weaving me back to my childhood. Candleglow shimmering out from the cracks of the rustic shrine. Laughter and the clink of sake glasses, the flutter of flute and drum as my mother and the other women danced for the kami, and for each other. The love-makings which were the secret key to the abundant harvests. The evening I peered in between the wooden seams, breathing the perfume of candles and incense, catching glimpses of a glow flickering around the women as if their bodies were the wicks of some great lantern. As I turned from my peephole I saw a white fox sitting, staring into a peephole on the other side of the shrine. She turned her face towards me and smiled, the way only a fox can smile, and then turned and trotted off, plumy white tail waving as she disappeared into the descending snow.

I don't think about the fire that ended that life, or the fire that ended the other lives I loved, or the high cliffs, or the deep seas, or the battles. I think about the glistening water as we sailed along the Inland Sea, and how gently it would rock us to sleep those nights. I remember the dolphins weaving in front of our prow, spray flying off their backs, how full of joy they were, how I longed to jump in with them, imagining what it would be like to shoot through the water at such speeds. How Atsumori and Kiyosune swam with me in the silks, a dance of equal joy and grace.

Returning from the woods, giddy and light, I meditate on the rock garden. Usually I do not enjoy the static stones as much as the gardens of living green, but I see today beyond any doubt that the rocks are also alive. Today they are pulsing with shifting light. How blind I was to think that they were boring. A rock remains long in one form. Yet inside there is a spirit that is as free and gay and colorful and dancing as any to be found in butterfly or flower. I see now, under its gray surface, there is a rainbow rippling, the rocks breathing and joyful. I find myself compelled to reach down and disturb the neatly raked surface, to displace the gravel into the shape of a couple of characters which say, "Hiro, I love you. Thank you."

The quality of light has changed. Evening approaches.

I change into my white robes, slip the cherry-colored jacket on top of it for warmth. I wrap Peony's baby clothes inside my robes, next to my heart.

A new arrangement of autumn leaves brightening my altar mimics red and gold flames. Hiro has left a note beside it. On very thin white rice paper, tremulous characters read, "Thank you for blessing my unworthiness with your presence. I will never forget you." Then the characters for love and forever, followed by his signature.

Tears come. Just a few. I hope he will find a woman who can love him and care for his children, to be the comfort and inspiration he is searching for. I fold his message and place it by my heart beside my favorite letter from Sessho.

I go back outside and walk around, watching the sunset. The trees catch the orange and red in their leaves, as if the sunset had bled out of those trees, coloring the sky. As the light fades, so does the last of my ambivalence. I kneel on the white reed mats of the ritual platform, completely at peace. The gold of the sun lingers over the forest in the west, and the moon rises, bathed in the sun's radiance. Then the moment of their communion passes, and the moon climbs, sharply silver, through the deepening air.

A servant brings out the finest mulberry scrolls with my inkstone and brushes so I can write my death poem.

He lays out the beautiful dagger that Tokushi sent me. I pick it up and examine it as the moon slips above the grasp of the trees. The handle is studded with moonstone jewels like drops of coagulated dew, the blade--I slide it out of the sheath to look at it--sharp and fascinating, like solid moonlight.

'The moonlight sharpens itself.

Sunset pulses in belly and throat

Ready to be released.'

I was going to write, ready to be released into the dark, but it is not at all dark, but very bright as the moon climbs over the trees. I am dazzled, sitting here clothed in white, the moon blade glimmering in front of me. I breathe in the silver of the moon, set that poem aside. It feels as if I could be here forever, floating in the moonlight, drifting at the edge of spirit.

As I watch the white orb, throbbing with it, I see that it is a door waiting to open, to take me through to the other world. Footsteps. Hiro, skirting the rock garden, coming towards me. He is dressed in gold and purple, wearing his armor, carrying his swords. He is dressed the way he was when I first saw him on the boat, before the killing that covered him with blood. He kneels, ritually washes his sword and dries it. Then he bows to me very formally, kneels on the ground before me, puts his hands together, a smaller bow. His face has assumed the impassive mask of the warrior. I feel a throb of sadness that I will never see him again, will never see the real Hiro, who I do love. But I understand that he needs to be in this state to do what he has to do, so I bow back, also formally and without trying to meet his eyes.

I smooth out another scroll, breathing in the moon, waiting for the inspiration for my death poem. I hear his steps coming up onto the dais behind me, walking very firmly, without hesitation, planting himself behind me, slightly to the right. I breathe in the moonlight, and my body becomes silver, transparent, shimmery, the soul ready, poised to leave. The light flows through my brush, shapes itself into my final composition.

I carefully set the poem aside. I am happy with how the character for moon looks like a window, the black ink on the white scroll the mirror image of the white moon against the night sky. I pick up the blade and unsheath it once again. It glitters so brightly. The cool air kisses my exposed neck. I hear a creak behind me and once again become aware of Hiro's presence.

I grasp the knife firmly, pointing it towards my belly, the seat of my hara. Soft as a whisper, Hiro raises his sword. I take one last breath, silently intoning my death poem as a prayer:

'Moon, in your brightness
Open your round door--
Make me a passage.'

Principal Characters

Akoyo, Taira—Son of Tsunemasa and On'na Mari

Antoku, Emperor—Son of Emperor Takakura and Tokushi; grandson of Lord and Lady Kiyomori.

Daigon-no-suke, Lady—Wife of Shigehira, lady-in-waiting to Tokushi.

Fujuri, Fujiwara—High Priestess of Inari at the Fukushima Shrine south of Kyoto. Mother of Seiko.

Go-Shirakawa, Retired Emperor—Father of Emperor Takakura, Grandfather of Antoku .

Harima, Lady—Sannayo's mother, Tsubame's grandmother.

Hiro--also known as Lord Yasuda—Seiko's captor--and lover--after the battle of Dan-no-nura.

Hiyadoshi—Older friend of Hiro's

Ieyeasa—Friend of Tsunemasa's.

Issho—Younger friend of Hiro's

Kaneyasu—Close friend of Shigemori's.

Kenreimon'nin—Tokushi's title when she became Antoku's mother.

Kiku Botan—Also known as Kikuko. Seiko and Sessho's daughter.

Kiyomori, Taira—Head of the Taira clan, father of Tokushi, Shigemori, Shigehira, Tomomori, Munemori and others; grandfather of Antoku.

Machiko—Seiko's trusted serving maid.

Matsu—Sessho and Seishan's youngest son.

Michinori, Fujiwara—Sometimes known as Shinzei. Important Court Official and ally of Lord Kiyomori. Brother of Fujiwara Fujuri, also Seiko's uncle.

Mochihito, Prince—Son of Retired Emperor Go-Shirakawa, brother of Emperor Takakura.

Munemori, Taira—Son of Lord and Lady Kiyomori, brother of Tokushi and Shigemori. Head of the Taira clan after Shigemori's death. On'na Mari's patron.

Murasaki, Lady—Author of Tales of the Genji. An important writer from the previous century. Seiko is sometimes called Murasaki as a form of flattery.

Nori-chan—Sessho and Seishan's daughter, who imagines herself as a woman warrior.

Noriyori, Minamoto—Son of Yoshitomo, half-brother of Yoritomo.

On'na Mari—A merchant's daughter who becomes Sannayo's comcubine. Later, she becomes a much sought after beauty at the Court and makes a marriage with Tsunemasa. Friends and lovers with both Seiko and the Empress.

Sannayo—Lieutenant Governor of Tajima province. Seiko's husband, Tsubame's father.

Seiko, Fujiwara—Daughter of Fujiwara Fujuri and Fujiwara Tetsujina. Raised to be an Inari Priestess, becomes the Empress's personal sorceress. Known for her poetry, sometimes called Murasaki. Mother of Tsubame and Kiku Botan, known as Kikuko.

Seishan, Taira—A cousin of Tokushi's. Seiko's lover and best friend. Married to Taira Sessho, mother of Nori, Tomomori, and Matsu .

Sessho, Taira—Governor of Tanba province, husband of Taira Seishan, father of Nori, Tomomori, Matsu and Kikuko.

Shigehira, Taira—Son of Lord and Lady Kiyomori, husband of Lady Daigon-no-suke. Important Taira Commander.

Shigemori, Taira—Oldest son of Lord and Lady Kyomori. Technical Head of the Taira clan after Lord Kiyomori takes Buddhist vows.

Takakura, Emperor—Son of Retired Emperor Go-Shirakawa, husband of Tokushi, father of Antoku.

Tetsujinai, Fujiwara—Poet and scholar, father of Seiko.

Tokiko, Taira—Lady Kiyomori, married to Lord Kiyomori, mother of Tokushi and Shigemori, grandmother of Antoku.

Tokushi, Empress—Childhood friend of Seiko's, Married to Emperor Takakura. Daughter of Lord and Lady Kiyomori.

Tomoe—Yoshinaka's consort; a famous woman warrior who fights for the Genji.

Tomomori—Sessho and Seishan's eldest son.

Tomomori, Taira—Son of Lord and Lady Kiyomori, brother to Tokushi and Shigemori. Military commander.

Tsubame—Seiko's eldest daughter.

Tsunemasa, Taira—Nephew of Kiyomori, half brother of Atsumori. Husband of On'na Mari. Known as a poet, musician and warrior.

Uryon-dai—Friend and lover of Seiko's. Her loyalty to the Empress and the Taira is questionable.

Yorimada, Minamoto—Uryon-dai's husband, Yorimasa's son.

Yorimasa, Minamoto—Distant relative of Yoritomo, ally of Lord Kiyomori until the revolt by Prince Mochihito.

Yoritomo, Minamoto—Son of Minamoto leader Yoshitomo, half-brother of Yoshitsune and NoriYori. Though Kiyomori spared his life, he later takes up arms against the Taira, hoping to restore the Minamoto (Genji) clan to its former glory.

Yoshinaka, Minamoto—Cousin of Yoritomo. Leader of the northern anti-Taira forces.

Yoshitomo, Minamoto—Leader of the Genji forces which attempt to overthrow Kiyomori and the Taira. His rebellion fails, but three of his sons, Yoritomo, NoriYori and Yoshitsune, resume his mission twenty years later.

Yoshitsune, Minamoto—Son of Yoshitomo, half-brother of Yoritomo. Principle Commander of the Genji forces.

Yukiie, Minamoto—Uncle of Yoritomo, commander of Genji forces.

Glossary

Amaterasu—the Sun Goddess and ancestress of Japan. The Royal Family of Japan are thought to be her direct descendants.

Badgers—Known as Tanuki in Japan, the clan animal of the Taira. Known for their fierceness, persistence, and sexual prowess.

Benten—One of the seven immortals. A kami of love and beauty, usually shown playing the lute. A patron of musicians.

Bodhisattva—an incarnation of the Buddha; an enlightened being.

Bridge of Birds—archway formed by all the magpies on earth, over which the Weaver and Herdsman may cross once a year during the Tanabata Matsuri festival.

Chodai—the chodai was a platform about two feet high and nine feet square, surrounded by curtains. Inside was a soft, private chamber covered with cushions and futons, used both for sleeping and for private conversations and encounters, almost a room within a room.

Floating World—A term specifically used to describe the pleasure houses in a city, but also sometimes used to describe the evanescence of the material world in general.

Fuchi—a fire Goddess/kami.

Fujiyama—Perfectly shaped mountain, home of the fire Goddess Fuchi.

Futon—a mattress used for sleeping, usually kept rolled up in a chest or closet when not in use.

Hachiman—The Japanese God/kami of war.

Hokkaido—Northern Japan.

I Ching—a Chinese form of divination using yarrow stalks, or cracks on tortoise shells held to the flames.

Ikebana—the art of flower arranging.

Imperial Regalia—Three treasures, believed to have been passed down from the Sun Goddess through an unbroken line of Emperors. The three objects are the Sacred Mirror, the jeweled bead strand, and the sword. The sacred sword was lost at the battle of Dan-no-nura.

Inari—Deity sometimes thought of as male, sometimes female, representing divine union. The Goddess/kami of abundance, sorcery, and the love which transcends death. Foxes are sacred to her, partly because they kill the mice which eat the grain, partly because of their seeming ability to materialize or dematerialize at will. The fox is a shape frequently assumed by sorcerers and sorceresses.

Itkushima Deity—Clan totem deity of the Taira, who protected the shrine to her on Miyagima Island. A triple Goddess who protects sailors.

Kami—the spirits inherent in all things. Sometimes used interchangeably with God, Goddess, deity, yet each being, whether waterfall, fox, boulder, or human, may also claim to have its 'kami'.

Kami-no-machi—Literally, the 'way of the kami'. Also known as Shinto (Shin-to means the way of the Gods), the indigenous religion of Japan. Kami guide and protect every activity of the natural world and human society. One of the primary objectives of Shinto is to create and restore harmony between the various kami. Brightness of heart, authenticity, and being a harmonizing force are typical goals.

Kannon—Buddhist Goddess of Compassion and Mercy.
Japanese form of Kwan Yin.

Kicho—sometimes called 'a screen of state'. A four to six foot tall frame, like a doorway, though sometimes as wide as it was tall, hung with curtains, open at the bottom. Court ladies generally sat behind a kicho when talking privately to any man who was not a relative or intimate.

Kishi-Mujin—ancient Mother Goddess of Japan.

Miyagima—Island containing a shrine sacred to the Itkushima Deity. The shrine is so sacred, only those with royal blood can enter it. Marked by a large Torii in the water.

Mochi—sweet rice cakes and dumplings, made from a special rice, sometimes stuffed with sesame, bean paste or other fillings.

Mt. Hiei—One of several mountains situated to the North-east of Kyoto, adorned with dozens of Buddhist temples and monasteries. The north-east was considered an 'unlucky' direction, so the monasteries were ostensibly to protect Kyoto with prayers and spells, though in reality, swarms of angry monks hoping to influence the politics of the Capitol often created the danger themselves.

Naga—Magical sea serpents.

Obon—Japanese festival of the dead, held in late July or early August (depending on the lunar calendar). Small rafts with candles commemorating the dead are set onto rivers at the conclusion of the festival.

Palanquin—a conveyance carried on men's shoulders, always elaborately decorated. Usually only members of the royal family and their attendants rode in palanquins. Lesser nobles rode in carriages, usually drawn by oxen or horses, though there was a type of carriage called a tegurama drawn by six to eight men which was used primarily during inclement weather when footing was too unstable for animals.

Sake—rice wine.

Sala flowers—grow on a tall evergreen called the Sala tree. Normally a pale yellow, Buddhist legend says they turned white and fell on the Buddha as he lay dying beneath them, becoming a natural shroud. The color of the sala flowers is a metaphor for the transience of life

Segan Sana—Goddess/kami of the Cherry Blossoms.

Shina Tsuhime—Goddess/kami of the winds.

Shrine—Shinto (kami-no-machi) place of worship. Often plain and austere.

Susano-o—the Storm God, unruly twin brother of Sun Goddess Amaterasu.

Sutras—Buddhist prayers.

Tabis—soft cloth slippers.

Tamayor-ihime—Triple Goddess of children, the ocean and the birth waters.

Tanabata Matsuri—Festival of the Weaver Star. The Weaver and Herdsman were two deities whose all-encompassing love for each other caused them to neglect their sacred duties. They were punished by being turned into stars (Vega and Altair), and set at opposite ends of the heavens. Once a year, in July, all the magpies of the world form a bridge over the Milky Way, which the Japanese called 'the River of Heaven' and the lovers cross over their wings to spend one night together. The Weaver is the patron of weaving, sewing, music and poetry.

Tatami—mats woven of rushes, in this era generally used for sitting on outdoors or for special ritual occasions.

Temple—Buddhist place of worship.

Torii—Sacred gates painted red marking the entries and pathways of Shinto shrines, usually consisting of a pair of upright posts topped with a pair of lintels. The torii represents the birth portal, and also evokes the place where birds perched and sang to entice the Sun Goddess from her cave.

Tsukihime—Moon kami.

Willow world—a term used to describe the pleasure houses inhabited by prostitutes of various levels. The women were said to be as pliable and graceful as willows.

Don't miss the first half of the epic series,

White as Bone, Red as Blood.

White as Bone, Red as Blood;
The Fox Sorceress,

Books may be ordered through:

Ingram

Amazon

Barnes and Noble

or at www.cerridwenfallingstar.com

Photo by Susanna Frohman

About The Author

Cerridwen Fallingstar is an experienced shaman devoted to creating magic, ritual and relationships that work. She lectures, teaches classes and offers counseling sessions utilizing tarot, hypnotherapy, soul retrieval, and other techniques. She is the author of three past-life novels; *White as Bone Red as Blood; The Fox Sorceress, White as Bone, Red as Blood; The Storm God,* and *The Heart of the Fire.* She is nearing completion on a non-fiction collection of teaching stories titled *Broth from the Cauldron.* She lives in northern California.

For information on classes, lectures, rituals and private sessions facilitated by Cerridwen Fallingstar, and to set up lectures and workshops in your own area, you may write to:

Cerridwen Fallingstar   or   www.cerridwenfallingstar.com
c/o Cauldron Publications
POB 282
San Geronimo, CA 94963

CPSIA information can be obtained at www.ICGtesting.com
Printed in the USA
LVOW11s1221010915

451993LV00024B/38/P